# DARK PASSION

"Why can't you admit that you want me?" His voice was thick with need.

"Because."

"Tell me."

She spread her hands on his chest, slowly lowering down until he could press his mouth to the juncture between her neck and shoulder. She shuddered, rubbing against his erection as his fangs replaced his lips, pressing just hard enough to send a thrill of anticipation through her.

He grasped her hips, sliding her over his rock-hard arousal in a movement that was meant to inflame her passion.

As if she needed any more inflaming. She was already about to combust.

"Tell me, Fallon."

"You frighten me."

He froze, his expression oddly vulnerable.

"You're scared of me?"

"Not you." Abruptly realizing she'd hurt him with her thoughtless words, she brushed her lips over his mouth. "The way you make me feel . . ."

# WHEN
# DARKNESS
# ENDS

## ALEXANDRA IVY

## ZEBRA BOOKS
## KENSINGTON PUBLISHING CORP.
http://www.kensingtonbooks.com

ZEBRA BOOKS are published by

Kensington Publishing Corp.
119 West 40th Street
New York, NY 10018

All Kensington titles, imprints, and distributed lines are available at special quantity discounts for bulk purchases for sales promotion, premiums, fund-raising, educational, or institutional use.

Special book excerpts or customized printings can also be created to fit specific needs. For details, write or phone the office of the Kensington Sales Manager: Attn.: Sales Department. Kensington Publishing Corp., 119 West 40th Street, New York, NY 10018. Phone: 1-800-221-2647.

Zebra and the Z logo Reg. U.S. Pat. & TM Off.

First Printing: June 2015
ISBN-13: 978-1-4201-2517-7
ISBN-10: 1-4201-2517-6

eISBN-13: 978-1-4201-3738-5
eISBN-10: 1-4201-3738-7

10 9 8 7 6 5 4 3 2 1

Printed in the United States of America

# Prologue

*Laigin (Ireland), 1014 AD*

The man woke with a blinding headache, stripped of his clothing as well as his memories.

With a groan, he sat up, shoving his tangled hair out of his face. It was immediately obvious he was in a damp cave. A strange place to wake. But not nearly as strange as the abrupt realization that something was terrifyingly wrong with him.

Despite the darkness he was able to see the limestone walls that had been chiseled by the water dripping from the low ceiling as clear as if it were day. And it was not only his sight that was unbearably acute.

He could smell the distant salt of the sea. And hear the faint scramble of a bug crossing the stone floor. He could even detect the warmth of two creatures that were rapidly approaching the cave.

What madness was this?

No man should have the senses of a god. Not unless he was a monster.

The dark thoughts barely had time to form before they

were interrupted by a hunger that thundered through him. He groaned. It was as if he hadn't eaten in weeks. Months. But it wasn't the thought of food that made his stomach cramp, he realized with a flare of horror.

It was . . . blood.

His mouth watered, the pain of his fangs ripping through his gums startling him as the image of the red, intoxicatingly rich substance filled his mind.

He had to feed.

Aye. That was what he needed.

Disgusted with the knowledge, he slowly rose to his feet, a virile strength running through his massive body even as his head remained thick with confusion.

His instincts urged him to leave the cave, to hunt down his prey and bury his fangs deep in their throats, but the tantalizing scent of fresh strawberries kept him frozen in place.

It appeared that his prey was willingly coming to him.

And they smelled . . . delectable.

Like an animal, he warily shuffled to the deepest shadows. From his vantage point, he silently watched the two slender creatures enter the cave. His eyes widened at the sheer beauty of the strangers. The male had hair the color of rust with bold green eyes set in a lean face, while the female possessed long tawny hair with eyes the shade of spring grass.

They looked like angels.

His fangs ached, his muscles tensing as he prepared to strike.

Angels or not, they were about to become dinner.

But before he could charge, the male held up a slender hand, the scent of strawberries becoming overpowering.

"Hold, berserker," he commanded, a tingle of magic in the air.

He frowned. "I am a berserker?"

"You were."

The confusion only deepened. "Were?"

"Two nights ago you were attacked by a clan of vampires."

He shook his head, his hand instinctively lifting to touch his neck.

"I survived?"

The pretty female grimaced. "Not as a human. The local villagers left you in this cave to see if you would rise as a vampire. Even now they are on their way to either witness your corpse or slaughter you." She held out a slender hand. "Come with us in peace and we will harbor you until you are able to care for yourself."

Vampire . . .

He went to his knees in shock.

Holy shite.

# Chapter One

*Ireland, present day*

Cyn, clan chief of Ireland and former berserker, moaned as he slowly regained consciousness. His brain was fuzzy, which meant it took a full minute to realize he was lying butt-naked on the cold stone floor of a cave.

Bloody hell. It had been a millennium since he'd woken in this precise cave, naked and disoriented. He didn't like it any better today than he had a thousand years ago.

What'd happened?

With a groan he forced himself to a sitting position, his body hardening at the intoxicating scent that teased at his nose.

Champagne?

A fine, crisp vintage that made his entire body tingle with anticipation.

For a blissful minute he allowed the fragrance to swirl around him. It was oddly familiar. And, surprisingly, it stirred a complex mixture of emotions.

Arousal. Wariness. Frustration

It was the frustration that abruptly forced him to recall why the scent was so familiar.

Muttering a curse, Cyn had a searing memory of following a beautiful fairy through a portal. No . . . not a fairy, he wryly corrected himself. A Chatri. The ancient purebloods of the fey world who'd retreated to their homeland centuries before.

He'd been there to help Roke locate his mate, but Princess Fallon had shoved him out of the throne room when it was obvious that Roke and Sally needed time to work out their differences, insisting that he leave them in peace.

He'd only been vaguely annoyed at first. He didn't trust the cunning Chatri as far as he could throw them, especially not their king, Sariel. But he wanted Roke to work out his troubles with his mate.

Besides, he was male enough to appreciate being in the company of a beautiful woman.

Or in the case of Fallon . . . a breathtakingly exquisite woman.

Her hair was a glorious tumble of rich gold brushed with hints of pale rose. The sort of hair that begged a man to bury his face in the silken mass. Her eyes were polished amber with flecks of emerald and framed by the thickest, longest lashes Cyn had ever seen. And her ivory features . . . gods almighty, they were so perfect they didn't look real.

He might be suspicious of Fallon, but that didn't mean he couldn't enjoy fantasizing about having her tossed on the nearby chaise longue while he peeled the gown off her slender body, he'd assured himself.

So he'd allowed himself to be distracted by the lovely female as he sipped the potent fey wine, not realizing the danger until his head began to spin and the world went dark.

Idiot.

He should have known that they were plotting something.

He might have a fondness for the fey, but that didn't mean he wasn't well aware of their mercurial natures.

And their love for luring the unwary into their clever traps.

With a low growl he turned his head, easily spotting the female who was sprawled naked on the ground, her golden hair shimmering even in the darkness.

He wanted to know how the hell she'd managed to bring them to the caves beneath his private lair. And he wanted to know now.

Cyn moved to bend beside her slumbering form, pretending that he wasn't acutely aware of the enticing temptation of her long, slender body and the fragile beauty of her pale face.

Sleeping Beauty . . .

A scowl marred his forehead. Aye. She was a beauty. She was also a powerful fey princess who'd managed to catch him off guard once.

It wasn't going to happen again.

"Fallon?" Cyn murmured, his voice deep and laced with an accent that hadn't been heard in this world for centuries. She heaved a sigh at the sound of his voice, but she remained stubbornly asleep. Cyn knelt at her side, knowing better than to touch her. The feel of that satin skin beneath his fingertips was guaranteed to make him forget he was pissed as hell at her little trick. "Fallon," he growled, his voice a command. "Wake up."

She gave a small jerk, her lashes fluttering upward to reveal the striking amber eyes with the shimmering flecks of emerald.

For a long moment she studied him in stunned confusion.

Understandable.

Most people found Cyn . . . intimidating.

At six foot three he had a powerful chest and thick muscles that marked him as a warrior. His thick mane of dark blond hair hung halfway down his back except for the front strands that he kept woven into tight braids that framed his face.

His features were chiseled along blunt lines with a square jaw and high cheekbones. His brow was wide and his jade green eyes heavily lashed. Females seemed to find him handsome enough, but there was never any mistake that he was a ruthless killer.

She sucked in a shaky breath as her gaze lowered to the barbaric Tuatha Dé Danann tattoos that curled and swirled in a narrow green pattern around his upper arms, emphasizing the perfect alabaster of his skin.

His lips twisted, wondering what she would think of the golden dragon tattoo with crimson wings that was currently hidden beneath the thick mane of his hair.

He'd earned the mark of CuChulainn that was branded onto his right shoulder blade after he'd survived the battles of Durotriges.

It marked him as a clan chief.

"Vampire," she muttered, as if having difficulty remembering who he was.

He narrowed his gaze, wondering what game she was playing. "Cyn."

"Yes . . . Cyn." Her confusion was replaced with a horror as if she were suddenly remembering who he was. A horror that only intensified when she belatedly realized they were both butt-naked. "Dear goddess." She shoved herself to a sitting position, curling her arms around her knees as she glared at him with angry accusation. "What have you done to me?"

"Me?" He made a sound of disbelief, unconsciously reaching to push a strand of golden hair off her flushed cheek.

"No . . ." With a flare of panic she was scrambling backward, a genuine fear flaring through the amber eyes. "Stay away."

Cyn muttered a low curse. Her pretense of confusion was annoying the hell out of him, but he didn't like the thought that she was afraid of him.

Strange when he'd devoted several centuries to terrifying his enemies.

"Settle down, princess," he murmured softly.

"Settle down?" A flush stained her beautiful face. "I wake up naked in the company of a strange vampire far away from my home and you want me to settle down?" She bit her bottom lip, her flush deepening to crimson. "Did you—"

"What?"

"Violate me?"

What the hell? Cyn surged upright. Six foot three of quivering, offended, naked male.

"No, I didn't damned well violate you," he rasped. "And if I had, I can assure you that you would not only remember, but you'd be on your knees thanking me for the privilege."

Her fear was replaced by a more familiar disdain. As if he was a bug that needed to be squashed beneath her royal heel.

"Why, you arrogant . . . leech."

He folded his arms over his massive chest. "At least I'm not a stuck-up prig of a fairy."

"If you didn't violate me, why are we naked?" she demanded, careful to keep her gaze locked on his face. Was she afraid his bare body might strike her blind? "And how did we get here?"

He snorted. "That's a question I should be asking you."

"I beg your pardon?"

"I'm a vampire."

Her lips thinned in annoyance, her chin tilted as she continued her ridiculous charade of innocence.

"Yes, I had managed to figure that out."

"Then you know that I can't create portals," he snapped, deliberately allowing his gaze to skim downward. Unlike the aggravating female, he had no problem enjoying a naked body. Especially one so appetizing. "Only the fey can do that."

She frowned, belatedly realizing she couldn't try and pin the blame of their abrupt teleportation on him.

Odd, she hadn't struck him as stupid.

Just the opposite, in fact.

"Fey aren't the only creatures who can create portals." She tried to hedge.

"Well, I obviously didn't do it."

"Neither did I."

He made a sound of impatience. Why was she continuing with this game?

"You expect me to believe you?"

The flecks of emerald shimmered in her eyes. "My father has forbidden his people to leave our homeland."

"Oh aye, and a daughter has never dared to disobey her father."

She cast a condemning glance around the barren cave. "Trust me. If I did decide to defy my father, I wouldn't choose to travel to this dump."

His low growl filled the air. He was a true hedonist. A vampire who reveled in rare books, fine wine, and beautiful women.

And in turn, women adored him.

*All* women.

But this female . . .

She wasn't the warm, willing, bundle of pleasure he was accustomed to. She was rude and prickly and downright dangerous.

"Watch your tongue, princess," he snarled. "This dump happens to be a part of my private lair."

"There." She pointed an accusing finger toward him. "I knew it. You kidnapped me."

Cyn rolled his eyes. Could this farce get any more ridiculous?

"The only one kidnapped was me."

"Why would I kidnap an oversized, ego-bloated vampire?"

Yeah. Why would she? It took him a minute to shuffle through his still-fuzzy thoughts.

"To keep me from protecting my friend," he at last concluded.

Hadn't she pulled him out of the throne room, leaving Roke at the mercy of her father, Sariel? And then she'd plied him with some wicked fey brew that had knocked him unconscious.

Aye. It made perfect sense that it was a nefarious plot to separate him from his friend.

At least it did until she glared at him in outraged disbelief.

"Are you completely mental? Your friend was exactly where he wanted to be."

Okay. She had a point.

Roke hadn't looked like he needed Cyn's services. In fact, the last he'd seen of his fellow vampire, he was wrapping his mate in his arms, his expression one of besotted devotion.

Bleck.

"Then perhaps you simply wanted to be alone with me." He flashed a smile that revealed his snowy white fangs. One way or another he was getting answers. "You wouldn't be the first female to use magic to get me into your bed."

She muttered something distinctly unladylike beneath her breath.

"I am a fairy princess."

"And?"

"And I don't share my bed with—"

He planted his hands on his hips, his expression daring her to finish the sentence.

"With?"

Her lips parted to complete her insult, but before she could speak there was a sizzle of power in the air. Cyn turned toward the center of the cave, his muscles coiled to attack as there was a faint pop, and then a tiny demon dressed in a long white gown appeared out of thin air.

Cyn gave a startled hiss, his eyes widening at the creature who could easily pass as a young girl with her small stature and long silver braid that nearly brushed the floor. Cyn, however, wasn't fooled. He recognized the strange oblong eyes that were a solid black and the sharp, pointed teeth.

This was no harmless juvenile.

She had enough power to crush him and his entire clan.

Even worse, she was an Oracle. One of the rare demons who sat on the Commission, the ultimate rulers of the demon world.

"Enough squabbling, children," she chided, folding her hands together as she studied them with an unnerving intensity.

"Holy shite." Cyn offered a belated bow. "Siljar."

Fallon crouched on the ground, her arms wrapped around her knees in a futile effort at modesty.

"You know this person?"

"Not person," Cyn corrected, shivering as Siljar's energy sizzled over his skin. "Oracle."

The amber eyes widened. "Oh."

"Forgive me." Siljar gave an absent wave of her hand and Cyn made a strangled sound of shock as he found himself covered by a plain white robe that hit him just below the knees. The Oracle gave another wave of her hand and Fallon was covered in a matching robe. "I haven't created a portal into the fairy homeland for a number of centuries."

Cyn scowled, ignoring Fallon's I-told-you-so glare. "You brought us here?" he demanded.

Siljar gave a nod of her head. "I did."

"Why?"

"Because I have need of you."

His acute hearing picked up Fallon's soft sigh of relief as she rose to her feet and brushed her hands down the satin robe.

"You need the vampire?"

"I have a name," he reminded the princess with a snap.

Siljar clicked her tongue, her gaze shifting from Fallon to Cyn.

"I need both of you."

Cyn stiffened. It was never, ever a good thing when an Oracle had need of him.

"Why?"

There was the unmistakable scent of sulfur as Siljar's expression tightened with anger.

"I fear the Commission is being tampered with."

Cyn arched a brow. Hadn't Styx sent word that they'd uncovered the plot by the strange demons who'd been holding Fallon's father captive?

"Aye, we know the Nebule planted a spy to pose as an Oracle," he said.

Siljar shrugged. "He has been destroyed."

Oh. Cyn grimaced. "You suspect there's another traitor?"

"That was my first thought," Siljar admitted. "But I believe that on this occasion the Oracles are being manipulated without their knowledge."

That seemed . . . unlikely.

"Why are you suspicious?" he demanded.

Siljar hesitated a second before revealing what was troubling her.

"Over the past few weeks I've found myself awakening as if from a trance to discover I'm seated in the Council Room," she at last said.

Cyn blinked in confusion. That was it? He'd been kidnapped and dropped naked in these caves because the old gal was becoming forgetful?

He forced himself to consider his words. Only an idiot implied that an Oracle might be going a bit batty.

"The past year has been stressful, especially for the Commission," he murmured.

"It has. And if I was the only Oracle to experience the strange phenomenon, then I would assume that your implication that I'm suffering from some sort of mental decay was right." Her lips twitched as he flinched at her blunt words. "I am, after all, quite old and it wouldn't be entirely unlikely that I would accidentally transport myself to a familiar location without realizing what I'm doing."

Cyn ignored Fallon's barely hidden amusement at his discomfort.

"But?"

"More than once I discovered I wasn't alone."

Cyn grimaced even as he heard Fallon suck in a startled breath.

Having Siljar suffering from an occasional blackout was one thing. To think of the entire Commission being controlled by some unseen force . . . bloody hell.

"The other Oracles didn't know how they got there either?" he rasped.

Siljar gave a somber shake of her head. "No."


When Fallon had opened her eyes to discover herself far removed from her fairy homeland, she'd been more annoyed than frightened.

Strange, considering that it was the first time in her life she'd ever awakened in a dark cave, stark naked, and in the company of an equally naked vampire.

Hell, it was the first time she'd ever been away from her father's vast palace.

She should have been freaking out.

Shouldn't she?

But while she'd tried to convince herself that he must be some sort of deranged beast who'd stolen her from her home for God only knew what sort of perverted reason, she couldn't truly make herself believe he was intending her harm.

She hadn't spent much time with Cyn, but while the massive clan chief was obviously a terrifying predator, she'd easily sensed he posed no danger.

No, that wasn't true, she wryly conceded.

He posed all sorts of danger, not the least of which was the unwelcomed excitement that sizzled through her whenever he happened to glance in her direction.

But she didn't for a second believe he would physically hurt her.

Not unless he believed she was a threat to his people.

The tiny demon in front of her, however, had just sent a chill of terror straight down her spine.

She knew of the Commission, of course.

Unlike most Chatri, the pure-blooded ancestors of the fey, Fallon had never been content with her secluded existence. Others might be happy in her father's royal palace, surrounded by lush gardens and meadows that were drenched in perpetual sunshine, but for her it was all too . . . flawlessly monotonous.

There was only so much perfection a woman could endure before she became bored out of her mind. Which meant that Fallon had been driven to develop a secret life just to keep her sanity.

No one among her people knew that she'd created a hidden chamber where she honed her skill at scrying until she could not only peer into other dimensions, but she could maintain several images at once.

Over the years she'd spent endless hours studying this world, fascinated by the rapidly changing cultures while her own life remained stagnant. She'd even kept up on the current fads and speech patterns, telling herself that she might have the opportunity to visit this world, even when she'd known deep in her heart that her father would never allow her to leave their homeland.

Now she wondered if she'd been mistaken in her belief that the powerful Oracles were both wise and fair leaders for the demon world.

"What would be the point of trancing you?" she demanded in confusion.

Siljar regarded her with an unblinking gaze. It was . . . creepy.

"My guess would be that they want us in the Council Room," she said.

Fallon forced herself not to wilt beneath that basilisk stare. "Why?"

"It's the place we gather to share information, and to settle disputes between demons," Siljar explained, abruptly pacing across the cave with jerky movements. As if she was trying to contain her emotions. "And in extreme cases it's where we share our power."

"Do you think it could be a demon who is trying to influence you to judge in his favor?" Cyn abruptly demanded.

"I asked myself the same question. We are currently negotiating a land treaty between the mountain ogres and the woodland sprites." Siljar gave a sharp shake of her head. Swish. Swish. Her white robe brushed the uneven floor. "But now I fear the plot is far more nefarious."

"Nefarious?" Cyn demanded.

Siljar nodded. "I think someone is trying to force the Commission to combine their powers to cast a spell."

Cyn grimaced. "Who or what could have the necessary strength to influence the entire Commission?"

Siljar halted her pacing, regaining her composure to turn and meet the vampire's troubled frown.

"That's what I need you to discover."

"You want me to spy on the Oracles?" Cyn rasped.

"Of course not," Siljar chided. "I want Fallon to spy on them."

Fallon's mouth dropped open, her blood running cold. "Me?"

Siljar lifted a brow. "You are a master at scrying, are you not?"

Oh . . . damn.

"How did you—"

"I know many things, my dear," Siljar smoothly interrupted.

Fallon shuffled beneath the dark, steady gaze. What else

did the tiny demon know about her? Not that Fallon had an exciting enough life to hoard many secrets, but still . . .

Cyn sent her a searching glance, as if surprised that she might have an actual skill.

Jerk.

"What does a master of scrying mean?"

Siljar answered. "Fallon can keep track of the Oracles, even when they travel between dimensions."

He didn't look particularly impressed. "How will that help?"

"She can see if there is anyone in particular who has contact with all of the Oracles," Siljar explained. "Or if there is someplace they travel where they could be manipulated."

"How close does she have to be to scry?" Cyn demanded of the Oracle.

Fallon muttered a low curse. Had she suddenly become invisible?

"Distance doesn't matter," she informed the vampire, not about to be treated as if she couldn't speak for herself. She'd had enough of that in her father's court. "The only thing I need is a location to start."

Without warning, Siljar was moving to stand directly in front of Fallon, her hand reaching to press against her cheek.

"There," the demon said, searing the image of a vast complex of caves into Fallon's mind. "You can track them?"

Fallon hissed in shock as the location locked in her mind and she realized just what was expected of her.

Crap. What was wrong with her? She should have told Siljar she couldn't scry. That she'd made some sort of mistake.

Instead she'd practically boasted about her skill.

As if she was trying to impress . . .

No. She locked out the disturbing thought.

Cyn was an arrogant lug with an oversized ego. Okay, he was gorgeous. And sexy. And his hard, warrior body was lickably delicious. But she certainly wasn't going to waste her time trying to impress him.

Siljar cleared her throat. "My dear, can you track them?" She repeated her question.

Fallon swallowed a sigh. It was too late to get out of her unwelcomed duty.

Besides, if her talent would help, then she surely had a duty to do whatever she could. "I think so," she said.

"Good." Cyn folded his arms over his chest. "Then she can return to fairyland?"

Fallon's mouth dropped open at his blunt words. "Why, you rude—"

Siljar held up a hand. "No."

Cyn's jade green eyes narrowed. "Why not?"

"Although it has been several weeks since you left Fallon's homeland—"

"Several weeks?" Fallon forgot her annoyance with Cyn as she sucked in a shocked breath. How was that possible? It felt as if it'd only been a matter of minutes since she was standing in the small reception room in her father's palace.

Siljar gave a lift of her hands. "Traveling through dimensions can often create temporal fluctuations."

She was lying. Oh, it was true that traveling through dimensions could screw with time, but Fallon suspected that the cunning Oracle had deliberately altered time for her own purpose.

With a low growl Cyn clenched his hands in frustration, clearly more pissed than suspicious.

"What's the date?" he demanded.

"The middle of January."

The vampire's icy powers pulsed through the air, making Fallon shiver.

"Shit," he rasped.

Siljar calmly smoothed her hands down her robe, pretending there wasn't a massive vampire filling the cave with enough power to make it collapse on their heads.

"As I was saying, I brought you here so Fallon could concentrate on her task without the interference of her father and her fiancé who are both searching for her."

Fallon widened her eyes. It made sense that her father would come in search of her. But her fiancé?

The prince barely remembered she was alive most of the time.

"Magnus is here?"

"Fiancé?" Cyn muttered, sending Fallon an oddly angry glare before turning his attention to Siljar. "You can't expect me to be her babysitter."

"I request that you give her your protection." Siljar spoke before Fallon could call him a jackass. "Which will be considerably easier if you remain behind the potent magic that hides your lair from prying eyes."

"And what about my people?" he snarled. "I've already been gone too long. They need their chief."

Siljar waved away his concern. "You surely have a trusted servant who can keep your presence here a secret and yet allow you to ensure the welfare of your clan?"

The chill in the air became downright frigid. "There are others more suited to taking care of a fairy."

Fallon met him glare for glare. "I couldn't agree more."

Siljar reached into the pocket of her robe, pulling out a small scroll.

"But they would not be more suited to deciphering this."

# Chapter Two

It wouldn't come as a shock to anyone that Styx was the Anasso, King of Vampires.

At six foot five with dark eyes, and the fierce Aztec features of his ancestors, he was the poster child for BADASS. Dressed in leather pants and white silk shirt that emphasized his massive chest, he had his long raven hair braided and decorated with tiny turquoise amulets. There was another amulet around his neck, this one a traditional medallion that held the power of his people. His size thirteen feet were shoved into a pair of shit-kickers that looked decidedly out of place in the elegant library.

Of course, there was no place in the sprawling mansion north of Chicago that he didn't stand out like a sore thumb. His home was filled with marble columns and painted ceilings and an explosion of gilt. And the furnishings weren't Louis XIV rip-offs. The furniture had actually come from the king's palace. Which meant they were so delicate, a poor vampire was constantly terrified it would crack beneath his weight.

Unfortunately his mate, Darcy, insisted that he needed a

lair that would impress the demon world. And if it made Darcy happy, then that was all that mattered.

The vampire walking through the door, however, was the exact opposite of Styx.

Not to say that Viper wasn't equally lethal. He hadn't earned a position as the Chicago clan chief because his eyes were as dark and beguiling as a velvet night sky. Or because his features were as beautiful as a fallen angel. Or because his long, silver hair shimmered like the finest satin.

He was one of the most ruthless killers to stalk the streets of Chicago.

But while Styx looked like death walking, Viper resembled an eighteenth-century dandy dressed in a dark velvet jacket that reached his knees and a ruffled pink shirt.

Crossing the priceless Parisian carpet, Viper headed directly to the side of the room, pouring himself a brandy before turning to face Styx who was leaning against the heavy desk.

"This had better be important," Viper growled, tossing the brandy down his throat.

Styx arched a raven brow as Viper set the empty glass on a low, walnut table.

"Did you get up on the wrong side of the bed?"

Viper nailed him with an exasperated glare. "I hadn't left my bed, Your Majesty. I was enjoying a rare evening alone with my mate."

Ah. That would explain the pissy mood.

Styx shrugged. "A pity."

Viper rolled his eyes. "You could at least pretend to be sympathetic."

"I would be more sympathetic if my own mate wasn't back in St. Louis," Styx muttered.

Darcy's sister had recently given birth to a litter of pureblood Weres and Styx had discovered himself living the life of a bachelor as the females fussed and cooed over the babies.

He tried to be patient, but it wasn't his greatest talent.

Oh hell, who was he kidding? It was at the bottom of the list of his talents.

Viper grimaced. "I've discovered that no mere male can compete with the allure of newborn babes. Even Shay insists on traveling to see them when there isn't a waiting line outside Salvatore's lair."

"Yes." Styx's annoyance with Darcy's absence eased at the thought of Salvatore, the King of Weres, being tormented by endless guests forcing their way into his lair. The arrogant hound was at the edge of snapping. "Poor bastard."

Viper abruptly chuckled. "Once again I detect a distinct lack of genuine sympathy."

"True." Styx smiled. Truce or not, it gave him genuine pleasure to think of the arrogant bastard ripping out his hair. "The dog deserves the aggravation."

"So why did you require that I come over tonight?" Viper demanded. "Just the pleasure of my sparkling personality?"

Styx's brief amusement disappeared. "Salvatore isn't the only one with unwanted houseguests."

"I thought Sariel was out searching for his daughter?" Viper said, referring to the King of Chatri who claimed that his daughter had been kidnapped by Cyn, the clan chief of Ireland.

Styx snorted. How the hell did this happen?

One day he'd been celebrating the survival of yet another end-of-the-world-disaster, and the next his house was filled with fairies.

*Fairies,* for God's sake.

It was enough to make any vampire consider burning the place to the ground.

"He is, but he has left Prince Magnus, his soon-to-be son-in-law, here."

His tone left no doubt of his opinion of the prince.

Viper scowled. "Why?"

"He claims that he wants Magnus to be here in case Fallon appears while he's gone."

"You don't believe him?"

"Of course not." As if Styx would trust the word of any fey. Let alone the King of Fey. "Sariel is convinced that Cyn kidnapped his daughter and that I'm helping them remain hidden. He planted that annoying twit in my house to spy on me."

Viper looked hopeful. "Did you want me to kill him?"

"Hell, no." Styx shoved himself away from the desk, his power filling the room with an icy chill. "If anyone is going to kill the prissy pain in the ass it's going to be me. Unfortunately I'm not prepared to start a war with the fairies, no matter how tempting."

"Ah." Viper flashed a smile. "Then you invited me to chain you to the dungeon wall so you don't do anything stupid?" He offered a mocking bow. "My pleasure, Your Majesty."

"You can shove that 'Your Majesty' up your ass," Styx growled.

His people knew just how badly he hated any symbol of authority. Well, except for his big-assed sword that could cut through an ogre with one swipe.

The one sure way to grate on his nerves was to call him by some stupid title.

Viper's smile widened. "Fine. What do you need from me then?"

"Nectar."

"Nectar?" The clan chief waited for the punch line.

When Styx merely studied him with growing impatience, he gave a shake of his head. "What kind of nectar?"

"How the hell should I know?" Styx made a sound of disgust. "The stupid prince keeps bleating about some nectar that is essential to his survival."

"He'll die without it?" Viper shrugged. "Problem solved."

Styx shook his head. After a week of enduring Magnus's moans and groans, he was ready to stake himself.

"Not if I have to listen to him complaining until he finally croaks." Styx shuddered. "I just want to shut him up."

Viper moved to stand near the windows that offered a stunning view of the moon-drenched rose garden.

"Understandable. No one likes a whiny fey. But I'm not sure why you called me." He turned back to send Styx a puzzled frown. "I don't have any nectar."

"You have clubs that cater to the fey."

"And?"

Styx swallowed a growl of annoyance. Viper was obviously in no mood to be helpful. No doubt it had something to do with being taken away from his beautiful mate.

"And at least one of them must have some damned nectar," Styx snarled.

Viper pulled his phone from his pocket, accepting that Styx wasn't going to allow him to leave until he had what he wanted.

"I suppose I could check around."

"Yeah, you do that."

With a grimace, the silver-haired vampire began contacting his various managers that ran his chain of demon bars. Styx didn't doubt at least one of them would have what he needed.

Viper's clubs were notorious for satisfying the desires of his guests. No matter how outrageous those desires might be.

"Got it," he at last muttered, glancing at Styx. "Tonya has a fresh batch."

Thank the gods.

"Tell her to bring it."

"Now?" Viper scowled, a businessman to his very soul. "The club—"

"Now."

Viper rolled his eyes. "Bring what you have to the Anasso's lair," he commanded the beautiful imp who was in charge of his club a hundred miles south of Chicago. "But don't try to travel directly into the estate," he warned. Styx had a layer of barriers wrapped around his home to prevent magic. He had a lethal dislike for unwanted guests popping in. "You'll have to stop at the edge of the estate and wait for an escort to bring you inside."

Styx reached behind him to punch a button that opened the intercom to his security team, warning them to expect the imp.

When he turned back, Viper had put away his phone and was adjusting the lacy cuffs of his ridiculous shirt.

"Have you had any word from Cyn?"

"Nothing."

Styx felt a familiar stab of frustration. When Roke had informed him that the clan chief of Ireland had disappeared along with the Chatri princess, Styx had assumed that they would turn up within a few hours. There were few women who wouldn't leap at the chance to spend some time alone with the charming vampire. But as the days, and then weeks passed, the mildly annoying incident had turned into a looming disaster. The Chatri were the ruling class of the fey and if they decided that the vampires had insulted their king, they could make things very unpleasant.

He gave a sharp shake of his head.

"If Cyn has returned to this dimension he's remaining well hidden."

Viper shook his head. "I know Cyn. He can be impulsive—"

"He's a damned maniac," Styx muttered, recalling the night the clan chief had released a herd of cows in King James's palace. It'd caused a near riot.

"But he would never kidnap a fairy princess," Viper insisted.

"Unless she wanted to be kidnapped," Styx pointed out.

"If that was the case then he wouldn't remain in hiding. He would confront Sariel head-on, not skulk in the shadows."

"I agree." Styx grimaced. "He's never been subtle."

"Which means he's in trouble."

Trouble.

It was a word that he'd heard too often over the past year.

Was it really too much to ask that he have one damned week without some disaster lurking?

"I have my Ravens searching for him," he said. "Between them and the fey there's no rock that will be left unturned. And once I have my hands on whoever is responsible"—his power made the electricity flicker—"there will be hell to pay."

"Yes, there will be, no matter who is responsible for kidnapping the princess," a male voice drawled from the doorway.

Styx's fangs lengthened, aching for the opportunity to drain the idiot who waltzed into the library as if he owned the place.

Prince Magnus was exactly what you would expect of a pure-blooded fey.

His long hair shimmered like the finest rubies in the light from the chandelier. His brow was wide, his nose a thin, noble blade, and his lips lushly carved. And his eyes were the color of cognac and rimmed with gold.

Tonight he'd put aside his usual flowing gown encrusted with jewels to wear a pair of black slacks and a jade green silk shirt, revealing his surprisingly muscular body.

A humorless smile twisted Styx's lips. The clothes had changed, but the outrageous arrogance was the same.

Viper moved to stand at Styx's side. "I presume this is Magnus?"

The Chatri lightly touched the large emerald pendant that was hung around his neck, the intoxicating scent of finely aged whiskey filling the room.

"Prince Magnus," the fey corrected, his expression pinched as if he had a corn cob stuck up his ass.

Styx wondered if his expression would be the same if it was a size thirteen boot stuck up there.

Viper smiled, deliberately exposing his fangs. "The last royal I met ended up as my dessert."

The pale, elegant features hardened, hinting at a dangerous power hidden behind the fey's pretense of namby pamby stupidity.

"I do not fear you, vampire," he said.

Viper tapped the tip of his fang with his tongue. "Then you're even more stupid than you look."

"Enough," Styx interrupted, not entirely pleased by the suspicion that Prince Magnus wasn't quite the harmless fribble he'd first assumed. "What do you want now?"

The prince sniffed, once again a harmless, aggravating pain in the ass.

"I smelled imp," he said.

Styx belatedly caught the scent of plums at the same time that Viper glanced in his direction.

"He's right. Tonya's here."

"Thank God for portals," Styx muttered, lifting a hand as the female imp appeared in the doorway. "Enter."

A hum of male appreciation buzzed in the air as the tall

woman with lush curves and a stunning mane of dark red hair sashayed across the carpet. Tonya was the sort of imp that could make any demon rejoice at being a male.

It was more than her pale, perfect skin and slanted emerald eyes. It was the blatant sensuality that oozed from her, enticing and provoking the male senses.

"You wanted nectar," she murmured, holding up a jar that contained a pale gold liquid.

Styx nodded toward the man standing near the marble fireplace.

"It's for him."

"Who . . ." The imp turned, her flirtatious expression freezing as she caught sight of the Chatri prince. "Oh."

"Well?" Magnus snapped his fingers. "Bring it to me, imp."

"Yes." Clearly bedazzled by the fey, Tonya obediently headed toward Magnus.

Waiting until she was standing directly in front of him, Magnus took the jar from her hand and sniffed at the golden liquid.

"Pedestrian," he muttered. "But I suppose it will have to do." Setting the nectar on the mantel, he turned his attention to the enthralled female. "Why are you not on your knees?"

Viper made a choked sound. "Oh hell."

Tonya blinked, as if coming out of a spell. "Excuse me?"

"You are a lesser fey," Magnus informed her, his superior tone enough to make any demon consider the pleasure of kicking him in the nuts. "You should be on your knees when in the presence of your master."

The emerald eyes widened; the scent of scorched plums making Styx rub his nose.

"Master?"

"I am Prince Magnus." The idiot gave a wave of his hand. "Bow before me."

"How about I do this instead?" the imp said, pulling back her arm before punching the prick directly in the nose. Viper shrugged as the prince cursed in pained disbelief. Turning his head, he met Styx's amused gaze.

"He really did ask for it."

Styx chuckled. "I think I just found my fey liaison."

Cyn unrolled the fragile scroll with a practiced care that would have surprised most people.

They only saw the wild berserker who would destroy anyone who threatened his clan. Or the impulsive hedonist who reveled in sensual pleasures.

His love for history was a hobby that he shared with very few.

"Where did you get this?" he asked, his voice reverent.

"It was presented to the Commission as a gift."

Cyn caught the scent of musty linen and charcoal as he studied the delicate hieroglyphs sketched on the scroll.

"Presented by whom?"

"No one can recall."

Hmm. That was odd. His gaze skimmed over the delicate symbols.

"What's it for?"

"I believed that it was a simple cleansing spell that would rid the caves of any lingering residues of magic." The female Oracle gave a lift of her shoulder. "When so many powerful demons are gathered in one place it is necessary every few months to purge the air so that the overspill of energy doesn't build up and interfere with our current spells."

Cyn was blissfully ignorant when it came to magic and residual buildup. He was, however, an expert when it came to the subtleties of language.

"You said you *believed*." He studied her tiny, heart-shaped face. "Now you don't?"

She gave a firm shake of her head. "No."

"Why not?"

"Because I can't remember who planted the idea in my head that it was a cleansing spell."

Cyn frowned in puzzlement. "You can't read it?"

"No. But there is a compulsion deep inside me to try and cast it."

"How would you cast it if you can't read it?"

"That is a question I have no answer for." Siljar stepped toward him, pointing to the glyphs. "Can you decipher it?"

"No." He frowned, sensing the age of the writing. "It's old. Very old."

"Fey?" the Oracle prompted.

"Maybe fey in origin, but—"

"What?"

"The marks are too straight." His finger traced an angled line that was topped by a section of triple dots. "The fey glyphs are curved and usually more . . . elegant." He gave a shake of his head. "This has the blunt simplicity of humans, but it isn't in any language I've seen before."

Siljar's expression remained calm, but Cyn didn't miss her tiny jerk of surprise.

She hadn't been expecting him to say human.

"But you have the means to translate it?" she at last demanded.

Cyn considered his response. He was impulsive, not suicidal. A wise vampire didn't say no to an Oracle.

Then again, he wanted nothing more than to get rid of his unwanted guests and check on his clan. He had full faith in Lise, whom he'd left in charge when Roke asked him to travel to America, but his clan would be frantic to discover what'd happened to him.

And more importantly, he wanted the damned fairy princess out of his hair.

Okay. That wasn't entirely true.

If he was honest, what he really wanted was her soft and welcoming and groaning with pleasure as he came deep inside her.

But that was about as likely to happen as him sprouting wings and a halo. Which meant he would be stuck for days with a haughty, prudish female who was way too fond of treating him like he was some sort of lesser being who should be kneeling at her elegant feet.

Yeah. A big "No, thank you," to that.

"Why not go to the fey?"

The dark gaze never wavered from his face. "I suspect the answer is in your library."

Cyn narrowed his eyes. How the hell had she known about his library?

"Is there a reason for your suspicion?"

"Erinna came to me shortly before she and Mika left."

Cyn stiffened. Erinna and Mika had been the two fairies who'd rescued him from these caves, taking him into their home even when he could so easily have destroyed them.

He'd never forgotten how they'd rescued him from the caves, and how they'd made him a member of their family. They'd been a part of his life for centuries, treating him as a true son. At least they had until they'd disappeared several days . . . No, wait. If it was January, then they'd left weeks ago, with only a short note to tell him not to search for them.

"What did she say?"

"She had a premonition after they took you into their home that you would be the savior of the fey." Siljar watched the disbelief spread over Cyn's face. "That's why they insisted you learn as much of their history as possible."

He adored his foster parents and he'd been happy to indulge their desire that he learn the language and writing of the fey. And even had listened to the endless stories that had been passed down by their ancestors.

But they tended to be highly dramatic, and it wouldn't take more than a stray dream, or the shape of a leaf, to convince them that he was supposed to be some sort of fey messiah.

Cyn shook his head in denial.

Bloody hell.

It had to be a joke.

"If they thought I could be their savior then why did they leave?" he demanded.

Siljar shrugged. "They sent word to me that Erinna had a new vision and they were going to check it out. They refused to give me any more information."

The growing fear that he was going to be forced to help the Oracle whether he wanted to or not was forgotten at Siljar's words.

It was one thing to accept that Erinna and Mika had taken off for their own pleasure. And another to think they'd put themselves in deliberate danger.

"Damn them." He shook his head, angry that he hadn't suspected there was more to their abrupt departure. "Why didn't they tell me?"

"Clearly they wanted to protect you."

His fangs ached. "That's not how it works. I keep them safe, not the other way around."

Siljar blinked, as if confused by his burst of anger. "It was their choice."

He wasn't going to argue the point. At least not with the Oracle.

Now when he found Mika and Erinna . . .

"Did they tell you what direction they were going?" he instead asked.

"They only said that they wanted to investigate the vision." The Oracle smoothed her hands down her satin robe, not appearing particularly concerned. "I don't think they were entirely clear on what they expected to find. They were, however, quite convinced that you would soon be needed to play your part in fey history. They asked me to keep an eye on you."

"Do I have a choice?" he muttered.

"No, your foster parents are depending on you." Siljar reached to place a hand on his arm. "We all are."

Cyn glanced down at the scroll in his hands. "Well, shit."

The Haven Estate was a sprawling work of art just half an hour north of Dublin.

The three-story Palladian-style mansion was built of white stone with simple, symmetric lines and a large portico that added to the air of splendid dignity. It was framed by lavish gardens that were formally terraced to lead to the large lake with a fountain in the center.

It was precisely the type of home one would expect for an aristocratic member of the Irish Parliament. And Sir Anthony Benson was exactly the sort of man that one would expect to be the owner.

Seated in a wing chair in the Green Drawing Room, Anthony was dressed in an emerald smoking jacket the precise shade of the curtains and a formal cravat that had gone out of fashion a couple centuries ago. His face was rounded and his pale brown hair had thinned until it was little more than a fringe around the edges. At a glance he looked like a comfortable, middle-aged man with a kind smile.

It took a much closer look to see that the clear gray eyes were as flat and cold as a snake.

Sipping his aged whiskey, Anthony studied the fairy prince who stood in the center of the room.

Yiant tried to appear indifferent to Anthony's basilisk stare, but his too-pretty face was damp with sweat and the slender hands that smoothed the silk robe covering his tall, reed-thin body weren't quite steady.

"You summoned me?"

"I did," Anthony said, his tone gentle as he pointed toward the ceramic pots that were arranged on a priceless pier table that had been in his family for six hundred years. "After examining your latest delivery I realized there was something missing."

The scent of freshly mowed grass filled the air as Yiant pushed back his thick mane of golden hair.

"I provided the phi potion," he said, referring to the potent mixture of rare herbs that Anthony needed to defy his mortality. The herbs could only be grown with fey magic. "As well as your favorite fey wine."

"You know what I want."

"We have no more of the potion," the fairy insisted, the pale green eyes wary. "I told you, it was very rare."

"Then create more."

"It is forbidden."

Anthony set aside his whiskey.

His family had held a treaty with the fairies for countless centuries. It had started when a distant ancestor had joined the clan of mystic druids.

It was a mutually beneficial arrangement.

The druids helped to protect the traditional lands of the

fey from human development and the fairies offered them extended life.

For his ancestors it'd been a religious duty. The land and the fey were a part of the magic that allowed the druids to thrive. It was in their self-interest to protect them both.

Anthony, however, wasn't content with being a lesser partner to a bunch of fairies. Especially not after discovering that there were far more dangerous creatures out there than just the fey.

He'd been forced to accept that humans were truly stupid. They blindly believed they were the lucky winners in the evolution lottery when they were surrounded by monsters that could destroy them.

Well, Anthony wasn't going to stand aside and allow it to happen.

If someone was going to rule the world, it wasn't going to be some damned demon.

It was going to be him.

Wisely he'd started slow. Patience was a powerful weapon that he wielded with a skill few other humans could master.

First he'd taken command of the druids.

Most of them continued to live in the past, barely understanding technology as they instead clung to worthless traditions.

Idiots.

Once he had a firm grip on the aging fools, he'd returned to Haven and established his position as head of the Benson family. Again.

It was always tricky when a human lived longer than was reasonably expected. It meant he had to leave and return as his own son. He'd done it three times in the past century.

Once he'd earned his place in the local society and worked

his way back up the political ladder, he'd been able to turn his attention to his connection to the fairies.

At first they'd only seen him as a benevolent friend.

He'd offered to extend their homelands by using his influence in the government to reclaim farmland as a sanctuary for . . . hell, what had he insisted was endangered? A pygmy shrew? Some sort of bat?

It didn't matter. The extra acres of land had allowed the Irish fairies to gather their tribe in one place. A rare occurrence in the modern age that not only consolidated their magic, but had given their prince a position of power among his people.

The fools had been gushingly grateful.

So grateful that they didn't realize that his generosity came at a price. Even after he'd gently requested that they share with him a rare Compulsion spell that had been forbidden by Sariel, the King of Fey.

They didn't know that he could make the potion even more powerful with his own skill with magic, weaving vast webs of compulsion that could trap even the most wary.

Then all he had to do was sit back and manipulate those in his command. Like a puppet master, tugging on the strings.

Or at least, he'd assumed they hadn't been aware of his secret efforts.

Now he had to wonder if the prince had started to suspect that Anthony was using the potion for more than swaying his fellow members of Parliament to vote in his favor.

"I understand, Yiant," he murmured, his tone still gentle. "And I truly admire your reluctance to break fey law. Your people will be proud to know that you kept your honor even if they are forced to abandon their homes."

The fairy licked his lips. Duty might tell him to sever

his connection to Anthony, but it was obvious that he was reluctant to jeopardize his own power among his people.

"There has to be another price I can pay," he said, his ambition a tangible force in the air.

"I fear not." Anthony rose to his feet, his smile one of regret. "Please give my regards to your mother, the queen, and tell her that I'm deeply sorry that we could not come to an agreement—"

"Wait."

"Aye?"

Lick, lick, lick of the lips.

"Perhaps something could be arranged."

Gotcha.

Anthony hid his smug smile. The prince was as easy to play as a fiddle.

"I really do think it would be for the best, my friend," he agreed with a sweetly encouraging smile. "It would be a pity to see the protected lands become a shopping center."

Yiant gave a stiff nod, turning to head for the door. "I will be in contact."

"Soon," Anthony warned, briefly wondering precisely what had prompted the unexpected display of defiance before he was abruptly interrupted by the scent of cherries.

Turning his head, Anthony watched as the mongrel stepped through the hidden panel at the back of the room.

Keeley was a half human/half imp male who'd sought Anthony's protection after the death of the previous Anasso. The too-handsome creature with pale green eyes and a mane of sleek golden hair had once been a playmate of the dissolute King of Vampires, and worse, he'd been related to Damocles, the imp who had contributed to the downfall of the once-powerful leader.

The imp had feared that Styx might retaliate against

those he held responsible for the destruction of his mentor and fled to Ireland.

Not an unreasonable fear.

So he'd allied himself with the druids, and over the past year, he'd earned a place in Anthony's inner circle.

It wasn't that he was more clever or talented or powerful than Anthony's other servants. Hell, his only real skill was creating portals.

But he was willing to follow any order, no matter how outrageous, and more importantly, he possessed an intimate knowledge of the caves where the previous Anasso had lived.

Caves that were now occupied by the leaders of the demon world, the Commission.

"You truly are evil, Benson," the imp murmured, crossing the Aubusson carpet.

Anthony adjusted his cuffs.

The imp had no idea just how evil he could be.

Not yet.

"I don't recall inviting you to my office, imp."

Wearing nothing more than a pair of faded jeans that emphasized his smooth, muscular chest, Keeley halted next to the wing chair.

"We have a problem."

Anthony frowned. "The prisoners?" he demanded, referring to the elder druids who refused to accept his vision for the future as well as the two interfering fairies.

His first thought had been to destroy them. A dead enemy was the best enemy. But he hated to toss away such a valuable resource.

It would be a sin to waste such potent blood.

So instead of burning them at the stake, he'd locked them in a Labyrinth spell that kept them safely imprisoned.

Keeley shook his head. "The spell still holds them."

"Then what has happened?"

"A friend from America sent me this."

The imp held out his phone to reveal a photo of a slender man with a long mane of hair that glistened like rubies even in the grainy image.

"A fairy?"

"A Chatri."

Anthony hissed in shock. It wasn't often anyone mentioned the pure-blooded ancients who were the ultimate rulers of the fey. They were written about in the secret druid legends, of course, along with dire warnings never to attract their attention.

It was said that an angry Chatri could kill with just the power of his light . . . whatever the hell that meant.

Anthony didn't know, and didn't want to find out.

"Impossible," he growled.

"Unexpected, but clearly not impossible," the imp drawled.

Anthony frowned. He didn't like sarcasm. It was the sign of a lazy mind.

On the other hand, he did like using his druid skills to punish those people who were stupid enough to annoy him. He liked it a lot.

Smiling, he ran his thumb over the heavy silver ring that circled his index finger.

A symbol of his authority that made the imp pale.

Satisfied, Anthony returned his attention to the image of the fairy.

"Who is he?"

Keeley had to clear his throat before he could speak. "He claims to be Prince Magnus."

A prince?

Then he wouldn't be alone.

Royals always traveled with guards.

"They retreated from the world centuries ago," he muttered. "Why would they return now?"

The imp returned the phone to his back pocket. "There're a dozen rumors, but no actual facts."

"Where is he?"

Keeley grimaced. "At the home of the Anasso."

The Anasso? Anthony lifted his brows. Things were getting stranger and stranger.

He didn't like strange any more than he liked sarcasm.

"He's with the vampires?"

"So it would seem."

Anthony paced toward the priceless Botticelli painting that hung on the back wall, silently contemplating his next move.

He wasn't a narcissist. He didn't believe that everything that happened in the world had something to do with him.

Then again, he wasn't stupid.

The return of the Chatri after so many years had the potential to ruin everything he'd worked so hard to achieve. He had to know if they intended to cause trouble.

He considered various ruses that might lure the Chatri to Ireland, only to dismiss them. He couldn't wait and hope the powerful fey might choose to arrive on his doorstep.

He needed to know now what they were planning.

The sooner the better.

"Bring him to me," he softly commanded, turning back to meet the imp's horrified gaze.

"What?"

Anthony picked a piece of lint off the sleeve of his smoking jacket, waiting for the imp to gather his composure.

"I believe you heard me," he at last murmured.

"Why me?"

"You have a connection to Styx, don't you?"

Keeley made a strangled sound, clearly not overjoyed at the promise of being reunited with his vampire friends.

"Not one that's likely to endear me to him," he managed to choke out. "He blamed my cousin Damocles for the destruction of the previous Anasso and he won't have forgotten that I was related to him. He'll kill me if I return to America."

"Nonsense." Anthony clicked his tongue. The fey, even half fey were annoyingly dramatic. "If he wanted you dead, you'd be dead."

"But—"

"Keeley, find a way to make him invite you into his home," he interrupted, his voice deceptively gentle. "I need to know if they've somehow managed to discover my plans."

The stench of cherries made Anthony's nose wrinkle as the imp fought his instinct to refuse the direct command.

A wise choice.

The vampire might kill him, but Anthony . . . ah, he would make the imp wish he were dead . . . over and over again.

"And if they have learned that you've been interfering with the Commission?"

A good question.

Anthony reached for his glass of whiskey he'd left on a small table next to the chair.

Unfortunately he didn't have a good answer.

"Then I suppose we will have to accelerate our timetable."

Keeley frowned. "Is that possible?"

"You sound concerned." Anthony sipped his whiskey, capturing the imp's nervous gaze. "You aren't getting cold feet, are you?"

"No." Keeley took a nervous step backward. Smart imp. "Of course not."

"Then bring me the Chatri."

Draining the whiskey, Anthony set aside the glass and headed toward the door. He was stepping into the formal gallery when he heard Keeley mutter behind him, "Bastard."

Anthony shrugged. The imp wasn't wrong.

He was a bastard.

# Chapter Three

Fallon gasped when Siljar disappeared as swiftly as she'd appeared.

One second she was patting Cyn's arm and the next . . . poof.

No smoke. No mirrors. No abracadabra.

Just there and then gone.

Damn.

What was wrong with her?

She should have insisted that the powerful demon return her to her homeland. Even with Sariel's interference she could have kept watch on the Commission. It wasn't as if she'd ever let her father or fiancé interfere in her fascination with scrying before.

It was easy to tell herself that it was the shock of waking up in a strange cave with a dangerous vampire, swiftly followed by the appearance of an Oracle demanding her help in spying on the Commission, that had rattled her brain. How could any poor female think clearly under such circumstances?

But a part of her knew that she'd allowed herself to be

steamrolled by the tiny Oracle quite simply because she didn't want to go home.

She'd spent centuries trapped in the glorious palace her father had created. She'd been petted and pampered and . . .

Trapped.

And worse, she'd known deep in her heart that she would never escape.

Not so long as her father considered the pure-blooded Chatri above the lesser fey.

So was it really surprising that she would be reluctant to give up this unexpected miracle even if it meant enduring the company of an obnoxious vampire?

It wasn't like she had to actually work next to him.

He was a clan chief. His lair should be large enough for them never to cross paths, right?

As if to prove her point, Cyn was abruptly heading toward the far end of the cave, his face grim although he held the scroll with obvious care.

Far more care than he was willing to give her. Jackass. With a swift step, Fallon had moved to place herself directly in his path.

"Where are you going?"

He came to a grudging halt, his gaze narrowed. "To have a shower."

"What about me?"

He shrugged. "Aren't you supposed to be spying on the Oracles or something?"

Her fists clenched. She'd never hit anyone before, but now seemed a good time to start.

"Now look here, you big lug—"

"You have an obsessive fascination with my size." He ran a slow, deliberate gaze down her tense body before leaning forward to whisper directly in her ear, "In case you're interested, I'm large everywhere."

The brush of his lips against her skin sent darts of white-hot excitement sizzling through her.

How was that possible?

She'd lived with the most beautiful men in the world. Her own fiancé, Magnus, was breathtaking. But never, ever had one of them made her so acutely aware of being a woman. As if Cyn had some magical ability to arouse her darkest, most intimate desires.

Jerking back, she sent him a glare. "Well, your head is certainly bloated."

His gaze lingered on her mouth. "If you're trying to charm me, it's not working."

She wouldn't lick her lips. She wouldn't.

Her tongue peeked out, swiping her lower lip with a provocative movement. Instantly Cyn's eyes darkened with a scorching heat.

Fallon stiffened. What was wrong with her?

"I'm not trying to charm you," she stubbornly denied.

"Fine."

Abruptly he'd stepped around her, clearly intending to leave her abandoned in the caves.

"Wait."

He sent an impatient glance over his shoulder. "Now what?"

"We're obviously stuck with one another for now," she said, pointing out the obvious.

"Do you have a point?"

Heathen. Barbarian. Hulking, gorgeous, pain in the ass. She counted to ten.

"You could at least try to be civil."

He folded his arms over his chest. "And what does 'civil' entail?"

"I obviously can't stay in these caves." She waved a dismissive hand toward the damp floor, shivering at the distinct chill in the air. "I'm assuming you have private rooms I could use. And I'll need food. Oh . . ." She glanced down to the plain, too-short robe. "And clothes. Silk."

Something dangerous lurked in the jade eyes. "Anything else, princess?"

"Nectar." She used her most grating princess voice. She was a guest here, dammit, not a prisoner. It was time that Cyn fulfilled his duties as a host. "Preferably from my homeland."

A stark, dangerous silence followed her daring command. The sort of silence that came before the strike of lightning.

Or a nuclear explosion.

Instead there was a flurry of movement as Cyn reached out to grasp her by the waist and with one smooth movement had her tossed over his shoulder.

Fallon gasped in shock. No man touched the royal princess. Not unless he wanted to be burned to a crisp by Sariel. And certainly they didn't haul her around like she was a sack of potatoes.

"What are you doing?" she finally managed to choke out.

Leaving the cave, Cyn headed up a narrow set of stairs carved into the stone.

"Let's get one thing straight, princess. This is my lair," he growled.

She slammed her fist against his back only to wince in pain. Crap, the man felt as if he'd been chiseled from granite.

"I wouldn't be so quick to boast about this shabby—"

Her furious insult came to an outraged halt as his large hand landed on her butt, giving the tender flesh a deliberate squeeze. Fallon's breath tangled in her throat. She was livid. Of course she was. But more than that she was . . . oh dear God, was she aroused? Was the intimate touch of his hand turning her on?

Or maybe being in this world was screwing with her hormones. Yes. That was a much better answer.

Belatedly aware they were moving through a long hallway lined with heavy tapestries, she gave his back another punch.

"Put me down, you barbarian."

"Berserker," he snapped.

"Is that supposed to be better?" she ground out, wiggling in an effort to dislodge his hand that was causing tiny sparks of pleasure to race through her body. "I told you to put me down."

Her wiggles were futile, but thankfully they'd reached a closed door and he was forced to release her butt to shove it open.

"My lair, my rules."

They entered what appeared to be a large room with a woven carpet in shades of silver and violet.

"What's that supposed to mean?"

"It means that I'm not your damned servant." He crossed the floor, abruptly dropping her on a massive four-poster bed with a feather mattress. "So long as you're beneath my roof you'll treat me with respect."

"Respect is earned, not commanded."

"Actually I just did." He planted his fists on his hips, using his powers to ignite the logs that were neatly stacked in the stone fireplace. "And you'd better pay attention."

"Or?"

"Or I'll return you to the caves and you can rot down there for all I care."

Fallon glared into the forcefully handsome face, catching a glimpse of snowy white fangs. Sensibly she knew she should be afraid of him.

He was a lethal predator who had her completely at his mercy.

But she wasn't afraid.

She was angry and frustrated and terrifyingly aware of the hard, male body barely concealed beneath the thin robe.

"I really dislike you," she muttered, trying to tug the robe down her legs.

"The feeling is mutual."

"I . . ." Fallon forgot what she was going to say as she belatedly noticed her surroundings. "Oh."

Cyn was instantly wary. "Now what?"

She forgot her urge to slap his arrogant face as she slowly scanned the pale ash furniture that filled the room.

Beyond the canopied bed, there was a chest set beneath a large stained-glass window that was composed in shades of indigo and saffron and crimson with threads of gold. The arched masterpiece not only provided beauty, but filtered out any potential sunlight. Near the fireplace was a rocking chair that matched the large armoire near the door. And nearer the bed was a delicate washstand.

There was a definite medieval vibe, but it was the exquisite craftsmanship that captured Fallon's attention.

With a soft sigh she shoved herself to her knees, reaching to skim her fingers over the delicate pattern that had been carved into the wooden posts of the bed.

Row after row of tiny flowers and woodland creatures flowed from the top of the post to the bottom, each one charmingly different in design. And the carvings were echoed on every piece of furniture, giving the room an ethereal beauty that tugged at her heart.

"It's beautiful," she breathed, feeling as if she were surrounded by a woodland glade despite the fact that the sun would never be allowed to stray beyond the window. "Really, really beautiful."

Cyn made a strangled sound, as if pushed to the very edge.

"Bloody hell, you could drive a saint to drink," he roared.

Ignoring the completely unfair accusation, she continued to stroke her fingers over the glossy wood.

"Where did you find the furnishings?"

"I made them."

She sent him a startled glance. "You?"

"Why do you sound so surprised?"

Fallon frowned at the hint of defensiveness in his tone. Was he embarrassed to reveal his artistic talent?

"This is fey in design."

"Oh." He shrugged. "I was taken in by fairies while I was a foundling. Mika trained me to carve."

Fallon couldn't deny a stab of curiosity.

She'd watched this world enough to know it was extremely unusual for any demon to foster another species, let alone a fairy taking in a savage vampire.

It would be like a human adopting a full-grown lion.

But she wasn't about to probe. Not when Cyn was already treating her as if she were some unwelcomed intruder who'd invaded his lair.

Like black mold.

"He must have been a master craftsman," she instead murmured.

"Careful, princess. That was perilously close to a compliment," he mocked.

Okay. That was it.

Turning her head, she stabbed him with a furious glare.

"Do you always have to be an ass?"

He abruptly grimaced, then without warning, he reached out to cup her cheek with his hand.

"No," he said, his thumb brushing her lower lip.

Fallon stilled, sensing the electric tension that sizzled between them.

"Cyn?"

His lips twisted at the sudden uncertainty in her voice.

"We're stuck together. At least for now," he said, his gaze lowering to her mouth. Almost as if he was imagining how it would taste beneath his own. "We need a truce."

Fallon shivered, the image of him tumbling her back onto the mattress and covering her with his hard body searing through her mind.

It was raw and primal and scary as hell.

*You're playing with fire,* a voice whispered in the back of her mind. *And you're the one who's going to get burned.*

She covertly inched back on the mattress. He carried with him a force field that threatened to suck her in.

"It should be simple enough." She managed to sound almost indifferent. Good for her.

His gaze remained locked on her lips. "Do you think so?"

"This is obviously a large lair. There's truly no need to spend any time in each other's company."

Something that looked like . . . hurt . . . flared through his eyes before he abruptly dropped his hand and stepped back.

"Right," he muttered, turning to head toward the door. "A perfect solution."

"Wait." Feeling ridiculously guilty, Fallon scrambled off the bed, her feet barely touching the floor as the door was being slammed shut.

With a shake of her head, she flopped back on the mattress, wondering why men had to be so . . . so impossible.

Cyn didn't know why he was so pissed as he left the room, slamming the door behind him.

Hell, he should be pleased the aggravating little fairy wanted to stay out of his way. This was his home. The place he indulged in his favorite vices.

The last thing he wanted was an intrusive, nagging, obscenely tempting . . .

He muttered a curse, storming toward a wide staircase to make his way to his private chambers that were built belowground. The entire castle was wrapped in spells of illusion as well as thick magic that prevented any stray trespassers. There were also heavy stained-glass windows that shielded the interior from the sun.

But old habits were hard to break. Especially for a vampire who was as old as Cyn.

Entering the cavernous room that was filled with ebony furniture and lush gold and black tapestries, Cyn crossed to the desk that was surrounded by floor-to-ceiling bookcases. Yanking open the top drawer, he pulled out a cell phone that was always kept charged and sent a text to his top lieutenant, using an encrypted code that warned her to meet him in his lair without alerting anyone as to where she was going.

Then, with long strides he entered the fully modern bathroom and stripped off the ridiculous robe, still bristling with a baffling sense of annoyance. Then, stepping into the shower he turned on the water, shivering beneath the icy blast.

Okay. He was attracted to Fallon. Maybe even more than just attracted. Despite her prudish nature and irritating arrogance, she was the most stunningly beautiful woman he'd ever seen. What man wouldn't be fantasizing about having her spread across his bed?

Or on a fur rug in front of a blazing fire.

Or in a moonlit meadow with a thousand stars spread above them.

Or . . .

He cursed again, scrubbing himself clean and stepping out of the shower.

He'd just pulled on a pair of faded jeans and a loose cable-knit sweater when there was the sound of approaching footsteps. Returning to the outer chamber, Cyn watched the female vampire stroll through the doorway.

A small smile curved his lips.

Lise looked like a china doll. A tiny body that was currently covered by tight black leggings and a long, flowing shirt. Straight black hair that was chopped just above her shoulders, pale, delicate features, and startling blue eyes that could disarm the most suspicious predator.

But the second she stepped into the room, any assumption that she was a dainty, submissive creature was blown all to hell.

Even with ten feet between them, Cyn could feel the unnerving pulse of her power beat against him.

That power combined with her brilliant intelligence would have made her a formidable clan chief, but Lise had refused to enter the battles of Durotriges. She claimed that her off-the-charts IQ prevented her from doing something so stupid as to become the leader of a bunch of barely civilized demons with authority issues. Cyn suspected her decision had more to do with a mysterious male from her past than any fear of commitment to a clan.

He never pressed for details. He wasn't about to lose the best lieutenant he'd ever had.

Halting in the center of the Turkish carpet that covered the stone floor, Lise allowed her gaze to take a slow survey of his large form.

It wasn't sexual. It was a well-trained warrior judging

whether or not Cyn's return was some sort of trick that would put the clan at risk.

When she was at last convinced he wasn't an illusion, or shape-shifter who'd assumed the identity of her clan chief, and that his mind didn't appear to be compromised, she took another step forward, an almost smile touching her lips.

"So. You live."

He flicked a brow upward. "Don't get all choked up."

She shrugged. "I knew you would return."

"I doubt the rest of the clan shared your confidence," he said, abruptly realizing his mind was only partially on his companion while the majority of his attention was focused on the startling acute sense of Fallon two floors above him. Bloody hell, had the female cast some fey spell on him? With a grim effort, he tried to slam the door on his unwelcome connection to the princess. "Did you have any challenges?" he demanded.

Lise's smile widened, giving a glimpse of her sharp fangs. "Oddly enough most of the clan think that I'm—"

"Scary as hell?" he completed in dry tones.

"Intimidating," she corrected. "Where have you been?"

"Fairyland."

There was a startled silence before Lise narrowed her gaze. "Is that a joke?"

"Actually it's a long story." He gave a shake of his head. He didn't want to discuss the fact he'd been magically transported out of the Chatri palace and caught in some dimensional limbo for weeks. He was still weirded out by the whole thing. "For now all you need to know is that no one can realize that I have returned."

A rare hint of surprise touched Lise's usually inscrutable face.

"Is there a particular reason why?"

"A request by an Oracle."

Lise grimaced. "A wise vampire tries to avoid the attention of the Commission."

No shit. Unfortunately Cyn hadn't been given an option.

"Too late," he muttered. "I'm just hoping to survive the next few days."

"What can I do to help?"

And that was what made Lise the perfect second-in-command.

No unnecessary dramatics. No annoying questions he obviously didn't want to answer. Just a request to know how she could assist.

"I will need you to continue with my clan duties."

"No problem." She studied his carefully guarded expression, clearly sensing that he was hiding something from her. "Anything else?"

"I'll need food."

Lise nodded. "I'll bring fresh blood tomorrow night."

"And fairy food," he commanded.

A startled blink. "Fairy food?"

Cyn ignored her response. "Nectar and the usual berries and nuts. And female clothing." He waved a hand toward his companion. "Slender like you, but a few inches taller."

Lise nodded, accustomed to Cyn's habit of filling his home with unexpected guests.

"Just one fairy?"

Once again he realized that he'd unconsciously reached out with his senses to lock on Fallon, a low hum of awareness vibrating through his body.

Bloody hell.

"Trust me, that's one more than I wanted to bring," he muttered.

Lise's power whipped through the room, forming a coating

of ice on the overhead chandelier, at the edge of frustration in Cyn's tone.

"Do you want me to get rid of her?"

"No." His power rose to match Lise's, an unspoken warning that his guest was not to be harmed. "She's here at the command of the Oracle."

Lise ratcheted down her rare ability to create ice as a weapon, studying Cyn as if he'd given away more than he intended.

"The mystery deepens," she murmured, her nose abruptly flaring as she tilted back her head to test the air. "What is that smell?" She shivered. "Delicious."

Cyn had already caught the unmistakable scent of champagne, his blood heating with a dangerous anticipation.

Damn.

"My unwelcome houseguest," he muttered, glancing toward the bank of security monitors that were discreetly attached to the wall in a shallow alcove above the desk.

Lise moved to stand at his side, her brows lifting at the sight of the female Chatri who was floating with elegant grace down the sweeping staircase.

"Unwelcome? She's beautiful."

Cyn snapped his teeth together.

No, not beautiful. Fallon was exquisite.

A walking work of art.

A lethal temptation that threatened to drive him over the edge.

"And a pain in the ass," he rasped, turning toward Lise as she gave a low chuckle. "What?"

"The best always are."

"The best what?"

She sent him a cryptic smile. "I'll leave you to figure that out."

"Thanks."

"I'll return later with the food and clothes."

With a mocking wave, Lise moved toward a hidden side door. The tunnel would take her directly to the small village that was built on a bluff overlooking the Atlantic Ocean.

Cyn gave a shake of his head, walking across the floor and out of his private chambers. He might not be the smartest vampire, but he had enough brains to know that he didn't want his personal space saturated with the intoxicating scent of the bewitching princess.

She had already managed to become a nagging constant in his brain when he was awake, she wasn't going to become a part of his dreams.

Not until she was soft and willing beneath him.

His long strides had him up the stairs and standing in the foyer that was paneled in a polished mahogany with an open beam ceiling and a massive stone fireplace. Absently he used his powers to light a fire beneath the neatly stacked logs. As a vampire he was immune to the distinct chill in the air, but he suspected that Fallon would be far more vulnerable to the temperature. The Chatri palace had been almost tropical during his brief visit.

He would have to remember to keep the lair warm.

Taking another step forward, Cyn watched as Fallon halted her descent down the stairs, her impatient expression being replaced by an annoying wariness as she caught sight of him.

"There you are, vampire."

A growl rumbled in his chest at her haughty tone. Why the hell had he bothered with the fire? The Ice Princess deserved to freeze.

"I have a name. Use it," he said, his fists planted on his hips.

"I don't take orders from you."

"And what about basic manners? Weren't you taught civilized behavior in fairyland?"

She held herself stiffly, her gaze trained on his face, as if forcibly preventing herself from checking out his body.

"You're right. I was being rude . . . Cyn."

Ah. His bad temper abruptly melted away.

Fallon, the fey princess, might not want to admit she was attracted to a savage vampire, but there was no mistaking the slight dilation of her eyes and the blush that tinted her cheeks.

He strolled forward, leaning against the carved post at the end of the stairs, eye to eye with Fallon as she stood on the bottom step.

"What do you want?"

"I need . . ." Her eyes abruptly widened, the emerald flecks in her eyes sparking with outrage. "Do you have a woman here?"

Cyn fought the urge to smile. "Jealous, princess?"

"Of course not." Her voice was just a tad too forceful. "I'm merely concerned considering that Siljar ordered us to keep our presence here a secret. You could have at least waited a few hours before breaking the rules."

"I'm a vampire with needs." He trailed a finger over her hand that was clutching the banister, relishing her tiny tremor before she was yanking away from his light caress. "So unless you're willing to fulfill them—"

"That's disgusting."

"Why?" he demanded. "You just made your list of demands, didn't you? You have needs that you want sated."

Her lips thinned. "I have to eat."

His hand moved to grasp a golden curl, sliding the silken strands between her fingers. "As do I."

She sucked in a sharp breath, but she didn't try to pull away, not even when his fingers moved to trace the faint blue vein running down the length of her neck.

"You were feeding?"

"Why do you care?"

"I . . ." Her chin tilted. "I don't."

He leaned forward, absorbing the intoxicating scent of champagne laced with an unmistakable hint of arousal.

"Liar."

# Chapter Four

Fallon told herself not to react to the annoying vampire as he joined her on the step, his hands landing on the banister so she was effectively trapped.

When she'd left the privacy of her room she'd been determined to be cool, controlled . . . civil.

It shouldn't be a difficult task.

She'd been playing the role of the perfect princess for over two centuries.

It should be child's play to slap a smile on her face and pretend she didn't want to stab a stake into the center of his chest.

But the second she'd caught sight of Cyn, her good intentions had shattered.

She didn't understand why her emotions became a tangled mess, or what made her nerves feel as if they'd been scraped raw, but she did understand that her reaction left her vulnerable.

"Cyn . . ." She forgot how to speak as his head lowered and she felt the touch of his lips against her throat. "Stop."

"Why?" His tongue traced the vein that he seemed to find so fascinating. "I smell your desire."

Fallon struggled to remember why she was convinced this was wrong. The gods knew it didn't *feel* wrong. Not when he was lightly scraping his fangs over her sensitive skin to send jolts of electric excitement shooting through her.

Oh . . . mercy.

She'd never met a man so tactile. His hands skimmed along the sides of her body, as if he was endlessly fascinated by her slender curves, while he continued to nip and nuzzle a path of kisses down her neck to the scooped neckline of her robe.

She instinctively reached to grasp his shoulders, her knees feeling oddly weak.

"I'm a princess," she forced herself to mutter.

She had to remind herself why she shouldn't be melting against his hard, savagely male body as his hands pressed against her lower back, urging her into contact with the thrust of his arousal.

His tongue traced the neckline of her robe. "I forgive you."

Fallon squeezed her eyes shut. He was stirring raw, primitive sensations that were threatening to overwhelm her.

"I mean my father has promised me to another," she said.

He slowly lifted his head, his brooding gaze locked on her flushed face. "Ah, the fiancé. Do you love him?"

She blinked in genuine confusion. "It isn't about love."

His gaze lowered to her lips. "Then it's about sex?"

"Of course not."

"There's no need to sound so shocked." His large hands gripped her hips, his incredible jade eyes dark with a sensual hunger that made her heart give a dangerous flutter. "The best relationships are based on lust."

Lust? Toward Magnus? She choked back the sudden urge to laugh.

"My marriage to Magnus is a—"

"What?"

"A melding of two powerful Houses."

His brows snapped together, an expression of disbelief on his painfully beautiful face. "Is that a joke?"

"Why would it be a joke?" Fallon was genuinely puzzled. Arranged marriages weren't uncommon among many species of demons. "My father is king and I am an asset he can use to solidify his position."

A chill cloaked around her. "An asset?"

"Yes." She warily tried to tug from his grasp. Why did he seem so angry? "Magnus brings to the marriage a large dowry and the loyalty of his very powerful House."

His hands tightened on her hips, his sensual charm decidedly absent. "And what does he get out of the deal?"

"His heirs will have royal blood."

The chill became downright frosty, making Fallon shiver. "So it is about sex."

Heat flooded her cheeks. She should tell him to go to hell. He had no business prying into her relationship with her fiancé.

But she didn't. It was almost as if his steady gaze was compelling the words from her mouth.

"It will be my duty to provide at least six live heirs," she muttered, revealing the truth that had been giving her nightmares since the engagement documents had been signed and her father had promised her future to a man who was little more than a cold, distant acquaintance.

"Duty?" Predictably he pounced on her revealing word. "Shouldn't that be a pleasure?"

"I don't know yet which it will be," she muttered.

"You mean . . ." Something that might have been satisfaction flared through his eyes. "You haven't slept together."

Her blush deepened. "It's forbidden until after we wed."

His hands slid up the curve of her waist, halting a tantalizing inch from her breasts. A low groan rumbled in his throat.

"He must be a fucking saint."

Fallon's mouth went dry. Her breasts were suddenly tingling, the nipples tight with a need she didn't understand.

"Not really." She grimaced. "Magnus is allowed to keep a harem."

A hot, dangerous hunger blazed in the depths of his eyes as her voice came out as a low, husky whisper.

"And you?"

It was growing difficult to concentrate on the embarrassing conversation. She'd never had a man span her rib cage with his big hands, his thumbs brushing the underside of her breasts. Or look at her as if he was imagining her naked.

"I'm expected to remain pure until the wedding night," she managed to rasp between dry lips.

A sound that was purely male was wrenched from Cyn's throat as he leaned into her, his lips stroking a cool path of destruction over her cheek to the edge of her mouth. She barely dared to breathe as his intoxicating sensuality wrapped around her like a cloak.

"And you call me a barbarian," he said, the tip of his fang lightly scraping her bottom lip. "I, at least, appreciate that a woman has the right to make her own choices."

*Her own choices . . .*

The fog of desire was abruptly pierced by a familiar pain.

For God's sake, did he think she wouldn't give everything she possessed—her fortune, her palatial quarters in the palace, and even her position as princess—if it would mean she could gain control of her life?

If she could be truly free?

Her hands lifted to press against his chest. "I don't want to discuss it."

"Fallon—"

"I need bowls," she abruptly interrupted.

He lifted his head, his brows arched. "Bowls?"

She gave another push against his massive chest. He was more than just invading her space. He was battering her with sensations that were as unfamiliar as they were unnerving.

"Yes."

Perhaps sensing she'd reached the limit of her endurance, Cyn reluctantly loosened his hold and backed off the step.

"I will have food delivered." He folded his arms over his chest, looking all broody again. "I assure you there's no need for you to slave in the kitchen."

As if she would know how to slave in a kitchen even if she wanted to.

"I need them to scry."

He gave a curt nod. "Fine. I'll take you there."

"If you'll just tell me where—"

With a blinding speed, Cyn was grasping her shoulders and sealing her mouth in a kiss that spoke of hunger and irritation and a smoldering frustration that was oddly echoed deep inside her.

Fallon was too shocked to immediately respond.

No doubt a good thing since she didn't have a clue if she wanted to slap his face or melt into his arms.

Instead she whipped up a less than convincing appearance of outrage as he pulled away.

"What's wrong with you?"

"I'll let you know if I figure it out," he growled, turning as if he intended to lead her to the kitchens. Then, without warning, he was whirling toward the front door, his fangs fully exposed. "Wait."

Fallon clutched the banister, her heart halting. Had her father found her? Or worse . . . Magnus?

"What is it?"

"Gargoyle," he snarled, the word barely leaving his lips before there was the sound of a small pop and a tiny creature with large fairy wings and stunted horns appeared in the middle of the foyer. "What the hell are you doing here?" Cyn demanded.

"Siljar sent me," the gargoyle said, spreading his arms and grinning at the furious vampire. "Lucky you."

Tonya had all sorts of reasons to be in a PMS mood as she switched on a lamp to battle the gathering shadows.

She was stuck in Chicago instead of taking care of the demon club that she managed for Viper. God only knew what disasters would be waiting for her when the Anasso allowed her to return.

She'd be lucky if the damned place was still standing without her to keep an eye on the volatile clientele who didn't consider a party started until someone was bleeding.

And now she was seated at the massive desk in Styx's library, staring at the mind-numbingly gorgeous Chatri prince who was strolling across the priceless carpet with enough arrogance to make her teeth ache.

A part of her wanted to grab the heavy crystal paperweight off the desk and toss it at his head. But a larger part of her wanted to rip off his black slacks and crisp white shirt and rub herself against his lean muscular body.

It was annoying as hell.

He was a rude, condescending ass who was clearly convinced she was far beneath his lofty royal position.

Precisely the sort of man she detested.

But the moment he walked into the room, she was zapped with such an intense sexual reaction that she felt physically compelled to reach out and touch him.

She tried to tell herself that it was merely a predictable reaction to being near a Chatri. They'd once been worshiped as gods by her people, hadn't they? The urge to become his ready, willing, and eager concubine was surely nothing more than a primitive instinct.

Or maybe she was just one of those women who had shitty taste in men.

She had, after all, believed herself to be in love with her boss, Santiago, who'd recently mated his beloved Nefri.

Whatever the cause, she found her nerves rubbed raw as the prince came to a halt in front of the desk, his expression haughty.

"Where is the Anasso?"

His power wrapped around her, the scent of aged whiskey teasing at her nose. She shuddered as a decadent pleasure bubbled through her blood.

"Do I look like a receptionist?" she forced herself to demand.

He narrowed his stunning cognac eyes. "You look like a lesser fey who should know her place."

Her hand reached for the paperweight. She wasn't going to throw it. Not yet.

"My place is at Viper's club, but because of you I'm stuck here."

He peered down the length of his noble nose. "It should be an honor to serve me."

"It's a waste of my time."

A frown touched his brows, as if he didn't know what to do with a female who refused to play by his rules. Then he gave a sharp shake of his head, the overhead chandelier catching the ruby highlights in the long length of his hair.

"I did not come here to speak with you," he said, his cultured voice holding the edge of an accent. "I need to see the vampire."

"Why?"

"It is not your concern."

Her fingers tightened on the paperweight. Styx hadn't forbidden her from doing bodily harm to the prince when he'd insisted she remain in Chicago.

Still, she didn't know how long she was going to have to deal with this aggravating male. After punching him in the nose it would probably be better if she resisted further bloodshed for as long as possible.

"Unfortunately it is," she said stiffly.

"I beg your pardon?"

"Styx has forced . . . requested that I be his liaison."

"And what does that mean?"

"Any requests you have for the King of Vampires must go through me," she informed him.

He made a sound of impatience. "That's unacceptable."

"No shit," she muttered. "But that's the way it is. So what do you want?"

Magnus studied her for a long minute, taking careful note of her stubborn expression. At last he heaved a resigned sigh.

"I wondered if he was aware there has been an imp circling the estate for the past hour."

"An imp?" Having expected some ridiculous demand, Tonya was caught off guard by the prince's question. With a smooth motion she was on her feet and heading toward the windows that overlooked the rose garden. When the Chatri had first made their appearance in Chicago, the King of Vampires' estate had been nearly overrun by fey who were desperate to catch sight of their one-time gods. Then Styx had sent his Ravens to warn the various imps, sprites, fairies, and nymphs that his house wasn't a damned tourist attraction and that he'd start putting fey heads on spikes if they didn't stay the hell away. It'd been enough to send the gawkers fleeing in fear. It seemed almost unbelievable that there would be an imp brave enough to invite the Anasso's wrath. "You're certain?"

Outrage touched the lean, beautiful face. "Of course I am certain."

"Male or female?" she demanded. "Did you get a good look at them?"

His gaze followed her hand as it slid into the back pocket of her leather pants to pull out her cell phone, lingering on the lush curve of her ass before it was abruptly jerking up to meet her taunting smile.

"A male," he said, his voice frigid although Tonya didn't miss the color that stained the pale honey of his skin. The prince had been sneaking a peek. "And I didn't see him at all."

Tonya's brief flare of amusement was forgotten as she studied him in confusion. "Then how do you know there's someone out there?"

"I can sense them."

She blinked in shock. "Even through the layers of magic?"

He shrugged. "It is my talent."

Her first thought was that he was lying. No one had the ability to detect an imp that was several hundred yards away and on the opposite side of the thick shields that protected the estate.

Then she realized that he had no reason to make up a story.

Not when he could so easily be proved wrong.

"I'll let Styx know." Tapping a brief text to the vampire who was no doubt just rising, she lifted her head to meet the cognac gaze that was studying her with an unnerving intensity. "Is there anything else?"

"Are all imp females so—" Words seemed to fail him.

"What?" She tilted her chin, her expression warning that

she wasn't opposed to planting another punch to his nose. "Beautiful? Clever? Sexy?"

"Outspoken."

Tonya shrugged. "We're all different, but most have no difficulty in sharing their opinion. Does that bother you?"

"True ladies—"

"Careful," she drawled, hiding her stupid reaction to his barely concealed disdain behind a façade of mocking indifference.

She was intelligent, capable, and most men found her sexy as hell. What did it matter if this prissy prince found her less than a woman?

"It is no wonder Sariel wished to separate us from this world."

Stepping forward, Tonya allowed her fingers to lightly stroke over his chest. "Are you afraid of a real woman?"

He stiffened, but he made no effort to slap away her hand. Instead his nose flared. Anger? Or was he breathing in her scent?

"The Chatri women are trained to be elegant, well-mannered companions who honor their mates," he muttered.

Tonya shivered as her fingers continued to trace the chiseled muscles beneath the silk shirt. She'd intended to torment Magnus the Magnificent, but suddenly her body was no longer connected to her brain.

Instead her thoughts were being fogged by the sensuous pleasure of at last touching him.

"They sound like schmucks to me."

His hands lifted to grasp her wrists, but he didn't pull her hands away. Instead his thumb absently stroked over her pulse that throbbed beneath the skin of her inner wrist.

"That word is unfamiliar."

Her gaze moved to linger on his lips. They weren't as lushly curved as most fey, but Tonya discovered a sharp-edged hunger to feel those hard, sculpted lines pressed against hers.

"Idiots," she said, speaking more to herself than explaining the meaning of the word.

His fingers tightened on her wrists, covertly tugging her closer to the enticing heat of his body.

"Because they appreciate a strong mate?"

She should pull away. Or better yet, push him away.

Anything to escape the surge of lust that was making her melt with a potent need.

Instead she glared into his beautiful face and leaned even closer.

"Because they've obviously allowed themselves to be bullied to the point that they're incapable of thinking for themselves."

His brows snapped together at her accusation. "I would never bully a female."

"No?" She lowered her voice to mimic his earlier words. "Why are you not on your knees, woman? I am your master. Yadda yadda."

He made a sound deep in his throat. "You are—"

"What?" she prodded, her heart thundering with sexual excitement.

"Extremely frustrating."

"Good."

He released a sharp breath, his gaze skimming over her face with a blatant confusion. "You are nothing like my women, so why do I want to kiss you?"

Her heart missed a necessary beat. "Maybe you like to go slumming."

The prince released her wrists so he could frame her face in his slender hands. "What is that?"

"Some men get a kick out of sleeping with women who they consider trash."

"Don't say that," he snapped.

"But you—"

"Hush," he growled.

"Did you tell me to—"

With shocking speed, he captured her lips in a kiss that demanded utter capitulation. For a second she stiffened, her survival instincts warning her that she was making a huge mistake. She was a common imp who worked at a demon club. He was a royal Chatri who would soon be returning to his home with his precious pure-blooded fiancée.

Then his tongue dipped into her mouth and she no longer gave a shit about the who or the why as a liquid heat seared through her.

Oh hell, yeah.

Tonya wasn't a virgin. She was a sensual woman who'd taken lovers over the years. All of them had been skilled enough to bring her pleasure. But none of them had created . . .

Fireworks.

She grabbed his upper arms, groaning as his fingers tangled in her hair and he deepened the kiss. He tasted of warm whiskey and raw male.

And magic.

A dazzling, wild magic that was uniquely fey.

Lost in the sensations that buffeted through her, Tonya missed the sound of footsteps. In fact, it wasn't until an unmistakable chill brushed over her skin that she realized they were no longer alone.

"Am I interrupting?" a deep male voice demanded.

With an unexpected quickness, Magnus was straightening and shoving her behind his lean body.

Tonya blinked in shock. Was he . . . trying to protect her?

"Not at all," the prince denied in aloof tones.

Styx moved forward, his expression stern although Tonya suspected there had been a brief twitch of his lips while he watched the male place himself squarely in front of her.

"Tell me about the intruder."

"I can take you to him."

Tonya shifted to the side to watch Styx deliberately pull out the large sword he had strapped to his back.

As if the King of Vampires needed a weapon to make him scary.

"This had better not be a trick, fairy," he growled.

Surprisingly Magnus didn't even flinch as he met Styx's narrowed glare. "I am Chatri royalty, not a common fairy."

"Whatever." Styx pointed the sword at the prince's throat. "Don't screw with me."

With a sharp shake of his head, Magnus was headed toward the door. "This is a madhouse."

Styx glanced toward Tonya, his expression pensive.

"Be careful, imp," he at last murmured. "There's more to this prince than he wants us to believe."

Tonya grimaced as she watched the men leave.

Yeah. She didn't need to be told that Magnus was hiding all sorts of unexpected surprises.


Styx followed the Chatri out of the house and into the vast grounds that were covered in a thick frost. Thankfully he was impervious to the brutally cold wind that whipped off Lake Michigan, but the fairy in front of him gave a sharp shiver, his steps slowing as he reacted to the frigid temperature.

Styx touched his sword to the center of the prince's back. "Stay in front of me."

Magnus picked up his speed even as he glared over his

shoulder. "If I wanted to hurt you, that sword wouldn't halt me."

"You'd be surprised what this sword can do."

"Vampires." Giving a shake of his head, the prince returned his gaze back to the shadowed garden, a golden glow abruptly surrounding his slender body.

Styx hissed, feeling the heat that the fairy was able to produce to keep himself warm. He'd never fought a Chatri, but he knew they could create a burst of energy that could destroy any number of demons.

Perhaps even a vampire.

Something to keep in mind.

They'd exited through a gate at the edge of his estate when Magnus came to an abrupt halt, holding up his hand.

"Hold."

"What now?" Styx growled.

He'd barely crawled out of bed when he'd received the text from Tonya. He was supposed to be spending the early hours of his evening on the phone with Darcy, not following a damned fairy on a wild-goose chase.

Magnus pointed toward the north. "The creature is hidden behind the large oak tree on the far side of the lake."

With a frown Styx moved to stand at the man's side, at last catching the faint scent of strawberries.

Imp.

Styx felt a newfound respect for the prince. There was no way in hell his own senses were acute enough to have picked up the fey from such a distance.

"Are you a tracker?"

Magnus gave a stiff nod. "I am."

"Impressive."

"Yes."

Styx rolled his eyes. "Wait here."

Moving forward, Styx gave a lift of one hand. The gesture

would signal his Ravens to circle the intruder, but to wait far enough away not to spook the creature until Styx had time to speak with him.

Then, moving with a silent speed that made him little more than a blur, he'd rounded the lake and approached the imp from behind.

Once close enough, he pressed the tip of his sword against the back of the creature's head.

"Don't twitch a muscle."

There was a squeak of terror, but the imp wisely froze as Styx slowly circled to study the overly pretty demon with pale green eyes and gold hair.

"Styx?" The imp drew in an unsteady breath, his fear drenching the air with the scent of strawberries. "It's me. Keeley."

Styx bared his fangs as a tidal wave of fury cascaded through him.

Keeley had been one of the bastards responsible for destroying the previous Anasso.

Leaning down, he grabbed the imp by his hair, lifting him off the ground and glancing toward his nearest Raven.

"Take him to the dungeon."

# Chapter Five

Fallon hadn't expected to sleep.

But after Cyn had escorted her to the kitchens and promptly disappeared, she'd gathered a dozen bowls and headed back upstairs. Then, choosing a room close to her private chambers, she'd filled each with water and infused them with her magic.

After that she had nothing to do but wait for the connection to the Commission to be completed.

It always took longer to scry for a person than a specific place. And the greater the magic of the person, the harder it was to get a lock on them. So tuning the bowls to the caves Siljar had seared into her mind, she set the magic to trip only for a demon of great power. Eventually she knew she would be able to track the movements of the Oracles, but it wouldn't be for several hours.

Unwilling to risk running into the vampire who seemed to have an uncanny ability to rattle her nerves, Fallon crossed the hall to her rooms and stretched out on the bed.

She'd only intended to rest for a few minutes, but obviously drained from expending so much magic she'd quickly tumbled into a deep sleep. It was past dusk when she woke and managed to drag herself to the shower.

Now, still dressed in the ridiculous robe with her damp hair left free to tumble down her back, she opened the door to her rooms, intending to check on her scrying bowls.

The last thing she expected to discover was a tiny gargoyle waddling down the hallway.

"Oh." She came to a halt, her brows lifting in surprise. Cyn had shared his opinion of Levet during the trip to the kitchens. And his determination to rid his lair of the "pest invasion." "I thought Cyn was going to make you leave."

The gargoyle sniffed, his fairy wings spread to reveal the brilliant crimson and blue patterns that were rimmed with gold.

"I do not answer to the vampires," he informed her, his ugly little features tight with outrage. "I have a higher calling."

"Of course." Fallon hid her flare of amusement. There was something excessively charming about the small demon being utterly unafraid of a vicious vampire ten times his size. "You said when you arrived that Siljar sent you. Are you a part of the Commission?"

"*Moi? Non.*" He gave a dramatic shudder. "I have discovered that being entangled in Oracle business always includes some daring adventure that ends with me doing all the work and some vampire or werewolf ending up with the beautiful maiden."

She blinked. "I . . . see."

"Still, I could hardly ignore Siljar's summons, or refuse her request that I assist Cyn and you in your efforts."

Fallon grimaced, easily able to imagine how happy Cyn was going to be when he crawled out of his coffin, or whatever it was a vampire slept in, and discovered the gargoyle still in his lair.

"So now Cyn has two unwelcome guests," she murmured.

Levet waggled his brows. "And one that is very welcome."

"I beg your pardon?"

"A female vampire just arrived," he explained. "They seemed to be very close friends."

Fallon narrowed her gaze. Cyn was entertaining *another* female vampire?

Was he suicidal? That could be the only excuse for deliberately trying to piss off Siljar.

"Indeed," she said between clenched teeth.

Levet tilted his head to the side. "Is something wrong?"

"Cyn clearly has difficulty following orders."

"Cyn follow orders?" Levet gave a light laugh. "From what I have heard, the clan chief of Ireland does precisely as he pleases whenever he pleases."

"You know him?"

Levet shrugged. "He spent a few nights at Styx's lair, but his reputation is widely known."

Fallon hesitated. She'd never enjoyed joining in the gossip that swirled around the royal court. Who cared who was flirting with whom, or which House was vying for more power?

Now she found herself incapable of resisting the urge to probe for information on her aggravating host.

"What reputation?" she at last demanded.

"He is a fierce warrior, naturally," Levet said, his tail aimlessly twirling around his clawed feet. "Berserkers are always dangerous savages."

Fallon frowned. She didn't need anyone to tell her that Cyn was a lethal enemy.

"Is that all?"

"*Non*." Levet waved a hand to indicate the vast medieval palace that served as Cyn's lair. "He is also a notorious hedonist who takes great pleasure in indulging his senses. His parties are legendary throughout Europe."

Fallon released her breath as a low hiss.

She'd already suspected the truth. No man could be so gorgeous and possess such irresistible charm without attracting hordes of women.

And he wasn't the sort of vampire to say "no" to a night of fun.

"I knew it," she muttered.

"Knew what?"

"He's what you would call a player, isn't he?"

Levet's brow furrowed with confusion. "Does that trouble you?"

Did it?

Hell, yeah.

And she didn't know why. Okay, she was attracted to him. Indecently, compulsively, unexplainably attracted.

But it wasn't like she was going to give in to her desires. Was she?

She wrapped her arms around her waist, telling herself that the small shiver was caused by the nip in the air, not the image she had of being spread across his bed while Cyn gently peeled off her robe, his fangs pressed against the vulnerable flesh of her throat.

A hot flash seared away any hint of a chill, sending a rush of color to her cheeks.

"Not as long as he realizes he can't play me," she forced herself to snap, acutely aware of the gargoyle's gaze that saw too much.

"Few women can resist the allure of a vampire," Levet said, heaving a deep sigh. "It is a baffling mystery of nature, like rainbows and unicorns and the breakup of the Backstreet Boys." He shook his head. "Unexplainable."

"Chatri females prefer men who are cultured, intellectual companions, not heathens," she lied with perfect composure.

"Is that right, princess?" a dark male voice drawled from behind her.

Oh . . . crap.

Slowly turning, Fallon watched as Cyn stalked toward her, holding two large bags.

He looked delectable in a pair of casual jeans that hung low on his hips and a cream cable-knit sweater that did nothing to disguise the massive width of his shoulders. The casual style should have made him seem less intimidating. Instead it only emphasized his lethal power and the impossible beauty of his fiercely male features.

But it wasn't just his undeniably gorgeous face and large body that made her heart slam against her ribs.

Halting just a few feet from her, the clan chief seemed to suck the air from the hallway, commanding attention by the sheer force of his presence.

A purebred male in the finest sense of the word.

She sternly squashed the urge to flutter like a damned dew fairy. She was a royal princess.

She didn't flutter.

At least not visibly.

"I thought you were entertaining a guest," she said, proud of her cool, aloof tone.

His gaze focused on the pulse that pounded at the base of her throat. "You seem fixated with who I might or might not be entertaining."

She tilted her chin. "My only interest is in completing my task for Siljar so I can leave here."

"And go where?" He stepped forward, his aggression suddenly prickling in the air. "Back to your fairy prince?"

She frowned. He almost sounded . . . jealous.

Which was totally ridiculous.

Her lips parted, but she found herself unable to speak beneath the intensity of his jade gaze.

Logic told her that she would eventually have to return to her homeland and fulfill the marriage contract. But she couldn't force the words past her lips.

Did she think that by refusing to admit out loud that she had no choice but to give in to her father's demands would somehow alter her future?

Thankfully Levet was moving to poke a claw at one of the bags as his nose twitched.

"Is that food?" he demanded. "Something smells delicious."

Cyn held the bag out of reach, glaring at the tiny demon. "Go away, gargoyle."

The wings twitched. "But—"

"I said"—Cyn leaned down, flashing his long, lethal fangs—"go away."

"Fine. I will hunt for my dinner." Blowing a raspberry toward the scowling vampire, Levet paused to offer Fallon a low bow before he was waddling toward the stairs.

Fallon sent her companion a chiding frown. "You truly have no manners."

Cyn shrugged. "I never claimed to be a gentleman."

She rolled her eyes. "Of course not. You enjoy being a brute."

He lifted his brows, his smile taunting. "Is that any way to speak to the man who holds your nectar?"

Fallon's stomach rumbled and her mouth watered as she abruptly realized she was desperately hungry.

Still she resisted the urge to snatch the bag from his hands.

Nectar didn't just appear out of thin air.

"How did you get it?"

"Lise is a vampire of many talents."

An unexplainable anger darted through her as she sucked in a deep breath and caught the faint scent of a female vampire clinging to his clothing. The same female vampire who'd been in the lair earlier.

"I can imagine," she said, her voice cold.

His lips twitched. "No, you truly can't."

Tiny sparks of magic warmed her palm. Her powers involved an ability to manipulate the environment around her.

Including creating small fireballs, as well as the blinding blast that could destroy most demons.

Not that she wanted to kill Cyn.

But she could singe the tips of those braids that framed his smug face.

Instead she held out an imperious hand. "May I have the nectar?"

He held the bags out of reach, his jade gaze skimming over her slender body. "What do I get in return?"

"What do you mean?"

"Quid pro quo." He stepped closer, his expression mocking. "I have food and nectar and clothes. What do you have for me?"

Her anger amped up another notch. Why did he take such pleasure in teasing and taunting and mocking her?

Was it because she was Chatri and her father had tried to separate his friend from his mate? Or was it because she was a naïve maiden with no knowledge of the games played between males and females?

No doubt his vampire friend was a master at pleasing a male.

Her hand dropped, her expression rigid. Full princess mode.

"It's your duty as my host to provide for my comfort."

"This isn't a hotel and I'm not your host," he drawled.

"What do you want?"

A slumberous heat darkened the jade eyes. "A kiss."

Her pulse spiked at his low words, heat flowing through her body.

"I don't know why you're determined to punish me," she muttered, trying to pretend that it was annoyance that stained her cheeks pink. "This situation isn't my fault."

He stepped forward, his gaze lowering to the unsteady line of her lips. "You think kissing me is a punishment?"

A punishment?

No. The thought of kissing him was . . . terrifying.

Gloriously, heart-stoppingly terrifying.

She took a deliberate step backward. "Where's your lover?"

His gaze narrowed as he tracked her sharp retreat. "Did you want her to join us? I didn't think a threesome would be your thing, but if you—"

"You're disgusting," she interrupted.

"A kiss, princess," he pressed. "I dare you."

Later she would blame her reaction on a mental melt-down.

She had, after all, been through enough over the past few hours to make any poor woman a little nuts.

Whatever the cause, she didn't hesitate as she stormed forward and without giving herself time to come to her senses, she grabbed the braids that framed his face and yanked his head downward.

She had a brief glimpse of Cyn's stunned expression before she was slamming her lips against his.


Cyn couldn't have been more astonished if the ground had opened up and swallowed him.

Aye, he'd deliberately provoked her. Who could blame

him? He'd spent hours pacing the floor of his bedroom, alone with his thoughts.

It wasn't that he was forced to remain beneath the ground. He'd made sure the castle was sun-proofed. But he'd known that if he gave in to the urge to leave the privacy of his chambers, he'd be headed straight for this female.

A knowledge that wouldn't have been so bad if it was sheer lust that was urging him to seek her out. He was a male. She turned him on. Simple. But it wasn't just sexual desire that had thrummed through him as he walked in endless circles.

No, it was a niggling fear that her room was too cold, and that she didn't have the proper food, and she might be missing her homeland.

Only sheer force of will kept him from giving in to the embarrassing need to seek her out and fuss over her as if he were some sort of demented mother hen.

Then dusk had fallen and Lise had arrived with the provisions he'd requested along with an update on his clan. He'd barely given her time to finish her report before he was heading out of his rooms and up the stairs to find the woman who'd plagued him for the past twelve hours.

The very fact that the need to see her had become a compulsion he couldn't ignore had set his temper on edge.

Still, when he'd tossed out his childish dare, he hadn't actually expected her to call his bluff.

Not until she was grabbing him by his hair and yanking him down for a kiss that blasted through him with enough force to wrench a groan from his throat.

Somewhere in the back of his mind he understood that this was supposed to be a "screw you" kiss. A punishment for his taunting.

But his body didn't care why her lips were pressed against his or why her fingers were spearing into his hair as he wrapped his arms around her slender form. It only knew that the aggravating princess was at last where she was supposed to be.

Drenched in the intoxicating scent of champagne, Cyn deepened the kiss, coaxing her from frustration to hunger. With a small moan, she parted her lips, inviting his tongue to dip into the welcoming heat of her mouth.

Cyn tightened his arms until she was lifted off the floor, kissing her as if he'd been starved for a woman. As if he'd been waiting for this precise moment for centuries.

He felt his body harden in exquisite anticipation.

Bloody hell. She was warm and soft and she tasted of sweet ambrosia.

One hand slid under her silken curtain of hair, gripping her nape in a gesture that was pure male possession while being careful not to bruise her ivory skin. Holding her so close, it was impossible to miss the fragile delicacy of her bones or the fact she weighed next to nothing.

Once again he was struck by that overriding need to care for her . . . to make sure she was protected.

Even from himself.

He allowed their tongues to tangle, briefly pressing her against his aching erection before he was easing back and allowing her feet to touch the floor.

She tilted back her head, her satin hair spilling over his arm with the stunning hues of a summer sunrise. Cyn's gaze skimmed over her flushed face, lingering on her lips that were still swollen from his kisses before meeting her stunned gaze.

"You're full of surprises, princess," he husked, his hands sliding up the slender curves to halt just below the gentle thrust of her breasts.

She shuddered, the scent of her arousal spicing the air

before she was abruptly jerking out of his grasp, her expression guarded.

"May I have my nectar?"

Cyn battled back his instinctive compulsion to pull her back into his arms, glancing down at the bags he'd dropped when he'd been overwhelmed by the need to touch Fallon.

Bloody hell, he was in trouble.

Big-ass-scary kind of trouble.

Baffled at how his life had been turned upside down so quickly, Cyn was on the point of full retreat when the sound of tiny bells had him grasping the hilt of his dagger that was holstered at his lower back.

"What's that?"

With obvious relief at the distraction, Fallon was turning to hurry into the room across the hall.

"My magic has activated," she said, moving to study the dozen bowls that had been arranged on the Persian carpet in the center of the floor.

Cyn halted near the doorway, studying the bowls with open suspicion. "Activated what?"

She turned to study his rigid posture. "Are you afraid of magic?"

Of course he was afraid. Magic was every vampire's worst nightmare. Okay, not his *worst* nightmare.

That would be looking like chicken shit in front of a beautiful woman.

Which was why he was squaring his shoulders and forcing his reluctant feet to carry him toward the bowls that flickered with eerie images that were as creepy as hell.

"I fear nothing."

Fallon smiled, not fooled for a second. "Such a big, bad vampire."

"Again with the big," he muttered. "Would you like me to show you—"

"Good, it appears that Siljar has called the Commission into session." She interrupted his peevish provocation, bending over a bowl closest to the stained-glass window.

Cyn frowned, forgetting his fear as he watched her tiny shiver. Dammit. He needed to find some way to keep the massive castle warm.

"Why is that good?"

"I can lock on them all at once."

Even without much knowledge of magic, Cyn recognized the amount of sheer talent, not to mention strength, it must take to keep a lock on a dozen of the world's most powerful demons.

"How long can you maintain your connection?"

She shrugged. "As long as I want."

Cyn felt an unexpected sense of pride spread through his heart as he moved to stand at her side, his fingers smoothing a stray curl behind her ear.

"No wonder Siljar was so anxious to get her hands on you." His lips twisted in a rueful grin as he felt tiny sparks of pleasure shoot from the tips of his fingers directly to his groin. "I know the feeling."

Instant arousal pulsed in the air, the scent of warm champagne making him hard with need.

His fingers drifted over the pale silk of her cheek, moving to outline the sweet temptation of her lips.

"Cyn," she breathed.

His mind was filled with delicious images of her mouth wreaking havoc as it explored his naked body, eventually taking his aching erection between those lush lips and . . .

"Hmm?" he murmured.

"What are you doing?"

"The hell if I know." His voice was a low growl.

"Your lover—"

"Lise is my most trusted lieutenant, not my lover," he

interrupted with a grimace. He'd been an idiot to ever have suggested there might be more between him and his clan mate.

"It doesn't matter." She licked her lips, the exotic emerald flecks in her amber eyes darkening with an unconscious invitation. "This isn't happening."

He slowly lowered his head, giving her plenty of opportunity to pull away.

"This?" He pressed a line of kisses down the length of her stubborn jaw. "Or this?" He gently bit her lower lip, allowing her to feel the razor-sharp points of his fangs.

Not a threat. A promise of the pleasure to be found in a vampire's arms.

She released a shaky breath, her lashes sweeping down in a futile attempt to disguise her primitive reaction to his touch.

"Don't mock me."

He pressed his lips to the vulnerable curve of her throat. His fangs ached to slide into her tender flesh, drinking deep of her rich, decadent blood.

"We're going to be trapped here together."

"And?"

"And there's no reason we can't enjoy our captivity."

For one delectable second he felt her melt beneath the soft exploration of his lips, her skin heating with an arousal she couldn't disguise. Then, as if she'd been struck by a sudden, unwelcome thought, her hands lifted to press against his chest, her head tilting back to stab him with an accusing glare.

"You intend to make me an addition to your harem."

Harem?

He was momentarily confused. Granted, he was a vampire who'd enjoyed his share of females. Sometimes more than one at a time. But his lovers had always been eager to be in his bed.

He'd never kept a stable of women who felt compelled to offer him their bodies.

Then his fangs lengthened as he recalled why she would be so suspicious.

Dammit. How dare she compare him to her faithless fiancé who kept a herd of females rather than devoting himself to pleasing this exquisite, utterly captivating creature?

"I'm not Magnus. I would never parade a pack of concubines beneath the nose of the woman who was to become my mate."

He instantly regretted the words as she paled, her eyes shadowed with a soul-deep pain.

"Don't."

"Hell, I'm sorry," he rasped. What the hell was wrong with him? This beautiful fairy princess was truly screwing with his mind. With a jerky motion he was turning, heading for the door before he could make the situation even worse. "I left your food and clothes in the hallway."

"Where are you going?"

His cowardly retreat never faltered. "To save the damn world."

# Chapter Six

Fallon was settled in the center of the floor, watching the images flicker in the bowls as she seethed over the vampire's assumption that she was going to become another notch on his bedpost.

Or at least, she told herself it was anger that was heating her blood and sending tiny quakes through her body. Because there was no way she was going to admit that it might be heart-pounding, gut-wrenching desire.

That was . . . unacceptable.

The oversized vampire was just like her worthless fiancé.

No, wait. That wasn't fair.

Magnus was an aloof, self-absorbed bastard who considered his giggling gaggle of groupies his right because he was a prince.

Cyn, on the other hand, was a charming brute who obviously adored women. And if Fallon was being completely honest with herself, she'd admit that her anger was directed more at her own reaction to his experienced touch.

She might not want to admit that she was as susceptible as the next female to a blatant playboy, but there was no doubt a very large part of her wanted to ignore her duty to her father and her virginal wedding bed.

How would it feel to forget she was a princess and just give in to the passion that exploded through her whenever Cyn was near?

A tiny shiver of anticipation raced through her body.

She sensed he would be a powerful lover. But tender. And thorough. Head to toe, and everywhere in between, thorough.

The sort of lover that would make a woman know she was in the hands of an expert.

Lost in the fantasy of being deliciously ravished by the vampire clan chief, Fallon was unaware of the tiny gargoyle who was silently crossing the room. Not until she nearly jumped out of her skin when a soft, male voice spoke directly into her ear.

"*Bonsoir, ma belle.*"

"Levet," she breathed in shock, not sure if she was relieved or annoyed at having her dangerous fantasies interrupted. She settled on relieved. Her body was still flushed and aching from Cyn's teasing caresses. Did she truly want to spend the rest of the night plagued by her unfulfilled desire? Or worse . . . give in to the temptation to track down Cyn and finish what he started? She made a choked sound, squashing the last thought as a white-hot excitement sizzled through her. Grimly she forced herself to focus on the small demon studying her with a shrewd gaze. "Did you find something to eat?"

"*Oui,*" the gargoyle assured her, patting his rounded little belly. "A farmer's wife was kind enough to share her shepherd's pie."

Fallon blinked in surprise. She'd spied on this world long

enough to know that few humans realized that there were demons living among them.

"She wasn't frightened to be visited by a gargoyle?"

"It is possible that she was not precisely aware of her generosity." Levet cleared his throat, his tail twitching. "It did not seem polite to wake her and ask her permission when she was sleeping so soundly."

Fallon hid a smile. "Very thoughtful of you."

"*Oui,* I am a very thoughtful demon." He gave a small sniff. "Unlike some."

Hmm. Fallon didn't need to be a mind reader to guess who he was referring to. "I assume you mean Cyn?"

Levet pursed his lips. "I am, of course, delighted to be of service to you, *ma belle,* but he could at least have allowed me to finish my meal."

"Be of service?"

Waddling across the room, Levet halted in front of the massive fireplace and spoke a low word of magic. Instantly the pile of logs caught fire, filling the room with a welcome heat.

"Cyn seems to believe that you will freeze to death if I do not ensure that there is a fire lit in each room you might enter," Levet muttered, turning to glance toward the empty pots that had held the nectar she'd consumed just minutes after Cyn had left. A blush touched her cheeks. It wasn't her fault she'd devoured the entire stash. She was an emotional eater. "He also insisted that I monitor your food intake."

Her brows snapped together. "Why?"

"He feared you might allow your magic to drain you if there wasn't someone near to remind you to replenish your strength."

"Oh." A perilous warmth spread through her heart. "He said that?"

Levet rolled his eyes. "It was really more of a growl."

"Did he say anything else?"

"*Oui*. I am to contact him immediately if I suspect that you are in danger of burning out."

"Burning out?"

"Using too much magic."

She shook her head, wondering what game Cyn was playing. Or maybe he was just demented.

That would explain how he could jump from the unwelcoming host, to the determined seducer, to the fussing mother hen. All in the space of a couple of hours.

His moods changed faster than a drunken dew fairy.

"I'm in no danger," she said.

A part of her wanted to be annoyed that Cyn would question her ability to take care of herself.

She might not be a kick-ass vampire warrior like Lise, but she wasn't helpless.

But a larger part was secretly savoring the sensation of having someone worry about her. When was the last time anyone had considered her needs? Among her people she was little more than a political pawn. Her feelings, her desires, her hopes and dreams were meaningless.

They certainly didn't spend any time fretting over the fear that she might be cold or hungry, or that she might be using too much magic.

"I have the bowls tuned to the various Oracles as well as triggered to warn me when someone enters the caves or if the Oracles leave," she continued, pointing toward the images that flickered on top of the water.

Levet moved to peer into the nearest bowl. "Clever."

Fallon bit her bottom lip, still obsessed with the fact that Cyn had sent the gargoyle to watch over her.

"So why is Cyn concerned?"

Lifting his head, the gargoyle glanced at her in confusion. "There is only one reason a male spends time thinking about whether a woman is eating or not, *ma belle*. Clearly he cares."

Her brows drew together as she remembered the sparks that flew between them whenever they were in the same room.

"If he cared, he wouldn't be so—"

"So?" Levet prompted.

Unpredictable? Fascinating? Gut-wrenchingly sexy?

"Annoying."

"He is a vampire." Levet's wings twitched, his gaze dangerously astute as he watched the hint of color touch her cheeks. "It is in their DNA to be a pain in the derrière."

Belatedly realizing she'd given away her fascination for the vampire who should mean nothing to her, she hastily tried to act as if her interest had nothing to do with her and everything to do with her sister who'd so recently become the mate of a vampire.

"What about Roke?" she demanded.

"Ah." Levet smiled, but Fallon sensed he wasn't fooled. "You have no need to worry about your sister. Roke is excessively devoted to her."

"And she's happy?" Fallon continued the game even though she had no need to ask the question.

She'd seen the way her sister and Roke looked at each other. The two were blatantly gaga for each other.

"*Oui*," Levet readily confirmed. "She appears to be very pleased with her mate."

Fallon nodded. She truly was happy for Sally. Even though

she hadn't known her sister when they were growing up, she sensed they could become friends if they were given the opportunity. Still, she couldn't deny a small pang of envy.

What would it feel like to be chosen by a male because he was so deeply in love with her that he couldn't imagine a life without her? To be consumed by his passion and to know he would never, ever stray from her bed?

"Good," she forced herself to say.

Levet tilted his head to the side. "And what of your mate?"

She glanced down at the robe she continued to wear. It would take time to gather the courage to try on the jeans and sweater that were now neatly folded in her room.

"Chatri don't mate," she admitted in low tones. "We have a more practical approach to relationships."

She heard the scratch of Levet's claws on the floor as he moved to stand beside her. "Practical?"

"Our marriages are arranged."

"Ah." The tiny gargoyle heaved a sigh. "That is often the choice among gargoyle royalty as well."

"It's . . ." She tried to come up with a word to describe her upcoming union with Prince Magnus. Bleak. Endless. "Efficient," she at last murmured.

"It is a suitable arrangement for some demons," Levet slowly agreed.

"Yes."

Fallon felt a small hand lightly stroke her arm, the comforting gesture pulling her out of her brooding thoughts.

"I sense your unhappiness, *ma belle*."

"Well, this is all very unsettling," she said, not wanting this creature's sympathy. "I've never been away from my father's palace."

Levet gave her another pat. "You are homesick?"

"Oh no," she breathed, trying to hide her tiny shudder at

the mere thought of being whisked back to the elegant palace and her inevitable fate. "I've always hoped to travel to this world." She grimaced. "Although my dreams hadn't included spying on the Commission or being trapped with a bipolar vampire."

Levet sighed. "*Oui,* bipolar vampires are usually reserved for our nightmares." He abruptly smiled. "Thankfully we will eventually discover the culprit and you will be able to explore this world."

Explore the world . . .

Fallon forced herself to snuff out the small spark of hope.

It would only lead to disappointment.

"My father will never allow me to remain," she said, her voice carefully composed. "Besides, I'll soon be marrying my prince."

Levet's fingers tightened on her arm, his expression filled with open sympathy. "I have learned that trying to live your life to please your family is a certain path to misery."

There was something in his lightly accented voice that assured Fallon that he did understand the burden of family duty.

"Did your family want you to wed a gargoyle of their choosing?" she asked softly.

"*Non.* They wanted me dead."

She sucked in a horrified breath. Good heavens. She thought her father was arrogant and overbearing.

At least he wasn't homicidal.

"Oh."

The gargoyle sent her a wistful smile. "If your father truly loves you, he will want you to be happy."

She swallowed a bitter laugh. Sariel didn't know the meaning of love. At least not the sort of love that humans lavished upon their children.

"Happiness is not valued among my people."

"Then perhaps you should remain among those who do value it, hmm?" Levet murmured, heading toward the door. "Something to consider."

Enough. Cyn slammed shut the thick book on fey history and rose to his feet.

He'd spent the past hours in his library, endlessly searching through books, manuscripts, and ancient scrolls in an effort to find hieroglyphs that would match the spell that Siljar had given him.

So far he'd found precisely nothing.

Oh. There were a lot of "almost" symbols, mostly fey in origin. But nothing that would allow him to decipher the spell.

Now he needed a break.

Grasping the scroll in one hand, he shoved himself to his feet and crossed the antique carpet to step through the door leading into the large study.

Then, pouring himself a large glass of the blood Lise had delivered earlier, he absently paced across the room to stare at the tapestry that his foster mother had made for him shortly after he'd finished building the castle.

It was a scene of a glistening white unicorn standing in the center of a flower-filled meadow with a pretty virgin kneeling at his side.

His foster mother, Erinna, had claimed he needed some reminder of purity to compensate for the debauchery that filled his lair.

Cyn grimaced as he realized that the female reminded him of Fallon.

The glorious golden hair. The delicate profile. The essence of innocence that shouted to his jaded soul with a siren's call.

His jaw clenched, the growingly familiar jolt of heat blasting through his body.

The female was rapidly becoming an obsession. Something that hadn't happened to him since . . .

*Since never,* a voice whispered in the back of his mind.

Polishing off the blood, he set aside his glass with a shake of his head.

What the hell was happening to him?

He'd known hundreds of women. Thousands. So why was this particular one driving him bat-shit crazy?

He was still debating the question when his peace was destroyed by the tiny gargoyle who waddled into the study.

Usually Cyn took pride in the satinwood furniture that he'd carved with his own hands, and the arched, stained-glass window that refracted the sunlight until it filled the room with a dazzling display of harmless colors.

Now he barely suppressed the urge to grab the creature by the tail and toss him out of the room.

"What do you want?"

The gargoyle sniffed. "I thought you would wish to know that I completed my duty."

"You made sure the rooms are warm enough?" he demanded.

It was ridiculous, but he couldn't shake his concern that Fallon might be uncomfortable in his lair.

"I did." Levet moved toward him, his tail rigid with outrage. "Not that I appreciate being treated as a servant."

Cyn arched a brow. "You don't want Fallon to be kept warm?"

"Of course I wish the *petite fille* to be warm. But I am a warrior of great renown. I should be given tasks that are suitable to my considerable talents."

"What you are is a pain in the . . ." Cyn's muttered words were forgotten as the gargoyle reached up to snatch the scroll from his hand. "Hey."

Levet frowned as he studied the spell. "What is this?"

Cyn narrowed his gaze as suspicion raced through him. "I thought that you said Siljar sent you."

"She did."

Cyn grabbed the paper back, ignoring the fact they were behaving like a couple of five-year-old humans.

"Then you should know what this is."

Levet wrinkled his snout. "Siljar wasn't in the mood to share why I was to come here. In fact, she was acting in a most peculiar manner."

"Obviously she just wanted an excuse to get rid of you."

The gargoyle stuck out his tongue. Ridiculous pest.

"I do not know why you are being so secretive." He pointed a claw at the spell in Cyn's hand. "It is not as if I can see what is written unless you remove the illusion."

"Illusion?" Cyn froze, a strange chill inching down his spine as he held up the yellowed parchment. "On this?"

"*Oui.*"

"How do you know?"

"Illusions happen to be my specialty." Levet preened, giving a flap of his wings. "Along with seducing beautiful women."

Cyn dismissed the gargoyle's bloated ego, his gaze lowering to the scroll.

"Why didn't Siljar notice? Or even Fallon?" he demanded. "They both should have been able to sense magic."

"It isn't a traditional spell."

"What do you mean?"

"The writing itself is the illusion."

Cyn shoved the scroll toward his companion. "Get rid of it."

"*Non*." Levet shook his head. "I cannot."

Cyn released a trickle of power, a humorless smile twisting his lips as the gargoyle shivered at the pinpricks of ice that filled the air.

"You just said that illusions are your specialty."

Levet rubbed his arms, his heavy brow furrowed. "If I break the illusion, the writing will disappear."

"Damn." Cyn shook his head. Why would a stranger leave a spell with the Commission that was hidden beneath an illusion? None of this made any sense. "Then what's the point?" he growled.

"Your eyes see this." A claw touched the fragile paper. "But your mind sees the truth."

Cyn scowled. "Are you deliberately trying to piss me off?"

"I am trying to explain—"

"Then say it in words I can understand," Cyn snapped. He hated magic.

Having to deal with it made him . . . irritable.

"The spell appears to be mumbo jumbo," Levet said, his brows abruptly lifting. "Have you truly been trying to decipher it?"

Cyn flashed his fangs. "Get on with it, gargoyle."

"Party do-do," the gargoyle muttered.

Do-do? It took Cyn a second to realize what the fool meant.

"Pooper, you prat."

Levet waved aside the correction. "But beneath the magic it is like a subliminal message that becomes lodged deep in your mind."

Reaching down, Cyn grabbed the pest by his horn, dangling him off the ground so they were eye to eye.

"Let me make this simple. I need to know what this

says." He waved the hieroglyphs in front of Levet's snout. "How do I do that?"

Levet pouted, but clearly realizing that Cyn's temper was reaching a critical edge, he resisted the urge to make some snarky comment.

Wise gargoyle.

"Perhaps a magical artifact would . . ." Levet gave a small squeak as Cyn dropped him without warning and headed toward the door that connected to his library.

"Bloody hell," he muttered.

"Where are you going?" Levet demanded, following him like a stray puppy.

"When Siljar said there was something in my library that might help I assumed she meant a book," Cyn muttered, too late realizing how dangerous it was to jump to conclusions. Reaching the doorway, he turned to point a warning finger at the gargoyle. "Wait here."

"But . . ."

Cyn stepped into the library and slammed the door shut behind him. No one, absolutely no one, was allowed in his private sanctuary.

He swiftly moved across the book-lined room to the hidden panel just behind his massive desk. Laying a hand on the wood, he waited for the magic his foster parents had cast to recognize his touch. With a faint click the panel slid open to reveal the small cupboard filled with Erinna and Mika's most prized possessions.

It'd been Cyn who'd insisted on bringing the collection of magical artifacts to his hidden safe. The rare potions, crystals, and amulets were worth enough to encourage any number of demons to try and get their greedy hands on them.

He didn't want his family taking unnecessary risks.

It was his duty to protect them.

Which was why he was so aggravated that they'd deliberately put themselves in danger.

Tucking his concern for them to the back of his mind, he grabbed a large crystal off the top shelf and returned to the study.

He'd barely stepped through the door when Levet was hurrying toward him, the fairy wings buzzing with excitement. Unlike Cyn, the gargoyle would be capable of sensing the magic of the crystal threading its way through the air.

"What do you have?"

"Truth," Cyn said, hoping his foster mother hadn't exaggerated when she'd said this particular crystal could not only force humans and weaker demons to speak honestly, but that it could see through written deception.

He could only hope it would work on an illusion.

"*Oui,* very clever," Levet breathed, not bothering to hide his surprise. "At least for a leech."

"Here." Cyn shoved the crystal and piece of parchment into his companion's hands. He might want to strangle the tiny plague to his existence, but gargoyles were capable of manipulating many different kinds of magic. "Remove the illusion."

Levet nodded, but he looked oddly wary as he held the crystal toward the unrolled parchment.

"Very well, but without knowing what is beneath . . ." There was the sound of a loud sizzle, then without warning a tangible cloud of evil spread through the room. Making a sound of disgust, Levet shoved the paper and crystal back into Cyn's hands. "*Mon Dieu.*"

Cyn shuddered. "What the hell?"

"It's coming from the spell," Levet said, backing away with a grimace.

"Is it dangerous?"

"*Non*. At least . . ." The gargoyle gave a small shrug. "I do not think so."

Cyn scowled. "Awesome."

There was the faint sound of footsteps, then the door leading to the hallway was shoved open so Fallon could rush into the room.

"Are you hurt?"

# Chapter Seven

Fallon hadn't known precisely what was causing the ripples of evil to sweep through the lair, but she hadn't hesitated to rush from her room to . . .

What?

To make sure that Cyn wasn't in danger?

How stupid was that?

He was a vampire. Hell, he was clan chief. And a berserker.

A demon would have to be demented to try and challenge him.

Still, she couldn't halt her agitated flight that led her to the large study.

Now she wiped her hands down the silky material of her robe, feeling like a total idiot as Cyn and Levet turned to watch her with matching expressions of surprise.

"Ah, *ma belle,* forgive me." Levet was the first to recover, moving toward her to press a kiss to the back of her hand. "I have managed to remove the magic that disguised the spell."

Her embarrassment was forgotten as her attention turned to the spell that Cyn held in his hand.

"Disguised?" She shook her head in confusion. "There was an illusion?"

"*Oui*."

Without even realizing she was moving, Fallon was standing next to Cyn.

"Why didn't I sense it?"

"It was woven into the writing," Levet explained.

"Odd." She bent to study the markings, relieved that the weird sense of evil was rapidly dissipating. "It looks the same."

"Almost." Cyn moved to a low table, smoothing the piece of scroll until it lay flat. Then, gesturing for her to join him, he pointed a finger at the hieroglyphs. "The basic patterns are similar, but now it's . . . in focus."

Fallon grimly concentrated on the symbols, refusing to acknowledge the tiny glow of happiness at being included.

Okay, he treated her as if she were a person with an actual brain. And he seemed to think she could contribute more than a pretty smile and the proper bloodline.

Still, that didn't mean he wasn't too large, too male, too . . . everything.

"Can you read it?"

"Not all of it." His shoulder brushed hers as he used his finger to trace the symbols. "It's a confused jumble of hieroglyphs. Fairy, imp, and even human. But I can read enough to get a general idea."

"Well?" Levet prompted, struggling to see over the edge of the table.

Cyn's finger halted at a hieroglyph that was made up of interconnecting circles. "This is a portal and these are the veils that divide the dimensions." He moved to a half-moon shape with a line through it. "I don't recognize this."

Fallon's breath tangled in her throat. "It's Chatri."

"What does it say?"

"Destruction."

There was a long, uneasy silence as they exchanged wary glances.

Finally Cyn asked the question that was obviously troubling him.

"Of the veils?"

Levet clicked his tongue, his wings drooping. "Not again."

"No." Fallon leaned forward, reading the part written in Chatri symbols. "It says 'the destruction of pathways.'" She pointed toward the end of the page. "And here. 'The entrances shall be forever closed.'" She paused, rereading the passages several times before she finally lifted her head to meet Cyn's searching gaze. "I think this is a spell to close portals. All portals."

Cyn frowned. "What does that mean?"

"It would mean the end of travel between dimensions," Levet said, his brow furrowed.

Cyn frowned. "That's it? That's all this spell does?"

"All?" Fallon pressed a hand to her heart. "It's . . ." She shook her head, too horrified to even come up with the words. The mere idea of closing travel between dimensions was insanity. Instead she turned her attention to the tiny gargoyle. "Is that possible?"

"That is the question, is it not?" Levet muttered, rubbing one of his stunted horns.

Fallon's shock shifted to fury. "If there is a spell that can prevent portals from being formed—even portals that open from place to place within this world—how would the fey travel?"

Cyn folded his arms over his chest, clearly baffled by Fallon's outrage.

"They would be forced to use human technology," he

said with a shrug. "Or use their feet like demons were meant to do."

She sent the vampire a frustrated frown, her earlier pleasure in being treated as an equal forgotten at his complete lack of empathy for the fey.

Was he always so annoying or did he make a special effort just for her?

"Don't you understand?" she snapped. "My people would be completely cut off from this dimension."

He gave another shrug. "You've been cut off for centuries."

"By choice," she said through gritted teeth. Then she grimaced, realizing she wasn't being entirely honest. "Or at least the choice of my father," she clarified.

Levet deliberately cleared his throat. "And fairies wouldn't be the only demons either forced to return to their homelands or be separated from their families for the rest of eternity."

The thick-skulled vampire abruptly stiffened. "Santiago."

"Precisely. Not that I particularly care about your ill-mannered friend." Levet gave a small sniff. "But lovely Nefri and her clan would be forever cut off from this world," he continued, referring to the vampires that had chosen to live beyond the Veil. "And there is no way to predict exactly what the closures will do to the demons who remain here."

"What does that mean?" Cyn pressed.

Fallon made a sound of disgust. "Typical. You didn't care what happened to the fey, but now that it affects vampires—"

"Magic comes into this world in many forms." Levet hastily interrupted. "Some is the natural residue from demons, but there is a great deal that seeps through the veils that separate our dimensions."

Fallon sucked in a deep breath, regaining her composure.

Damn the oversized, arrogant . . . aggravatingly gorgeous vampire. She'd never realized she even possessed a temper until he'd come crashing into her world.

"This spell would stop the magic?" she asked, determined to concentrate on the looming disaster.

Levet nodded. "*Oui.*"

Naturally Cyn had to intrude. "What happens to the demons who depend on it?"

"All demons depend on magic to survive." Levet deliberately held Cyn's gaze. "Even vampires."

His jaw clenched. "You didn't answer the question."

"It's impossible to know for certain," the gargoyle confessed. "But there's a very real possibility that our powers will begin to fade until we—"

"Die," Cyn completed the sentence.

The harsh word hung in the air before Levet gave a slow nod of his head.

"That is my fear."

Fallon pressed a hand to her throat. As a Chatri princess she could return to her homeland, but what of all the lesser fey who would die? Not to mention all the other demons who would be trapped and condemned to a slow, painful death.

"Why would anyone even consider closing the portals?" she choked out.

"I intend to find out. But first . . ." Cyn glared in Levet's direction. "Can you get in touch with Siljar? She needs to know what we've discovered."

The gargoyle wrinkled his snout. "I can try."

Taking several steps backward, the gargoyle gave a dramatic lift of his hands, his eyes closed as he sent some sort of mental message to the Oracle.

Beside her, Cyn made a sound of disgust, his lips parting

as if he were about to share his opinion of Levet's less than subtle style.

But before he could speak there was an ominous electric charge in the air, and without warning Levet was flying backward to hit the wall with a sharp thud before sliding to the ground.

With a muttered oath, Cyn was striding across the floor to grab the gargoyle by the horn, hauling him back to his feet.

"What the hell was that?"

"It would appear that Siljar isn't in the mood to be bothered right now," Levet muttered, rubbing his backside.

Fallon bit her bottom lip. That didn't sound good.

"What does that mean?"

Levet gave a shrug. "Either she is truly busy and does not wish to be disturbed. Or—"

It was Cyn who finished the sentence. "Or she's under the control of someone, or something."

Oh hell. It was just as bad as she feared.

"Do you think the person who is trying to manipulate the Commission sent them this spell?" she demanded.

"Aye," Cyn muttered.

"So what do we do?"

Cyn returned to her side, staring down at the dangerous hieroglyphs.

"I have to discover who is behind the spell." His jaw clenched. "And stop them before they can force the Commission to cast it."

She frowned. "Don't you mean *we?*"

He sent her a stern glance. "I'm going to take care of this. You need to return to fairyland."

"*Mon Dieu,*" Levet muttered, gingerly inching toward the door. "I believe that is my cue to leave."

Neither of them noticed the gargoyle exiting the room, both intent on winning the glaring contest.

"I was brought here just as you were," she reminded the arrogant man. "I have a duty."

His gaze narrowed. "That was before we realized the magnitude of the danger. I'm sure Siljar would agree that you should travel back to your home."

Fallon tilted her chin. "And I'm sure she'd expect me to complete the task she gave me."

"Fallon—"

"No," she interrupted.

It wasn't that she was particularly courageous. Or that a part of her didn't want to rush back to her father's palace where she'd be removed from the danger. But she'd been brought to this world for a reason, and she wasn't leaving until the job was done.

No matter what the oversized vampire might say.

Turning, she headed for the door.

"Wait," he growled from behind her. "We aren't done discussing this."

Her retreat never faltered. "A discussion implies an equal exchange of ideas. You were giving me a command and expecting me to obey." Reaching the door, she paused to glance over her shoulder. "I don't take orders from you."

A scowl pinched his brows together, his fangs fully displayed, but before he could continue the argument, she was out the door and headed back to her rooms.

Over the next few hours, Fallon spent her time either monitoring the bowls or resting in her bedroom.

She wasn't hiding from Cyn. Of course she wasn't.

It was just that . . .

Okay, she'd been hiding. With a grimace, she forced her

feet to carry her down the stairs and through the vast catacomb of rooms.

Being around the vampire clan chief was like being thrown into a raging storm.

She'd lived her life in endless golden peace. No changes. No surprises. Just one sunny day after another.

Now she was suddenly staying in a dark castle, spying on demons who could crush her with a mere thought, and stuck with a vampire who turned her into a woman she didn't recognize.

She should have been horrified. Instead, she'd never felt more alive.

Suddenly she was surrounded by a whirlwind of emotions. Fear, annoyance, excitement, and a potent desire that haunted her even when she was asleep.

It was no wonder her instincts were warning her to try and minimize the impact of this world on her.

It would be hard enough to return to her homeland when this strange adventure came to an end. How much harder would it be if she allowed herself to become even more addicted to the intoxicating feelings that sizzled through her?

But waking just as dusk was falling, Fallon had come to a firm decision.

No more hiding.

She didn't know how much time she was going to have in this world. She was going to savor every second.

With her decision made she'd hopped into the shower, then defiantly pulled on the jeans and lavender sweater that Cyn had given her. With her hair left loose to tumble down her back and her cheeks flushed, Fallon barely recognized herself in the mirror.

Gone was the perfectly groomed princess, and in her place was the real woman beneath the façade.

Her father would be horrified.

Moving from room to room, Fallon had finally halted in the paneled chapel, her fingers reaching to lightly trace the delicately carved altar. She didn't need to be told that it was the work of Cyn. It was obvious in every perfect line and curve that created the image of a sturdy tree growing out of the tiled floor.

Right on cue Fallon felt the distinct chill that warned a vampire was approaching.

Slowly turning, she watched as Cyn appeared from the shadows, her breath squeezed from her lungs as she took in his large body covered by a pair of faded jeans and a cashmere sweater that was the precise jade green of his eyes. His blond hair was still damp from the shower and the braids that framed his bluntly chiseled face were threaded with tiny glass beads that caught the dim candlelight.

He was a big, gorgeous warrior with the soul of an artist.

Precisely the sort of man that had filled her girlish fantasies.

Excitement fluttered through the pit of her stomach, her heart pounding as he strolled past the pews to stand directly in front of her.

For a long minute he studied her in silence, taking a slow, thorough survey of her slender body. Starting at her feet that she'd left bare, his gaze traveled up the jeans that hugged her long, slender legs and then over the sweater that outlined the curve of her breasts. His nose flared, his hands clenching at his side as if he were battling a strong emotion.

"Exploring, princess?" he at last demanded, meeting her wary gaze.

Fallon stiffened, instantly assuming he was angry. "Is that against the rules?"

"There are no rules," he instantly hastened to assure her. "You're welcome to go wherever you want in my lair."

"I am?"

He stepped close enough for her to feel the cool rush of his power wrap around her. Her skin prickled with awareness, her mouth dry as she resisted the urge to close the small space between them and press against his broad chest.

Crap. What was it about this vampire that set her senses on fire?

And why the hell couldn't she feel this same blistering exhilaration with Prince Magnus?

It might not bring her complete happiness, but it certainly would make the marriage less of a burden.

"As you have pointed out, you are my guest," he said, pretending that he couldn't catch the scent of her stirring arousal.

"And only a few hours ago you were trying to get me to leave." Her lips flattened. "In fact, you've been trying to get me to leave since we woke in the caves."

He shrugged. "Clearly that's not going to happen. At least not in the foreseeable future. So in the meantime I want you to feel at home here."

Fallon frowned. Okay, something was wrong.

Cyn had been bossy, irritating, and insanely sexy since he first intruded into her father's palace. But he'd never played the role of gentleman.

"Did you take a fall down the stairs?" she demanded.

He arched a brow. "Excuse me?"

"You are behaving almost civilized," she said, not bothering to hide her suspicion. "I assume you must have taken a severe blow to the head."

His lips twisted with a hint of regret. "This has been . . . difficult for both of us."

She grimaced. "We can agree on that."

"We can also agree that it's not helping for the two of us to be sniping at each other," he said.

Fallon hesitated. She might be a complete innocent, but

she sensed that she'd instinctively nurtured the nagging antagonism for a reason. Still, it seemed childish to toss his tentative olive branch back in his face.

"I did suggest we try to avoid one another," she reminded him.

His gaze lowered to the vulnerable curve of her mouth. "I have a better solution."

"You do?"

He had a hold of her hand and was tugging her toward a side door before she could guess his intentions.

"Come with me."

Fallon told herself to pull away from his light grasp. Hadn't she been determined to enjoy her short time in this world? And that meant relishing a few hours of choosing what she wanted to do rather than being told where she had to be and what she had to wear and how she had to behave.

But curiosity overcame any annoyance at being tugged around like an untrained puppy. Why spend the night roaming the ancient castle alone when she could have Cyn as a guide?

Her capitulation had nothing to do with the white-hot flames of anticipation licking through her.

Did it?

Trying to pretend her heart wasn't racing and her stomach wasn't fluttering, Fallon allowed herself to be led down a flight of stairs that had been hidden behind a marble statue.

"Where are we going?" she asked as they traveled deep beneath the castle. "I don't need another tour of your caves."

His pace slowed as they reached a narrow tunnel. "Patience."

Fallon grimaced. Patience was the one quality that she'd been forced to develop just to survive in her world.

Now she didn't want . . .

Her spurt of irritation was forgotten as he shoved open a heavy door and allowed a flood of sunlight to fill the tunnel. Horror raced through her as she tried to drag him away from the killing rays.

"Cyn."

"Trust me," he murmured, resisting her frantic tugs and instead urging her forward.

Accepting that the sunlight posed no danger to her companion, Fallon cautiously stepped through the doorway and into . . . paradise.

With a gasp she took in the large meadow that was spread before her.

A cloudless blue sky seemed to spread above them, stretching toward the horizon with no beginning and no end. Below her feet was a carpet of crisp spring grass and tiny daisies where butterflies danced and floated on the cool breeze. In the distance she could see a babbling brook that was shaded by large weeping willows. And in the very center of the field was a marble grotto with fluted columns that might have been plucked from a Greek villa.

An illusion. It had to be.

And yet it was so perfectly created that she could feel the heat of the sun, smell the rich earth, and hear the distant chirp of birds.

"Oh," she breathed, turning her head to discover Cyn watching her with an unreadable expression. "How?"

"My foster mother," he said, his brow flicking upward as her lips twitched. "What's so amusing?"

She wrinkled her nose, allowing her toes to curl into the soft grass. Spell or not, it felt good to have the sun warming her chilled body.

"The thought of two fairies being your parents."

"It was an odd situation." A fond smile softened his features. "Still, I never forget that I owe them my life."

She watched as he angled his face toward the sky, intrigued by the fey who'd obviously loved this vampire enough to bring him the sun.

"Why do you owe them your life?"

"Newly made vampires who aren't taken in by their sire rarely survive," he murmured, his eyes closed as he savored their magical surroundings.

Fallon felt an unexpected flare of panic at the mere thought that this magnificent male might have died before he'd ever had a chance to crash into her life.

"I've never understood why vampires would create children and then abandon them," she muttered.

Cyn shrugged. "It's something that Styx is slowly changing. Lucky for me, Erinna and Mika found me in the caves below this lair and took me into their home."

She glanced around the meadow, awed by the amount of magic it had taken to create such a special place.

"They obviously love you."

"Aye. Yet another rare gift for a vampire." He opened his eyes, taking her hand to lead her toward the grotto. "I have another surprise."

Feeling as if she'd strayed into some sort of dreamworld, Fallon allowed herself to be led across the meadow, climbing the marble stairs. Cautiously she stepped past the columns, her eyes widening at the sight of the blanket spread across the floor with a large basket and a bottle of champagne chilling in a bucket of ice.

She sent a startled glance toward Cyn. "A picnic?"

The vampire moved to settle next to the basket, pouring them both a glass of champagne before he pulled out the plate of sliced fruit that had been dipped in nectar.

Exactly as she liked it.

"You need to eat."

She blinked, slowly sinking onto the blanket. Okay, it was one thing for him to make an effort to be polite. But why would he arrange this beautiful meal?

Maybe he really had fallen down the stairs and rattled his brains.

Difficult to come up with another explanation.

"I did eat."

"Hours ago."

She thought back, recalling that she hadn't touched the tray that had been left outside her bedroom door before leaving to explore the castle. But how had he known?

Unless . . .

"Are you having Levet spy on me?" she demanded.

Taking a slice of apple, he pressed it to her lips. "If I have to have him in my house then he can at least make himself useful."

Fallon took a bite of the fresh fruit, shivering as the taste exploded in her mouth. There was something unbearably intimate about being fed from his hand.

"I don't understand why you're being so nice," she said softly, her expression unconsciously vulnerable.

His fingers lingered, lightly tracing the curve of her lower lip. "It might be hard to believe, but I'm usually considered to be a charming bloke."

"If you say so," she forced herself to mutter, the insult losing its punch as she shuddered at the feel of his cool fingers skimming the length of her jaw.

"You possess an uncanny ability to . . ." He hesitated, as if he was searching for the words. "Get under my skin."

She narrowed her gaze. "Get under my skin" sounded remarkably like "annoy the hell out of me."

"What does that mean?"

His finger traced the vein that ran the length of her throat. "I want you."

Heat blasted through her at his unexpected words, her body tingling with a bone-melting awareness.

She wanted to believe that it was a predictable reaction to a male so bluntly stating his hunger for her. After all, she'd never had a man treat her as if she were a desirable woman. Not when the male Chatri knew that any interest would be seen as a direct insult to the king.

What woman wouldn't feel all hot and bothered?

But a part of her knew that her reaction had nothing to do with her innocence and everything to do with a gorgeous hunk of a vampire who made her want to forget about duty and fiancés and bury herself in his arms.

"Cyn," she murmured, not sure if she was pleading for him to stop or to throw her back on the blanket and ravish her.

Not that her body was conflicted. It wanted the ravishing.

"But it's more than that," he continued, his lips twisting as he grabbed another slice of apple to feed to her. He waited until she'd eaten the fruit before he continued. "Even when you're not around, my thoughts turn to you. I need to know that you're taking care of yourself and that you're—"

A frisson of excitement fluttered through the pit of her stomach as his fingers tangled in her hair, his gaze brooding as he studied her upturned face. She could physically feel the hunger that hummed through his body.

Or maybe it was her own hunger.

Either way it was making her tremble with a delicious sense of anticipation.

"That I'm what?" she asked.

"Not unhappy."

She met his piercing gaze, sensing the intense emotions that smoldered just beneath the surface.

Was he angry? Frustrated? Wishing he'd never followed his friend into her homeland?

"Why do you care?"

His lips parted, his fangs fully extended. "That, princess, is a question without an answer."

# Chapter Eight

Wearing a cloak that covered him from head to toe, Sir Anthony Benson felt a sharp stab of relief as a shimmering breach suddenly appeared in the middle of his attic.

It'd taken Yiant only a few hours to return with the potion that Anthony had demanded, but he'd hesitated to complete the spell. He needed to speak with Keeley before he headed into the lair of the Oracles. If the Chatri were in this world because they sensed his plot, then he needed to take extra precautions.

But as the hours passed with no sign of the imp, he'd at last started his preparations. Whether Keeley had given in to his cowardice and run or he'd been killed by the King of Vampires, Anthony couldn't wait any longer.

The spell of Compulsion he'd built layer by slow layer around the Commission would already be starting to fade. And just as dangerous, his connection to one Oracle in particular was reaching a critical point.

A fact that had been emphasized when it'd taken him three attempts to magically command the demon to leave the caves and form the breach that he needed to travel halfway around the world.

Not for the first time he regretted his inability to use Keeley or one of the local fairies to create a portal to take him to the woods that surrounded the Oracles' lair. Unfortunately, while he could mask his scent with a disguise amulet, there was no way to hide the power surge of fey magic that a portal demanded.

The Oracles would know he was coming before he could ever step foot near the caves.

On the other hand, a breach caused by one of their own would never be noticed.

Reaching into the pocket of his cloak, Anthony curled his fingers around the bottle of potion as he stepped into the breach. Immediately he was stung by a hundred pinpricks of electricity; it felt as if he were being attacked by a swarm of bees. This was why most people avoided traveling through a breach.

Locked on the demon who'd created the opening, he forced himself to move steadily forward, chanting a lethal spell as he at last stepped out the other side.

He was prepared to destroy any threat that might be lying in wait.

Shivering as the icy breeze tugged at his cloak, Anthony backed against the tree, struggling to see through the thick darkness that shrouded the woods. Unlike the supernatural creatures, he didn't have night sight that could penetrate the predawn shadows.

When nothing leaped out to kill him, Anthony altered his spell to produce a small ball of light that floated just above his head.

The illumination was enough for him to catch sight of the eerily beautiful woman who stood in a small clearing, her long copper hair floating around her oval face that was dominated by a pair of green eyes speckled with pure silver.

Phyla looked like she should have been strutting the

catwalks of Paris, not hidden in a damp cave near the Mississippi River. But the beautiful demon attired in a long, nearly see-through white gown, was one of the most powerful Oracles. A bonus when she was creating a breach for him or encouraging the Commission to complete the spell he'd given to her, but a pain in the ass when she was trying to escape his control.

Sweat beaded Anthony's face despite the chill as he covertly pulled the bottle from his pocket and dabbed a small amount of the potion on his fingers. Then, moving forward, he took the female's hand and offered a deep bow.

"Bless you, mistress," he murmured, releasing the spell of Compulsion as the potion transferred from his hand to hers. "As always I'm grateful for your assistance."

The demon briefly tried to fight the spell, inwardly sensing she was about to break free. Then, as the potion spread through her body, the woman's tension eased. Slowly her features softened, a hint of confusion darkening her eyes.

"Do I know you?" she asked, her words coming out as a low hiss.

Anthony smiled with smug satisfaction. The potion enhanced his powers far beyond those of a normal druid, giving him complete control of the demons who thought they were superior to humans.

Arrogant bastards.

"I am nobody," he said. "You will soon forget my presence."

"This is wrong." The woman pulled her hand free, stepping back with a fluid movement that reminded him of a serpent. "I should not be here."

Anthony's smile remained. The spell had come close to snapping, but he could feel his connection to the demon strengthening with every passing second.

"You have merely come for a stroll." The words were

spoken as a command. "Now you need to return to your private rooms. You are tired."

She gave a blink. "Yessssss. I am tired."

"Go now."

The demon turned, slowly making her way toward the caves. Anthony didn't bother to wait for her to disappear before he was headed up the bluff that overlooked the Mississippi River. Thanks to Keeley, he was familiar with a hidden entrance into the lair that would allow him to avoid the Commission and their numerous servants.

A vital requirement for him to spread the potion and re-inforce his spell of Compulsion.

Fallon knew she was in trouble.

Wandering through the magical meadow with Cyn at her side, she tried to convince herself it was time to return to her rooms.

She'd finished the plate of fruit and even polished off the bottle of champagne. There was no reason to linger, was there? Not unless she was willing to admit that she simply wanted to spend time with the vampire.

Turning her head, her eyes clashed with the steady jade gaze, the twist of his lips assuring her that he was as baffled as she was by the strange compulsion that kept pulling them together.

"Tell me about your life," he abruptly demanded, bringing them to a halt next to the shallow brook that flowed over shelves of rocks that created tiny waterfalls.

She shrugged. "There's not much to tell."

"What do you do with your days?"

A flippant response trembled on her lips before she caught sight of the tight line of his jaw and felt the icy prickles of his power in the air.

Cyn was clearly battling the urge to unleash his primitive desires and toss her onto the grass to satisfy the need that continued to pulse between them. It was up to her whether they kept up the pretense of two civilized companions, or if she provoked him into . . .

She clenched her teeth, refusing to allow the image of being pressed into the soft ground as Cyn covered her with his larger body to form.

At the moment they were standing on the edge of a precipice. One wrong move and they'd tumble over the edge.

Not yet prepared to take that irrevocable step, Fallon licked her lips and began chatting with a burst of nervous energy.

"We tend to be a social species, as well as highly competitive, so each House hosts lavish gatherings."

His lips quirked. "I've been to a few fairy clubs. I will admit that they know how to throw one hell of a party."

She blushed. Over the years she'd accidentally peeked into a few of the fairy clubs when she was scrying, and was shocked by the drunken orgies that seemed to pass as entertainment among many demons.

"Not those types of parties," she muttered. "We host teas and soirées and nightly balls. They're intended to display the wealth and stature of our House, not to—"

"To actually have fun?" he finished for her, a wicked glint of amusement in his eyes.

She wrinkled her nose. "I hardly think that overindulging in spirits and having sex with multiple partners is my idea of fun."

He reached to carefully brush a stray curl off her cheek. "Then what do you do for fun, princess?"

She hesitated. What *did* she do? The majority of her time was devoted to her role as princess, of course. When she wasn't expected to join her father, she was in her rooms peering into her scrying bowls. But for fun?

She was still struggling for an answer to the simple question when she was interrupted by the chime of a distant bell.

Cyn was on instant alert, his hand reaching for the dagger that was strapped beneath his sweater.

"What is that dinging?"

"I need to check the bowls," she said, hurrying back across the meadow.

Cyn jogged at her side, leading her back to the door hidden by the illusion. "Is the bell a specific warning?"

"Yes." She was forced to wait while he triggered the lock before they could return to the tunnel that ran beneath the castle. "One of the Oracles left the caves."

"This way."

He led her in the opposite direction from where they'd entered, rounding a corner to reveal a staircase that led them directly to the upper floors.

Fallon never slowed as she hurried up the steps and then down the corridor so she could enter the room where she'd arranged the bowls.

Walking in a slow circle, she pinpointed the bowl that had set off the alarm.

"Here."

She lowered herself until she was kneeling on the carpet, peering into the water. The images flickered across the surface, revealing a slender woman with red hair walking back into the caves.

Odd.

Why would a demon leave the lair only to return minutes later?

"A Manasa demon. It must be Phyla," Cyn murmured, leaning over the bowl.

Fallon stiffened, ridiculously wondering just how well he

knew the beautiful demon. Then she gave a sharp shake of her head.

What was wrong with her? This was no time to be distracted by her childish stab of jealousy.

Focusing on her demon, Fallon touched the edge of the bowl, carefully angling the bowl to the side. The water tilted, distorting the images as they began to flow backward. As if she'd pressed a rewind button.

"Holy shite," Cyn muttered. "How far can you go back?"

"Only a few minutes," she said, removing her fingers from the bowl as she reached the limit of her powers.

Instantly the water settled back in the bowl and Fallon spoke a low word of command, freezing the image as she caught sight of a distinctive simmer that was barely visible among the thick trees shrouded in darkness.

"What is that?" Cyn demanded, his broad shoulder brushing hers as he leaned over the bowl.

Fallon kept her gaze locked on the bowl even as her senses were leaping with acute awareness of the man kneeling at her side.

It wasn't fair. He shouldn't be able to make her ache with this intense need without even trying.

"She created a breach," she explained, wrenching her thoughts back to the vision that filled the bowl.

"Isn't that the same as a portal?"

"No." Fallon shook her head. "A portal is creating a passageway through dimensions that is controlled by a fey's magic. This is a temporary rip in the space that will collapse within an hour."

He sent her a wry glance. A silent reminder of his opinion of magic. Then he asked the obvious question.

"So why would she have created a breach and then returned to the caves?"

"If she didn't intend to travel then she must have let something through."

He shifted his attention back to the bowl. "Can you search the area?"

"Yes."

Releasing the magic from its stasis, the images flickered until she and Cyn were seeing the area in real time. Fallon gave a wave of her hand. Slowly she began a thorough sweep of the area. At first there was nothing to see but trees. And rocks. And an abandoned farmhouse.

It was Cyn who abruptly pointed at the cloaked form that was disappearing into a shallow cave that had been hidden by the undergrowth.

"There," he muttered. "Can you follow him?"

"Aye, aye, sir," she muttered, locking her magic on the cloaked form.

Without warning she felt his fingers lightly grasp her chin, tugging her face to meet his teasing gaze.

"Do you deliberately taunt me?"

Fallon sent him a chiding frown, only to ruin it when she shivered at the delicious feel of his fingers stroking along the line of her jaw.

"I don't like being given orders," she informed him.

The teasing faded from his eyes, his gaze lowering to her lips. "Then why are you even considering returning to your father?"

Her heart missed a beat as she hastily lowered her gaze. She didn't want anyone to know just how the mere thought of returning home made her heart squeeze with panic.

It was just so . . . disloyal to her family.

"Because I understand my duty," she forced herself to say.

His humorless laugh echoed through the room. "A martyr to appease your father's arrogance?"

The fact that he was right only pissed her off. "What does it matter to you?"

He leaned down, filling her vision with the savage beauty of his face. "You know why."

She did. He wanted her.

And the goddess knew that she wanted him. Desperately.

But sating her lust with a man who made a habit of seducing women was hardly a legitimate reason to betray her family and perhaps ruin her life forever.

Was it?

With a muttered curse, Fallon jerked her gaze back to the bowl. No more distractions.

Thankfully Cyn seemed equally determined to concentrate on the reason they were kneeling on the hard floor, and careful not to touch, they watched in silence as the shadowed form squeezed through a narrow crevice at the back of the cave.

Her brows lifted in surprise as she realized he was entering a tunnel that led to the lair of the Commission.

"What the hell?" Cyn leaned forward. "Why would a cloaked human male be creeping through the tunnels that have been claimed by the Commission?"

She glanced at him in surprise. "How do you know it's a human male?"

His gaze remained trained on the shadowed form as it weaved its way from one tunnel to the next, occasionally halting and brushing his hand over the wall.

"The way he walks," Cyn said in absent tones.

"You can barely see how he walks beneath that cloak."

"I'm a predator. I've devoted centuries to studying my prey." He nodded toward the bowl. "That's a human male."

She rolled her eyes. "Arrogant."

He shrugged aside her insult. "I know what he is, not who he is or why he's in the tunnels."

"Maybe I can focus on his face."

Fallon held her hand over the bowl, a trickle of sweat inching down her spine as she concentrated her magic on the hood that covered his head. It was one thing to set the bowls and leave them locked on a specific place. The pull of power was a steady drain that she could offset with the proper nutrition and rest. It was another to manipulate the scrying. Such a blast of energy couldn't be compensated for.

The image of the man narrowed to the shadowed opening of his hood, giving a hint of unremarkable features.

"He's looking for something. Or someone," Cyn murmured as the stranger turned in a slow circle, his head tilted back. Then without warning, he came to a halt, seeming to peer directly at them through the bowl. A low growl rumbled deep in his throat. "Can he sense you?"

"No, it's impossible," she assured him, even as a cold chill inched down her spine.

"*Impossible* is a dangerous word, princess," he warned.

"But—"

On the point of explaining the numerous reasons that there was no way the man could detect her scrying, Fallon had the breath knocked from her as Cyn shoved her to the side. At the same time a visible bolt of magic shot out of the water and slammed into the vampire.

With a small cry Fallon watched as Cyn fell backward, his body crashing onto the floor with enough force to tumble a vase off a nearby table.

Ignoring the shattered porcelain, Fallon crawled toward the unconscious vampire, dread clenching her stomach.

"Cyn," she rasped, desperately grasping his shoulders to give him a shake.

He was lying so still. As if he was . . .

No. She couldn't allow herself to think the worst.

Torn between staying with Cyn and needing to find some

way to help him, Fallon compromised by screaming at the top of her lungs.

"Help. Someone help."

Absently smoothing back the braids from his too-pale face, she kept herself between his unconscious body and the bowl. Later she would try to figure out how the hell the cloaked figure had managed to send magic through her scrying bowl, but for now she simply needed to make sure that Cyn wasn't hit again.

Preparing to go in search of help, Fallon was relieved when the door was pushed open and Levet stepped into the room.

"What has that bully of a vampire . . ." The gargoyle's words came to an abrupt halt as he caught sight of Cyn collapsed on the floor. "Oh. *Bravo, ma belle.*"

"It wasn't me," she rasped. "He's truly hurt."

Easily sensing her panic, Levet crossed the carpet to lean over Cyn with a puzzled frown. "Human magic." He lifted his head to meet her worried gaze. "How?"

"Through my scrying bowl."

The fairy wings fluttered in shock. "Truly?"

"Can you help him?"

"*Non.*" The gargoyle gave a shake of his head. "A vampire can only receive strength from their own kind."

Fallon surged to her feet. She didn't know exactly where to find the beautiful Lise, but she had to be close by.

"His clan—"

"Styx," Levet interrupted, halting her step toward the door. "The king?"

"*Oui.*" A grimace wrinkled his tiny snout. "He might be an annoying creature, but he is the most powerful vampire and his position as the Anasso means he has a connection to Cyn."

It made sense.

Her own father could share his powers with his people when they were in need, giving them strength or assisting the healers on the rare occasion when one of them was grievously wounded.

Still, he was half a world away.

"I can't form a portal without knowing where I'm going."

Levet squatted down beside Cyn, his hand pressing to Cyn's chest. Fallon felt a tiny tingle of magic flow through the air as the gargoyle did his best to keep the vampire's life-force from slipping away.

"Can you travel to your fiancé?"

Fallon stiffened in confusion. Did the creature think that she was going to run away when Cyn was hurt?

"Why would I want to do that?"

"He's staying with Styx." Ignoring Fallon's gasp, Levet glanced up with a worried expression. "I suggest you hurry."

# Chapter Nine

Styx had reluctantly returned to his lair an hour before sunrise.

Darcy had urged him to remain in St. Louis where she was helping her sister with her new litter of pups, but Styx declined. He'd told her that a vampire didn't accept the hospitality of the King of Weres. Which wasn't exactly a lie. While he currently had a truce with Salvatore, it wasn't that long ago they'd been mortal enemies.

But the truth was that he was feeling growingly uneasy.

It wasn't just the fact that his mate wasn't in his bed where she belonged.

Or that Cyn was still MIA.

Or that his lair had somehow become a hotel for the Chatri.

Or even that he had a treacherous imp locked in his dungeons.

It was quite simply that Styx had been through too many near-apocalyptic disasters not to sense trouble when it was brewing.

Entering the house from the gardens, he headed straight toward the dungeons. He was in no mood to run into the prissy Prince Magnus.

He paused to speak with the two vampire guards on duty before he traveled along the narrow pathway between the cells. Each small cubicle was built to hold a specific demon, with the fey cages at the very back of the room.

Built of iron with powerful hexes scraped into the walls, they added to the spells that already dampened the magic in his lair.

Not even the strongest fey could create a portal here.

Clearly hearing his approach, Keeley was standing near the door when Styx pushed it open.

"It's about time," the imp groused, his golden hair limp and his clothes rumpled. Standing in the barren cell that held nothing but a narrow cot, the creature looked nothing like the arrogant fey who used to prance through the lair of the previous Anasso. "I thought you had forgotten I was down here."

Styx bared his fangs. Damn, he hoped the bastard gave him a reason to rip open his throat.

"Do you really want to start this conversation by pissing me off?" he asked, his voice lethally soft.

Only a bully raged and yelled. A truly dangerous predator never lost control of his emotions.

Belatedly recalling his life was hanging in the balance, Keeley performed a deep bow. "Forgive me, Your Majesty. It was my fear speaking."

"You should be afraid." Styx leaned his shoulder against the doorjamb, folding his arms over his massive chest. "You betrayed my master and led him to his ultimate death."

Keeley straightened, his face pale. "It wasn't me. Damocles was the one who brought the drug addicts to poison the Anasso."

"With your assistance," Styx pressed, carefully monitoring the imp's face.

He wasn't particularly interested in dredging up the past.

He had his own share of guilt when it came to the death of his master. But he wanted to see the imp's reaction to the reminder that Styx had every reason to want him dead.

"I had no choice." The fey licked his lips, the smell of tainted strawberries filling the air. "I was as much a victim as the Anasso."

Styx wrinkled his nose. Pathetic worm.

Still, he'd gotten his answer.

Keeley was terrified of him. So what the hell could drive him to try spying on this lair with the certain knowledge he would be caught?

"Why are you here?" he abruptly demanded.

The pale green eyes shifted to peer over Styx's shoulder, as if he was looking for something. Or someone.

"I . . . heard you have a Chatri here."

Styx grimaced. He suspected every fey in the world had heard the elusive Chatri were here. It'd taken the threat of death to run off the hordes that had gathered outside his gates trying to catch a glimpse of the royal family.

It seemed like a reasonable excuse, but Styx wasn't buying it.

"Unfortunately I have a number of demons who are convinced they have a right to stay in my lair. What's so special about the Chatri?"

"They are gods to us," he said, the words sounding as if he'd memorized them. "How could I resist the opportunity to see one in the flesh, so to speak?"

Styx narrowed his gaze. "Why don't I believe you?"

"I have no idea." Keeley pressed two fingers to his heart, a layer of sweat beading his forehead. Not that it meant anything. Most demons tended to sweat when confronting the King of Vampires. "I swear my only interest is in the Chatri."

There was enough truth in his words to make Styx hesitate.

Perhaps the cunning little twit did travel to Chicago because of the Chatri, but there was more going on here than a simple wish to catch sight of a pure-blooded fey.

"I've forbidden the public to gawk at my lair," he at last said.

"Oh, I didn't know." Keeley pasted on an unconvincing smile. "I've been out of the country."

"And now that you do know you will leave?"

"Of course." The smile slowly faded beneath Styx's steady glare, the sweat trickling down the side of his face. "Although—"

"What?"

"I can't help but be intrigued by the sudden return of the ancients." The imp nervously cleared his throat, his gaze continuing to dart over Styx's shoulder. "Have they said why they have returned?"

"I assume if they wanted you to know they would tell you."

That should have been the end of the conversation.

If his interest was nothing more than casual interest, then he would have accepted Styx's contemptuous refusal to gossip about his houseguests.

Prodding a vampire was like poking at a snake.

A good way to get bit.

"You can't blame my curiosity," Keeley grimly continued. "The Chatri have been gone for so long that many of our younger generation have begun to believe they're mere myths. It must be a compelling need to lure them from their homelands."

So. This was more than mere nosiness.

But what?

"Extremely compelling," he murmured, hoping to lure the imp into exposing the true reason he'd been spying on the lair.

Beating it out of him would, of course, be more fun. But there was always the chance the annoying weasel would lie.

"Does it have anything to do with fey business?" Keeley at last asked.

"No."

"Are they considering a return to this world?"

Styx didn't have to fake his shudder. "God forbid."

"Then the Chatri sense trouble?"

Ah. They were getting somewhere.

"What possible trouble could they be sensing?"

"I . . ." The imp nervously licked his lips. "There's always some sort of disruption in the demon world," he finished lamely.

"True, but you were referring to a specific incident."

Realizing he'd said too much, Keeley gave a strained laugh. "Don't be silly."

The temperature dropped as Styx narrowed his eyes. "I'm many things, but I'm never silly."

Keeley made a choked sound. "I didn't intend to insult you. I was merely speculating on why the Chatri were here."

"I can smell lies, Keeley," Styx warned. For now he was willing to use verbal intimidation since the imp's interest seemed locked on the Chatri. The second he suspected the bastard was a threat to vampires, he intended to rip out his heart. "Why are you here?"

"I told you." Keeley took a covert step backward, wise enough to know Styx was reaching the end of his patience. "Curiosity."

Styx tapped one of his massive fangs with the tip of his tongue. "Try again."

Keeley instinctively raised a hand to cover his neck. As if that would stop Styx from ripping out his throat.

Idiot.

"I wanted—"

The stammered words were abruptly interrupted as Styx

caught the sound of his name being called from the entrance of the dungeon.

Without hesitation he was headed out of the cell and closing the door firmly behind him.

"Wait," Keeley cried. "Where are you going?"

Styx ignored the imp. No one would dare to disturb him unless it was important.

With long strides he was moving down the line of cells and out the heavy door that was closed behind him by the guards. Then, stepping out of the security room, he found Jagr waiting for him.

The leader of his Ravens was a towering Goth warrior with dark blond hair and features that looked like they'd been carved in granite. Dressed in black leather with a sword in his hand, he was an imposing sight.

"Talk to me," Styx commanded.

"A female appeared just outside the gates, demanding to see you," Jagr said, his tone revealing his opinion of unwanted visitors. "She claims to be Fallon."

Styx jerked in surprise. "Christ."

"Do you want me to call for the starchy prince?" Jagr asked.

With a sharp shake of his head, Styx moved to jog up the nearby staircase. He'd waited weeks to discover the location of his brother. He intended to find out what the hell happened.

Now.

"Not until I've had a chance to talk to her."

"Are you sure? We aren't entirely certain just what powers she has." Jagr easily kept pace at his side, his expression even more grim than usual. "For all we know she's responsible for causing Cyn's disappearance."

"Then it's all the more imperative that I speak with her."

Jagr muttered a low curse. "You're a pain in the ass to guard. You know that, Styx?"

Styx sent his friend a wry smile. "You can take comfort in the knowledge I'm too stubborn to die. Where did you put her?"

"I left her on the front veranda," Jagr grudgingly revealed. "Do you want me to come with you?"

"No." Halting at the top of the steps, Styx nodded back toward the dungeons. "Keep an eye on the prisoner as well as the prince. I don't want any fey surprises biting me in the ass."

With the unwavering loyalty that made him Styx's most trusted Raven, Jagr gave a nod. "You got it."

Confident his back would be protected, Styx headed directly to the foyer, catching the intoxicating scent of champagne as he pulled open the door.

His brows arched at the sight of the tall, slender female with a golden tumble of hair that held highlights of a cresting dawn. Her eyes were a rich amber flecked with emerald and her features perfectly carved.

Hell, who would blame Cyn for wanting to disappear with this female?

Of course, he wasn't yet sure that Cyn had gone anywhere willingly.

Folding his arms over his chest, he silently studied her tense expression and the way she was twisting her hands together. As if she was struggling to keep some raging emotion under control.

"You wanted to see me?" he demanded.

She flinched at his frigid tone, but grimly held her ground. "Are you the king?"

"I am."

"Thank God," she breathed, shivering as a sharp breeze whipped through the air. In the hour just before dawn the temperature in Chicago dipped well below freezing. "You have to help."

"Help who?"

"Cyn."

Styx stepped forward. Fallon might look as fragile as a fairy, but there was always the danger one of the Chatri could form a burst of light that was lethal to demons.

"What have you done with him?"

"Not me," she protested. "It was . . ." She bit her lip, her eyes darkening with regret. "I don't know. I can explain when we get there." She held out her hand. "Come with me."

Styx flicked a brow upward. He didn't doubt she was genuinely frantic, but there was no way in hell he was going to be led into a trap.

"Come where?"

She hissed with impatience, waving her hand toward his house. "I can't create a portal here. I'll have to do it outside the magical barriers you have around your lair."

"You think I'm just going to follow you into a portal?" He shook his head. "I'm not the smartest vampire in the world, as Darcy will happily assure you, but I'm not stupid."

Her lips thinned, her chin tilting to a stubborn angle. "Cyn has been injured and I don't know how to help him. Levet said to come to you."

Styx stiffened, not sure if he was more troubled by the thought that Cyn was hurt or that Levet was somehow involved.

"You know the gargoyle?"

She nodded. "He's staying with us."

"Where?"

"At Cyn's lair."

"Impossible." Styx had his people out searching for the missing clan chief for weeks. There was no way they wouldn't have known he was back in Ireland. "I would have heard if he'd returned to his home."

"We had to keep it a secret," she insisted.

Styx narrowed his gaze. A convenient story.

"Why?"

She glared at him with rising frustration. Styx had seen that look before. He didn't doubt she was considering the pleasure of zapping him with her fairy power.

"Because that's what the Oracle ordered us to do."

Oracle. Styx frowned. First Levet and now one of the Commission? Christ. Had everyone known where Cyn was but him?

"What Oracle?" he snapped.

"Siljar," she said. "She's the one who took us from my father's palace."

"Meddlesome . . ." Styx bit off his furious words. He should have known without asking it would be Siljar. The tiny Oracle always managed to dump Styx into a shitload of trouble. "What did she want from Cyn?"

"I can't tell you." Tears filled her beautiful eyes, her voice thick with fear. "Please, you have to believe me."

He did.

He didn't have the power to read her mind, but he could sense the sincerity of her words.

Not that he was happy at the thought of traveling around the world through a magical portal.

He'd rather have his fangs pulled.

"Shit," he muttered, accepting that he had no choice. Cyn needed him. End of story. "If you don't kill me, Jagr will." Pulling the sword from the sheath angled across his back, he stepped out of the house and headed down the stairs. "Let's go."

Fallon didn't hesitate. With a speed that caught him off

guard, she was sprinting past him, her bare feet barely seeming to touch the frozen ground.

Together they headed down the long drive and out the front gate, halting in the middle of the quiet suburban street. Then, with a wave of her hand, she was creating the portal that Styx couldn't see or feel.

Grimacing, Styx allowed the female to grab his arm and lead him through the invisible opening. No matter how prepared he might be, it was still a jolt to step from the public street into complete darkness.

God Almighty, he hated traveling this way. A vampire was meant to use his two feet to go from point A to point B, not be magically jerked through dimensions.

The sensation of being surrounded by complete emptiness barely had time to form before Fallon gave another wave of her hand to open the portal and they were stepping into a large room with stone walls and an open-beamed ceiling. On the far wall a cheery flame burned in the massive fireplace and the opposite wall was dominated by an arched stained-glass window that Styx had seen before.

Cyn's lair.

Instinctively stepping away from Fallon so he had room to fight, Styx swiftly scanned his surroundings, making sure that there were no lurking enemies. Only then did he turn his attention to the large vampire who was stretched out on the floor, surrounded by bowls of water and one tiny gargoyle.

"Christ," he muttered, barely capable of sensing Cyn.

With a graceful flutter, Fallon was moving to kneel beside the unconscious vampire, her face pale with worry.

"He won't wake and he was too heavy for me to move to his bed," she breathed.

"It was best to leave him," Styx absently assured her, squatting beside Levet. "What happened, gargoyle?"

"Magic," Levet answered, his leathery skin more ashen than usual as he struggled to maintain a hold on Cyn's fading life force.

Styx's initial suspicions returned in a rush. "Fey?"

Levet gave a sharp shake of his head. "Human."

Fallon ran her fingers through Cyn's hair, her touch unconsciously intimate. "Can you help him?"

"I can add my strength to his and hope it's enough to heal him."

Styx gently pushed aside Levet's hand and replaced it with his own. He'd slice out his tongue before he'd admit it, but for once he was glad the irritating creature had been around. His efforts had quite possibly saved Cyn's life.

Pressing against Cyn's chest, Styx concentrated on the thread that connected him to his people. Then, with a ruthless determination, he was shoving his power through the bond and into the unmoving vampire.

This was one gift as Anasso he truly appreciated.

Focused on his brother, he forgot about his audience, flaming the spark of life until he could sense Cyn regain his awareness although his eyes remained closed.

It was at last Fallon who broke the heavy silence. "What can I do to help?"

Lifting his head, Styx continued to offer Cyn his strength to aid in his rapid healing. "He'll need to feed to regain his full strength."

"Do not look in my direction," Levet grumbled, hurriedly heading out the door. "I am no *à la mode* for a leech."

Styx didn't bother glancing at the retreating gargoyle, instead concentrating his gaze on the beautiful princess. "Fallon?"

Surprisingly she abruptly surged to her feet, her face pale. After her possessive way of touching Cyn, he'd assumed that they were already lovers. Now he sensed that he'd touched a raw nerve.

"I'm certain he must have a store of blood in the kitchen," she muttered.

Styx frowned. "It won't be as effective as yours."

"Why not?"

"The greater your magic, the more pure your blood," he said. She bit her bottom lip, clearly uncomfortable with his pressure. Not that Styx gave a shit. The Chatri packed powerful magic. If her blood would help Cyn heal faster then that's what he was going to get. "He needs you."

"I . . ." She muttered something beneath her breath before giving a grudging nod of her head. "Fine."

A hand suddenly grabbed his arm, and Styx glanced down to see Cyn's eyes were opened, his expression tight with pain.

"Styx?"

"I'm here, amigo," he reassured his friend, leaning forward so Cyn didn't try to sit up.

Fear flashed in the jade eyes. "Fallon . . ."

"She's fine." Styx flicked his glance toward the hovering Chatri princess. "And very persistent."

Cyn managed a weak smile. "Aye. She's as stubborn as an Irish stoat."

Styx heard the female make a startled sound of irritation, but his only concern was for the vampire who remained dangerously weak.

"You must feed. Fallon has agreed to offer her vein."

Once again Styx was caught off guard as Cyn's fingers dug into his arm. "No."

What the hell? He allowed a growl to rumble deep in his chest.

"Don't be an idiot. You need blood."

Cyn grimaced. "Not Fallon's."

There was a low hiss before Fallon was headed toward the door, her body stiff with wounded dignity. Even if she'd

been reluctant to offer her vein, it clearly pricked her pride
that Cyn would refuse her gift.

"Obviously the clan chief considers my blood unworthy.
I'll return with his preferred vintage," she muttered. "I hope
it chokes him."

# Chapter Ten

Cyn grimaced as Fallon slammed the door behind her retreating form. He knew he'd offended her. Again. But on this occasion he wasn't sorry.

Better have her pissed at him than suffering the potential fallout from him taking her vein.

Styx glared down at him, his hard expression saying he thought Cyn had lost his mind.

And he wasn't wrong.

His life had gone from a peaceful existence of glorious hedonism to chaotic frustration.

From the second he'd seen Fallon, he'd been careening from one upheaval to another. But it wasn't being a pawn for a powerful Oracle that had his nerves scraped raw.

That little achievement belonged solely to the Chatri princess.

So why hadn't he followed the urgings of his logical mind that had warned him to avoid the female? As she'd pointed out more than once, his lair was big enough to make sure they could go weeks without running into each other.

*Because you haven't been able to resist the primitive need to seek her out,* a voice in the back of his head whispered.

And every passing minute in her presence had only made matters worse.

He'd gone from fascinated to obsessed to desperate. Bloody hell, he needed to have her naked in his arms, his fangs buried deep in her throat as he felt her climaxing around his erection.

That was precisely why he'd slammed the door on any risk of making his compulsion a permanent part of his life.

"Do you want to tell me what the hell is going on?" Styx demanded. "Her blood is—"

"Dangerous," Cyn interrupted.

The Anasso blinked. "Because she's a Chatri?"

"Because she's a female I find far too tempting."

"Ah." Immediately understanding why Cyn was reluctant to exchange blood with a female who could be his potential mate, Styx's expression altered from annoyance to curiosity. "Tell me what happened."

Cyn planted his hands on the floor and forced himself to a seated position despite Styx's protest. He was still weak, but he'd be damned if he remained lying on the floor like he was some invalid.

"Siljar isn't going to be pleased if I share."

"Too damned bad." Styx's tone revealed his current opinion of the Oracle. "I'm tired of her expecting vampires to clean up the Commission's mistakes."

Cyn hesitated, then with a small shrug he offered a condensed version of what had happened since arriving back at his lair.

By the time he finished, Styx had surged to his feet and was pacing the room with a growing restlessness.

"A spell to close dimensions?" the Anasso growled, the

lights flickering as his power threatened to fry the electrical system that Cyn had spent a fortune to install. "That's—"

"Crazy?" Cyn offered, his smile wry. "Welcome to my world."

Styx continued to pace, his displeasure a tangible force in the air. "And also vaguely familiar," he finally muttered.

"What do you mean?"

Styx came to an abrupt halt. "There's something about this whole situation that gives me an itchy sense of déjà vu."

Cyn felt a strange chill shoot down his spine. Styx was right. He couldn't pinpoint why this felt so freakishly familiar, but suddenly he was certain that he'd either heard or read or been told of another spell that offered a similar annihilation.

"Aye. I know what you mean." He scrubbed a hand over his face. The icy sense of premonition had settled like a heavy ball of dread in the pit of his stomach. "I need to return to the library. Maybe there's something in the history of the fey that can help us."

There was the crisp scent of champagne before Fallon shoved open the door and stepped inside. Her chin was still tilted to a militant angle as she crossed the room and dropped two bags of blood onto his lap.

"Here."

He offered her a rueful smile. Hard to believe that he'd once considered himself an expert in pleasing a woman.

"Thanks."

She sniffed, spinning as if prepared to head back out the door. "I'll leave you two alone."

"Wait," Styx commanded.

She hesitated, her rigid body revealing she desperately wanted to tell the King of Vampires to go to hell. But, of course, she didn't. She'd been trained to play the gracious lady. Only Cyn was allowed to see the fiercely independent woman beneath the glossy façade.

The knowledge of that sent a blaze of satisfaction through him.

Turning back, she met Styx's dark gaze with a wary expression. "Yes?"

Styx pointed toward the bowls that continued to flicker with a dozen separate images. "I don't claim to be an expert on scrying, but I've never heard of anyone being able to use them as a weapon."

She wrapped her hands around her waist, as if assuming Styx was blaming her for the attack on Cyn.

"Neither have I," she snapped. "Certainly no human should have the power to connect to my magic."

Styx studied her with a gaze that could make grown men piss their pants. "You're certain he wasn't fey?"

"Ask the clan chief." She shot Cyn a dark glare. "He's the one who was convinced the attacker was a human male."

Having drained the two bags of blood, Cyn rose to his feet, relieved when his legs held his weight. His strength was rapidly returning, but he wasn't fully recovered. That bastard magic-user. He was going to pay for attacking him.

For now, however, his only concern was mending the breech with Fallon.

Stepping forward, he took her hands in his, gazing down at her wounded eyes. "Truce, princess," he murmured softly. "I promise you can tell me what a huge jackass I am later."

Her lips pursed, but seeming to realize she was overreacting to his refusal to take her blood, she heaved a resigned sigh.

"Fine," she muttered. "Jackass."

Cyn hid his smile as he turned back to Styx, keeping one of Fallon's hands tightly clenched in his.

"He was a human," he assured his Anasso, trying his best to recall what had happened before he'd been hit by the bolt of magic. "He looked like he was sneaking through the back tunnels of the Commission's lair and then he halted as if he could sense us watching him. A second later . . . he hit me with his damn spell."

Styx scowled. Cyn knew his king well enough to realize the older vampire didn't like mysteries. Or the Commission. Or strangers attacking his people.

"Do you think he's part of the conspiracy to close the dimensions?" Styx asked.

"Aye," Cyn swiftly answered. "It's too much of a coincidence for him not to be involved."

Styx nodded. "Agreed."

Cyn grimaced. "The question now is how do we discover who he is?"

"I'm more interested in how to protect you," Styx said, his gaze moving to Fallon. "No more snooping on the Commission."

Cyn felt Fallon flinch at the direct command, but this time she didn't allow her ingrained manners to overcome what she believed to be right.

"That's not your decision to make," she informed the towering warrior.

Styx narrowed his gaze. "Are you trying to get Cyn killed?"

Fallon refused to bend, but Cyn didn't miss her tiny step closer to him. A step that pleased the hell out of him.

"I'm trying to halt a looming genocide," she said.

"She's right, Styx," Cyn swiftly agreed. "As much as I want to put a halt to this, we can't risk the Oracles being under the compulsion of some unknown enemy."

Styx studied them with a speculative expression, silently considering their options.

It didn't take long.

They didn't have enough information to do anything but follow Siljar's orders. Not when they risked making matters worse.

"What do you need from me?" Styx demanded.

"For now . . ." Cyn forgot what he was going to say as the rich scent of aged whiskey threaded its way through the air. "What the hell?"

"Magnus," Fallon said, the word so low he barely heard it.

"The fairy prince?" Cyn growled even as there was a weird prickle of energy that brushed over his skin.

At the same time, a tall man with a long mane of shocking red hair appeared in the center of the room.

"Chatri prince," the stranger complained, glaring down the length of his noble nose. "It's not difficult to remember."

Fury slammed into Cyn with unexpected force. This too-pretty man with his cognac eyes and arrogant expression was Fallon's fiancé. The man who thought he had the right to claim the female at his side.

Without warning, Cyn was lunging forward, intending to plant his fist in that perfect fairy face.

"Cyn, no," a voice snarled, as a massive pair of arms wrapped around him, holding him in place.

Cyn grunted, struggling to break free of the painful bear hug. An impossible task. Even if he'd been at full strength.

Trapped by the unmovable object known as Styx, Cyn was forced to content himself with glaring over the Anasso's shoulder at the unwelcome intruder.

"How the hell did you get in here?"

The bastard calmly smoothed a hand down the sleeve of his jade silk shirt that he'd tucked into a pair of black slacks, pausing to pick an invisible piece of fluff from his sleeve.

"I followed my fiancée's imprint."

Fiancée? Oh hell, no.

Cyn gave another furious attempt to break free. "What does that mean?"

It was Fallon who answered. "A Chatri with royal blood can trace a portal created by another fey."

The pompous prince sent her a warning frown. "How I arrived is no business of the vampires."

"It is if you don't want to become dinner," Cyn warned.

Magnus curled his lips. "You don't frighten me, leech."

"Then you're an idiot," Cyn shot back.

"Stop," Styx commanded, turning his head to send Magnus a warning glare. "The penalty for trespassing in a vampire's lair is death."

The prince held up a slender hand, a strange glow surrounding his fingers. "Just as the penalty for kidnapping a Chatri princess is death."

"No, Magnus." Fallon took a sudden step forward, her face pale. "I wasn't kidnapped."

Magnus never allowed his gaze to stray from the vampires. "Do not contradict me, female."

"She'll do whatever the hell she wants to do," Cyn barked.

The cognac eyes narrowed. "She belongs to me."

No fucking way.

A red mist exploded in his mind, short-circuiting any attempt to think.

Instead it catapulted him into action.

He was going to rip off that fairy head and . . .

"God. Damn." Styx spread his legs wide, his face tight with the effort of holding on to the crazed vampire. "Get him out of here before Cyn shows you just what happens when you piss off a berserker."

\* \* \*

Fallon sucked in a sharp breath, trying to rid herself of the nasty sense of panic that she always felt when in the company of her fiancé.

Magnus was never cruel. At least not physically.

But he'd lived among the Chatri royalty who firmly believed that females were little more than property. He'd bought and paid for her; now he expected her to fulfill her role as the submissive, always-dutiful fiancée.

He was the adored alpha male and she was nothing but another female expected to kneel at his feet.

Unfortunately for both of them, Fallon had never truly accepted the part she was expected to play. And it was even worse now after being away from her homeland.

*Or maybe it is worse because you've been with a man who's treated you as if you are more than a thing*, a treacherous voice whispered in the back of her mind. Even when they were fighting, Cyn made her feel as if she were an equal opponent. And when she'd been in his arms . . .

With a smothered gasp, she hurried to grasp Magnus's hand and tugged him out the door. This was no time to think about the shocking pleasure she'd felt when Cyn kissed her. Not when her fiancé was calling on his powers as if he intended to use them against the furious vampire that Styx was barely restraining.

Good Lord. The violence in the air threatened to drown them all.

"I need to speak with you," she muttered.

Once they reached the hallway, Magnus snatched his hand free, his eyes glowing with a frustrated anger.

"We will speak once we have returned to our homeland." His gaze flicked over her casual attire, his disdain obvious. "And after you've changed into proper attire."

Endless years of training had Fallon bending her head in

apology; then, with a swell of long-suppressed defiance, she forced herself to meet the cold cognac gaze.

She'd been brought to this world for a reason. And the attack on Cyn only stiffened her determination. The mysterious enemy now knew they had been spotted. It was very likely they would step up their pressure on the Commission to complete the spell.

She had to discover who was responsible before it was too late.

That duty was greater than any contract her father signed.

"I can't return," she said, her voice low but steady.

"You are my fiancée." The words were cold, clipped. "You will do as I say."

His power beat against her, but Fallon squared her shoulders, refusing to be intimidated.

"Not this time."

Magnus went rigid, his nose flaring. "You dare to defy me?"

Was that what she was doing?

Fallon gave a sad grimace, staring at the man who was supposed to be her life partner. She'd never been foolish enough to believe that he actually cared about her as a woman, but she assumed he would at least be concerned about her as an investment.

"You haven't even asked how I got here. Or if I've been harmed," she pointed out, wrapping her arms around her waist. "Or if I want to return."

With a sharp motion Magnus turned to the side, almost as if he were trying to disguise his reaction to her soft chastisement.

Which was ridiculous.

The prince believed himself omnipotent. He couldn't possibly feel guilt.

"I see your short time in this world has already started to corrupt you." He proved her point with his stark chastisement. "The sooner you are back in your father's palace the better."

She heaved a sigh. "I told you that I can't leave. The Oracles have commanded my service."

"The Commission has no authority over the Chatri."

"Maybe not." Fallon had no knowledge of the hierarchy between her people and the Oracles. To be honest, she didn't care. This was about saving lives, not playing political games. "The danger this world faces might eventually threaten our people as well."

He turned back with a frown. "What danger?"

"I'm not allowed to say."

There was a silence, almost as if the prince was actually intrigued by her demand to stay. Then his expression was wiped clean, his inner thoughts hidden by his mask of royal superiority.

"I will not argue with you," he informed her. "Either you return with me now or you can consider our marriage contract null and void."

Fallon was stunned. She'd expected him to be angry. To even try to bully her into returning with him.

But never to end their contract.

He'd bartered for years with Sariel to earn the right to marry her. His House had spent a fortune to celebrate their coming union, gloating in their elevated social status and inscribing Fallon onto their family tree with Magnus's blood.

They would be horrified to be publically demoted.

Of course, their humiliation would be nothing compared to hers. A woman who was jilted by her fiancé not only lost the protection of her lover, but her own family. It was the ultimate insult.

And all because she'd refused to obey his command?

Surely not even Magnus could be so cruel?

She studied his handsome face, noticing the way he re-fused to directly meet her gaze. He was hiding something from her. Something that was pushing him to cause this break between them.

But what?

She was the last princess that was unwed. There was no other female Chatri who could offer him more.

"You"—she licked her dry lips, wondering if this was just an empty threat—"wouldn't do that."

"The choice is yours." There was no compromise. "Return with me now or risk becoming a pariah among your own people."

Fallon hesitated.

She didn't love this man. And the last thing she wanted was to be his wife. But the thought of being treated as an outcast for the rest of her life was horrifying.

Was she truly willing to sacrifice her position, her repu-tation, and her father's respect to help a world that wasn't her home?

For a heartbeat she wavered.

It would be so easy to give in to Magnus's demands. She could return home and live the life that had been expected of her. No fuss, no muss.

And no happiness.

Or she could stay and risk losing everything.

Then she caught sight of Cyn standing as rigid as a statue in the doorway and her decision was made.

"No."

The soft refusal hung in the air, seeming to pulse there before it shattered the fragile bond that had been forced between her and Magnus by a toxic combination of family and duty and pride.

The refusal captured the prince's full attention. For a long moment he studied her pale face, something that might have been regret at last flaring through the cognac eyes.

"Fallon—"

"You heard her," Cyn growled, moving to stand at Fallon's side.

"Stay out of this, vampire," Magnus snapped, angling his body so he could keep an eye on both Cyn and the King of Vampires who joined them in the hallway.

Cyn pulled back his lips to reveal his fangs. Not that he needed the lethal display. The icy flood of his power was already causing the floor to tremble beneath their feet.

"You have your answer. Now leave," he told the prince.

Magnus held Fallon's gaze, his expression unreadable. "You understand what this means?"

She did.

And it made her heart break.

Perhaps sensing her pain, Cyn stepped toward Magnus, his hands clenching as if he was considering the pleasure of punching the intruder.

"Time to leave, you pompous prick."

"I am happy to leave." Magnus offered a mocking bow, his gaze never leaving Fallon's pale face. "Your father will no doubt wish to speak to you once he learns of your reckless disregard for his position. If nothing else, he will need you at his side when he publicly shuns you."

Without warning, Styx had reached out to grab Magnus's arm.

"Sariel isn't going to know about this," he warned, his expression grim. "At least not yet."

Magnus gave a low hiss, his honey tinted skin glowing as he allowed his power to flow through his body.

"This is not your concern."

"Tough," Styx snarled, pointing a finger directly into the prince's handsome face. "This is what's going to happen.

You're taking me back to my lair and then you're staying there with your mouth shut until the Oracles get their shit together and I can either kick you out or kill you."

Magnus narrowed his gaze, but shockingly he kept his power firmly leashed. He didn't even fight against the vampire's grip.

Weird. Very weird.

"You are not my king," he muttered.

"No, but I can promise you that Sariel won't be pleased to discover you've made an enemy of the Commission," Styx said. "Now let's go."

"This will not be forgotten." Magnus lifted his hand, but instead of sending a bolt of energy toward the Anasso as Fallon dreaded, he instead formed a portal and led Styx into the opening.

"You owe me, amigo," Styx warned Cyn before he abruptly disappeared with Magnus.


Cyn remained silent as Fallon took an instinctive step toward the spot where her fiancé had just disappeared.

Rage ripped through him.

He wanted to yank her into his arms. To kiss her until her pale cheeks were flushed and he'd replaced the scent of the damned fairy prince with his own. Territorial? Hell, yes.

Unfortunately he couldn't risk touching her. Not when he continued to vibrate with the savage need to tear apart the male who had dared to try to take her away.

Instead he was forced to watch her stand in the center of the hallway, her golden hair tumbled around her shoulders and her amber eyes wide with a distress that sliced through his heart.

She looked like a lost waif.

It was . . . unbearable.

He stepped to stand close enough to feel her intoxicating heat wrap around him, easing the frigid fury that had nearly sent him over the edge.

"Fallon?"

"He's playing his own game," she said, her voice distracted.

Cyn didn't know what he'd expected, but it wasn't that.

"Who's playing a game?" he demanded.

"My ex-fiancé." She gave a slow shake of her head. "Styx is powerful, but Magnus possesses the magic of royals."

Belatedly Cyn recalled Roke telling him about Sariel's ability to fry the Nebule demon to a gooey tar. He'd said that it'd destroyed everything in its path. He'd also admitted that it was a talent that his mate, Sally, had inherited.

It'd never occurred to him that Fallon might have the same dangerous power.

Bloody hell, he was lucky not to be a smudge on the floor.

"The burst of light?" he asked.

"Yes." Her expression remained absent, as if she was pondering some deep thought. "It's lethal to most demons."

"He's not stupid." Cyn shrugged. Magnus might have all sorts of fairy magic, but it wouldn't protect him if he harmed Styx. "If he'd killed the Anasso there would be nowhere he could hide from us. We would destroy him."

She continued to study that empty spot where Magnus had disappeared. "Still, he could have used his magic to disable Styx long enough for him to escape. So why would he have let himself be forced back to the king's lair?" The question wasn't directed at him. Hell, he wasn't sure she was even aware he was around. "And why didn't he try to force me home? It was almost as if he was hoping I would break our engagement."

A rational part of him knew that Fallon was right to be concerned if her prick of an ex-fiancé was acting out of character. But he wasn't in the mood to hear another word about the glorious, fucking golden prince.

He'd been to the edge of death, and before he could fully recover, he'd been driven into a berserker frenzy. Who could blame him for being a little twitchy?

"Is he a threat?" was the only thing he wanted to know.

"No."

Satisfied, he crowded her against the wall, using his larger size to keep her trapped. "Then forget about him."

He heard her breath catch in her throat, her heart thundering, but her expression remained troubled.

"Easy for you to say," she muttered.

His fingers tangled in her hair, his voice coming out as a rough growl. "You told me that you didn't love him."

"I don't."

Something dangerous eased in his chest as he allowed his fingers to lightly stroke through the satin strands.

"Then why are you upset?"

"I'm going to be shunned."

He grimaced. He didn't know the ins and outs of fairy society—thank God—but he did know that any demon would be traumatized at being disowned by their people. Even vampires who could be solitary creatures instinctively created clans. It wasn't just a need for protection, but a sense of belonging.

To have that torn away because she felt it was her duty to use her skills to halt a looming genocide must feel like the worst sort of betrayal.

Someday he intended to beat the shit out of Prince Magnus and King Sariel for daring to treat this exquisite creature with anything less than utter devotion. But for now he couldn't deny that their stupidity played directly into his hands.

"Does that mean you can't return to your homeland?" he asked, his fingers sliding from her hair to outline the faintly pointed tip of her ear.

She was such a fairy.

Licking her lips, Fallon visibly struggled to concentrate even as the warm scent of champagne drenched the air.

"I can return, but I will no longer be allowed to attend any social functions or to be seated with my family during meals. It will be . . . difficult."

His hand glided down to cup her jaw so he could tilt back her head.

"Stay," he said.

She stilled, an unmistakable yearning darkening her wide eyes before she was hurriedly trying to disguise her vulnerable reaction. Her life among the Chatri had taught her not to reveal her deepest desires.

"Don't be ridiculous."

"Why is it ridiculous?"

"You've been trying to get rid of me since I—"

He brought an end to her argument by the simple process of covering her mouth with his own.

Bloody hell.

She was right. He should be encouraging her to kiss and make up with her stupid fiancé so she could return to fairyland. She was in danger here.

And if he was being brutally honest, he was doing a piss-poor job of protecting her.

But the mere thought of her leaving . . .

He shuddered, deepening the kiss as excitement exploded through him. Oh God, the taste of her. Honey. And sunshine. And pure female temptation.

He groaned, dipping his tongue into the moist heat of her mouth. She was addictive. Like a drug that had entered his system and filled him with a need that threatened to overwhelm him.

"Stay," he whispered against her lips, his hands greedily exploring her long, slender curves.

She shivered, her hands tentatively pressing against his chest. "How can I?"

He nibbled at the edge of her lips, his hand slipping beneath the border of her lavender sweater. Instant arousal seared through him at the feel of her satin-smooth skin beneath his fingertips.

"Will you die if you don't return to your homeland?" he demanded, tracing her lower lip with the tip of his tongue.

His elongated fangs throbbed with the need to sink deep into the tender flesh, but he was careful not to accidentally draw blood. There's no way he would force a mating on her. Not after she'd nearly been manipulated into one by her bastard of a father.

"No, but—"

He stole her words with another kiss. Her family considered her nothing more than a pawn who could be sacrificed when she no longer served her purpose. They didn't deserve her.

"Then stay."

Cyn leaned back just far enough so he could pull the sweater over her head, his gut twisting at the sheer beauty of her.

Fallon didn't possess the lush body of most fey. No. His princess was all sleek lines and graceful curves. Like a pure-blooded racehorse.

Perfect.

"Stay where?" she husked, her nails digging into his chest as he allowed his fingers to skim up her narrow rib cage to cup her small breasts with reverent care. "I have no home, no family, no one who can help me."

Cyn struggled to concentrate. He knew it would be a difficult task to convince her that she belonged with him. Especially when she was still raw from her fiancé's abandonment. But the hunger that had been growing from his first sight of this tempting female was thundering through him, making it almost impossible to think of anything beyond wrapping her impossibly long legs around his waist so he could sink himself into her tantalizing heat.

"You have me," he murmured.

"You want me to become a part of your harem?"

He yanked his head up to glare at her wary expression. Was she deliberately trying to piss him off?

"Why the hell do you keep harping about my nonexistent harem?"

"Why else would you ask me to stay?"

Cyn swallowed his urge to laugh. He wasn't about to tell her that he thought she might be his mate.

In the past few days she'd been kidnapped from her homeland, commanded to spy on the Commission, forced to share a lair with a vampire, jilted by her fiancé, and potentially shunned.

Now didn't seem the best time to pile on the fact that he had no intention of ever letting her go.

"We still have to save the world, remember?" he asked, his gaze drifting to the unsteady line of her lips.

She tilted her head to the side, unconsciously offering the temptation of her exposed neck.

"And that's the only reason?"

He pressed the heavy thrust of his arousal against her, groaning at the incandescent sensations that exploded through him.

"Isn't that enough for now?" he asked, his lips feathering kisses down the length of her throat.

"No other women?" she stubbornly demanded.

"Only you, princess." He nuzzled the pulse that raced at the base of her throat, his fingers skimming down the flat plane of her stomach to unsnap her jeans. "Only you."

She shivered, her slender arms tentatively wrapping around his shoulders. Cyn growled in approval, dipping his head to lick a rose-tipped breast. She gasped with shocked pleasure, her fingers tunneling into his hair.

"Will you stay?" He had to hear the words. He had to know that she wasn't going to suddenly disappear on him.

"Yes," she whispered.

Tugging the nipple between his lips, Cyn skimmed his hand down the length of her spine, lingering on the curve of her buttocks. His cock twitched at the sensation of her soft, feminine flesh beneath his hand. He wanted to feast on her. To spend the entire night exploring her from the top of her glorious curls to the tips of her tiny toes that she never remembered to cover with shoes.

But not tonight, he conceded as he grabbed the bottom of his sweater and yanked it over his head.

His hunger was a burning force that threatened to consume him. A slow, delectable exploration would have to wait until he'd dulled the edge of his lust.

More than once.

"Touch me," he pleaded softly, unzipping her jeans and urging them down her legs until she could step out of them.

She hesitated only a second before he felt the timid brush of her fingers down his back. He moaned, rocked by the raw pleasure at her shy caress. He did not know how it was possible that an untutored innocent could set him on fire, but there was no denying her power.

With a groan, he branded her with a kiss of possessive

demand, his muscles clenching as he gained access to the warmth of her mouth.

Sweet honey. And sunshine.

And innocence.

Christ. A shudder raced through him. It should have terrified him. There was no way in hell he deserved such purity. Not with his jaded soul.

But he'd discovered long ago to grasp happiness when it was offered.

And that was exactly what he intended to do.

Not giving her a chance to protest, Cyn had her swept off her feet and cradled against his chest. Leaving her clothes abandoned on the hallway floor, he entered her bedroom and kicked shut the door.

He wasn't going to risk being interrupted.

Gently laying her on the wide mattress, Cyn wrestled off his heavy boots before he was shedding jeans. At last naked, he stood and simply savored the sight of his princess.

She was . . . a work of priceless art.

Hair like a cresting dawn spread around her ivory face. Her eyes an exotic amber with flecks of emerald that burned like green fire. And her slender body wearing nothing but the tiny thong looked so perfect, it might have been chiseled from marble by the hand of a master.

Shivering beneath the intensity of his slow survey, Fallon licked her dry lips.

"Cyn?"

He perched a knee on the edge of the mattress, planting his hands on each side of her shoulders.

This would be her last opportunity for second thoughts. Once he took her there would be no going back.

For either of them.

Almost as if sensing this last step had to be hers, Fallon

lifted her hand to slide it over the tense muscles of his chest. Distantly he was aware of a chilled rain pelting against the stained-glass windows and the crackle of the wood burning in the fireplace, but his sole focus was on the woman who was spread like a pagan offering beneath him.

Holding her burning gaze, Cyn smoothed his fingers up the inner flesh of her thigh, tugging her legs apart so he could catch a glimpse of her glistening clit. He growled deep in his throat, shaking his head as she lowered her hands to cover the evidence of her arousal.

"Don't hide from me, Fallon," he murmured, swooping down to scatter soothing kisses over her face. "I need to know you want me."

"I . . ." Slowly her muscles eased, her hands returning to his chest as she met his searching gaze with a trust that sliced straight to his heart. "I do."

Something moved inside Cyn at the soft words. Something so large that he was certain that the world would never be the same.

His kisses became more heated as he followed a path over her cheek and down her throat. He paused to lick and suckle her straining breasts, chuckling softly as she arched her back off the bed in a silent plea for more.

He lingered, teasing the tight nubs with lips and then with his teeth, careful not to break her skin with the aching points of his fangs. She hissed in pleasure, her nails digging into his chest as she experienced her first taste of passion.

Promising himself that some night he would discover if he could make her climax just by caressing her breasts, Cyn slowly moved down her quivering stomach. Each kiss was lingering, deliberate. A sensual promise that was intended to stroke her desire to a fever pitch.

Cyn lifted his head, capturing her startled gaze as he settled between her legs, his fingers sliding delicately through her feminine heat.

"Oh," she breathed, a flush staining her cheeks.

He waited, allowing her to adjust to the sensations that were bombarding her. Only when she released a quivering sigh of pleasure did he slowly replace his fingers with his tongue. She gave a small gasp that settled into a groan of ecstasy as his tongue dipped into her moist heat.

His eyes slid shut in pure bliss.

Her honey was sweeter here, the crisp, utterly feminine scent of champagne intoxicating him.

Over and over he teased at her tiny bud of pleasure before dipping his tongue into her body, bringing her tantalizingly close to the edge of completion before pulling back.

At last she gave a choked groan of need. "Please . . . Cyn."

"Yes," he husked, unable to wait another moment.

Running one fang along the sensitive inner length of her thigh, he briefly allowed himself to relish the image of drinking deep from that tender spot.

Someday . . .

Until then he had another hunger to satisfy.

One that was hammering through him with enough force to make him groan.

He needed to be buried deep inside her.

Crawling onto the mattress, he stretched out beside her and gathered her in his arms. Then, holding her gaze, he rolled onto his back until she was perched atop him. She blinked, pressing her hands against his chest as she regarded him in puzzlement.

"I'm twice your size and double your weight. This will be more comfortable for you," he muttered, barely able to form the words as her legs naturally draped on either side of his hips, her hot clit pressed against his erection.

She bit her bottom lip. "I don't know what to do."

Tenderness clenched his heart. She looked so beautiful, but fragile, vulnerable.

He had to make sure she never regretted giving him her innocence.

"Like this," he murmured, reaching to guide her hand to his fully erect cock.

His entire body clenched with agonized pleasure as she delicately curled her fingers around him, nearly torpedoing him straight into an orgasm. Bloody hell. He was supposed to be an experienced hedonist, not a randy schoolboy.

"Did I hurt you?" she asked.

"Christ, no. It's perfect. You're perfect," he groaned. "I need to be inside you."

She fumbled awkwardly as she attempted to adjust him, and gritting his teeth, Cyn managed to avoid embarrassing himself. Then, with a low groan, he was at last pushing the crest of his erection into her entrance.

She was tight.

Gloriously tight as he forged his way inside her. A moan was wrenched from his throat at the sensation of her silky heat clenched around him like a glove. God. Damn. Nothing had ever felt so good.

"Cyn," she moaned, her hair tumbling forward to brush his chest as Cyn grasped her hips and lifted her upward before plunging back into her with a slow, maddening tempo.

"Fallon," he echoed, the savage pleasure already twisting his lower stomach into a tight ball of anticipation. "My sweet princess."

Her lips parted as she matched his rhythm, her beautiful

face flushed with the same desire that blazed through him. He lifted his head off the mattress, the beads in his braid rattling as he latched on to one nipple. At the same time he reached between them, using his finger to stroke over her clit.

She whimpered, meeting his thrusts with a frantic enthusiasm that had him swiftly rushing toward his release. With a muttered curse, he angled his hips upward, pressing ever deeper as his pace increased.

He muttered ancient curses as his head dropped back to the mattress, his entire body on fire.

It felt so good.

Too good.

His fingers tightened on Fallon's hips as she made a strangled sound of sheer bliss, her slender body arching as she was overwhelmed by her climax. Cyn watched in fierce satisfaction as she shook with a stunned shock at her first orgasm. But all too soon the feel of her channel gripping his cock with tiny ripples had him thundering toward his own release. With one last thrust, he was shouting out as he came with a violent force that he felt to his very soul.

Urging the trembling Fallon to lay against his chest, Cyn wrapped his arms around her body, his cunning mind already plotting his next step in binding her to him.

Making love to this woman had been fabulous. Mind-blowing.

But he wanted more than sex from her.

He wanted her bound so closely to him that she never, ever wanted to leave.

# Chapter Eleven

Fallon struggled to catch her breath, slowly drifting back to earth.

Okay. That was . . . Words failed her.

She'd expected the shattering climax. Cyn was a sexually attractive male who had the sort of experience to make any woman melt into a puddle of satisfied, boneless bliss.

But she hadn't understood just how intimate the joining would be.

He hadn't just touched her. Every stroke of his fingers had sent shock waves of pleasure deep inside her body. His kisses hadn't been a mere meeting of the lips. He'd intoxicated her with the deep, slow brush of his tongue and scrape of his fangs as they'd traced the line of her throat. And the cool press of his skin against hers hadn't just aroused her to a fever pitch, he'd branded his enticing male scent deep into her flesh.

And when she'd reached her climax, she felt as if she'd been flung into the stars, tossed free from her body, only to return an entirely different woman.

Lost in her ridiculous thoughts, Fallon allowed Cyn to roll to the side, snuggling her tight against his body.

"Are you okay?" he asked softly.

Was she?

Fallon blinked, still struggling to regain command of her fragmented thoughts.

"I don't know," she admitted.

"Hell." Cyn jerked his head up so he could stare down at her in concern. "Was I too rough?"

"No. I just . . ." She sucked in a deep breath, trying to slow the pace of her thundering heart. "I didn't realize it would be like that."

His worried expression was replaced by a slow, wicked grin. "Oh, princess, I can promise you that it's never like this."

She frowned. Was he mocking her innocence?

"What do you mean?"

"What happened between us was rare." He leaned down to kiss the tip of her nose. "Extraordinary."

A thrill of excitement fluttered in the pit of her stomach. It *had* felt extraordinary. As if . . .

With a muffled curse she slammed a mental door on her dangerous thoughts.

Cyn had shared this bed with a thousand different women.

She was just the next willing body.

Nothing extraordinary about that.

"I suppose you feel you have to say that."

The words had barely left her lips when she found herself flat on her back and an angry vampire perched on top of her.

"Stop."

Her eyes widened as she caught sight of his grim expression. "Cyn?"

"You can accuse me of enjoying more than my fair share of life's pleasures, but don't you dare try to cheapen what just happened between us," he growled.

"I didn't," she protested.

The jade eyes narrowed. "You just implied I was pulling out some stock answer after a random hookup."

She lowered her lashes, a blush staining her cheeks. "I just don't need you to pretend that I'm any different from the other women you've been with."

"Holy shite." He impatiently brushed back one of the braids that framed his handsome face. "Aye, I've been with plenty of females, but they came to me knowing that our time together was all about fun."

Her lips pressed together as a stab of . . . something sliced through her heart. God. Could it be jealousy?

"Exactly," she forced herself to mutter. "I'm no different."

Wrong answer.

She shivered as the temperature dropped. Climate control was a definite issue when dealing with a moody vampire.

"But those women weren't you." He leaned down until they were nose to nose. "Making love might not have mattered to you but it was bloody special to me."

"Of course it mattered," she muttered.

"Why should I believe you?" he demanded. "You did, after all, just break up with your princely fiancé. For all I know, this was revenge sex."

Fallon pressed her hands against his naked chest, floundering as he neatly turned the tables on her.

"This had nothing to do with Magnus."

"You did save your virginity for him. How can I be sure that you didn't just sleep with the first man available to punish him?"

She sucked in a shocked breath, sheer horror racing through her at the mere thought of any other man touching her.

"You know that's not true. I would never be with someone that I didn't . . ."

Her words trailed away as she realized she was revealing far more than she wanted to.

Thankfully he didn't press her to finish her sentence. Instead he gazed down at her with an unnerving intensity.

"Just as I would never lie to you," he asserted. "If I tell you that you're special, that's exactly what I mean. You're special."

Her lashes fluttered downward, shielding her expressive eyes. She felt vulnerable. Stripped dangerously raw. Which was no doubt why she'd tried to convince herself that Cyn considered her nothing more than a convenient body.

She was rattled enough by the physical intensity of their lovemaking without adding in the tangle of emotions that seethed just below the surface.

"I've never felt special," she breathed, her fingers unconsciously stroking over the satin-smooth skin of his chest.

He muttered a low curse, his lips skimming her furrowed brow. "Because your fiancé is an arrogant prick who wouldn't recognize a female of worth if she bit him on the arse."

True. But that hadn't been her point.

"I never had expectations from Magnus," she corrected, feeling a familiar sadness pierce her heart. It didn't seem to matter how many years passed. She would always be that little girl who ached for her father's love. "But it would have been nice if Sariel had bothered to notice me as more than a piece of property to be bartered for his own gain."

"Forget him." He lifted his head to study her with a somber expression. "He doesn't deserve your loyalty."

"It's not that easy. He's my family."

Something flared deep in the jade eyes. "Not anymore," he reminded her in a soft voice.

Fallon flinched at the blunt reminder that she would soon be shunned.

God Almighty. Once she'd cursed the tedious peace of her days. She hated playing the role of submissive princess. She hated having her life ruled by her father, and later by Magnus. She hated the fear that she would never travel beyond her homeland.

But now the tumultuous changes in her life were all happening too fast.

"You're right," she rasped, her voice thick with pain. "I've been . . ." She couldn't even speak the awful words.

"Don't," he growled, holding her gaze as his fingers threaded through her tangled hair. "I've got you."

She blinked back her tears. "You don't understand."

"No?" His gaze lowered to the dejected droop of her lips. "I was abandoned by my sire before I even woke as a vampire. I would have died in those caves. Hell, for all I know, he intended to kill me."

Fallon grimaced. "Okay, maybe you do understand."

"Aye." His expression softened. "But I found a new family. And I've never stopped appreciating what they did for me."

Shying away from the mere thought of never seeing her homeland again, she slid her hand beneath his hair, her fingers brushing over the dragon she'd seen tattooed on his shoulder blade. It was a stunningly beautiful symbol of his position.

"Is that why you became a clan chief?"

"In part." His fingers combed through her hair, his touch soothing even as it began to stir the familiar heat in the pit of her stomach. "It was a terrifying experience to awake alone with no memory of who or what I was. I intended to make sure that I never felt that vulnerable again."

She twitched beneath the heavy weight of his body, her mouth going dry as she felt his cock harden against her hip.

The heat was beginning to spread through her, those delicious tingles of anticipation making her shiver.

Good . . . Lord.

She was supposed to be a proper princess, not a harpy in heat.

"What was the other part?" she demanded, trying to distract herself.

The jade eyes darkened as Cyn reacted to her unmistakable arousal, his fangs visible between his lips.

"I'm a bossy, conceited bastard who likes to be in charge."

"You'll get no argument from me," she said, her breath hissing between her teeth as his lips brushed her forehead before skimming down her cheek.

"I also like protecting my family." He nuzzled the edge of her mouth, one hand still tangled in her hair while the other traced the curve of her hip. "Nothing and no one is allowed to harm those I consider mine."

*I consider mine . . .*

The words should have made her panic.

Her entire life had been filled with overbearing males thinking she belonged to them. First her father and then Magnus.

The last thing she wanted was another man with a caveman mentality.

But it wasn't panic that was making her heart flutter, or her stomach quiver.

"We should discuss what happened," she abruptly announced, needing a distraction.

"Discuss?" Cyn chuckled, placing a gentle kiss on her lips. "I'd rather share a physical demonstration."

"I didn't mean—"

"Our astonishing bout of mind-blowing sex?" he smoothly

interrupted, using his fang to trace the vein that ran down the side of her throat.

Sparks of pleasure shot through her. She moaned, battling against the impulse to tilt back her head and urge those fangs to sink deep into her throat.

Cyn had already made it clear he didn't consider her blood worthy of his finicky appetite.

"We need to find out who the man was sneaking through the caves," she clarified.

"I would suggest that we contact Siljar, but I'm no longer confident that the Commission hasn't been compromised," he said, his thoughts clearly not on the mysterious cloaked figure. Not when his hand was slowly stroking up to cup her breast. "Clearly the Oracle Phyla has some connection to the magic-user."

Fallon gripped his shoulders, her nails digging into his skin. "I can try to scry for him."

That got his attention.

Jerking up his head, he glared down at her.

"No."

She blinked, startled by the unequivocal refusal. Then she got pissed.

"I've spent my entire life being told what I can and can't do by men," she snapped, wishing she had the strength to shove him off her. Well, maybe she wouldn't actually shove him off. Not when his thumb had found the tip of her breast and was teasing it with a skill that was making her back arch in silent invitation. But she wanted him to know her days of obedience were over. "From now on I intend to make my own decisions."

His grim expression eased as his lips twitched at her bluster. "This has nothing to do with your newfound independence, princess."

Her eyes narrowed. "It sounded like you just told me no."

"I have a reason, I swear." He dropped a kiss on the tip of her nose. "Just let me explain."

Fallon pressed her lips together. Why did she find the oversized leech so damned charming?

"Fine."

"We've already alerted the magic-user that the tunnels are being spied on."

"And?"

"He can't be certain who was watching the Oracles' lair or why," he said. "But if you continue to try and scry for him, then he'll know that he's been busted."

Fallon frowned. She still wasn't sure how the magic-user had managed to sense her scry or how he'd used the connection to attack them. The mystery was going to gnaw at her until she figured it out.

"Isn't that what we want?" she demanded.

"Not if we aren't in a position to capture him."

She didn't miss the fierce edge in his voice. Cyn clearly itched to repay the magic-user for nearly killing him.

A predictable male reaction.

"What does it matter if it stops the spell?" she demanded.

"Because we can't be sure that he doesn't have a partner with the power to trigger the Oracles into completing the spell. Or an even worse plot if this one fails."

Hmm. She supposed it was possible that there was more than one enemy. And more than one plot.

Still, she sensed that she was being played by a master.

"I think you're just trying to keep me from scrying," she accused.

A half smile tugged at his lips as his gaze lowered to her naked breasts. "It won't break my heart to know you aren't putting yourself in danger."

"I have to do something to help."

"You can continue to keep track of the Oracles."

"And?"

He shrugged. "And assist my search through the history books in my library," he offered, his head lowering so he could use his tongue to trace the line of her jaw. "I agree with Styx. There's something familiar about this. I'm hoping I've read about a similar spell in one of the books left behind by Erinna and Mika."

Fallon grimaced. Growing up, her father had insisted that she spend hours in his library memorizing the various family bloodlines and where they fit in the complex social ranks. As if she actually cared whether the eldest daughter of the Morcella House should be greeted before the third son of the Vestres House.

"I thought everyone in this world used something called Google?"

Cyn gave a soft laugh. "Or we could stay here and forget about the Commission and evil magic-users."

Fallon swallowed a groan as his fangs scraped down the length of her neck. Oh. Yes. This suddenly seemed like a much, much better idea. Already her body was melting in anticipation, her legs parting so he could settle more firmly against her.

Losing herself in the pleasure of Cyn's touch was far preferable to worrying about shunnings, and ex-fiancés, and crazed magic-users.

Still, a tiny voice in the back of her head whispered that indulging her seemingly endless hunger for this vampire wasn't without risk.

Unlike Chatri males, Cyn didn't make her feel as if she were a mindless object he needed to control. Just the opposite.

When she was in his arms she had the unshakable sense she was . . . cherished.

A sensation that was as dangerous as Magnus's indifference.

No. *More* dangerous.

Her fiancé might have considered himself her master, but he'd never had the ability to truly touch her. Not on an emotional level.

But Cyn . . . he was inching perilously close to stealing her heart.

"We can't," she breathed.

He nibbled along the line of her collarbone. "Of course we can."

Her eyes slid closed, swiftly forgetting why this was a bad idea.

"Cyn."

His thumb circled the tight nub of her nipple. "Aye, princess?"

"We should be searching for the magic-user."

"We will," he assured her. "Later."

Clearly determined to divert her, he captured her lips, his tongue urging hers to part and allow him entry.

She quivered, briefly yielding to the desire pounding through her before she turned her head just enough to break the soul-melting kiss.

"Wait."

"No more waiting." Denied her lips, Cyn allowed his mouth to explore the line of her jaw to discover the sensitive hollow behind her ear. "I've hungered for you since the minute I caught sight of you."

The air was squeezed from Fallon's lungs, her head tilting back to allow greater access to his talented lips.

"You thought I was trying to trap your friend," she reminded him.

"That didn't keep me from wanting you." He stroked a path of searing kisses down the curve of her neck, lingering on the frantic pulse that beat at the base of her throat. "Just as you wanted me."

"You think you're so irresistible?"

"I think that the heat between us is combustible." He lightly nipped her shoulder, careful not to break her skin with his fang. "Admit it." His tongue traced a path toward the curve of her breast. "You were fascinated by me."

A whimper was wrenched from her throat as his lips closed over her tender nipple.

Her heart stopped beating as he caught the tip of her nipple between his teeth. "What makes you think I noticed you at all?"

"I know when a woman wants to see me naked." He lifted his head, watching her expressive face as he reached for her hand and pressed it against his arousal. "When she wants to touch me like this."

"Really?"

Unable to deny temptation, she wrapped her fingers around his cock, exploring down to the heavy testicles before slowly skimming back up to the broad tip.

"Aye." He shuddered, his palm sliding over the curve of her waist until his fingers were squeezing the soft flesh of her backside in a promise of pleasure to come.

Her mind went momentarily blank. What was she going to say?

Oh yes.

She was trying to convince him that he wasn't nearly so irresistible as he believed.

"I'd never seen a vampire in the flesh. Of course I was staring."

"Admit it." Without warning he was rolling onto his back, arranging her so she was lodged on top of him. Pleasure jolted through her as her already damp flesh was pressed to his thick cock. "You didn't have to stay with me after you pulled me from the throne room."

"Someone had to make sure you didn't go berserker and destroy our home," she moaned.

"Not someone . . . you." His hands moved to cup her breasts, his eyes darkened with a stark hunger. "There was no way in hell you were going to allow any other female near me."

"You're so vain." Her accusation ended on a gasp as he rolled her tender nipple between his thumb and finger.

"Why can't you admit that you want me?" His voice was thick with need.

"Because."

"Tell me."

She spread her hands on his chest, slowly lowering down until he could press his mouth to the juncture between her neck and shoulder. She shuddered, rubbing against his erection as his fangs replaced his lips, pressing just hard enough to send a thrill of anticipation through her.

He grasped her hips, sliding her over his rock-hard arousal in a movement that was meant to inflame her passion.

As if she needed any more inflaming. She was already about to combust.

"Tell me, Fallon."

"You frighten me."

He froze, his expression oddly vulnerable.

"You're scared of me?"

"Not you." Abruptly realizing she'd hurt him with her

thoughtless words, she brushed her lips over his mouth. "The way you make me feel."

A fierce relief flared through his eyes before he lifted his head so his lips could travel over the curve of her breast, at last latching on to her aching nipple.

She sucked in a sharp breath, a ruthless pleasure thundering through her.

"Oh . . . Cyn."

"Passion is nothing to fear," he muttered.

Nothing to fear? Perhaps not for him. He'd made seduction an art form that he practiced on a routine basis. She wasn't a laughably naïve princess who was ripe to tumble in love with the first man who aroused her desire.

Not that she was about to confess the truth.

At least not the full truth.

"It's not just passion. You make me . . ." She lost track of her words as she studied his starkly chiseled face. Dear heaven, he was just so beautiful.

Not pretty. Not like Magnus. He was too male for that. But there was a compelling savagery to his features that reminded her of the lethal beauty of a wild animal.

Predator.

His lips twitched as if he suspected he'd managed to disrupt her thoughts. "You were saying?"

An instant stab of annoyance jerked her out of her brief reverie.

"You make me psychotic," she said. It wasn't a lie. "One minute I'm furious with you."

"And the next?" he prompted.

"I want to rip off your clothes," she bluntly admitted. "Until I met you I never lost my temper."

"Boring." He urged her back down so his mouth could

return to its torment of her nipple. "I like when you forget to be the perfect princess."

She shuddered, her fingers somehow finding their way into the thick satin of his hair.

"It's not boring. It's peaceful."

As if sensing her struggle against the demands of her body, Cyn tilted back his head to study Fallon with a gaze that sent tiny tremors down her spine.

"Is that what you want? Peace?"

She bit her lip.

Of course it wasn't. She'd endured enough peace to last an eternity.

And if she was brutally honest with herself, she would admit that the ferocious tangle of emotions that catapulted her from one extreme to another was exactly what she'd always wanted.

Oh, she hadn't hoped for a threat to the world. Or the potential shunning.

But she was eager to experience the thrill of never knowing what was going to happen from one minute to the next. To opening herself up to a life that wasn't neatly planned and had the potential to break her heart.

She wasn't going to be a coward.

"No, I don't want peace."

He reached up to frame her face in his hands, tugging her down to kiss her with an urgency that spoke of need and yearning and . . . possession.

"What do you want?"

Fallon sighed. She didn't know what the future held with this vampire, but she would be a fool not to savor every moment he remained with her.

Her hands smoothed over the sculpted muscles of his chest. His skin was a cool, silken temptation. Yum. She gave a small moan of need, allowing her lips to glide over his face and down the strong column of his throat.

She shivered as she sucked in a deep breath of his erotic male scent.

Storm clouds and lightning.

"I love how you smell," she whispered as she continued her provoking caresses.

"I'm supposed to be seducing you," he growled, his hands clutching her hips as he sought to regain command.

Bossy.

"You seduced me last time," she whispered, moving steadily lower. "It's my turn."

"I wasn't finished."

"Do you want me to stop?"

He muttered a curse as she reached the taut muscles of his lower stomach. "Hell, no."

She gave a soft laugh, oddly pleased by his violent reaction to her touch. Feminine power. Who knew it could be so intoxicating?

Deliberately rubbing her body back up the length of his, she shivered at the sensation of their naked skin rubbing together.

"Tell me how to please you," she murmured.

"Just having you near pleases me," he said in thick tones. "Christ, I've waited for you for longer than you could ever possibly imagine," he murmured.

Oh. She faltered, not knowing how to react.

As if realizing he'd revealed more than he intended, he slid his arms up the curve of her spine.

"Now, my turn to play," he informed her, drawing her toward his waiting lips.

"But—"

Not giving her time to protest, Cyn branded her lips with

a kiss of pure hunger. Bolts of pleasure sizzled through her, making her feel as if she were struck by lightning.

The power felt wild . . . untamed.

As if Cyn had released the berserker who lived deep inside him.

Planting tiny, restless kisses over her face, he slid his lips down the length of her arched neck. Fallon's breath was slammed from her lungs as he tugged her upward, catching the puckered nipple between his teeth. She gave a soft gasp as he licked and tormented her, her back arching as excitement buzzed through her. He turned his attention to the other breast, deliberately urging her desire to a fever pitch.

Oh . . . Lord. She needed more.

She needed to feel him stretching her as he slid his cock deep into her body.

But even as she struggled to slide onto his waiting erection, he was ruthlessly hauling her up to her knees. With a strangled moan she glanced down to watch his mouth explore the clenched muscles of her stomach, his tongue darting out to send shivers of delight through her.

She hissed, her fingers tangling in his hair as his lips explored the curve of her hip and down the inside of her thigh.

Okay. Perhaps she shouldn't be in such a hurry.

Cyn seemed to know what he was doing.

Then his tongue found her moist cleft and she forgot how to think.

Feeling her entire body clench as his tongue stroked the highly sensitive flesh, Fallon gazed down at the vampire who was rapidly becoming a necessary part of her life.

He made her feel beautiful, and desirable, and just a little wicked.

Everything a woman wanted to feel.

Tightening his hold on her hips, Cyn found the mysterious center of her pleasure, gently sucking until her entire body clenched with her looming orgasm.

"Cyn," she breathed. "I need—"

"I've got you," he assured her, guiding her back so he could position her over his straining cock.

Then slowly he breached her tight passage.

Fallon hissed as she tentatively pressed downward, groaning at the delicious burn.

Suddenly she understood why he kept assuring her that his large size was a good thing.

Actually, it wasn't a good thing. It was a fantastic thing.

His teeth clenched as he allowed her to go at her own pace, sinking down one slow inch at a time.

It wasn't until she was fully seated that he tightened his hold on her hips and began to move.

Savoring his deep, steady pace, Fallon laid her hands on his chest, following the instinct to roll her hips to meet his upward thrust. She smiled with satisfaction as he gave a low shout as his fingers tightened on his hips.

She might be naive, but she was a fast learner.

"You're going to be the death of me, princess," he panted.

Fallon leaned down, sucking his lower lip between her teeth. His hips jerked off the mattress, as she bit the tender flesh at the same time she scored her nails down his chest.

Fallon chuckled, loving the sensation of having Cyn in her thrall. It might be nothing but an illusion that he was offering her, but it gave her a heady sense of power.

In this moment there was only the two of them.

No past.

And no future.

Shoving away the worries that waited just beyond the

bedroom door, she concentrated on the sensation of Cyn's deepening thrusts, her soft pants filling the air as she hovered on the cusp of bliss.

Cyn tightened his grip, his face burying in the curve of her neck. Then, still pumping into her at a furious pace, he tilted his hips for an even deeper penetration, sending her into a shattering climax.

Fallon shuddered in ecstasy, convulsing around him as he cried out with the violent pleasure of his own release.

# Chapter Twelve

Anthony Benson woke to find he was lying on the floor of his foyer.

Grimacing, he forced himself to the kitchen to devour the meal he'd prepared before leaving his private estate.

It was difficult enough to layer the magic through the caves of the Commission. Even with the potion to amplify his power, it drained him to the point of exhaustion. But to be forced to send a blast of energy to disrupt whoever had been spying on him had depleted what few resources he had left.

He was fortunate he'd managed to reach home before he collapsed.

Once he felt the magic returning to his body he took a quick shower and pulled on his usual uniform of slacks and a brown tweed jacket. Only then did he head to his library where he paced the floor with short, jerky steps.

Who the hell had been scrying the caves?

And why?

Had they been searching for him?

A trickle of fear inched down his spine. No. It was impossible.

Halting at the table below the large bay window, Anthony

poured himself a large shot of whiskey. If anyone suspected that he was manipulating the Oracles, he would have been destroyed before he could reach the caves.

It was more likely that the Commission had decided to beef up their security.

Which still posed a problem.

His cloak would have hid his identity, but if the Oracles were aware that there was someone sneaking through the tunnels, it would make it almost impossible for him to return.

Which meant he had to hope this last Compulsion spell would be enough to gain complete control of the Commission.

But first . . .

He drained the whiskey and set his empty glass on his desk.

The imp Keeley should have returned by now. Which meant he'd either been captured or turned traitor.

Either way, Anthony needed to shut his mouth before he could start squealing and ruin everything.

Reaching into his pocket he pulled out his phone and sent a short text to Yiant.

Minutes later the slender fairy appeared, attired in ornate robes that revealed he'd been in the middle of some flamboyant fey celebration.

Offering a low bow, Yiant straightened to offer Anthony a patently false smile. "My lord, I am honored by your invitation, but as I said, I truly have no more potions."

Anthony waved aside the overly practiced words. Really. Dealing with the fey was like dealing with the slimy politicians in Dublin. Cunning, slippery bastards who would stab you in the back without hesitation.

Thankfully he had them by the nuts.

And he wasn't afraid to squeeze his grip when necessary.

"I need you to make me a portal," he said.

The fairy frowned. No doubt he'd hoped for a quick return to his party. "To where?"

"The King of Vampires' lair."

Pure shock drained the color from the fairy's face. "You want me to take you to Styx's lair?"

"Unless he's been replaced," he mocked.

"But . . . it isn't possible."

Anthony adjusted the cuff of his tweed jacket, his voice dangerously soft. "You really need to stop saying that to me."

Yiant licked his dry lips. "I mean that his home is protected by layers of magic that prevent the opening of a portal."

Anthony shrugged. "Have you been there?"

"Naturally I traveled to pay my respects after he'd settled at the lair with his mate."

"And to scout the terrain in case you wanted to spy on the Anasso?"

"Of course not," the fairy denied, his eyes wide with innocence.

A lie. One that Anthony ignored.

He had no interest in demon power games. All that mattered was that Yiant had been to the vampire lair, so he could create a portal.

"Then you will take me as close as possible."

Yiant was shaking his head before Anthony finished speaking. "The vampires will kill us. The Ravens patrol the grounds."

"I don't intend to linger long enough for the vampires to know we're there. Besides, it will soon be daylight there."

"But—"

Anthony slashed a pudgy hand through the air. "This isn't a request."

* * *

Pacing from one end of the library to the other, Tonya told herself to go to bed.

It wasn't as if she could be a damned liaison when the two people she was supposed to be liaisoning between were both too busy with the exquisite Chatri princess to need her services.

Her hands fisted, her jaw clenched as she recalled her brief glimpse of Fallon as she'd led Styx from the porch to the front gate.

She'd been perfect, of course. Tall and slender with a glorious cloud of golden hair and the features of an angel. And she'd moved with a hypnotizing grace, making Tonya feel like an awkward lump in comparison.

It was no wonder that Magnus had been so eager to follow them when he'd caught the faint, champagne scent of his fiancée.

Now the two would be happily reunited and no doubt headed to their fairy home where they would live happily ever after.

Blah, freaking blah, blah.

Telling herself that she'd be happy to see the last of Magnus, Prince of Chatri, Tonya watched as the automated curtains silently slid across the windows to block out the cresting sun. It wasn't as if she cared about the bastard.

No. Way.

The fierce words had barely formed when her heart gave a renegade leap at the sound of angry male voices echoing through the hallway.

Mere seconds later Styx and Magnus stormed into the library.

Halting in the center of the room, Magnus spread his arms, his expression mocking. "Satisfied, my lord?" he sneered. "I have returned as you commanded."

Styx narrowed his gaze, clearly in a mood. "Not nearly.

Keep your fairy ass in this lair. If I have to chase you down
I'm not going to be happy."

With his warning delivered, the Anasso turned on his
heel and headed out of the room, slamming the door behind
him.

"As if he has the right to tell me what to do," the prince
muttered.

Tonya's lips twisted with grim amusement as she studied
the painfully beautiful male face. It was obvious the prince's
arrogance was taking a battering from the King of Vampires. So why had he returned?

And without his fiancée.

"What did Fallon want with Styx?"

"She needed him to repair the vampire who'd been injured."

Tonya blinked in confusion. "Cyn was injured?"

"Yes."

"Oh my God, is he okay?"

Magnus sent her a glance of disgust. "Why should I care?"

Tonya narrowed her gaze. "Hey, don't be pissy with me.
I didn't do anything."

"I'm not pissy," Magnus denied, his slender fingers
toying with the emerald pendant hung around his neck.
Tonya suspected it was an unconscious habit that revealed
he wasn't quite as composed as he wanted her to believe.
"I'm quite justly aggrieved."

She shrugged. The two men were too alpha not to strike
sparks off each other.

"Styx isn't happy unless he's making someone feel aggrieved. I wouldn't take it personally."

"I'm indifferent to the vampires."

"Of course you are." She rolled her eyes. "Then what has
you so aggrieved?"

"My fiancée has broken our marriage contract."

Tonya stilled. A tangle of emotions twisted her stomach into a painful knot.

"Oh," she at last breathed. "I didn't know that was possible."

"It's extremely rare." Magnus paced toward the fireplace, the scent of aged whiskey teasing at Tonya's nose. "Only a fool would choose such an extreme path."

Tonya watched as he poured himself a glass of the nectar that had been left on the mantel to warm.

He sounded so . . . cold. As if he didn't care that the female he'd chosen as his wife had decided to remain with Cyn.

"What do you mean by 'extreme'?" she prodded.

"She will be shunned by our people." He finished the nectar and set aside the glass. "It is the worst fate a Chatri can suffer."

Tonya shuddered. She'd pissed off her father and brothers when she'd chosen to work for a vampire in a demon club, but they hadn't actually shunned her.

She just wasn't invited to feast days.

A sweet bonus as far as she was concerned.

"What did she do to break the contract?"

"She refused to return to our homeland."

Tonya waited for the rest of the story. And waited. At last she gave a shake of her head.

"That's it?"

Magnus arched a brow, the firelight shimmering over his stunning hair. Even dressed in casual slacks and a green silk shirt, he managed to look unearthly. Ethereal.

"I gave her a direct command."

Tonya's petty jealousy toward the impossibly lovely princess was buried beneath a surge of outrage. She moved forward, not halting until she had to tilt back her head to glare at the prince who stood there with such supreme indifference.

"You . . . pig."

Magnus blinked. "I beg your pardon?"

"You're allowing the woman you once intended to make your wife to be shunned because she didn't obey your command?"

"It's her duty."

"While your duty is doing whatever the hell you want, including kissing me?" she accused.

A sudden flush touched his cheeks, an emotion she couldn't read flaring through the cognac eyes.

"You didn't object at the time."

Tonya grimaced at the direct hit.

Of course she hadn't objected. Hell, she'd been an eager participant, even though she'd known he belonged to another.

Once again, she'd allowed her stupid hormones to overcome her common sense.

Christ. What was it with her and being attracted to the wrong guys?

Not only wrong, but completely inaccessible?

No doubt a psychiatrist would tell her that it was simply a case of wanting what she couldn't have.

She thought it was a pain in the ass.

"Because I was temporarily insane, you moron," she snapped, lifting her fist to bang it against his chest.

Scowling, he grasped her wrist, careful to keep from bruising her pale skin. "Why are you so angry?"

Tonya had a dozen reasons.

Most of them had to do with her unwanted attraction to an arrogant jackass who could treat his fiancée as if she were some disposable piece of property.

"Why did she refuse to return with you?" she demanded.

His lips curled in disdain. "She claimed that an Oracle

had demanded her services, but it was obvious that she has developed feelings for the vampire."

"Oracle?" Tonya was momentarily distracted. "What Oracle?"

"Ask your precious Anasso."

She frowned at the odd words. "He isn't mine."

Magnus tightened his hand on her wrist, tugging her close enough that the heat of his body seared through her tiny, spandex dress.

"You answer to him."

"Wrong," she countered. "I answer to Viper, who pays the bills. Not all of us happen to be a princess."

He leaned down until they were nose to nose. "You are too outspoken."

"Tough shit." She didn't back down an inch. If he thought he could intimidate her, then he was in for a very big disappointment. She dealt with drunken trolls on a regular basis. "Why are you here?"

"Where should I be?"

She desperately tried to pretend that the stroke of his thumb against her inner wrist wasn't sending arrows of pleasure darting through her body.

She didn't want to be so vulnerable to his touch.

"You came to search for Fallon, didn't you?"

His gaze moved slowly over her face, at last stopping to study the full curve of her lips. "I did."

"Now you've found her." She pointed out the obvious, not sure why she was pressing him. "Why don't you return to your homeland?"

His fingers skimmed up her bare arm, even as his expression tightened with annoyance. "You sound as if you're trying to get rid of me."

An unexpected pain sliced through her heart at his words.

No. Oh God, no.

She wasn't idiotic enough to want him to stay, was she?

"Once you're gone I can return to my real job," she forced herself to say. "The club needs me."

His hand moved beneath her hair, cupping her nape with an oddly possessive grip. "And that's the only reason?"

She ignored the question. "Are you staying because you hope Fallon will change her mind?" she instead demanded.

He frowned, as if confused by the implication he might be harboring a secret desire to reunite with his fiancée.

"Change her mind?"

"That she'll return home with you." Her lips twisted as she pretended she didn't care what his answer would be. "Agree to become your obedient little wife?"

There was no hesitation. "The contract is broken."

"A new contract could be written." She carefully watched the impossibly beautiful face, searching for . . . what? Pain? Regret? Guilt? Relief? "If you truly want her as your wife."

"It's done."

She made a sound of impatience. "And it doesn't hurt?"

"Why should it?"

For some reason his flat tone pissed her off.

"God. You're a piece of work," she muttered. "Did you care for the poor woman at all?"

He held her gaze, his expression strangely knowing. "Would you prefer that I be suffering at the loss of my fiancée?"

Tonya's annoyance faltered. Did she want him to be pining for Fallon?

Hell, no.

In fact, if she was being honest, a part of her was fiercely happy he wasn't brokenhearted.

Still, she needed to know he was capable of feeling *something*.

"I'm just trying to understand how you could be so indifferent."

His lips flattened. "Our engagement was not based on emotion. It was a means to improve the status of our mutual Houses," he grudgingly admitted. "We both understood our duty."

He was in full prince mode. Cold. Aloof. Committed to his social position.

Tonya shivered. Why did she keep searching for some indication he was more than an arrogant snob?

"So now you return to find another sacrificial lamb?"

"Eventually."

It was exactly the response she'd expected, so why did she abruptly want to knee him in the nuts?

"Why not now?" she asked through clenched teeth. "There's nothing to keep you here."

Without warning the cognac eyes darkened and his fingers tangled in her hair so he could tilt back her head.

Then, swooping downward, he claimed her lips in a kiss that demanded a response.

Tonya trembled, a blast of sheer pleasure nearly sending her to her knees. God Almighty. She'd managed to provoke a response. But it wasn't the one she expected.

Drowning in the scent of whiskey, Tonya parted her lips, allowing him greater access. Their tongues tangled, his power wrapping around her like a blanket.

For a crazed moment, Tonya forgot all the reasons she didn't want this man.

It didn't matter that he was a ruthless prince who had recently condemned his fiancée to a painful shunning. Or that he was on the point of returning to his homeland to choose another to become his wife.

When she was in his arms all that mattered was that she felt needed and beautiful and heart-meltingly cherished.

He eased the demanding pressure of his mouth, giving her lower lip a sharp nip. "You don't want me to leave."

"Of course I do," she tried to bluff. "I told you . . ." The words were stolen as he covered her mouth with demanding lips. With a low groan she at last pulled her head back to study his flushed, impossibly beautiful face. She felt drunk on the excitement that bubbled through her like the finest nectar. "Why are you kissing me?"

His expression was brooding as his hand skimmed down the curve of her spine, cupping her backside with an intimacy that stole her breath away.

"I don't have a damned clue."

Lost in one another, neither heard the door opening. It was at last the blast of icy air that had them turning to discover the Anasso watching them with obvious impatience.

"Again?" Styx growled. "You two really need to get a room."

With a low hiss, Magnus was abruptly shoving her behind him, protecting her disheveled appearance from Styx's all too perceptive gaze.

"What do you want now, leech?" he snapped, a faint golden glow surrounding his body as his power kicked into overdrive.

Tonya gasped as Magnus's heat surrounded her in a protective shield.

It was dangerously easy to underestimate this lethal Chatri.

Styx scowled, but perhaps sensing that Magnus was at the point of snapping, he pulled back his own aggression, careful not to glance at Tonya as she peeked around the prince's shoulder.

"I need your help," the Anasso said.

Magnus made a sound of impatience. "What now?"

"The imp is dead," Styx said, his voice flat. "I need to know how the hell it happened."


Cyn was seated in a leather wing chair, absently stroking his charcoal pencil over the sketch pad that he held in his hands. At the same time, he was keeping a careful watch on Fallon as she restlessly paced the floor.

Even dressed in jeans and a casual blue sweater, with her hair pulled into a haphazard ponytail, she managed to look stunningly beautiful.

Of course, she'd been even more exquisite when she was lying naked in his arms, he ruefully concluded.

Unfortunately, as much as he wanted to pretend that the world outside his lair didn't exist, he couldn't entirely ignore the imminent threat to demons. So while he'd wanted nothing more than to keep her in his bed, he'd grudgingly given in to duty. Well, first they had been in a long, delicious shower together, and then he'd insisted that she eat the dinner left in the kitchen by Lise.

Only then did he bring her to the library to sort through the vast collection of books while he struggled to clear his mind and connect the dots.

Dammit, there had to be a reason why this all felt so familiar.

Sorting through a millennium of memories, Cyn was yanked out of his inner thoughts when Fallon came to an abrupt halt in the center of the priceless carpet.

"Arrgh," she breathed, glaring at him in exasperation.

He hid his surge of amusement. It was becoming obvious that his soon-to-be mate wasn't a scholar, despite her shrewd intelligence.

She preferred far more interactive pastimes. Like scrying. Or . . .

Hastily shoving aside the memory of Fallon's thorough, agonizingly slow exploration of his body in the shower, he concentrated on her obvious frustration.

The sooner they discovered what the hell was going on, the sooner he could have her in his bed.

"Troubles, princess?" he asked.

She held up the heavy leather-bound book she'd been reading. "I don't know what I'm supposed to be looking for."

He set aside his pencil, astonished at the sense of right-ness he felt to see Fallon in his most private sanctuary.

This room was the one place that he never allowed his guests to enter. Not only because it contained priceless man-uscripts given to him by his foster father, but because this was the one place he could simply . . . be.

No women, no games, no outrageous behavior that made him infamous throughout the vampire world.

He'd never thought to willingly invite a woman into his refuge.

Then again, Fallon wasn't just a woman.

She was his mate.

The other half of his soul.

"You're supposed to be searching for a spell that closes dimensions," he murmured, not surprised when she nar-rowed her eyes at his bland tone.

"Half the time it doesn't even say what is happening," she groused, glancing down to read from the book that was dedicated to ancient nymph history. "'A great and terrible darkness rose from the bowels of the earth to seek destruc-tion upon the bright and shiny people,'" she quoted, giving a shake of her head. "What's that supposed to mean?"

He shrugged. "The fey do have a love for melodrama."

She tossed aside the book, deliberately allowing her gaze

to take a slow survey of his body that was casually sprawled in the chair.

"What are you doing?"

"Sketching."

The amber eyes narrowed. "Aren't we supposed to be searching for a way to save the world?"

"I am."

"How?"

"This helps me think."

She placed her hands on her hips, her expression revealing her disbelief.

"Really?" Her eyes widened as he turned the sketch pad so she could see his work. "Oh."

She moved forward, taking the sketch pad from his hands to study the image of herself standing in front of a small cottage in a pretty dale.

"Where is this place?" she asked.

Cyn rose to his feet, reaching to tuck a stray curl behind her ear. "My foster parents' home just a few miles south of here." His heart gave a painful twist at the thought of the cottage being empty. Dammit, as soon as he found them he was going to have a long chat with them. "I'll take you to visit as soon as they get back."

Her expression softened, as if she sensed the worry for his foster parents that gnawed at him.

"They don't live here?"

"They visit, but they prefer their own space," he said, taking the sketch pad from her and tossing it onto the chair. Grabbing her hands, he pressed her palms flat against his chest. He needed to feel the warmth of her skin seeping through his fisherman sweater. He'd always been more tactile than most vampires. No doubt a result of having been taken in by fairies. Now, however, his craving for touch was limited to this one particular female. "They said my lair was too big."

Keeping one hand against his chest, she lifted the other to lightly tug on the narrow braid that lay against his cheek.

"Are you sure it wasn't the orgies that ran them off?"

Ah. He knew jealousy when he heard it.

He didn't bother to hide his pleased smile.

"You really are obsessed with those orgies."

Another tug on his braid. This one sharp enough to cause a prick of pain. "Do you deny them?"

Cyn hesitated, choosing his words with care. He wasn't ashamed of his past. He lived with an open lust for pleasure that was shared by those who moved in and out of his lair.

Still, he didn't ever want Fallon to think that she was one of a long line of lovers.

"In the past I filled this lair with friends. And my clansmen are always welcome to stay," he slowly admitted.

"So it was like the . . ." She halted, clearly struggling for the words. "What was the name? Playboy Mansion?"

"As I said." He leaned down to place a kiss on top of her head, soaking in the scent of warm champagne. "The past."

"Why the past?" She absently pulled the braid through her fingers, her head lowered as if she was trying to pretend that his answer didn't matter.

Cyn cupped her chin, gently forcing her to meet his somber gaze. "You know why."

He heard her breath catch in her throat, her eyes darkening with a potent combination of fear and gut-deep yearning.

Time halted as their gazes locked, both sensing the vast, unyielding bond that was slowly, irrevocably forming between them.

For Cyn it was the natural progression of finding his mate.

For Fallon . . . His lips twisted as panic rippled over her face.

Clearly she wasn't ready to accept the threads that were tying her to him on a fundamental level.

With a skittish movement she was tugging free of his light grasp, her cheeks flushed as she tried to pretend her heart wasn't thundering a hundred miles an hour.

"Are you worried about your parents?"

Wise enough not to press, Cyn gave a slow nod. "Yes. I wish they would have been honest with me. It was bad enough when I thought they'd taken off without saying good-bye." He didn't try to hide the edge in his voice. "Now I have no way of knowing whether they're okay or not."

She offered a sympathetic smile. "They no doubt wanted to protect you."

"I don't want their protection," he growled, glancing toward the mantel where he had a charcoal sketch of the two fairies who'd rescued him from the caves and taken him into their home. "If they'd stayed we could have faced the threat together."

She didn't bother to point out that his foster parents would die rather than place him in danger. Which meant that she was already learning he had a fierce belief that he was supposed to be the defender.

A good sign.

"What were they doing before they left?" she instead asked.

Pain twisted his gut at his last memory of watching Erinna and Mika strolling away from his lair, hand in hand.

If someone had harmed them . . .

He shook his head, refusing to even contemplate the possibility.

"They'd gone to Dublin to speak with the druids," he said.

"About what?"

Cyn shrugged. When his foster parents had visited to say they were traveling to Dublin, he hadn't paid much attention. It wasn't like it was out of the ordinary. And they'd been careful not to allow him to sense they might be troubled.

"They didn't say." He grimaced, belatedly wishing he'd pressed for more details. "After the meeting they intended to stay for a gathering of the Irish fairies."

"And they never returned?"

"No." He gave a frustrated shake of his head. "I assumed they decided to remain with their tribe. Or that they were traveling. They often take off during the winter months, although they'd never disappeared without leaving a note for me," he explained. "If I'd thought for a second they were in danger—"

"You couldn't know; you can't blame yourself," she hastily assured him, moving close enough to lay her hand against his chest. "Besides, they more than likely are in hiding, waiting for the danger to pass. Fey are very clever creatures."

His lips twisted. His princess hid a soft heart beneath her prickly independence.

Fate had chosen well for him.

"Very clever," he agreed, his hands spanning her waist and urging her against his body.

Instant heat flared through her eyes as he urged her against the thickening length of his arousal, but she pressed her hand against his chest.

"Tell me why you feel that this is familiar."

He smiled, his hand sliding upward to cup her breast. "This?"

"No." She shivered, clearly struggling to recall what she wanted to say. "I mean the spell that the Commission is going to cast."

"I was afraid that's what you meant," Cyn admitted, ruefully allowing his hands to drop.

When he took Fallon back to his bed he wanted her full attention.

"Well?" she prompted.

"It isn't the spell itself that teases at my memory. I wasn't even aware that it was possible to close the dimensions," he admitted. "It's more the overall threat to destroy demons."

"Have you been able to track the source of the hieroglyphs?"

"No, but I suspect that it has a fey history, but the actual spell is more human . . . Shit."

She looked alarmed. "What?"

Cyn restlessly paced toward the heavy arched doors. Shoving one open, he stepped onto the balcony that overlooked the vast lake that surrounded his lair. In the moonlight he could easily make out the lights of the village that was the only civilization among the rugged hills and broad valleys.

There was no worry any of his clansmen would catch sight of him. There were layers of magic wrapped around the castle to keep any prying eyes from seeing anything more than a thick mist.

He walked to place his hands on the stone balustrade, his thoughts catapulted three hundred years in the past.

For long minutes he silently shuffled through his memories, following a single thread until it reached the dramatic confrontation just a year ago.

There was a light touch on his arm as Fallon joined him on the balcony. "Cyn, what is it?"

"A human magic-user," he muttered, turning his head to meet her concerned gaze.

"Do you know him?"

He shook his head. "No, but I've heard of other humans who tried to destroy demons."

"Who?"

"The witches." With a sudden surge of determination, Cyn pulled his cell phone from the pocket of his jeans. "I have to speak with Dante."

She blinked in confusion. "Who is Dante?"

"One of my brothers. I hope he might have some answers." He quickly texted a message to his friend. "I'll have him meet us outside Styx's lair once the sun sets in Chicago. You can open a portal so he can travel here and look at the spell."

She hesitated, perhaps sensing he didn't want to discuss his suspicions until he had a chance to speak with his fellow vampire.

Smart and beautiful.

"If he has answers, does that mean we can stop looking through all these musty books?" she asked.

He chuckled, wrapping his arms around her waist. "My books are not musty."

She grimaced. "Fine. They're not musty, but I'm tired of research."

The desire that was a constant, exhilarating buzz in the pit of his stomach abruptly spiked as he gazed down at her beautiful face.

Bloody hell. His erection was already aching to be buried deep inside her addictive heat.

"Good," he growled, stroking his lips over her forehead. "Because I have a better way of passing the night."

She shivered, her lips parting in an unconscious invitation. "Cyn."

"But first . . ." Taking her hand, Cyn led her back into the library, heading straight to his desk. Pulling open the top drawer, he pulled out the delicately carved box he'd hidden there before he'd taken Fallon on their picnic. Then, with a small smile, he placed it in Fallon's hand. "Here."

She glanced at him in confusion. "What is this?"

He brushed the back of his hand down the satin softness of her cheek. "My musty books didn't have much information on the elusive Chatri, but they did reveal that the fey royalty have an unquenchable thirst for pretty baubles."

She blinked in surprise. "When did you research the Chatri?"

"As soon as we arrived here," he ruefully admitted.

Slowly she took the lid off the box, giving a soft gasp at the sight of the diamond and ruby necklace that had been designed in the shape of a hummingbird.

"Oh." She lightly traced the delicate gems that shimmered with a living fire in the moonlight.

Smug satisfaction raced through him. The handful of references he'd found on the Chatri had spoken of their love for treasure, but it was his own instinct about his mate that warned him she wasn't the sort of woman who would be impressed by size or monetary worth.

She was unique. So only the most rare, the most exquisitely crafted treasure, would impress her.

"Well?" he prompted when she continued to stare at his unexpected gift.

"You"—she paused to clear her throat—"are a very dangerous man."

# Chapter Thirteen

Magnus was left alone in the dead imp's cell while the vampires transferred the various prisoners and did a thorough sweep of the house. Crouching beside the body, he monitored how quickly the body disintegrated.

He wasn't a healer, but he'd trained as a warrior, despite his royal blood. He'd been taught how to determine the death of a fey.

Hours later he was still maintaining his vigil as the imp became nothing more than a faint sparkle of sand on the lead-lined floor. He was rising to his feet when he sensed Tonya entering the dungeon along with the King of Vampires.

His hands clenched. This was absurd. Tonya was a mere imp. And worse, she didn't have the slightest knowledge of how a true female should behave.

She was rude. Outspoken. And she had zero respect for his position as prince.

So why did he keep kissing her? It was as if his body disconnected from his brain, was urging him to touch her with a compulsion he couldn't seem to resist.

And why did he feel more vibrant—more intensely alive—whenever she was near?

The answers shouldn't matter to him. Just like he shouldn't be curious as to why the imp had come to Styx's lair and was now dead.

He should have already returned to his homeland. It would take time for the formal dissolution of his engagement and then the tedious negotiations to choose someone else to become his fiancée.

His House was depending on him to elevate their stature among the Chatri.

Slowly rising, he smoothed his expression to one of aloof boredom as Tonya stepped into the cell swiftly followed by Styx.

"How did he die?" the Anasso curtly demanded, displaying his usual appalling lack of manners.

Not that he particularly wanted to indulge in idle chitchat with a leech.

"Magic," he revealed.

Styx scowled at the unwelcome revelation. "Impossible."

Magnus folded his arms over his chest, deliberately holding the vampire's gaze. It wasn't really a challenge. It was the only way he could keep himself from staring at the sinfully sexy woman who was hovering near the door of the cell.

"Then you explain what happened," he said.

Styx stabbed a finger toward the complex engravings on the cell wall. As if Magnus could have missed them.

"The hexes in the dungeons prevent any magic, even if it could pass through the layers of protection that are wrapped around the estate."

"That would be no barrier if the spell had already been cast."

A blast of icy air slammed into Magnus. The King of

Vampires wasn't pleased at the knowledge his barriers weren't as impenetrable as he believed.

"Explain," he snapped.

Magnus glanced back down at the sand that had lost its sparkle. He knew of only one way to kill an imp who was surrounded by defensive hexes.

"Long ago witches kept private assassins."

"Are you saying the imp was an assassin?"

"Not necessarily." He returned his attention to Styx. "My point is that the witches would place a death spell on their servants. If they were captured then they could detonate the spell before the assassin could reveal the name of their master."

The vampire peeled back his lips, revealing his massive fangs. "So the killer could be anywhere."

"No," Magnus said in decisive tones. He'd never encountered a witch powerful enough to perform the spell, but he knew enough about magic to know that it must have its limitations. "They would have to be close enough to speak the word of power."

"How close?"

"It would depend on the strength of the magic-user."

The vampire glared at him, the air becoming downright frigid. "How close?" he repeated.

"A few hundred feet," Magnus muttered.

Styx's features tightened, his eyes narrowed. "Interesting."

Magnus didn't find it interesting. He found it . . . disgraceful.

No fey should die by such a cowardly attack.

"I suppose that I'm expected to track down the witch?" he commanded, not about to admit that he was remotely interested in the mystery.

A Chatri prince should be above such mundane curiosity.

"Once the sun sets," the vampire at last said.

Magnus frowned. Styx wasn't stupid. He had to know the quicker that Magnus was on the hunt, the better the chance of finding the culprit.

"The scent will be faded."

Styx studied him for a long moment. "I don't trust you," he at last said.

Tonya muttered something about men and the size of their privates beneath her breath, but Magnus kept his gaze locked on the vampire.

"If I intended to flee I would have done so when we were in the portal," he said, his tone edged with an arrogance that was certain to annoy the leech. "Chatri are capable of creating more than one opening. You would never have realized I hadn't returned to Chicago until too late."

"I have a dead imp." Styx refused to back down. No surprise. Vampires were overly aggressive creatures who should be kept caged for the safety of all demons.

"Yes, we've already established that," Magnus drawled.

Styx stepped toward him. "And the most likely suspect for the murder is standing in front of me."

"Are you suggesting I might have killed the imp?"

"I don't suggest. I'm flat-out saying that you're a suspect."

Magnus lifted his hand, a glow beginning to dance over his skin. Styx might be the King of Vampires, but a Prince of the Chatri had a potent magic. If the leech wanted a fight, then he could have one.

The scent of plums filled the air as Tonya was abruptly standing between the two of them.

"Why would he want to kill an imp?" she demanded.

Styx's gaze remained locked on Magnus. "There could be any number of reasons."

"Ridiculous." Magnus sneered, trying to pretend that he

didn't care that the beautiful imp had clearly risked her own neck to halt the looming violence. What did it matter if she cared whether or not he was hurt by the Anasso? It didn't. Of course it didn't. "I wasn't even here, if you'll recall."

Styx shoved aside his obvious logic. "You could have killed him, then followed me to Cyn's lair. It would have given you the perfect alibi."

"If I'd decided to kill the imp I wouldn't sneak around." He released a trickle of his power, melting the frost that had formed on the walls. "I am a Chatri. It's my right to offer death to any fey."

"I'll watch him," Tonya abruptly said, turning to glare at him over her shoulder.

As if the sudden tension was his responsibility.

Styx's icy expression abruptly softened as he glanced toward the female who barely came to the middle of his chest.

"Viper will kick my ass if anything happens to you," he ruefully admitted.

Magnus deliberately moved until he was standing at Tonya's side. He didn't like the casual intimacy between this woman and the King of Vampires.

It made him itchy.

"I would never harm a female," he snapped.

Tonya gave a toss of her head. "I can take care of myself, thank you very much."

Styx's lips twitched as his gaze briefly flicked toward Magnus before returning to Tonya. Then, with a smooth motion, he had reached behind his back to pull out a handgun.

"Here." He offered the gun to Tonya. "Can you use it?"

Taking the gun, Tonya tested its weight before lifting it to aim it at a spot on the far wall.

"I can shoot the balls off a gnat," she assured the vampire.

"Good." Styx gave her a nod of approval before turning to point a finger at Magnus. "You."

"What?"

"If you find an intruder you will follow their scent, but you won't confront them or allow them to know we have managed to discover their trail," Styx commanded. "You will mark their location and return here."

Magnus glowered in outrage. "You do realize that I'm not your servant?"

"Don't get caught."

Seemingly confident his orders would be carried out, Styx strolled out of the cell, the sound of his pet Ravens instantly falling into step behind him as they left the dungeon.

"Bastard," he rasped, barely resisting the urge to send a bolt of power toward the retreating vampires.

Not to kill.

But he could singe their asses.

Perhaps sensing his childish urge, Tonya moved to stand directly in front of him, blocking his path to the door.

"Are we going?"

Magnus sucked in a deep breath, drenching himself in the scent of wild plums. "I don't know why I should do the bidding of a leech who has the manners of a demented troll."

"Neither do I." She studied him, her expression unreadable. "But you're going to search for the killer, aren't you?"

He was.

He didn't know why. His logical mind told him that this was none of his business. That he should return to his home and forget he'd ever traveled to this world.

But some inner instinct warned him that there was something going on here that was important.

Something that might affect the Chatri unless it was stopped.

Silently calling himself a fool, Magnus stepped around the too-tempting imp and headed out of the cell.

"You should stay here."

Predictably Tonya was immediately at his side, her pretty features set in a stubborn expression.

"No way in hell."

He shook his head. No doubt he should have told her that she had to join him on the hunt. She was just contrary enough to have demanded that she be left behind.

How did males in this world ever deal with such continual insolence?

"It could be dangerous," he growled, climbing the steps and heading toward the foyer.

Tonya easily kept pace at his side. "Darling, I spend my evenings preventing the most lethal demons in the world from killing each other in a drunken rage," she drawled. "Besides, I'm supposed to keep an eye on you."

"Fine," he muttered, his voice carefully nonchalant. "Come if you want." Reaching the door, he glanced at her with a frown. "But you will not call me darling. I am a prince."

"Whatever you say, princy poo." She deliberately glanced at the door, the gun still in her hand. "Let's do this thing."

"You . . ." He bit off his exasperated words, yanking the door open and leading the way out of the house and down the path to the front gate.

The late-afternoon sunlight drenched the estate in a pale light, but the breeze was brutally cold and the ground frozen hard beneath their feet.

Without thought, Magnus warmed the air around himself, extending the heat to protect the female walking at his side.

She sent him a startled glance. "What are you doing?"

He kept his senses locked on his surroundings, sorting through the hundreds of scents that floated on the air.

"It's freezing," he murmured absently. "My powers will keep you warm."

"Oh."

He turned to regard her, in puzzlement over her strangled tone. "Does it bother you?"

"I . . ." An odd flush stained her cheeks. "No. Of course not."

Intending to press her on her peculiar behavior, Magnus was distracted by the unmistakable scent of fey.

With a swift jog he was headed through the gate and toward a large oak tree across the street. Bending downward he touched the shallow indents in the ground.

"Here." He blocked out the various smells, focusing on the two distinct sets of footprints. "A fairy and a human."

Tonya crouched beside him, lightly touching the scorched grass where a portal had opened.

"A witch?" she demanded.

Magnus shook his head. "No, but I sense magic."

"A lot of magic," she agreed softly, clearly capable of picking up the prickles of raw energy that had been left behind by the human.

Straightening, Magnus allowed himself to lock on the residual magic left behind by the portal. It wasn't as easy as following the pathway of another Chatri, but he was one of the rare trackers who could at least retrace the portal to the general area.

With a lift of his hand, he released a bolt of energy, slicing an opening between dimensions in the precise spot as the first portal.

Tonya surged upright, her expression wary. "What are you doing?"

"Following the trail."

"But—"

He held out a hand as he prepared to step into the opening. "Are you coming or not?"

She hesitated, nodding her head toward the nearby mansion. "I don't think Styx will be happy."

Magnus made a sound of disgust. "As if I care."

"I'm beginning to wonder if you're staying just to aggravate the King of Vampires."

Magnus shrugged. That was as good an explanation as any other.

# Chapter Fourteen

Anthony stepped out of the portal and into his library with a sense of relief. It didn't matter how many times he traveled through dimensions, he never became used to the sense of electricity dancing over his skin.

And it only made it worse that after leaving Chicago he'd forced Yiant to take him to a private sanitarium in Amsterdam to visit the woman who was his current wife. It was a duty he forced himself to perform despite his annoyance with Clarice. He'd chosen her from one of the finest families in Dublin, using her standing among society to elevate his career in politics. Who knew she would be such an ill-bred bitch, snooping through his things and having him followed until she'd discovered he was using fairy potions to keep himself from aging.

His first thought was to kill her.

She wouldn't be the first or last wife he'd had to get rid of.

But then he realized that after a suitable time of mourning he would once again be expected to remarry.

It was far better to keep the one he had . . . only slightly modified.

With one burst of power he'd crushed her mind, leaving

her locked in a deep coma. Then he'd placed her in a distant hospital. Unfortunately he had to make the occasional visit to keep his in-laws from complaining.

Now he walked straight across the library to pour himself a large glass of whiskey. He needed something to rid himself of the stench of antiseptic and fading flowers.

"Wait." Draining the fiery liquid in one gulp, he abruptly turned his head as he heard the unmistakable sound of retreating footsteps. He glowered at the fairy who was clearly attempting to slip away unnoticed. "Where are you going?"

Yiant licked his dry lips. "I must return to my Court. It is a feast day."

Anthony rolled his eyes. "Every day is some ridiculous feast day among the fey."

"Traditions are important to us."

"Not as important as keeping me happy," he reminded the fool.

Yiant looked petulant as he straightened the thick folds of his elaborate robe. "What do you want of me?"

"I need you to remain here for the next few days."

"Why?"

Anthony leaned against the edge of his desk. "I might need to travel."

"What of my people?"

"They'll no doubt survive without you sitting on the throne and basking in your own importance," he mocked.

The fairy visibly restrained his temper. A wise choice. Anthony was at the end of his considerable patience.

"I will at least need a few changes of clothing."

Anthony swiveled to touch a button that was hidden beneath the lip of his desktop. There was a faint creak, then a hidden door slid open to reveal a narrow staircase.

"I'm sure Keeley left his belongings behind. Feel free to use whatever you want. He won't be needing them."

Yiant grimaced, but the reminder that Anthony had just destroyed the imp who'd been locked in Styx's dungeons, had him grudgingly heading toward the secret passageway.

"As you command."

Waiting until the door closed behind the fairy, Anthony left the library and headed down to the tunnels hidden beneath his estate.

Halting at a thick, wooden door, he carefully unwrapped the layers of protective magic. It took nearly half an hour before he was able to enter his inner sanctum, and another half hour before he was safely sealed inside.

Only then did he light the candles that revealed the vast, cavernous room.

Dug deep into the limestone, it was larger than a football field and in the center was a ring of standing stones. Towering nearly a hundred feet high, they were precisely spaced with lintel stones that connected them at the top.

Even at a distance Anthony could feel the power that radiated from the circle. He smiled as he moved forward, intoxicated by the pulses of energy.

This was the true magic.

A mystic power that came from the earth.

Nothing at all like the vile, unholy powers that the demons used.

Such toxic magic had to be purged from the world, along with the creatures who spread their infection among humanity like a disease.

Stepping between the stones, he entered the circle. He grimaced as he realized the usual sense of peace that entered him in this place had faded since his last visit. For centuries the powers of the druids had been used to create harmony. It wasn't intended to become a weapon.

An unfortunate sacrifice necessary for the greater good,

he assured himself, stepping to the center of the limestone floor where he'd placed his wooden altar where a small fire was burning.

Anthony offered a small prayer before he was peering into the dancing flames.

There was no heat, no sound from the fire. It simply floated above the altar, feeding off the spell he'd cast months ago.

Leaning forward, he opened his senses, allowing the magic to seep deep inside him.

He trembled at the heat that scoured through him, a cleansing flame that threatened to melt his very bones.

Balanced somewhere between agony and ecstasy, Anthony first concentrated on the prison that kept the elder druids from interfering in his plans.

A smile touched his lips. He could see each of the four druids aimlessly wandering through the maze of magic. It had been his first attempt at creating a labyrinth. Now he understood why it'd been banned.

Confident the elder magic-users were effectively trapped, Anthony turned his attention to the spell that he'd cast in the depths of the Commission's tunnels.

Unlike the labyrinth, the Compulsion spell was a complex spiderweb of magic. Dozens of filaments linking him to the Oracles, each one too fragile to force them to obey his commands. But with each layer of magic the filaments were threading together, creating an unbreakable bond that would give him complete control.

Choosing one of the threads, Anthony closed his eyes as he focused on the connection. Two thousand miles away he sensed the Mosnoff demon who was deeply asleep. He paused, making certain that the demon didn't realize that Anthony was delving into his mind.

As the demon remained asleep, Anthony cautiously gave

a tug on the thread. On cue the Mosnoff sat upright, his eyes snapping open as he rose from the narrow bed and crossed the barren cavern. Then, ignoring the sweat that trickled down his face, Anthony urged the Mosnoff to reach for the delicate crystal that was carefully stored in a velvet-lined box.

Anthony gave another tug on the thread, forcing the demon to pluck the crystal from the box. More sweat dribbled down his face as the demon instinctively tried to resist Anthony's compulsion.

It'd been a battle they'd fought several times, although the Mosnoff had no memory of Anthony's "tests."

Usually Anthony could compel the demon to this point, and then the Mosnoff would refuse to go any further.

This time, however, he grimly forced the demon to cross the room to the fireplace that warmed the chilled cavern. Then, with one last burst of power, he coerced the Mosnoff to toss the irreplaceable family heirloom directly into the flames.

The crystal landed in the fire, the soul that had been stored inside the quartz swiftly becoming unstable. Within seconds it had reached a critical point and combusted into a hundred tiny shards.

Through the thread, Anthony could feel the horror as the demon watched one of his beloved ancestors being lost to the flames.

Still, Anthony managed to maintain control long enough to urge the Mosnoff back to his bed and back to sleep.

Only when the demon was snoring did Anthony release his hold and lift a shaky hand to wipe the sweat from his face.

He'd done it.

Granted, he'd only be in control of one Oracle, but it was

one of the strongest of the Commission. And he'd made the demon destroy one of his relatives.

An act that could only be forced by having complete command of the creature.

Stepping away from the flame, Anthony sucked in a deep breath.

He had to believe that the experiment proved he had gained the necessary control to compel the Oracles to complete the spell.

It didn't matter whether or not Keeley had revealed his plans. Or if the Chatri were here to try and stop him.

He could feel time swiftly slipping away from him.

If he was going to strike it had to be soon.

Grimacing at the fine tremors that shook his body, Anthony turned to head back to his house. Before he did anything, he had to rest.

He was still in the circle when a silvery chime echoed through the cavern, making Anthony stiffen in outrage.

"Intruders." Turning on his heel, he headed back to the altar. "Damn."

Tonya stepped out of the portal with a shiver.

The air was certainly warmer despite the fact it was night, but there was a weird sensation that brushed over her skin.

As if she'd just stepped through an invisible web.

Tonya hated spiders.

"Where are we?" she demanded, unconsciously brushing her hands over her bare arms. Dammit, why had she decided to wear a barely there spandex dress?

Okay, that was a stupid question.

She'd put on the outfit because she wanted to make Magnus drool.

Now she wished she'd chosen a pair of jeans and a sweat-shirt.

Moving to stand beside her, Magnus glanced around the untamed fields that were divided by waist-high fences built of gray stone. In the distance were rolling hills and a thatch-roofed cottage that was tucked into a small valley.

"Ireland," he at last said.

"How odd."

Magnus narrowed his gaze. "More than odd."

She sent him a confused frown. "What are you talking about?"

"Cyn is the clan chief of Ireland," he said, the words clipped.

"That's not a newsflash," she muttered, wondering what bug had crawled up the prince's ass this time.

"Now we track the killer to his homeland."

Ah. Now she got it.

"Are you implying Cyn was the killer?" she demanded.

His features tightened at her blatant incredulity.

"He did send Fallon to lure Styx away from his lair, no doubt knowing that I would follow."

"Why would Cyn sneak around?" She shook her head. "If he wanted the imp dead, then he could have demanded that Styx hand over his prisoner. It's not like Styx would have cared what happened to a fey who'd already betrayed him once."

He waved aside her logic in his usual princely fashion. Jackass.

"Perhaps he feared the imp had information he didn't want the King of Vampires to know."

"Information?"

Magnus shrugged, his gaze scanning the dark country-side, almost as if he sensed some sort of approaching danger.

"He's holding a Chatri princess in his lair," he said, his tone absent. "We can't truly know that he isn't using her for his own nefarious purpose."

A sharp, unexpected jealousy sliced through her heart.

It was . . . insane.

She was never jealous. She had no interest in holding on to a lover who'd turned his attention to another female. After all, there were plenty of males anxious to earn a place in her bed.

But there was no mistaking the ugly anger that was twisting her stomach at the mere mention of Fallon's name.

"So you're suddenly worried about your fiancée?" she ground out.

He sent her a wry smile. "Did you not want me to display more compassion?"

"Whatever," she muttered, giving a toss of her head as she headed toward a narrow lane.

The voice of reason had told her not to come with Magnus on his search for the magic-user. It'd warned her that spending more time in this man's company was a mistake.

One of these days she was going to listen to that voice.

"No." Without warning Magnus was grabbing her arm, yanking her to an abrupt halt. "Wait."

Tonya tugged her arm free. Magnus might be a horse's patootie, but he'd never been a bully.

"What the hell?"

Magnus grimaced. "A trap."


Cyn moaned as Fallon wrapped her legs around his waist, allowing him to sink deeper into her warm, welcoming body.

It didn't matter that he'd spent the past six hours ravishing this female. He was fairly certain that he could spend the next century exploring her from the top of her silken hair to her tiny toes and still feel obsessed with the need to have her in his arms.

Lightly scraping his fangs down the length of her neck, he gripped her hips and plunged into her silken heat, a groan wrenched from his throat.

"Cyn," Fallon breathed, her fingers tangled in his hair as she arched beneath him. "Please."

He shuddered, the violent urge to sink his veins into her flesh an overwhelming need.

Bloody hell.

His every instinct was screaming to mark this woman, to complete the mating so she would be bound to him for all eternity.

Instead he buried his face in the champagne scent of her silken hair, increasing the tempo of his thrusts.

Until Fallon was willing to accept that they were destined to be together he wouldn't force the issue.

She'd spent her entire life being bullied by the men who were supposed to respect her. She'd been told what she could and couldn't do.

She had to come to him freely.

"Please what, princess?" he roughly demanded, trailing his lips down her collarbone. "What do you need?"

Her fingers tightened in his hair, her hips lifting off the mattress to meet him stroke for stroke.

"I need . . ." Her words broke off in a strangled groan as his lips found the tip of her breast. "You. Just you."

He used his tongue to lash the sensitive nub, treasuring her soft moan.

He might not own her heart—at least not yet—but her exquisite body was his.

All his.

"You've got me," he teased, sliding his hand between their bodies to find the precise spot of her pleasure. "And I've got you."

"Yes." She yanked his hair as she went rigid with pleasure beneath him, her inner muscles squeezing his cock as she came with a violent force. "Oh . . . yes."

Cyn surged up to take her lips in a savage kiss, giving one last thrust as his orgasm slammed into him.

"And I'm not letting you go," he murmured against her mouth, the words so soft he wasn't sure she could even hear them.

With a last lingering kiss, he allowed his hands to run over her slender body. The need to maintain a physical connection with Fallon was an unbearable ache.

Until they mated . . .

No. With a last nuzzle against her throat, Cyn forced himself to untangle his body from Fallon's lingering hold.

He couldn't dwell on his primitive urges.

Not now.

Once the threat to the world was over and the good guys had succeeded, he intended to do a full-throttled, good old-fashioned courtship.

He would win her heart, and then he would earn her soul.

Climbing off the bed, he reached for the cell phone he'd left on the small table, not surprised to discover there was a message from Dante.

The younger vampire had no doubt been intrigued by Cyn's cryptic voice mail.

"Dante's at the front gate," he murmured.

With the liquid grace that always managed to fascinate him, Fallon slid off the bed and swiftly began pulling on her clothes.

Cyn hid a grimace as his body instantly hardened. God Almighty. His intense reaction to this female was almost embarrassing.

Turning to hide his fully erect cock, he slid on his jeans and sweater, shoving his feet into his boots before turning back to watch Fallon pull her hair into a long, complicated braid.

"There's no need to travel with me," she said, no doubt sensing his reluctance. "It must be getting close to dawn in Chicago."

What would she say if he told her that his reluctance had nothing to do with going to pick up Dante, and everything to do with leaving the protection of his lair?

Not only was there an unknown magic-user out there with enough power to kill a vampire and compel the Commission, but there were any number of other dangers that were always lurking in the dark.

And if he forced himself to be entirely honest, there was a part of him that was suddenly remembering that the prince she'd so recently intended to marry was going to be far too near for Cyn's peace of mind.

It wasn't that he was jealous . . .

Oh hell. Of course he was jealous.

Fallon could say all she wanted about her engagement being nothing more than a duty, but the fact was that she'd been planning to spend the rest of eternity with the too-pretty prince.

What if Magnus had a change of heart?

What if he decided that he wanted to reclaim Fallon as his fiancée?

The mere thought made his fangs ache to rip a chunk out of the prince of priss.

"We don't know that your fiancé won't decide to cause trouble," he muttered, his tone sour.

She gave a startled blink. "What could he do?"

"I don't want him anywhere near you."

Something that might have been disappointment darkened the magnificent amber of her eyes.

"You don't trust me?"

Shit.

Realizing he'd managed to wound her, Cyn stalked forward, cupping her chin to force her to meet his fierce gaze.

"More than I've ever trusted anyone in my very long life," he said. "But right now I can't allow you out of my sight."

She studied his tense expression. "I don't understand."

He knew better than to try to explain that a vampire on the cusp of mating was like a rabid animal when a male tried to get to close to his woman.

She already knew that vampires could be savage creatures. He didn't want to terrify her with his inner berserker.

"You will," he promised, lowering his head to press a quick kiss to her lips before he was straightening to regard her with a brooding gaze. "We should go."

She gave a shake of her head, pulling away from his grasp to head out of the room.

"I'm beginning to suspect that testosterone does strange things to the male mind."

"You have no idea," he muttered, following her out of her private rooms and down the stairs.

He'd adamantly insisted that she open the portal in the foyer. When she'd traveled to bring Styx to the lair, she'd been followed by her fiancé. If Magnus made a sudden appearance in her bedroom, there was nothing that would keep him from shredding the bastard into small, unrecognizable princely parts.

Now, as they moved down the stairs, he realized there was an added bonus to his demand of using the foyer.

The sexy sway of her hips as she took each step.

Reaching the bottom of the stairs, Fallon moved to stand in the center of the paneled foyer, the firelight highlighting the beauty of her delicate features.

A faint smile touched her lips as she glanced toward the flickering flames, no doubt aware that he'd made certain that there were fires in every room of his vast lair.

He should have known the minute he began fretting over whether or not she was cold that he was in danger, he wryly acknowledged.

She made no comment, instead raising her hand to form the portal. Cyn waited until she gestured for him to approach, then, squashing his instinctive dislike for magic, he grabbed her fingers in a tight grip.

There was a sensation of nothingness, then a darkness surrounded him. He clenched his teeth, convinced that he could feel prickles of electricity dancing over his skin despite the fact he couldn't sense magic.

Only seconds later the darkness was abruptly replaced by a shadowed, tree-lined street that was covered by a new layer of snow.

Cyn sent a swift glance around, making sure there was nothing but the lone vampire who was waiting for them in front of Styx's front gate.

At last certain there was nothing about to leap out of the shadows, Cyn turned his attention to the raven-haired vampire who was watching him with a mocking silver gaze.

"Dante."

The vampire moved forward to slap Cyn on the shoulder, a smile on his finely chiseled features.

"It's been a long time, my friend."

"Too long," Cyn said, grinning as he ran a glance over Dante's casual black jeans and shit-kickers. Long before Dante had been captured by the witches and made the guardian of the Phoenix, they'd traveled through Europe, indulging in every vice they could discover. "I have yet to meet your mate."

Dante shook his head, the pair of golden hoops hanging from his earlobes catching the moonlight.

"I'm not sure I want you to," he said. "I haven't forgotten your fatal attraction to women."

Cyn rolled his eyes. Dante hadn't been hurting for women. They'd found his bad-boy vibe absurdly exciting. But, of course, the annoying vampire had to remind Fallon of Cyn's unfortunately exaggerated reputation.

Predictably the princess made a sound of resignation. "Is there anyone who doesn't know about your unsavory habits?"

Flipping off the laughing Dante, Cyn fixed his attention on the female at his side.

"They weren't unsavory."

"No?"

He grimaced at her disbelieving expression.

"Okay, they might have been a tad unsavory, but they're in the past."

"The scourge of Europe has been tamed?" Dante drawled.

Cyn glared at his friend. "You aren't helping."

"Payback's a bitch."

"Payback for what?"

Dante lifted a dark brow. "Surely you haven't forgotten those twin nymphs in St. Petersburg who you—"

"Enough," Cyn growled. He was going to have to have several long, painful conversations with his fellow vampires about sharing unnecessary stories about his past. "Are you ready?"

Dante's smile faded, his gaze flicking toward the massive house hidden behind the high gate.

"Yes, I don't want to leave Abby alone for long."

"Isn't she inside?" he demanded in surprise. Dante rarely left his mate behind.

Dante shrugged. "Yes, but most demons are too terrified to stay in the same room with her, including the Ravens."

Ah. He'd assumed that Dante had chosen to live in a remote lair outside Chicago because he wanted to be alone with his new mate. After all, Cyn fully intended to make his castle off-limits to stray visitors once he'd convinced Fallon they were destined to be together.

He hadn't actually considered how difficult it might be for demons, including his fellow vampires, to make casual chitchat with Abby. As the vessel for the Goddess of Light, she could fry them all to a smudge of ash without breaking a sweat.

"Styx isn't here?" Cyn asked, knowing that the Anasso would never allow Abby to feel unwelcomed.

"No, he just left for St. Louis to retrieve his mate." The wicked humor returned to sparkle in Dante's silver eyes. "He was muttering something about cold beds and mangy werewolves who lure females from their mates with a litter of babies."

"Poor bloke." Cyn gave a shake of his head. There weren't many things worse than having Weres as in-laws . . . Wait. He grimaced, suddenly recalling his own potential in-laws. He didn't doubt for a minute that the King of Chatri would do everything in his power to take Fallon away. Including trying to kill him. He squared his shoulders. A worry for another day. "Ready?" he asked Dante.

"Yes."

Grabbing his friend's arm, he reached for Fallon's hand, shivering as they were instantly surrounded in the electric darkness of her portal.

Seconds later they were once again standing in his foyer.

Cyn shook off the momentary disorientation at being yanked through dimensions, and glanced toward Fallon who was calmly studying Dante as if she hauled vampires around on a regular basis.

Cyn, on the other hand, was already growing twitchy at having Dante so close to his potential mate.

It didn't matter that his friend was already bound to another female. Or that Fallon wasn't the sort of female to give herself to more than one man.

Until he completed the mating, his instincts were set on "kill now, ask questions later" mode.

Cursing at the unwelcome violence that trembled through his body, Cyn swiftly headed toward his library. Behind him, he could sense Dante and Fallon trying to keep pace with his long strides, but they thankfully didn't demand to know why he was doing the speed-walking routine.

At last they entered the library, and Cyn moved to the desk where he'd left the scroll given to him by Siljar.

"Damn," Dante muttered behind him, turning in a slow circle as he inspected the shelves that towered two stories and the ceiling that had been painted with a Greek fresco. "Why the hell did you keep this such a secret?"

"Did you think I was going to allow a bunch of demons who were barely housebroken to trash my books?"

"Hey, I was housebroken."

Cyn snorted. "Which is why you destroyed my favorite tapestry when you used it for target practice?"

Dante sent Fallon a sorrowful glance. "How do you endure living with him?"

A flustered heat stained her cheeks. "Oh, I don't . . . I mean—"

"This is the spell," Cyn interrupted her embarrassed stutter, moving to hand the scroll to his friend.

Dante glanced down, a frown tugging his brows together. "I can't read hieroglyphs," he at last muttered, lifting his head to meet Cyn's steady gaze. "That's Roke's expertise. And you know more about the fey than any other vampire I've met. I'm not sure how I can help."

"I'm hoping you can give me information on another spell."

Dante handed the rolled-up parchment back to Cyn. "I'm listening."

"You battled witches who tried to destroy demons."

A chill entered the air as Dante's expression became stony. "I did, along with Abby."

"They used magic?"

"Yes."

"How did they cast it?"

Dante moved to pour himself a glass of whiskey, still clearly raw from the battle. It didn't matter if it was hours, months, or centuries ago, a male didn't get over seeing his mate in danger.

"They captured Abby, intending to use the power of the Phoenix."

Cyn watched his friend toss back the drink, regretting the need to bring up such difficult memories. It was only because he couldn't shake the suspicion that this was somehow connected that he was forcing the issue.

"Why did they need the Goddess of Light?"

Dante shrugged. "Not even an entire coven of witches working together could achieve the power needed to cast that particular spell." A cold smile twisted his lips. "Unfortunately for them the Phoenix was in no mood to cooperate. She zapped the bitches."

Cyn had heard the basic story of Abby's ability to destroy the witches, but he needed a firsthand account of the details.

"What was involved in casting the spell?"

"I wasn't there for all of it." The temperature plunged another twenty degrees and Cyn could see Fallon shiver, a golden glow surrounding her as she used her natural powers to warm herself. Cyn felt a ridiculous prick of annoyance. It wasn't that he wanted her to be cold, but he'd taken pride in making sure his lair was always warm enough for her to be comfortable. Dante set aside his empty glass, unaware he was causing Fallon discomfort. "According to Abby, the Queen Bee of the coven, Edra, strapped her to an altar and put a small amulet on her chest," he grimly explained. "The witch said it would draw on the power of the Phoenix."

Cyn arched a brow.

That sounded way too easy.

"That was all there was to casting the spell?"

"No." Dante's expression twisted with disgust. "She'd sacrificed one of her own witches. Like most dark magic, this one demanded blood."

Fallon stepped forward, far more familiar with all this hocus-pocus than Cyn.

"The amulet would focus the magic and the blood would be the catalyst."

Dante nodded. "Exactly." He sent a curious glance toward Cyn. "You want to tell me what all this is about?"

"Siljar will have my ass," Cyn growled. "But I need your help."

Dante grimaced. "This is Oracle business?"

"Aye. It seems that someone, perhaps more than one, has been manipulating the Commission."

Dante looked shocked. "Impossible."

"My word exactly," Cyn said in dry tones. "Siljar, however, is convinced that they're being coerced into performing this spell."

Dante's gaze lowered to the scroll in Cyn's hand. "Does she have a suspicion of what the spell is supposed to do?"

"One designed to shut down any travel between dimensions."

Dante looked confused. "Why would the Oracles want to do that?"

It was Fallon who answered. "They've been tricked into believing that it's a simple cleansing spell."

Dante muttered a curse. "Manipulating the entire Commission takes some serious mojo."

"No shit," Cyn muttered.

"What happens if they complete the spell?" Dante asked.

Cyn tossed the spell on his desk. "Demons die."

Dante looked more resigned than surprised. "Sounds familiar."

"That's what I thought." Cyn glanced toward his vast collection of books. He had thousands that spoke of fey powers, but very few that concentrated on human magic-users. He gave a frustrated shake of his head. "Did any of the witches survive your battle?"

"A few," Dante admitted. "You suspect they might be involved?"

Cyn gave a restless lift of his shoulder. He didn't know what the hell he suspected.

Only that he couldn't shake his sense of déjà vu.

"It's difficult to know, but I think we should consider the possibility," he said. "What happened to the spell books?"

"If any were bound to Edra they would have been destroyed

when she died." Dante reminded Cyn of the witches' habit of magically connecting themselves to their most private papers so they would turn to ash the moment of their death. "But to be honest, they were the last of my concern."

"Understandable." Cyn nodded toward the spell on his desk. "But it would be nice to know if they had the same hieroglyphics."

# Chapter Fifteen

Sensing Cyn's rising frustration, Fallon briskly headed toward the desk. Sitting in the large wooden seat she pulled out a piece of paper and pen.

She didn't have any battle skills, or special magic that could help reveal the identity of the magic-user. But she'd trained her entire life to bring order out of chaos.

Okay, her chaos usually included fairy balls and complicated seating arrangements, but still, the principle was the same.

Watching her with a lift of his brows, Cyn leaned against the edge of the desk.

"What are you doing?"

"Making a list," she said, trying not to feel foolish.

If she couldn't scry to track down the human, she had to do something.

His brows inched higher. "A list?"

She held his curious gaze. "I'm a princess. That's what we do."

Dante choked back a laugh. "Princess, eh? Aiming high, my friend."

Cyn ignored the other vampire, his attention remaining fixed on Fallon.

"A list of what?"

"What seems to be similar between the two spells." She put the pen to paper and began to write. "Both are designed to specifically affect demons, both are performed by human magic-users, and both need a large power source to complete them." She glanced up at Dante. "Would the Commission have the same power as a goddess?"

"More," he said without hesitation.

"You sound certain," Cyn said in surprise.

Dante's lips twisted into a humorless smile. "The Commission has more or less allowed Abby and I to live in peace. They would have her locked and isolated in some sort of prison if they weren't certain that they can control her if necessary."

Cyn nodded. "True."

Dante tilted his head to the side. The dark-haired vampire was built on smaller lines than Cyn—of course, everyone but the Anasso was built on smaller lines—but there was no missing the lethal power that chilled the air around him.

"What makes you believe that the person responsible is a magic-user?" he demanded.

Cyn touched the spell that was lying next to Fallon's arm. "This spell is fey in origin, but I suspect that it's been altered by humans."

Dante clearly sensed there was more. "And?"

Cyn hesitated, waiting for Fallon to give a small nod before revealing the talent she'd kept carefully hidden.

"Fallon was scrying the Oracle's caves and caught sight of a shrouded male sneaking through the back tunnels," he said, unconsciously raising his hand to his chest where he'd been hit by the vicious spell. "We suspect he was performing some sort of magic."

"A Compulsion spell?" the vampire shrewdly deduced.

Cyn shrugged. "That would be my guess."

Fallon frowned, abruptly realizing that they were missing an obvious flaw in their reasoning.

"If the magic-user completed his spell and has the Commission under his sway, why is he waiting? Shouldn't he be forcing the Oracles to close the dimensions?"

"I was trapped by the witches for over three hundred years," Dante said, his anger toward those who held him captive a tangible pulse in the air. "Controlling more than one person with compulsion is massively difficult. I know less than a dozen witches who are capable of compelling more than two or three humans at a time. To try and leash a dozen Oracles . . ." He shuddered. "It would take more power than I can even imagine."

Cyn tapped his finger on the smooth surface of the desk, clearly in deep thought.

"Or several layers of lesser magic," he at last said.

Dante nodded. "Yes. That would make sense."

"You mean he performed the spell several times?" Fallon asked.

"Aye," Cyn agreed. "And each one tightens the magic-user's control over the Oracles."

Fallon absently chewed her bottom lip. "But when he does—"

"He can command them to cast the spell," Cyn finished her terrifying thought.

Dante's expression was grim as he placed his hands on his hips.

"Do you want me to try and track down the witches that were connected to Edra's coven?"

Cyn nodded. "It would be a start." He paused as he

pulled out his phone, his brows pulling together as he read the incoming text. "It's Styx," he muttered. "He wants us in Chicago."

"Now?" Dante asked.

"Aye." Cyn's frown deepened. "Bloody hell."

Fallon rose to her feet, instantly concerned. "What is it?"

"He wants me to bring the gargoyle."

"Levet's here?" Dante growled.

With exquisite timing, the diminutive gargoyle stepped into the room, his wings dazzling in the firelight.

"Did someone call?"

Dante rolled his eyes. "Why me?"

Levet scrunched his snout, sending the dark-haired vampire a mocking glance.

"Clearly you were created beneath a lucky star."

Sensing the brewing violence, Fallon hurriedly crossed to put herself between Levet and the scowling males.

"We must travel to the King of Vampires," she informed the tiny demon.

"Ah." Levet gave a small sniff. "I suppose I am expected to save the world once again?"

"It's quite likely," Fallon agreed.

"Truly?" The gray eyes widened with horror. "*Mon Dieu.*"

Dante strolled forward. "I thought you enjoyed being Savior of the World?"

Levet's tail twitched as he cleared his throat. "Of course I do, but it hardly seems fair to constantly pig out all the glory."

"Pig out?" Cyn demanded, moving to stand beside his friend.

"Hog, you imbecile," Dante said with a shake of his head. "It's hog all the glory."

"*Tout ce que,*" the gargoyle said. "I feel I should allow some other demon to enjoy the pleasure of being a savior."

Cyn gave a short laugh. "Very generous."

"*Oui.*" Levet preened, ignoring the blatant sarcasm. "I am a giver."

"You're something, all right," Dante muttered.

Fallon hid her delight with Levet. It was rare for two vampires to be so obviously annoyed by such a little creature. He clearly had a special talent.

Still, she didn't want to see him harmed.

"We should go," she said, heading out of the library to lead the way back to the foyer.

Once there, she concentrated on reopening the portal she'd so recently closed.

She'd just stabilized the portal when she felt the brush of cool fingers along the nape of her neck. Fallon shivered, her entire body going up in flames.

Damn. How did he do that?

One touch and all she wanted was to melt into his arms.

"It won't be too much of a strain to take all of us through the portal?" he softly demanded, speaking low enough so his question wouldn't carry.

Clearly he didn't want to embarrass her if she had to admit she didn't have the power to transport them.

Her lips twitched. Not by his display of concern. Cyn had already proven that he possessed an instinctive need to protect females. But the fact that he actually accepted she might have a pride that could be wounded . . .

It was a hell of a lot more than her father or Magnus had ever offered her.

No wonder women found him irresistible.

"No," she assured him. "Once the portal is open, I can easily transport a large number of people."

"Damn." Dante's expression held a hint of admiration. "It's no wonder the fey worship the Chatri."

Cyn's fingers lightly skimmed down her throat, a mysterious smile curving his lips.

"Aye, I worship one of my own."

She blushed at being the center of attention, hastily reaching to touch Levet's wing while Dante laid his hand on Cyn's shoulder.

"Is everyone ready?"

"*Non,*" Levet said with a heavy sigh. "But I do not suppose my opinion matters."

"Go," Cyn growled, shoving the gargoyle into the waiting portal.


Magnus couldn't deny a grudging respect for Tonya as they walked the pathway that meandered through moonlit fields, a large forest, along the edge of a loch and up and over the series of low, rolling hills.

She made no complaints despite the fact that she was hardly dressed to be trudging for miles. And more importantly, she didn't badger him with questions even knowing that their surroundings were an illusion.

But at last she'd had enough, coming to a halt so she could kick off her ridiculous high-heeled shoes.

"Stop," she muttered. "I'm exhausted."

"Fine." He stood beside her, grudgingly accepting that it wasn't going to be as easy as he hoped to break free of their prison. "We will rest for a short time."

"Will you tell me what the hell is going on?"

He paused. If she were a Chatri female, he would have told her not to worry her pretty head and offered a vague assurance that everything would be well.

But Tonya was nothing at all like the women he was accustomed to.

She was stubborn, and independent, and she would be completely pissed if he tried to lie to her just to make her feel better.

Ridiculous female.

"When we stepped out of the portal we were caught in a Labyrinth spell," he said.

"Labyrinth?" She shook her head. "I've never heard of it."

"The ancient druids used to cast them to trap unwary fey."

She looked puzzled. "Why?"

"They could force them to share their potions that magnified the druid magic."

"Oh." She cast a glance around the empty landscape, almost as if she expected a cloaked druid to appear from the shadows. "I knew that sorcerers were rumored to force the fey to prolong their lives with potions, but I always thought druids were peaceful."

"Sariel discovered what they were doing and threatened to slaughter every one of them if they used fey magic again," Magnus said.

"He did?" The emerald eyes widened in surprise. Magnus grimaced. Why did she assume that the Chatri males were ineffectual wimps? Sariel had enough power to make most vampires quake in fear. "Well, I suppose the threat of complete genocide would make a druid think twice about disobeying the royal command."

"It should have." Magnus waved a disgusted hand toward the fields. "Clearly our time away from this world has emboldened the magic-user."

"Why would a druid want to trap us?"

It was a question that had been nagging at Magnus since he'd realized they'd triggered the spell.

"It could be nothing more than a precaution used by the druid to ensure he wasn't followed," he said, choosing the most logical explanation.

"Or?" Tonya prompted.

"Or he learned a Chatri had returned and was afraid I might punish him for breaking our law," Magnus said, knowing he couldn't overlook that this might be more personal. "The death of the imp could have been used as a way to lure me here with the intent to kill me."

Tonya shivered, but she didn't panic. Magnus gave a faint shake of his head. Why did he feel a stupid prick of pride at her composure? Dammit. Her foolish courage might very well lead her into danger.

"Tell me about the spell," she demanded. "What does it do?"

"It works like a maze," he grudgingly revealed. "The magic has us locked in a bubble where we can move forward but we can't leave."

"Holy shit," she muttered. "It's Hotel California."

He frowned. Hadn't he told her they were in Ireland?

"What?"

"Never mind." She waved a hand toward the distant loch. "If this is a maze, then why does the scenery keep changing?"

"I have been using my power to alter our perception," he said.

"Why?"

"Because the spell shouldn't be capable of holding a Chatri," he said, his voice edged with frustration. "And certainly not a prince."

"Of course not." Tonya rolled her eyes.

"I am a prince because my bloodline possesses superior powers."

"Arrogant ass."

Magnus scowled. Annoying female. Did she think he was bragging?

He had been born with a power that was second only to the king. Which was precisely why Sariel had chosen him to wed his daughter.

"It's truth, not arrogance," he snapped.

She folded her arms under her breasts, emphasizing their lush beauty.

Not that he actually noticed, he hastily assured himself, wrenching his appreciative gaze from the decadent swell of her bust that was showcased by the low scoop of her neckline.

"If you're so freaking powerful, then why are we still stuck?" she taunted.

"The spell has been modified." He used his senses to touch the illusion surrounding them. As soon as he brushed against the magic it instantly shifted, the hills replaced by a barren tundra. He made a sound of disgust. "I should be able to break the illusion and find our way out. Instead, a new illusion simply replaces the old."

"Then how do we get out?"

"We can't."

She sucked in a shocked breath, revealing the first crack in her grim composure.

"Are you shitting me?" she rasped, the scent of stewed plums filling the air. "We're stuck in this . . . illusion for eternity? Just the two of us." The emerald eyes darkened with an indecipherable emotion. "I must have died and gone to hell."

Outrage flared through him. How dare she imply that it would be a punishment to spend an infinity in his company? She should only be so lucky.

Aggravating female.

"Fey don't believe in hell," he said stiffly.

"I do now," she muttered, hunching her shoulders. "So what do we do? Sit here and twiddle our toes for the next millennium?"

His annoyance was forgotten as he caught a glimpse of the fear she was trying so hard to hide.

She was terrified beneath her prickly sarcasm.

Barely aware he was moving, he stepped forward, his voice unconsciously gentle.

"I said we couldn't get out, but the spell is connected to the druid."

"And?"

His fingers brushed a soothing caress over her cheek. "Eventually I'll follow the trail of magic to its source."

Her expression was guarded, although he was pleased to note she didn't try to pull away from his touch.

"You really think you can?"

This time he didn't take offense at her seeming lack of confidence in his abilities. Eventually she would be forced to admit that he possessed more than superior manners and an exquisite taste in clothing.

For now he contented himself with opening his senses to the thread of magic that he'd latched on to as they'd stepped out of the portal.

He didn't doubt that it belonged to the druid who'd cast the spell. Which meant it was only a matter of time before he managed to get a lock on the bastard's exact location.

Then there would be no mistake that he possessed more than his fair share of power.

"Yes," he said, deliberately concentrating on the illusion around them.

Before, he simply nudged their surroundings, searching for the way out of the maze. This time, he actively molded the magic to create the image he wanted.

With a wave of his hand the darkness was replaced by a

brilliant blue sky and dazzling sunlight. Another wave and the field was a carpet of green grass with a babbling brook in the distance.

"But first you need to rest," he said.

"Oh." The imp glanced around in surprise, her eyes widening as she glanced down at the daisies that were springing to life around his feet. "Does that always happen?"

He shrugged. "When I stay in one place long enough."

She appeared oddly fascinated by the flowers that now began to spread among the grass.

"Amazing," she breathed.

Magnus squashed the ridiculous urge to show off with a burst of power that would create a profusion of blossoms. Instead, he concentrated on creating a blanket along with several plates of food so Tonya could replenish her strength.

Taking her hand, he urged her to take a seat on the blanket, waiting until she was settled before he was joining her and reaching for one of the plates.

"Are you hungry?"

"I'm starving," she admitted, taking the plate and studying the fresh fruit and bread that was dipped in honey. "Is it real?"

"Of course."

She gingerly grabbed a slice of the bread, taking a bite. Her eyes slid closed as she relished the food without apology.

Magnus watched in fascination. This female was no delicate princess and yet there was a raw earthiness that enchanted him in a way he couldn't explain.

"Yum," she moaned, opening her eyes and leaning forward so she could press the bread to his lips. "Here. Try it."

He pulled back, suspicious of her teasing. "What are you doing?"

"Don't you want a taste?"

"I . . . yes." He took the bread from her hand, his gaze never wavering from her face. "You puzzle me."

She reached for a golden pear. "What do you mean?"

"One minute you are snapping at me and the next you are feeding me," he said.

"You make me crazy," she muttered, sinking her teeth into the soft flesh of the fruit.

Magnus groaned as she licked the juice from her lips.

Was she being deliberately provocative? Not that it mattered.

He was hard. Aching. The need to have her in his arms was a force that overwhelmed everything.

Including the fact that they were trapped in a druid spell.

"The feeling is mutual," he assured her, leaning forward to wrap his arm around her waist.

Then, with one tug, he had her lying across his lap, the food forgotten.

He studied her with a brooding gaze, his hand cupping her face as he tried to determine what it was about this woman that continued to captivate him.

She trembled, her body molding against him with remarkable perfection.

"Magnus?" she breathed.

"Hush," he murmured.

He didn't want to talk. Or think. He just wanted to feel.

"Don't tell me—"

He stole the words from her lips as he crushed her mouth in a kiss that demanded her complete and utter surrender.

# Chapter Sixteen

Cyn shoved the gargoyle out of his way as they exited the portal in front of Styx's lair.

It was bad enough to be traveling through some magical rip in the fabric of space without having the aggravating creature constantly beneath his feet.

With a flap of his wings, Levet scurried out of his way, turning his head to send a glare in Cyn's direction.

"There's no need to push," he groused, his eyes abruptly widening, his snout flaring as he took in a deep breath. "Ah, Darcy is home. And Abby. I must—"

"Stay where you are, gargoyle," the large Aztec warrior commanded, stepping from the shadows of a nearby tree.

Levet placed his hands on his hips, his tail stuck out straight.

"You are not the boss of me."

"Thank God," Styx muttered, folding his arms over his chest as he glared at the gargoyle. "You, however, are going to do exactly what I say. Got it?"

Levet stuck out his tongue. "Bully."

Cyn stepped toward his king, his body angled to put Fallon behind him. Not that he thought Styx had any intention of harming the Chatri princess, but there was no battling the primitive need to keep other males at a distance.

"What's up?"

"I don't know for sure," Styx admitted, offering a brief nod to Dante who had moved to stand on the other side of Cyn, his gaze constantly scanning the dark street for any sign of danger. "Before I came to your lair I'd discovered an imp sneaking around my estate."

Dante gave a short laugh. "You've had a lot of fey loitering since the Chatri royalty decided to use your lair as their personal hotel."

"Don't remind me," Styx growled, belatedly glancing in Fallon's direction. "No offense."

"What about the imp?" Cyn asked, skimming over the awkward moment.

Interspecies relationships were always challenging.

The temperature dropped as Styx bared his fangs. "He was related to Damocles."

"Damn," Dante drawled. "It was ballsy of him to come here."

"My thought exactly," Styx agreed, clearly still holding a grudge against the imp who'd helped to destroy the previous Anasso.

"Did you kill him?" Dante asked.

"I threw him into the dungeon." Styx grimaced. "I wanted to know why he'd risked his life to spy on me."

Cyn hid a smile. There was a time when Styx would have cut out the bastard's heart without giving a shit what information he might have.

Becoming the leader of the vampires had given him at least a small amount of restraint.

A very, very small amount.

"Did you get answers?"

Styx gave a sharp shake of his head. "When I returned from your lair he was dead."

There was a collective sound of astonishment.

It would be easier to sneak into a harpy's nursery than Styx's dungeon.

"How?" Cyn asked.

Styx flashed his fangs. "Magic."

"Is that even possible?" Dante muttered, referring to the hexes that were etched into the walls.

Styx shrugged. "That's what the Pestilent Prince claimed."

Dante lifted his brows. "Pestilent?"

"Magnus." Styx's tone revealed his opinion of the Chatri royal. "He said that witches used to have the ability to activate a death spell in an assassin that remained dormant until they set it off with a word of power."

"You think a witch killed the imp?" Cyn asked with a frown. It didn't make sense to send an imp that was already on Styx's shit list to try and kill him.

An assassin had to blend into the shadows, not piss off the mark and get themselves thrown into the nearest dungeon.

Of course, the creature might have just been there to spy on Styx.

"I don't know," the king admitted. "I assume it could have been anyone capable of magic."

Cyn glanced toward Styx's lair. "Where's the prince?"

"He was supposed to track whoever had killed the imp then return here." Styx's jaw tightened. "He never showed."

Cyn shrugged. It was hard to give a shit what happened to the annoying twit.

"Isn't that a good thing?"

"He has Tonya with him." Styx's lips twisted into a humorless smile. "Viper has threatened to have me disemboweled if she isn't returned."

Cyn glanced toward the silent woman who'd moved to stand at his side.

"Would Magnus kidnap an imp?"

She shook her head. "Absolutely not. A Chatri male is trained from birth to treat females as mindless creatures, but they would never, ever bring harm to one. It would go against everything he believes in to hold her against her will."

Cyn grudgingly nodded. He might think Magnus was a silly ass, but he didn't truly believe he'd hurt Tonya. And he doubted that Styx did either.

He studied the Anasso's grim expression. "You're worried about more than Tonya."

"I don't like coincidences," Styx rasped. "You were nearly killed by a human magic-user and now one has just destroyed my prisoner before I could question him."

"You think this is connected to what's happening with the Oracles?" Cyn demanded.

"I intend to find out."

Cyn knew Styx was right.

It could be nothing, but they couldn't afford not to discover if there was a connection.

"What do you need?"

"I want to find the prince."

Before Cyn could answer, Fallon was walking toward the center of the street, her expression distracted.

"He was here," she abruptly announced. "Along with a fairy and . . . a magic-user."

Styx joined her, bending down to study the faint marks on the road that revealed where a portal had been opened.

"Human," he murmured, glancing up at Fallon. "Can you trace him?"

Cyn was instantly at Fallon's side, his arm wrapping protectively around her shoulders as he glared at his king.

"Are you out of your bloody mind?"

Styx slowly straightened, holding up a hand as he sensed Cyn's barely restrained fury.

"Easy, brother."

Brother, his ass.

"The Oracles already put her in danger," he said, his voice flat with warning. "I'm not going to allow you to put her in even more."

Fallon clicked her tongue with impatience. "Isn't that my decision to make?"

Cyn kept his gaze locked on Styx.

"No." Blunt. Uncompromising.

Levet sucked in an audible breath. "*Sacre bleu*. I thought you were supposed to be some female killer?"

Cyn sent the tiny pest a furious glare. "What did you say?"

"Lady killer, idiot," Dante corrected.

Levet wrinkled his snout. "Either way, he is remarkably incompetent."

Wicked humor glinted in Dante's silver eyes. "Can't argue with that."

Cyn couldn't either. Especially when Fallon was roughly pulling away from him.

"Princess—"

She faced him squarely, her hands on her hips. "Do you intend to tell me what I can and can't do?"

He grimaced. Holy shite. His every instinct was screaming at him to lock her away so she couldn't be hurt, but he'd be damned if he acted like her father.

"No."

"Good answer," Dante murmured.

Fallon sent him a last warning frown before turning toward Styx.

"What do you need from me?"

Styx sent Cyn a rueful smile before concentrating on Fallon.

"I want you to open a portal that will take us to Magnus."

She paused, her brow wrinkled. "I can't sense him."

"What does that mean?" the king rasped.

Fallon gave a small shrug. "He's either returned to our homeland or there's some sort of magical barrier that's interfering."

Styx looked like he wanted to cut something with his big sword.

Or someone.

"Damn."

Cyn's stab of relief lasted less than the time it took Fallon to tilt her chin to a familiar angle.

Stubborn.

"I can follow his portal," she said, refusing to meet his narrowed glare.

"Thank God," Styx muttered. "I need you to open a passageway for the gargoyle."

Levet gave a small squeak. "*Moi?*"

Styx kept his gaze locked on Fallon. "You're not to leave the portal. Levet will get out and search for Magnus."

Levet toddled forward. "Why me?"

"You're the self-proclaimed Knight in Shining Armor," Styx reminded the creature. "Aren't you anxious to make sure that Tonya hasn't been kidnapped?"

Levet's wings drooped, cleverly trapped.

"I suppose it is my duty," he grudgingly conceded. "How will I return home?"

"Trust me. A few hours in your company and the prince will be itching to bring you back," Styx assured him in dry tones.

With a reckless lack of self-preservation, the gargoyle

marched forward and pointed a claw toward the massive Anasso.

"You are fortunate that Darcy has made me promise not to turn you into a newt."

Styx rolled his eyes before returning his attention to Fallon.

"You understand that you're not to leave the portal?"

"She won't," Cyn said, his expression unyielding. "I'm going with her."

Fallon glanced at him with a hint of resignation. "Cyn."

He held up his hands. "I swear I won't interfere."

She hesitated, then with a shake of her head she gave a wave of her hand, opening the portal.

"Let's go."


Anthony had just returned to the secret chambers beneath his house when he heard the sound of an alarm.

"Now what?" he snarled, heading toward the circle of stones. A few seconds later he was staring into the fire that burned on the altar in time to watch a portal open just a few feet from his front door.

"Goddammit," he breathed. "How the hell did they find me?" Hissing with exasperation, he sent a pulse of magic through the flames.

Time had just run out.

# Chapter Seventeen

Fallon held the portal open, warily glancing at the precisely manicured gardens that surrounded the large mansion. The sun had just set, leaving behind a faint band of violet and orange on the distant horizon, but it was dark enough to be safe for vampires and gargoyles.

"Magnus was here," she said, baffled by the strange prickle of magic that she could feel even without leaving the protection of the portal. "But I still can't sense him."

Cyn studied the mansion before his attention shifted to the placid, bucolic countryside.

"Here?"

"Why do you sound so surprised?" she asked.

"I recognize that scent," he muttered.

She frowned. "Magnus?"

"No." He shook his head, his expression distracted as if he was lost in some deep thought. "But there's no longer any doubt this is connected to the Oracles."

"Then we should have a look around," she said. If there was something out there that could help them locate the magic-user then they had to track it down.

Cyn was jerked out of his preoccupation, his brows snapping together.

"Don't even think about it."

Her lips parted, but before she could remind him that she didn't take orders from him, Levet was lightly tugging on her hand.

"He is right, *ma belle*. We do not know the danger."

With a sigh of frustration she bent down to speak directly to the demon who looked too small to be a Knight in Shining Armor.

"You'll be careful?"

"Do not concern yourself." The gargoyle lightly patted her cheek. "I am quite accustomed to risking my life to—"

"Would you just get on with it?" Cyn snapped.

"Leeches," Levet muttered, sending a sour glance toward the hovering vampire before planting a kiss on the back of Fallon's hand. "*Au revoir, ma belle*. We shall soon be reunited."

"Just go," Cyn growled.

"Hey," Levet squeaked as the ground beneath their feet gave a violent shudder, sending the gargoyle tumbling out of the portal.

"Bloody hell." Cyn grabbed Fallon as the ground continued to quake. "What did the idiot do?"

Fallon allowed Cyn to hold her upright, her energy entirely focused on keeping them from being squashed.

"It wasn't Levet," she said between clenched teeth.

Struggling to keep the bubble of protection around them, Fallon lifted her hand. She didn't have time to form a proper opening so she sliced a small rift, hoping they could escape. But whatever was forcing the portal to collapse slammed shut the fissure before it could properly form.

Cyn growled as the air was suddenly filled with painful pricks of electricity.

"What's happening?"

"The portal is collapsing," she rasped, her strength rapidly draining. Damn. She had to get them out before they were crushed between dimensions.

"How?"

She shook her head, giving another slash of her hand as she tried to find a way out.

"I don't know."

Perhaps sensing her growing weakness, Cyn wrapped an arm around her waist and pulled her back flat against his chest.

"Can we get out?"

"I don't know." She was trembling, feeling the darkness squeezing ever tighter. "Every time I open a rift it closes before we can get out," she rasped.

His arm tightened around her. "Shit."

She grimaced. "Shit" just about summed it up.

She was coming close to burning out. She would have one last chance to get them out before bad, bad things happened.

"Brace yourself," she muttered, gathering the last of her strength.

Caution wasn't cutting it. She could only hope that she could blast their way out before her bubble of protection was shattered.

She felt him go rigid. "For what?"

She didn't bother to answer him. Instead she closed her eyes, sending the last of her powers zinging toward the side of the portal.

There was a loud sizzle as her magic hit another magic and for a horrified minute Fallon feared that it might boomerang back toward them. What had she done?

Then, just as she braced herself for the impact, there was a sudden shift in the air pressure and without warning an explosion sent both of them hurtling out the side of the portal.

Cyn gave a shout of surprise, squeezing her tight against him as they were thrown forward. Fallon grimly held on as she tried to control their plunge through space. The last thing she wanted was to survive the catapult from the portal only to fry Cyn by landing someplace where it was daylight.

Of course, it was impossible.

She was still trying to lock on to Cyn's lair when they were out of the portal and making a painful landing onto a rough, stone floor.

Her first thought was that it was dark. Really dark.

Hooray.

Her second thought was that it wasn't much fun to be squashed between a massive vampire and sharp-edged rocks.

Cyn rolled to the side, a low groan wrenched from his throat as he forced himself to his feet.

"Where are we?"

Fallon shoved her tangled hair out of her face, managing to get to her knees as she peered through the murky darkness.

They were in a cave of some sort, but it wasn't like the one beneath Cyn's lair. She could sense the heavy weight of earth that extended well above them. As if they were deep in the bowels of a mountain.

Had her fear of the sun led them to a place where light never, ever penetrated?

Hard to say.

"I don't know," she admitted, sucking in a deep breath once she was sure the rough landing hadn't cracked any ribs. She was studying the nearby stalagmite that was coated in some strange, shimmering goo when an icy breeze sent a rash of goose pimples over her skin. Suddenly she stiffened, a wave of dread sweeping through her at the foul odor that made her stomach heave. "Ugh. What is that stench?"

"Troll," Cyn muttered, the word sounding like a curse. "Can you get us out of here?"

Fallon grimaced. Her royal blood meant that she recovered far faster than most fey, but at the moment she felt as if her magic had been sucked dry.

"I need a few minutes," she admitted.

Cyn nodded, as if he'd been expecting her response. Then, without warning, he was muttering a low curse as he bent down to scoop her into his arms.

Fallon stiffened. "What are you doing?"

"Hellhounds," he muttered. "Hold on."

Cradling her against his chest, he barely gave her time to wrap her arms around his neck before he was smoothly running across the cave and into a narrow shaft that was angled upward.

Fallon glanced over Cyn's shoulder at the large hounds that were entering the cave. They were nearly as big as a pony, with crimson eyes that flashed with malevolent hatred in the darkness. They had huge fangs and dripped acid onto the stone floor with an audible sizzle.

She shuddered. Yeah, it was a relief they hadn't ended up on a sun-drenched beach, but did the alternative have to be a troll nest guarded by hellhounds?

Obviously it did, she silently conceded, burying her head against his chest as Cyn ducked the dangling stalactites and leaped over cracks in the floor at a speed that made her head spin. It wasn't until he came to an abrupt halt that she glanced up to discover his face set in a bleak expression.

"Why did you stop?" she demanded, shivering at the nearing howls of the hellhounds that echoed eerily through the small cave they'd just entered.

Cyn gently set her on her feet, pulling a large knife from a sheath strapped beneath his sweater.

"We're being herded."

Herded? She frowned, wondering if it was some slang word.

"What does that mean?"

He moved to place himself between her and the opening to the cave, his legs spread wide.

"The hounds aren't attacking, they're deliberately trying to force us deeper into the mountain."

Oh. Herded. Like cattle.

"Why?" she asked, even as a small voice in the back of her head warned she didn't want to know the answer to that particular question.

"Trolls prefer to eat their dinner while they're still alive."

Her heart stopped. Yep. Much better not to know.

"Oh."

He glanced over his shoulder, his expression more determined than concerned.

"Stay behind me."

There were more howls joining the first. Three. Maybe even four.

"There's too many," she warned.

A slow smile revealed his large fangs, his jade eyes glowing with anticipation.

"Someday, princess, you're going to trust me," he promised, then with a lightning-quick motion he was surging forward to meet the charging hellhounds.

Fallon's breath lodged in her throat as the four hounds swiftly surrounded him, their sharp barks loud enough to hurt her ears.

Cyn turned in a slow circle, meeting the evil crimson gazes. Fallon clenched her hands. It looked as if he were daring them to attack.

It was only when the largest of the hounds leaped forward that she realized he'd been deliberately provoking the leader of the pack.

With a savage snarl the beast snapped his fangs at Cyn's throat, the acid from his mouth spraying onto his sweater and burning through to the flesh beneath.

Fallon winced, but Cyn seemed unaware of the damage as he grabbed the hellhound by the head and with one massive twist of his hands snapped the creature's neck. The other hounds hesitated, clearly smart enough to recognize that Cyn wasn't going to be easy prey.

The pause gave Cyn time to use his knife to cut out the leader's heart. Fallon grimaced even as she approved of his precaution.

Most demons had to have either their head or their heart removed to prevent them from returning to life.

Tossing aside the bloody carcass, Cyn curled back his lips to flash his fangs in direct challenge.

The hounds whined, clearly wanting to scurry away in fear. But almost as if they were being driven by some outside force, they charged toward Cyn.

With a swing of his arm, Cyn sliced the knife through the nearest hound's upper chest, sending it to the floor with a snarl of pain. The next two he easily sidestepped, kicking one in the side with enough force to send it sailing into the far wall.

There was a crunch of bones as the hellhound slid to the ground in an unconscious heap.

Never hesitating, Cyn was turning just in time to grab the hellhound who was pouncing on his back. Grabbing it by the muzzle, he crushed the monster's mouth, slicing his knife through its chest to remove the heart with obvious expertise.

Fallon grimaced at the carnage, but she couldn't help but

admire the smooth skill that Cyn displayed as he tossed aside the dead hound and bent to deal with the one that had healed the wound on his chest and was rising to his feet. With a few more slices of the knife he ensured the beast wouldn't be getting back up again.

Good . . . Lord.

Distracted by the bloody battle, Fallon barely noticed that the hideous stench that permeated the air had suddenly intensified. Not until she was actually gagging at the foul odor.

Spinning around, she watched as a massive, lumbering monster stepped out of a side tunnel.

She gasped, stepping back as she studied the seven foot creature who awkwardly headed toward her.

She'd never seen a troll in person, and she had the sudden hope that she never had to see another one.

It wasn't just the size or the grotesque features that made her shudder. Or even the large tusks that protruded from his lower jaw.

It was the frenzied hunger in the crimson eyes.

He was looking for dinner.

And she was going to be the main course.

She forced her stiff lips to part. "Um . . . Cyn."

Cyn was headed toward the final hellhound lying unconscious across the floor when he sensed the troll entering the cave just behind Fallon.

Raw fear jolted through him as he watched the nasty creature reach for Fallon.

Oh hell, no.

With a speed that few other demons could match, Cyn was surging forward, planting himself between the troll and Fallon before the bastard could touch her.

"Stay back," he commanded in clipped tones.

The crimson eyes narrowed, a howl of frustration sending a shower of dust from the ceiling as the troll realized his easy meal had just become a fight to the death.

"You no scare me, leech," the troll lisped, his gaze shifting to the knife that Cyn held in his hand.

Cyn understood the demon's confidence.

A troll had thick skin that couldn't be pierced by a traditional weapon. Not even Cyn's fangs could gnaw through the barklike hide. It took a blade that had been enchanted with magic to cause any damage.

Thankfully Cyn's knife had been given to him by his foster father and it had been forged with powerful hexes etched into the steel.

"Then let's play," he taunted, edging toward the middle of the cave. Not only did he need room to maneuver, but he wanted the troll as far away from Fallon as possible.

The troll obediently shuffled forward while Cyn located the spot he intended to strike. In the demon's lower stomach there was a large artery that he could reach with his knife. Once it was severed the troll would die within minutes.

Holding his position, Cyn abruptly ducked as the beast swung a massive fist toward his face. At the same time he struck out with his knife.

The troll grunted, turning just enough for Cyn to miss his mark.

Shit.

He dodged another swing of the fist, shoving the troll with enough force to send him stumbling backward.

With a snarl of fury the troll swiftly regained his balance, lowering his head as he charged forward.

Cyn ignored the tempting target. The skull was the thickest part of a troll. He could waste the rest of the night trying to batter his way through the impenetrable bone.

Instead, he braced himself, waiting until he could smell the stench of the troll's rotting breath. Then, with a quick twist, he was stepping out of the path of the raging beast.

Going too fast to halt his frenzied attack, the troll ran headfirst into the side of the wall. The impact wasn't enough to hurt him, but the tumble of sharp rocks that fell from the ceiling knocked him to his knees.

Muttering curses, the troll forced himself to his feet, giving a shake of his head as he turned back to glare at Cyn.

"No more play," he growled, the crimson eyes filled with hate.

Cyn flipped the dagger into the air, his smile taunting. The more incensed the troll, the lower his IQ.

"Bring it on, big boy."

A roar shook the air as the troll once again charged. Cyn held his knife ready, but once again the cunning troll managed to avoid a killing strike. At the same time, he managed to clip Cyn on the side of the head, knocking him to the ground.

A tactical mistake for Cyn as the creature managed to get past him with surprising speed.

It was far too easy to be lulled by the troll's slow, graceless motions. They could be remarkably quick when they wanted.

And worse, while they might be a few bricks short of a full load, they possessed a lethal cunning that made them dangerous in a battle.

Still in the process of rising to his feet, Cyn watched as the bastard managed to reach Fallon, grabbing her by the arm.

Cyn didn't know if the monster intended to try and escape with the princess or to use her as a bargaining chip. And in the end, it didn't matter.

Even as Fallon lifted her hand as if she intended to hit the troll, he was leaping between them, a red mist filling his mind.

Gone was the vampire who fought with a cold, deadly skill and in his place was the berserker who would tear apart the world to protect his female.

With a growl he was streaking across the small space, slashing the knife toward the troll's face. Instinctively the troll ducked to avoid the painful blow, and Cyn lowered his hand to stab at the bastard's stomach.

The troll screeched, releasing his hold on Fallon as he jumped backward.

Cyn used the opening to turn and push Fallon on the other side of a large stalagmite.

Even caught in his berserker rage, Cyn had enough sense not to tell her to run. It was too risky for her to leave the cave. Not when they didn't know how many trolls might be living in this particular nest.

Turning back toward the evil creature, he had no time to avoid the large arms that wrapped around him and hoisted him off the ground. He grunted as the arms tightened, cracking his ribs. Being squeezed wouldn't kill him, but it hurt like a bitch.

Arching backward, Cyn abruptly snapped his head forward, slamming his forehead into the monster's nose. Pain blasted through him as he fractured his skull, but the blow at least made the troll drop him so he could hold his hands to his face.

Going to his knees, Cyn grimly tried to shake off the blackness that threatened to consume him. Before he could stand, however, the troll was giving a bellow of fury as he raced forward to kick Cyn in his broken ribs.

He thought he heard Fallon cry out, but the berserker

rage was pulsing through him, allowing him to continue to fight even when every movement was an agony.

There was a startled grunt from the troll as Cyn surged to his feet and with one powerful leap was smashing into the large body with enough force to make the troll flail his arms in an effort to maintain his balance.

It was all the opening that Cyn needed.

With an underhand swing of his hand, Cyn slammed the knife into the troll's lower stomach, grimly smiling as the magical blade slid through the thick, outer flesh and found the soft organs beneath. Cyn swiftly twisted the dagger, grimacing as the rancid odor of bile filled the air.

Hissing his shock, the troll glanced down, watching his life spill onto the stone floor. Then, with a wheezing breath, he began to topple forward.

Cyn jerked the knife free, leaping to the side to prevent being crushed as the troll fell face-first.

Moaning as the sudden movement sent shards of pain ripping through him, Cyn allowed his gaze to dart toward Fallon.

He'd expected to find her hidden behind the stalagmite where he'd left her. But the space was empty. His gaze frantically scanned the shadows, a sharp fear slicing through him at the sight of her standing several feet away, her hand held out as the hellhound crouched, preparing to leap.

Bloody hell. He'd forgotten that he'd left the stupid beast alive when the troll made his untimely entrance.

Now he watched in horror as the hound surged forward.

No. He raced forward, knowing he would never make it. Time seemed to halt, his heart twisting with an unbearable terror as the hellhound parted its fangs as he prepared to rip out Fallon's throat.

Then, just inches from her tender flesh, the hound was abruptly surrounded by a golden glow.

Cyn slowed, his eyes widening as the light intensified, becoming a blinding glare as it consumed the demon until it was reduced to a pile of . . . goo.

"Holy shite," he muttered, his gaze moving toward Fallon who calmly lowered her hand and turned to meet his stunned expression.

"Did you think I was helpless?" she demanded.

He gave a rueful shake of his head. It was far too easy to forget she was a royal fey with the sort of powers that made most demons tremble with fear.

Now his gaze ran over her glorious beauty, his heart filling with a tidal wave of pride that was only marred by the lingering terror at how close he'd come to losing her.

"There's a vast difference between helpless and frying a demon to a crispy critter," he dryly informed her.

"Maybe next time you'll think twice before trying to tell me what to do." She sniffed, trying to hide the fact she was shaking like a leaf.

His foolish, dangerously brave mate.

Moving forward, he wrapped her slender body in his arms, pressing his cheek against the top of her head as he absorbed the intoxicating scent of vintage champagne.

"Highly unlikely," he warned her with a rueful smile.

Intelligent enough to realize she'd be wasting her breath to argue, Fallon instead tilted back her head, her hand lifting to run her fingers down the braid that framed his face.

"You were—"

He grimaced as she struggled for the word.

"Terrifying," he suggested, knowing he must have looked like a brutal savage during the battle with the troll. Nothing at all like the pampered warriors she was used to.

She shook her head, absently wrapping his narrow braid around her finger.

"Splendid," she gently corrected.

Braced for her disgust, Cyn closed his eyes as relief raced through him.

He didn't understand why fate would offer a barely civilized berserker this elegant, exquisitely sophisticated fairy as his potential mate. But he intended to make sure he devoted his life to earning her love.

"I like splendid," he said in rough tones.

She released his braid to lightly touch the large bump on his forehead.

"But I prefer not to see it again," she murmured.

"I'll keep that in mind," he assured her, frowning as she gave a violent shiver. "You're freezing."

She shrugged. "I don't want to waste my energy keeping myself warm."

"That is my duty."

With one smooth motion, Cyn swept Fallon off her feet and moved to the distant corner of the cave. Then, with a muffled groan at the pain from his shattered ribs, he sat on the floor with the princess cradled in his lap.

As much as he wanted to take her far away from the stench and gore, they both needed to rest.

Holding her tight in his arms, he concentrated on warming the air around them.

He didn't have the same talent as Fallon, but he could maintain the heat for a short period of time.

"How do you do that?"

"I'm a vampire of many talents." He pressed his lips to the top of her head. "Rest, princess, I've got you."

They sat in silence for a long time, both simply happy to have survived.

Cyn leaned his back against the wall of the cave, marveling at how perfect the slender princess fit against him. It wasn't just the feminine curves that were molded to his chest, although they were right up at the top of the list. Or the feel of her breath as it brushed his throat. Or even the satin hair that tickled his jaw.

It was the pure beauty of her soul as it settled against his.

Cyn allowed the peace to ease away the last of his fury, relieved to feel his bones begin to mend. He couldn't sense any predators near, but considering his luck lately, he intended to be ready for . . . hell, anything.

Time drifted past, then at last, Fallon tilted back her head to reveal the color had returned to her cheeks.

Thank God.

"You said that you smelled something familiar before we were attacked," she reminded him.

Lost in the fantasy of the pleasure he intended to share with this female the minute they returned to his lair, Cyn forced himself to recall his shock when the portal had opened.

"Aye," he said. "Druids."

She blinked in surprise. "Do you think they're involved?"

Did he?

Cyn hesitated. As a vampire he had little contact with the druids. They tended to be shy and reclusive, preferring to devote themselves to their studies. They did, however, often reach out to the fey to assist them with their efforts to repair the earth from the endless damage caused by modern technology.

His foster parents occasionally traveled to consult with the elders, even inviting them to visit their small cottage.

Which was how he recognized their scent.

"They're human magic-users, some of them dangerously powerful," he said. "And my foster parents were going to speak with them shortly before they disappeared. That makes them obvious suspects."

Her brow furrowed. "If they were so obvious then why didn't you mention them before?"

"Because they've been devoted to peace for centuries," he answered. "So far as I know they've never used their magic as an offensive weapon."

"Would they have the magic to gain control of the Commission?"

Cyn frankly didn't know. The elders might possess powerful magic for humans, but did they have the strength to compel the Oracles?

"Perhaps," he hesitantly said. "If they were doing it in layers as we suspect."

She stiffened in his arms, her eyes widening. "Wait. I seem to remember my father saying that he'd had to forbid the druids from performing certain spells."

Cyn lifted his brows. "What spells?"

She hesitated, clearly searching her memory for details. "I'm not entirely sure, but it had something to do with using fey potions."

"Potions." A heavy ball of dread lodged in the pit of his stomach.

The human magic alone was dangerous, but with the potions magnifying it . . .

Shit.

"Yes." She grimaced, clearly sensing unease. "Father threatened to destroy them if he caught the druids abusing the fey."

"It seems a few have decided to go rogue," he muttered, wishing that Sariel had done more than threatened the humans.

"But why would they want to close the portals?"

Cyn felt his fangs lengthen. That, at least, was one question that was easy to answer.

"I would assume they intend to try and finish what the witches started," he said.

"What?"

"Rid the world of demons."

There was a tense silence as she slowly absorbed his words. "Do you think they have Magnus?"

Cyn struggled to disguise the sharp-edged anger that raced through him.

Bloody hell. He was ancient even by vampire standards.

Far too old to be caught in the throes of a petty jealousy.

Or at least he should be.

Unfortunately he couldn't halt the urge to track down the prince and smash in his too-pretty face.

"It's possible," he ground out.

The amber eyes darkened with concern. "Will they hurt him?"

He instinctively wrapped his arms tighter around her delicate form.

As if he could physically prevent her from thinking about another man.

No. Not just another man.

The fiancé who she'd once promised to share eternity with.

"Do you care?" he rasped.

She studied him with a puzzled expression. "Of course I care. No matter what happened between us, he's one of my people."

Knowing he was being foolish, Cyn returned his attention to their current troubles.

Nothing was more important than halting the Commission from performing the deadly spell.

"We need to share this with Styx," he said. "Can you travel yet?"

"Yes, but it's daylight there," she reminded him.

He rearranged her on his lap, pulling out his cell phone. "Damn," he muttered as he glanced at the screen. "No service. Can you take us back to my lair?"

She gave a small nod, holding up her hand as the world faded to black.

# Chapter Eighteen

Anthony stood in the center of the stone circle, dangling an amulet in one hand while he tossed a strand of gray hair into the flames that burned on the altar.

The amulet would allow him to focus his magic, while the hair would call to the one he was seeking.

Muttering the words to his spell in a low breath, he felt a familiar tug of power deep inside him. He allowed it to spread through his body, at last releasing it in a small burst to open a hole in the thick illusions that held his prisoners.

The flames flickered and with an audible pop the magic grasped the druid that Anthony had been seeking, yanking him into the stone circle to land at Anthony's feet.

The opening slammed shut and Anthony bit back a groan of agony.

Druid magic was intended to work in harmony with nature. When he forced it to mold the environment to meet his needs, there was always a price.

Usually a painful price.

He grasped the edge of the stone altar, waiting for the recoil of magic to pass. The greater the magic, the more unpleasant the whiplash.

At last confident that his knees would hold him upright, Anthony straightened and watched as the elder druid rolled onto his back with a low moan.

The man was dressed in a worn brown robe with his long silver hair pulled into a tail at his nape. His face was narrowed and lined with age, while his hands were swollen from the arthritis that had nearly crippled him over the past few years.

Once Caydeyrn had believed himself to be the oldest and most powerful of the druids. Then Anthony had returned from his latest sabbatical, revealing that he hadn't died as they'd all hoped.

The fool had tried to condemn Anthony to death, claiming that his determination to rid the world of demons made him a traitor.

Idiot.

It hadn't taken Anthony long to prove that his place was at the top of the druid hierarchy, and that he was willing to destroy anyone who tried to stand in his way.

With a rattling cough, the elderly man forced open his eyes.

In the firelight he looked every one of his hundred plus years, his narrow face ashen and his pale blue eyes watery as he glared at Anthony.

"You . . . fiend," he hissed. "You should be shamed to show your face to me."

Anthony narrowed his gaze as he watched the druid struggle to a seated position.

"The shame is yours, old man," he spit out, feeling the annoyingly predictable frustration surge through him.

Why could they not understand he was doing this for all of them?

Humans were meant to rule the world, not demons.

To stand aside and allow the evil creatures to maintain

their stranglehold on power was nothing less than a sin against nature.

Caydeyrn tilted his chin, putting on his holier-than-thou expression.

"I have lived a righteous life devoted to caring for the weak and the helpless," he said in lofty tones. "I have protected our mother earth and—"

"You are a coward who sold your soul to demons to protect your own ass." Anthony interrupted the tediously repeated speech.

God. How many times had he had to listen to the claims of lofty morals that were nothing more than a shield to hide the druids' lack of a backbone?

"I honor the treaties of our ancestors."

"Treaties?" Anthony made a sound of disgust. "There were no negotiations. No concessions offered. We were neutered by the fey king and our blessed ancestors lay down and took it."

Caydeyrn hunched his shoulder, clearly unwilling to admit that the ancient druids had allowed the King of Chatri to turn them into a bunch of sniveling weaklings.

"We devoted ourselves to peace," he said.

"You became servants in the name of peace."

"Better a servant in peace than a master in death."

The condescending tone made Anthony's teeth clench.

He crouched down, meeting the watery blue gaze with open disdain.

"So pious," he hissed.

"It is who we are."

Anthony shook his head. When he'd first returned, he tried to work with this man and the rest of the elders.

Well, perhaps he hadn't tried to work *with* him.

After all, he was born to lead, not follow.

But he'd been happy to allow the other druids to become

a part of his inner circle as he sought to rid the world of demons.

It was entirely their own fault that he'd been forced into drastic actions when they refused to follow his commands.

"No, it's what we have allowed ourselves to become," he reminded Caydeyrn. "Once we stood tall, capable of ruling the world."

The old man shook his head, clearly refusing to admit even to himself that the druids had once been destined for greatness.

"Ruling the world is your dream." He gave a slow shake of his head. "Not ours."

"Because you're weak."

"I have a heart," Caydeyrn snapped, still filled with his bloated sense of self-worth despite the weeks he'd spent locked in the Labyrinth spell. "To commit mass murder for the sake of your own glory . . ." The older man gave a dramatic shudder. "It is wicked."

Mass murder?

Anthony rolled his eyes. The old man was truly a drama queen.

"The demons aren't people. They're a cancer that must be destroyed before they take over the world."

The druid grimaced, something that might have been pity twisting his features.

"Anthony, you've allowed your lust for power to corrupt your soul." His lips flattened. "I blame the witches. You should never have traveled to meet with them."

Anthony surged upright. Over ten years ago, he'd traveled to meet with Edra. At the time her coven had been responsible for guarding the human vessel for the Goddess of Light.

The witch claimed that they had discovered a spell capable of ridding the world of demons. Anthony had been dubious. Such a spell would take far more power than a mere coven of witches could conjure, even if they could somehow tap into the power of the Phoenix.

He'd declined her invitation to include the druids in her daring scheme. A stroke of luck considering that a year ago the vampires had managed to destroy Edra before the spell could be completed.

Or maybe it'd been the Goddess of Light who'd struck the killing blow.

Anthony had never gotten a clear answer. And truly it didn't matter.

He'd learned from their mistakes.

Of course, his caution hadn't halted him from traveling to Edra's home to steal the spell just hours after her death.

He wasn't going to rush into certain disaster, but he wasn't going to ignore the potential opportunity.

So he'd waited and plotted, searching for the best means to ensure the spell's success.

The key, of course, was finding a suitable power source.

Nothing human could possibly have enough strength to actually close down the portals. And even among demons only the Commission had the necessary magic.

For weeks he'd been convinced it was impossible.

Then his insatiable research had uncovered the fey potion that could amplify the druids' power.

Suddenly he had a plan to actually accomplish what the witches had failed to.

"They opened my eyes to the possibilities," he murmured, his lips twisting at the memory of Edra's arrogant command that the druids combine their power to assist in the casting of the spell. "Of course, there was no way that I was going to join forces with them. The bitches thought I was willing to bow to them while they took control of the world. That was never going to happen."

Caydeyrn grimaced. "So instead you stole their spell."

Anthony shrugged. It'd been sheer luck that he'd been on his way to visit Edra less than a half an hour after her death. It meant that he'd been able to jerk the fragile scroll out of her dead fingers and protect it from being destroyed by the binding spell that all witches put on their personal papers.

"They were dead," he said. "Obviously they didn't need it anymore."

The older man heaved a heavy sigh, his condemning expression becoming one of deep pity.

"Your father would be so disappointed."

Anthony jerked as the druid hit an unexpected nerve.

His father, Henlin, had not only been a highly respected leader, but he'd been beloved by both druids and fey. The sort of man that could draw people to him with the sheer force of his personality.

Anthony had been in equal awe of his father, wanting nothing more than to walk in his footsteps.

But unlike Henlin, Anthony had no personal charm to earn the approval of his peers. And worse, he couldn't disguise his disgust for the demons who were constantly seeking his father's advice.

It was painfully obvious from a young age that he would have to use force to claim the position he so desperately desired.

"You know nothing of my father," he rasped.

"I know that he was a man of great honor." Caydeyrn pressed despite the fact that Henlin had died long before he'd ever been born. "He is a legend among the druids."

Without realizing he was moving, Anthony had reached for the dagger he'd laid on the altar, his entire body clenched with fury.

"Don't," he warned in a lethally soft voice.

Either indifferent or blind to the danger, Caydeyrn refused to back down.

"I only speak the truth."

Anthony lifted his hand, distantly aware that his hand was shaking.

"My father was blind."

The pale blue eyes narrowed. "He saw you clearly enough," the older man accused. "Which is why you killed him."

With one swipe of his arm, Anthony was slicing the knife through Caydeyrn's throat.

That shut up the old fool, he grimly acknowledged, mechanically reaching for a wooden bowl as the druid tumbled to the ground, blood leaking from a thin red line at the base of his neck.

Adjusting the bowl beneath the dead man's neck to capture the blood, Anthony sat back on his heels and grimly struggled to squash the memory of his father.

It hadn't been his fault that Henlin refused to listen to reason.

He'd devoted years to proving to his father just how dangerous the demons were to their world. But had the stubborn old man believed him? Hell, no. In fact, he'd dared to bring one of his fey whores into their home.

That had been the final straw as far as Anthony was concerned.

Henlin was clearly determined to put his love for demons above the welfare of humans. It was time for him to go.

So he'd done what was necessary.

Slamming a mental door on the image of his father staring up at him with a deep sadness as his own son had shoved the dagger into his heart, Anthony rose to his feet.

This was no time for maudlin reminiscing.

Holding the bowl filled with the druid's blood, he peered into the flames, sending a silent message to the fairy sleeping upstairs.

Twenty minutes later a wary Yiant entered the stone circle, his long curls freshly brushed and his jade robe immaculate. Just as if he was about to enter a ballroom.

Anthony narrowed his eyes as he realized the little prick had kept him waiting so he could fuss over his appearance.

"It's about time," he growled, taking pleasure in the fairy's abrupt horror as he caught sight of Caydeyrn lying dead on the floor.

"Blessed saints." Yiant took an instinctive step backward. "What have you done?"

"We must all make sacrifices." Anthony glanced at the motionless corpse. "Some of us more than others."

Yiant was shaking, his eyes wild. "This is madness."

"Get yourself together, fairy," Anthony snapped. "I need to travel to the Oracles."

"No." Yiant took another step back, his horror turning to anger as he glared at Anthony's calm expression. "This is wrong."

Anthony moved forward. How dare the stupid fey believe he could judge the leader of the druids?

"It's too late for regrets, fairy. We're in this together."

Yiant shook his head. "I didn't know what you were doing."

Anthony gave a sharp, humorless laugh. "You spineless bastard. You might not have been familiar with the finer details of my plan, but you knew that I wasn't using the potions to sway a handful of humans into voting for more land for the fey," he scoffed. "But you were reveling in your power as I helped you to expand your royal domain, so you didn't bother to ask any questions that might have unpleasant answers."

The fairy paled, but typically he was swift to try and defend his lust for glory.

"Everything I've done has been for my people."

"I can say the same thing," he mocked, his face abruptly hardening. He only had a limited amount of time to use the blood before it started to lose its potency. "Open the portal to the Oracles, Yiant."

The fairy shook his head. "I can't."

"I did mention the need for sacrifices." Anthony deliberately glanced toward the dead druid. "Do you wish to be the next?"

"I mean I can't locate them with a portal." Yiant licked his dry lips. "I've never been to their lair."

"Damn." Anthony ground his teeth. This was all Keeley's fault. The imp was supposed to be here to take him to the caves. Instead he'd forced Anthony to kill him. Ungrateful wretch. Now he had little choice but to get as close as possible and find some other means of transportation. "Return me to the King of Vampires."

Tonya knew she should be desperately searching for a way out of the labyrinth.

Just a few months ago she'd been held captive by a crazy-ass vampire spirit and nearly lost her mind. The mere thought of being trapped again was enough to make her shudder with horror.

But oddly, she was having trouble remembering that she was stuck in an elaborate spell.

Perhaps it was the cloudless blue sky and the rolling meadow filled with flowers. It was hard to feel threatened when in a setting more suitable for a Disney movie than a prison.

Or more likely it was the man standing at the edge of the blanket, his eyes closed as he concentrated on trying to break through the illusion.

Prince Magnus.

Tonya shook her head, a wry smile touching her lips.

The Chatri male continued to bewilder her. One minute he was an arrogant jackass whom she wanted to slap, and the next he was making her melt with his kisses.

She wanted to believe her fascination was nothing more than the predictable reaction of a woman who was forced to be in the constant company of a handsome, occasionally charming male.

After all, she'd wasted years thinking she was in love with her vampire employer, Santiago.

Unfortunately she wasn't stupid.

Sure, she'd felt a mild affection for Santiago. He was a gorgeous, sexy, über-alpha predator. Just the sort of male to make a female's pulse go pitter-patter.

But with Magnus . . .

Her nose wrinkled.

Hell, most of the time she didn't know what she felt, but she did know that the thought of him returning to his home and leaving her behind was enough to make her heart twist with a savage pain.

Christ.

Slowly rising to her feet, Tonya was at the point of wandering toward the babbling brook when an electric charge filled the air.

She turned to watch as Magnus snapped open his eyes, his slender body stiff with surprise.

"What is that?" she demanded, her voice low enough to avoid being carried on the soft breeze.

"A portal has opened." Then, reaching to grasp her hand, he was tugging her along a pathway that magically appeared directly in front of them. "This way."

She swiftly fell into place beside Magnus, her eyes widening.

"Levet," she muttered in surprise.

Magnus glanced at her in confusion. "Gargoyles can't travel by portal."

She shrugged. There was no mistaking the distinct scent of granite.

"Someone must have brought him."

He slowed his pace, his hair shimmering like the finest rubies in the sunlight.

God . . . he was a gorgeous beast.

"Yes," he murmured, his expression distracted. "Fallon."

Tonya sucked in a sharp breath. The mere mention of the princess was enough to make her gut twist with jealousy.

Childish?

Of course.

But there didn't seem much she could do to change her reaction.

"She's here?"

He gave a slow shake of his head. "No. Strange." The pathway abruptly came to a halt as a large patch of daisies appeared complete with a tiny gargoyle soundly asleep in the middle of the white blooms.

"Gargoyle." Magnus reached out his foot to nudge the slumbering Levet with the tip of his leather boot. "Wake up."

Tonya frowned. "Don't gargoyles sleep when it's sunny?"

"This is an illusion," the prince reminded her, reaching down to grab Levet by one stunted horn. "The sun has no effect on him."

"There's no need to be rude," Tonya muttered as Magnus gave the dangling creature a sharp shake.

Magnus curled his lips. "I do not like him."

"The feeling is entirely mutual, fairy," a groggy Levet retorted, opening his gray eyes to glare at the man holding him several feet off the ground.

"Chatri," Magnus snapped. "How did you get here?"

"Fallon," Levet answered. "She opened a portal."

Magnus pulled his brows together. "Why?"

Levet struggled to free himself from Magnus's grasp, his wings fluttering in outrage.

"To search for you."

The prince swore beneath his breath. "Who allowed her to put herself in such danger?"

Levet folded his arms over his tiny chest, a stubborn expression on his ugly features.

"Release me."

Magnus scowled, but with a flick of his hand he dropped the gargoyle onto the pathway.

"Answer my question," he commanded, barely waiting for Levet to regain his balance. "Who gave her permission?"

"I do not believe she asked for permission." Levet grabbed his tail, carefully wiping the dust from the tip. "Indeed, she insisted that she was capable of making her own decisions."

"She has been in this world too long," Magnus muttered, ignoring the woman at his side. "She has forgotten what it means to be a Chatri princess."

Tonya clenched her teeth at the stiff words, her heart feeling as if it were being crushed.

Dammit.

Just a few days ago she would have assumed that they implied that the prince was a cold, egotistical bastard. Now she understood that Magnus preferred to hide his emotions behind the façade of royal arrogance.

The more he felt, the more fiercely he pretended indifference.

He was truly frightened for the young female.

Which was admirable, she grimly told herself. Of course it was. But if he was still in love with the perfect princess, then why wasn't he with her?

And why the hell didn't he keep his lips to himself?

Not nearly so self-contained, Tonya pulled back her arm and punched him in the center of his chest.

"You . . . jerk."

Magnus blinked, clearly more astonished than hurt by the blow.

"You struck me."

Tonya planted her hands on her hips. The man was staring at her as if she'd grown a second head.

Not surprising. She'd bet good money she was the first woman who'd ever dared to raise a hand to his royal perfectness.

"You're lucky I didn't kick you in the nuts."

Levet dropped his tail and moved to stand at her side.

"Truly, you are lucky," he assured Magnus. "I witnessed her make a grown orc cry with just the heel of her stiletto." He paused to give a dramatic shudder. "It was terrifying."

Tonya tilted her chin. She'd taken pride in her ability to defend herself when the drunken orc had tried to rape her. Prince Magnus, on the other hand, would expect her to give a womanly scream and hope that some big, powerful male came rushing to her rescue.

That was no doubt what a proper Chatri princess would do.

"I suppose you're horrified?" she challenged. "A woman shouldn't be strong enough to take care of herself."

A mixture of emotions flashed through the cognac eyes, his pale skin flushing.

Was he . . . embarrassed?

"You are not a royal princess," he at last said in a tight voice. "You are not expected to—"

"You should shut up now," Levet said with a grimace.

"Listen to Levet," she warned as Magnus glared at the tiny creature.

Not entirely stupid, the prince hastily veered the conversation away from his chauvinistic views of women.

"Where is Fallon now?"

"I am not certain." Levet's brilliant wings drooped as he stared at a small scorch mark near the daisies. "She was to follow your portal to bring me here, then she was expected to return to the Anasso's lair. But there was an explosion."

Tonya pressed a hand to her throat. Oh shit. She might be sick to death of hearing about the perfect Princess Fallon, but she would never wish her harm.

"What kind of explosion?" she demanded.

Levet touched a small wound on his shoulder that was rapidly healing.

"Magical."

"Damn," Magnus muttered.

Tonya instinctively reached out to lightly touch his arm. She wasn't so petty that she couldn't sympathize with his fear that the woman he'd once intended to marry was seriously hurt.

"*Oui*." Levet gave a sad nod. "I am not sure how badly Fallon and Cyn were injured."

Magnus lifted his hand, using his power to search for the entrance to the portal.

"I can't find it," he rasped.

Tonya watched him with concern. "Why not?"

"The portal collapsed."

Levet gave a small gasp. "Then she must have escaped, *oui?*" There was an edge of pleading in his voice. "A portal cannot close while a fey is inside it."

"We must believe she is well." Magnus dropped his hand, his expression unreadable as he turned his attention to Levet. "Why were you sent?"

"The Anasso wanted me to track you."

Predictably Magnus stiffened, his expression indignant. "Why?"

"To rescue you, of course."

Tonya lifted a hand to hide her sudden smile. The prince was literally quivering with fury.

Not just because a vampire had dared to assume that he would need rescuing, but that he'd sent Levet to perform the deed.

"Styx sent a stunted gargoyle to rescue me?" he snarled.

"Hey. I am not stunted," Levet protested, spreading his wings with blatant pride. "I am pleasingly compact. And my magic is *légendaire*."

Magnus shook his head in disgust. "You are—"

Tonya hastily interrupted the brewing squabble. She'd had enough.

"Can you see through illusions?" she asked the gargoyle.

Easily distracted, Levet turned his attention to the sun-drenched meadows that surrounded them.

"Certainly," he assured her before wrinkling his little snout. "These, however, are unusual."

Magnus made a visible effort to control his annoyance. "It's a labyrinth," he said in a flat voice.

Levet lifted his brows in surprise. "Druid?"

Magnus nodded. "Yes."

"Ah." Levet lifted his hands. "I have just the spell to break it."

"No," Tonya cried, all too familiar with Levet's dubious skill at magic.

She'd once seen him destroy a small warehouse when a pixie had dared him to prove he could create fireballs.

Unfortunately the word had barely left her lips when Levet released his spell only to have it smash against the walls of illusion and splinter with a resounding boom.

The earth shook, sending the three of them tumbling to the ground as tiny shards of magic shot over their heads like lethal missiles.

Tonya covered her head, waiting for the dust to settle before she at last glanced up to watch Magnus surge to his feet, his face tight with fury.

"What are you doing, you fool?" he grated.

Tail twitching, Levet shoved himself upright. "I am trying to get us out of here." His wings fluttered. "Where is the love?"

"Love?" Magnus clenched his hands, painful pricks of heat filling the air as he obviously battled against the urge to melt Levet to a puddle of tar. "You nearly killed us."

Tonya cautiously straightened as Levet gave a shrug. "*Bien*. Then you get us out."

Magnus narrowed his gaze. "I assure you that I am perfectly capable of getting us out." His lips flattened as the overly proud prince recalled he'd already devoted several fruitless hours to escaping the labyrinth. "Given time."

"Wait," Tonya breathed, her gaze captured by a silvery circle that hovered in midair. "What is that?"

"Ah ha," Levet cried, pointing his claw toward the hole that was slowly growing larger. "You see."

"See what?" she muttered, a chill inching down her spine

as she caught sight of three shadowed forms that were headed directly toward the opening.

"I created a rip in the spell," the gargoyle boasted, clearly proud of his accomplishment.

"Oh." She shivered. There was something coming. And she wasn't entirely convinced it was a good thing.

"Yes, oh," Magnus muttered, moving to wrap a protective arm around her shoulders. "Druids."

# Chapter Nineteen

Fallon stumbled forward as her portal opened directly into Cyn's massive foyer.

Instantly Cyn had wrapped an arm around her waist, his expression worried.

"Are you okay?" he asked, his gaze sweeping over her face.

Fallon resisted the urge to grimace. Unlike many of her sisters, she'd never been overly vain. It wasn't as if her beauty was anything exceptional among the Chatri.

But as Cyn's jade gaze lingered on the shadows of weariness beneath her eyes and his fingers gently combed through her tangled hair, she couldn't deny a pang of regret. She knew she looked like a bedraggled mess, while Cyn was as indecently gorgeous as ever.

He'd just fought hellhounds and a full-grown troll, but his hair was smooth as silk, the narrow braids framing his face without so much as a fleck of dust.

How was that fair?

"I'm fine," she said, her lips twisted in a wry grimace as she glanced down at her clothes that were coated with muck. "I just need a hot bath and fresh clothing."

His fingers lightly skimmed down her neck, an urgent hunger smoldering in the deep jade of his eyes.

"Or no clothing," he murmured.

An answering need surged through her, the intensity of her desire overwhelming.

She wanted to shove him onto the floor of the foyer and rip off his clothes so she could explore every inch of that hard, male body with her lips.

Then she wanted to straddle him and . . .

Her breath caught as she forced herself to take a step back.

Not only was she shaken by the shocking images that were seared into her brain, but she remained acutely aware she was covered in filth.

Hardly sexy.

"I thought you were going to contact Styx?" she reminded him.

He grimaced, reluctantly pulling his cell phone from the pocket of his jeans.

"It won't take long," he promised, placing a lingering kiss on her lips. "Keep the water warm."

Fallon hurried to her rooms, her heart racing with anticipation. Cyn didn't have to worry about the temperature of the water. At the moment she was fairly certain her body heat could make it boil.

Lost in the delectable thought of sharing her bath with a very large, very naked vampire, Fallon allowed herself to be distracted.

A dangerous mistake she realized as she stepped into her room to discover a female vampire standing in the middle of the floor.

She froze, her gaze flicking over the stranger who looked completely harmless with her delicate features and big blue eyes. Not that Fallon was fooled for a second. Even at a distance she could sense the power that pulsed around the tiny figure that was barely covered by a pair of spandex pants and T-shirt that looked like it'd been painted on her.

Lise.

She recognized the scent from the first night they'd awoken at Cyn's lair.

Now Fallon narrowed her gaze as she studied the female's silky black hair that just brushed her shoulders and the exotic tilt to her blue eyes.

Of course the vampire was drop-dead gorgeous.

And no doubt she was completely independent with no need of anyone to help her kill a rabid troll.

The perfect partner for a clan chief.

Feeling distinctly grimy and at a total disadvantage, Fallon instinctively retreated behind her façade of Chatri princess.

"I don't recall inviting you into my room."

The female offered a cold smile, her fingers deliberately stroking down the blade of the dagger she had holstered around her slender waist.

"Sorry."

The insincerity was palpable.

"I doubt that." Fallon folded her arms over her waist. A tiny voice in the back of her mind warned her that she should probably be terrified. It was obvious the vampire wasn't there for a social call. And if she'd decided that Fallon had overstayed her welcome, she could rip out her throat before Fallon could halt her. But it wasn't fear that she felt as she met the female glare for glare. "What do you want?"

Lise strolled forward, deliberately allowing her power to press against Fallon.

"A little woman to woman chat."

Fallon refused to back away. She'd been raised among Chatri royalty.

If Lise wanted a bitch contest . . . it was on.

"What do we have to chat about?"

The woman arched a dark brow. Was she surprised that Fallon hadn't dropped to her knees and pleaded for mercy?

"Let's start with Cyn," she drawled, her voice frigid.

Fallon scowled. "He claimed you weren't his lover."

"I'm not, but he is my chief."

"And," Fallon prompted, knowing the relationship between Cyn and this female went way beyond simple clansmen.

"And he's the man who turned me from my path of self-destruction," she reluctantly admitted, the words sounding as if they were wrenched from her lips. "If not for Cyn I would be dead by now."

A portion of Fallon's resentment toward the female eased at the confession.

"He does have a savior complex," she muttered, easily able to imagine Cyn rushing to the rescue of this fragile-looking female.

He just couldn't help himself.

The blue eyes remained hard. Obviously Lise wasn't interested in any girl bonding.

"He is a strong, loyal leader who is beloved by his people," she rasped.

"He means a lot to you," Fallon said. "I get it."

Lise bared her snowy-white fangs. "No, you truly don't."

Fallon held up a slender hand at the woman's foul temper. Yeesh.

"Fine. Then tell me."

There was a tense silence, as if Lise was deciding between explaining her fierce loyalty to Cyn or just sticking the dagger in Fallon's heart. Thankfully the female landed on the side of explanations.

"Cyn has never been a typical chief."

Fallon rolled her eyes. There was nothing at all typical about Cyn.

"Yeah, no surprise."

Lise ignored her, instead pacing toward the large stained-glass window. Fallon grimaced, knowing that the female had deliberately insulted her by turning her back to her.

She was implying that she wasn't afraid of Fallon because she was too weak to be a real threat.

Bitch.

She was lucky that Fallon knew just how much Cyn depended on his top lieutenant. Otherwise she might just send a pulse of light to singe her perfect little ass.

Then she wouldn't be so damned smug.

Instead she bit her lip and ignored the rudeness.

To be honest, she wanted to know more about Cyn and his clan.

Even if it meant enduring the less than charming Lise.

"When he started his clan he didn't choose vampires who were the most dangerous warriors or who had skills that could bring him wealth," Lise said, her finger tracing a small dragon that was nearly hidden among the ornate patterns in the glass.

"Then how did he choose them?"

"He took in those who needed his protection."

"Oh."

Fallon's heart melted. Just like that.

She'd spent most of her life surrounded by those who believed the pursuit of purity was the ultimate goal. They couldn't understand that the so-called "flaws" in the lesser fey were what made them so vital. So capable of embracing life with joy.

And so they'd locked themselves away in a virtual prison

and convinced themselves that they weren't bored out of their minds.

Cyn clearly understood that it took more than big muscles or clever tricks to make a worthy clansman.

It took heart, and soul, and a willingness to put the needs of others before themselves.

Lise turned, a wry smile twisting her lips. "I tried over and over to convince him that it was a mistake. After all, gathering the weak and misfits would make us vulnerable to attack."

"He can be somewhat stubborn," Fallon said, feeling a ridiculous sense of pride in his refusal to sacrifice his principles. Almost as if she'd started thinking of Cyn as her own.

She hastily shoved aside the dangerous thought, grimly concentrating on her uninvited guest.

"Somewhat?" Lise gave a short laugh. "It's easier to budge the Cliffs of Moher than to force Cyn into changing his mind."

"Why didn't you leave?"

"Because I owed Cyn my life. Besides—" The woman abruptly bit off her words.

"What?"

Lise leaned against the sill, looking all cool and badass. Damn her.

"The vampires he collected might individually be less than the pick of the litter, but once we came together our talents melded to make us one of the wealthiest, most feared clans in all the world," she said, her hand once again playing with the dagger at her side. "But it's a strength that comes from Cyn and the clan's unwavering loyalty to him. Without him we wouldn't survive."

Suddenly Fallon had endured enough.

She was tired, filthy, and in no mood to be polite to a female who clearly considered her some sort of threat.

"Why are you telling me this?"

The blue eyes narrowed. "Because he's placing you above us."

Fallon blinked at the unexpected accusation. "That's not true."

"Of course it is," she rasped, abruptly straightening to glare at Fallon with barely leashed anger. "He's been away from his clan for weeks."

"That wasn't my fault."

"But rather than taking his place as chief and reinforcing our bond as a clan, he's been pandering to your needs," Lise continued, overriding Fallon's protest.

Pandering?

Fallon squared her shoulders. Enough. She didn't care what this female thought of her, but she'd be damned if she'd be blamed for Cyn's recent distraction.

"Not my needs," she denied. "The needs of the Oracles."

Lise gave a wave of her hand, dismissing Fallon's claim.

"You don't know Cyn very well if you think he would let some mystery duty to the Oracles come between him and the people he considers his own."

Fallon shook her head. What was she being accused of? Enchanting Cyn with some mysterious magic?

"This is much bigger than you seem to believe," she said in stiff tones.

The blue eyes were hard as sapphires. "Perhaps, but his preoccupation has nothing to do with duty and everything to do with a fairy."

"Chatri," Fallon snapped.

"I don't care." Lise prowled forward, any pretense of civilization stripped away to reveal the dangerous predator beneath the pretty façade. "All that matters is what you intend to do with Cyn."

Fallon stood her ground. One hint of weakness and the other woman would devour her.

"Do with him?" she demanded. "What does that mean?"

Lise halted directly in front of her. "If you intend to return to your homeland then you should go now."

Fallon stiffened, as the vampire at last struck a raw nerve.

She had no homeland.

No place where she belonged.

"Not that it's any of your business, but I doubt I will be welcomed in my father's palace," she said with a quiet dignity, struggling to disguise her aching sense of loss.

She wasn't going to allow the other female to see her vulnerable.

"Then you intend to stay here?" the woman pressed.

"In this world?"

Lise hissed in impatience, "In this lair."

Fallon unconsciously lifted a hand to her throat, caught off guard by the piercing yearning that flooded through her.

"I don't . . ." A flush stained her cheeks at the realization of just how badly she wanted this lair to be her home. "I mean—"

"Decide," Lise snapped.

Fallon abruptly crossed the floor toward the nightstand where she'd left a pitcher of nectar. Anything to hide her expression from the bitch's unnervingly shrewd gaze.

"What does it matter to you?" she muttered, troubled by the tangle of emotions that were twisted into a painful knot in the pit of her stomach. "Unless you hope to get rid of me so you can attract his attention."

"Honey, if I wanted his attention, I would have it."

Fallon snapped her head around, meeting the mocking blue gaze.

"Then what's your problem with me?" she demanded through gritted teeth.

The female squared her shoulders, at last revealing the reason she'd so rudely intruded into Fallon's room.

"A vampire mates only once." There was a deliberate pause as Lise watched Fallon's mouth drop open with shock. "If you care for him at all you'll leave before—"

"Mate?" Fallon interrupted, the breath wrenched from her lungs. As in forever together, til death do us part? She gave an unconscious shake of her head, ignoring the violent thunder of her heartbeat. Cyn might be eager to have her in his bed. And of course he was driven by his need to protect her. But a mating . . . no. "That's impossible," she breathed.

"So I assumed. After all these centuries I believed he was immune." Lise allowed her gaze to flick over Fallon in blatant disgust. "Then you arrived and he can't seem to think of anything beyond bedding you."

Heat stained Fallon's cheeks. She would never get used to the casual ease that most vampires discussed the most intimate subjects with.

"I'm not the first woman whom he's"—she stumbled for an appropriate word—"enjoyed."

Lise sneered at Fallon, no doubt amused by her prudish awkwardness.

"No, but you're the first woman who has enthralled him," she retorted, her power pushing against Fallon. Not enough to cause pain, but a definite warning. "So take him or leave him. It's not fair to steal his heart and then break it."

A blast of cold air had both females turning to watch the massive vampire step into the room.

"That's enough, Lise," Cyn said, his expression impossible to read.

"You know I'm right," Lise said.

Moving forward, she reached out to lay her hand on Cyn's arm. The two might not be lovers, but obviously Lise assumed she had the right to interfere in his most personal business.

Even worse, Cyn pressed a light kiss to the female's forehead, before stepping back.

Fallon narrowed her gaze, barely leashing her violent urge to rush across the room and punch the aggravating woman in the face.

"Return to the clan," Cyn commanded. "We will speak later."

Lise stubbornly refused to budge. "I won't have you live with regrets."

He grimaced. "Trust me."

"You, I trust. Her"—Lise turned her head to glare at Fallon—"not so much."

Fallon clenched. That was it. Allowing her lips to curve into a challenging smile, she took a deliberate step forward.

She'd never, ever been a confrontational person. In truth, she'd do anything to avoid a conflict. Including becoming engaged to a man she barely liked.

Now she realized that she was more than ready to go head to head with Lise.

For Cyn she would fight.

As if sensing that Fallon had reached her last nerve, Cyn sent Lise a warning glance.

"Go," he commanded. "I'll contact you later."

"Fine, but I'm keeping my eye on the fairy."

Flashing her fangs toward Fallon, the vampire strolled from the room, swaying her tiny ass.

Fallon narrowed her gaze.

Someday she was going to bitch-slap that vampire.


Cyn wasn't invited to join Fallon in her bath, still he couldn't hide his small smile of satisfaction as the bristling female returned to the room dressed in jeans and a casual top.

When he'd first realized that his lieutenant had snuck into his lair, he'd been furious. Not that he thought for a second she'd harm Fallon. Not when she clearly suspected that Cyn had bonded with the Chatri princess.

But Lise had her own issues when it came to mating, and he knew that she would do her best to bully Fallon.

Then he'd rushed into the room and discovered that his princess didn't need his protection.

Not only was she standing up to the lethal vampire, but she was bristling with something that could only be jealousy.

The thought was enough to make him as giddy as a dew fairy drunk on mead, he wryly acknowledged.

What the hell had happened to the male who'd skimmed through life without any messy emotions? The one who would have found a jealous female a source of irritation now nearly danced a damned jig at the sight of furious amber eyes that blazed with emerald flecks.

*Oh, how the mighty have fallen.*

Unaware of his dark humor, Fallon planted her hand on her hips, looking every inch the arrogant Chatri royalty.

"Your clanswoman doesn't like me."

Cyn chose his words with care. He had every intention of convincing Fallon to remain with him in this lair. For the sake of peace he needed the two women to call a truce.

"Lise is a little touchy when it comes to unrequited love."

Fallon went rigid. "She loves you?"

He shook his head, moving forward. One day he intended

to track down the bastard who'd hurt Lise and chop off his head.

"Not me," he instantly denied. "Another male broke her heart."

There was a long pause. As if she was deciding whether or not to believe him.

Then she gave a shake of her head, clearly dismissing Lise and her abused heart.

"She said—"

"Now isn't the time for this discussion," Cyn broke in, already knowing where the conversation was headed.

Eventually he would reveal that she was his mate.

But not until they'd managed to deal with the crazed magic-user.

He wanted lots of time and maybe Fallon handcuffed to the bed when he shared the news.

She studied him with a wary expression. "Cyn."

"Since I wasn't invited to share your bath, I need a shower," he abruptly announced, latching onto the first distraction that came to mind.

"Wait." Her wariness deepened. "I think we should—"

His words were abruptly interrupted by a clang of bells that echoed through the room.

Cyn winched, his sensitive ears ringing. "What the hell?"

"My bowls," she muttered and headed out of the room before he could halt her.

Cyn cursed, swiftly chasing after her. "Where are you going?"

"The alarms have been tripped," she said without slowing. "That means someone's entered the Oracles' cave."

He darted across the hall and into the opposite room. While he'd been hoping for a distraction, this wasn't it.

"Wait." He managed to catch her arm and spin her around to meet his worried scowl.

She made a sound of impatience. "What's wrong?"

Wrong?

Was she kidding him?

His chest still hurt from the blast he'd taken from the damned magic-user.

"The last time the alarms were tripped we were nearly killed," he reminded her in dry tones.

A shadow briefly darkened her eyes as she recalled her terror when he'd been knocked unconscious, but her expression remained grimly determined.

"I'll be careful," she said, lifting her hand to lightly touch his cheek as he scowled at her in frustration. "I promise."

"Damn."

Loosening his grip on her arm, Cyn followed her hurried steps to the bowls that were vibrating from the force of the bells. Thankfully the noise came to an end as Fallon gave a wave of her hand.

In the blessed silence they knelt beside the nearest bowl, Cyn's muscles clenched as he prepared to knock Fallon out of the path of danger.

Ignoring his tension, Fallon waved her hand over the bowl, using her magic to guide the images from one end of the massive cavern to the other.

Cyn remained on alert, even when it appeared there was nothing to see beyond the Oracles resting in their various caves. He didn't know much about magic, but he was sure that it didn't accidentally set off alarms.

At last Fallon pulled back her hand and the image floating in the water settled on a narrow tunnel at the back of the cavern.

"Look," she breathed.

Cyn deliberately leaned so he was between Fallon and the bowl, his gaze narrowing with fury.

"Druid." The word came out as a curse. Silently he

studied the cloaked figure that was once again skulking through the shadows.

This time, however, he wasn't pausing to strengthen his previous spell. He was, instead, heading into a dark cavern that held an ancient altar in the center of the floor.

Fallon grabbed Cyn's arm, peeking over his shoulder as the druid moved to place a bowl on the flat top of the altar.

"He has the blood for the sacrifice."

Cyn surged to his feet. The druid wasn't there to lay another layer of magic.

Time had just run out.

"He's getting ready to start the spell," he growled, glancing toward the ornate clock on the mantel and doing a swift calculation. "Bloody hell."

Fallon straightened, her expression troubled. "Cyn?"

His gut twisted with fear. "It's still an hour until daylight there."

She bit her bottom lip, as if she were holding back her instinctive protest.

"You intend to travel to the Oracles?"

He shrugged. "We have to stop him from casting that spell."

"But we don't know how."

Cyn might not be capable of halting magic, but he was a master at putting an end to his enemies.

"Oh, I know how."

She blinked in surprise. "You do?"

Cyn bared his fangs. "The druid can't perform magic if he's dead."

# Chapter Twenty

Magnus studied the breech.

Was it real or merely another part of the complicated illusion?

He ignored the three men draped in heavy cloaks. Instead, his gaze lingered on the ragged edges of the rift and the abrupt change from sunny meadow to a dark, craggy landscape with a distant stone castle in the background.

It had to be real.

An illusion would never be so sharply defined. It would have faded from one scene to another.

Even as he came to his decision, the stupid gargoyle was waddling to stand at his side.

"Do you want me to turn them into newts?" he demanded, pointing a claw toward the robed men who seemed unaware of the breech.

"No." Magnus shot the gargoyle an annoyed glance. "You've done enough."

"So I have." Levet puffed out his tiny chest. "But I have yet to hear one word of thanks."

Magnus shook his head. Was the creature mentally damaged?

That reckless burst of magic might have killed them, but

was the gargoyle shamed? No. He strutted around as if they should all be grateful.

"Stay here and keep your mouth shut," he commanded.

Levet folded his arms over his chest. "Ungrateful fairy."

With a shake of his head, Magnus started toward the breech. He wasn't going to waste his time arguing with a three-foot chunk of granite.

"Wait." A slender female hand landed on his forearm, bringing him to a halt. Turning his head, he met Tonya's worried gaze. "What are you going to do?" she demanded.

He nodded his head toward the shadowy figures on the other side of the breech.

"I'm going to convince the druids to release us from the labyrinth."

"You think they'll let us go?"

He shrugged. "I can be very persuasive."

The imp remained blatantly unconvinced. "There are three of them."

"They're human."

"Yeah, and they managed to trap us in this spell," she muttered.

His brows snapped together at her obvious lack of faith in his abilities. Never in his very long life had his capacity to accomplish his goals been in doubt. He was a prince. A Chatri royal.

It was simply assumed he would succeed, no matter what the odds.

Being treated as if he could barely tie his own shoes was an experience that was beginning to wear on his nerves.

"Do you believe I am too weak to—"

His sharp words were interrupted as the gargoyle gave an irritated snap of his wings.

"Can you be offended later?" he requested, pointing toward the breech. "We've been spotted."

Magnus hissed as he realized he'd allowed Tonya to distract him long enough for the three robed men to crawl through the opening and head in their direction.

With one smooth step, Magnus had moved to block Tonya from the approaching men.

"Stay behind me."

He felt an elbow punch into his ribs as the imp moved to stand at his side.

"Not a chance in hell."

He sent her an exasperated glare. "There is no discipline in this world."

She lifted her gun and clicked off the safety.

"Oh, there's plenty of discipline at my club," she murmured, flashing a wicked smile. "But you have to pay extra."

He knew what she meant by extra.

He'd heard about the vampire clubs and their twisted perversions.

But he wasn't repulsed by her taunt.

Instead, a vivid image of being strapped to a bed by a leather-clad Tonya while she did bad, bad things to his willing body nearly sent Magnus to his knees.

Oh . . . hell.

He sucked in a deep breath. "I will never understand you," he muttered.

She gave a lift of her shoulder. "Perhaps that's a good thing."

Yes, he mused, a savage sensation clenching his heart, perhaps it was.

Disturbed by the strange thought, Magnus jerked his attention back to the approaching humans.

As Tonya had pointed out, they weren't completely helpless. He wasn't going to be caught off guard again.

"Halt," he commanded.

The three stopped several feet away, the middle one lifting his hands to push back the hood of his robe.

Magnus judged him to be in his late sixties in human years, although it was impossible to gauge his age without knowing if he'd used potions to prolong his life. His head was shaved bald, and his narrow face was lined with wrinkles.

"Fairy," he murmured, offering a small bow.

Magnus uttered a low curse. "For all that's holy . . ." He glared at the startled druid. "I am a Chatri, not a fairy."

"Truly? An ancient?" There was a murmur of astonishment before the nearest druid stepped forward, his arm outstretched as if he actually intended to touch Magnus. "I have never—"

"Stay where you are," Magnus snapped.

The hand abruptly dropped, but a reverent expression remained on the lean face.

"How did you enter the labyrinth?" he asked in soft tones.

Magnus wasn't amused by the faux innocence. The druids clearly hadn't expected the spell to be breeched and now they were scrambling to cover their asses.

"Do not lie," he snarled. "You obviously trapped us."

"Not us." The druid gave a frantic shake of his head as his companions took a hasty step backward. "We are imprisoned as well."

"Ridiculous."

"It's true."

"Why should I believe you?"

The older man gave a helpless lift of his hands. "It was our leader, Anthony Benson, who created the labyrinth."

Magnus studied the druid, searching for signs of deception. Despite the man's seeming sincerity, Magnus refused to believe he wasn't involved.

"Why would he place his own people in the spell?"

The druid grimaced. "Because we attempted to halt his crazed plan to destroy the demons."

Magnus frowned at the unexpected claim. What sort of trick was this?

"What plan?" he snapped.

"He has a spell that closes the veils between dimensions," the older man explained.

Closes the veils? Momentarily stunned, Magnus tried to imagine the consequences of such a reckless plan.

It went beyond the inconvenience of not being able to travel by portal. Or moving from one dimension to another.

The veils were arteries that fed magic from world to world.

If they were closed . . .

It would create a catastrophic ripple of death and mayhem.

And not just in this world.

"Impossible," he muttered, his hands clenching into tight fists. "A human doesn't possess the power to cast such a spell."

"He intends to compel the Commission to perform it," the druid said, his expression somber.

Magnus nearly laughed. A human capable of compelling the Commission was even less likely than closing the dimensions. Then he abruptly recalled his ex-fiancée's insistence that she'd been commanded to help the Oracles.

Was this connected? He grimaced. It had to be.

"That must be what Fallon was hiding from me," he muttered, a chill inching down his spine.

Tonya touched his arm. "What's going on?"

He covered her fingers with his hand, his attention remaining locked on the druid.

"I'm not entirely certain, but whatever it is will have to wait until we are released," he said, his gaze narrowing in suspicion. Whether the druid was being honest about Anthony Benson and the spell to close dimensions or not, Magnus was far from convinced that these men were innocent bystanders. "Remove the spell."

Impatience touched the lean face. "I told you, we are trapped just as you are."

"Or more likely you were sent to distract us," Magnus accused.

"I assure you that we want nothing more than to get out of here so we can stop Anthony."

As if Magnus would take the word of a mere human. They were notorious liars.

"I need more than assurances," he said, reaching up to remove the priceless emerald pendant from around his neck.

Tonya sent him a worried glance. "Magnus, what are you doing?"

"Trust me," he said.

She nodded without hesitation.

"I do."

His heart gave a funny flutter. He didn't know why it mattered that she believed in him, but it did.

Grimacing at his idiotic thoughts, he returned his attention to the druids.

"On your knees," he commanded, waiting for all three men to cautiously bend down. Then he moved forward, touching the emerald to each of their foreheads, before he moved back to hold the gem up to the light. "Swear that you speak the truth."

It was the leader who answered first. "I swear on the graves of my forefathers that I speak the truth."

"Now you two," he said, carefully watching the emerald as they swore they weren't lying.

Magnus hissed as the color of the gemstone remained a clear, unclouded green.

"Damn," he breathed, glancing toward Tonya. "They're speaking the truth."

She arched a brow. "You wanted them to be lying?"

"I can't force them to break the spell and release us if they don't know how," he said.

"Ah, I believe that is my cue," Levet abruptly announced, stepping forward to lift his hands in a dramatic motion. "Allow me—"

"No," Magnus snapped, glaring until the demented creature lowered his hands and gave a flap of his wings.

Beside him, Tonya gave a sudden shiver, her brow furrowed as she glanced around in confusion.

"What is that?"

Magnus didn't have to ask what she meant. He could feel the strange vibration beneath his feet. As if the ground was preparing to collapse.

The humans surged to their feet, the leader sending Magnus a glance of pure terror.

"Anthony has released the spell."

"Surely that's a good thing?" Tonya demanded. "We should soon be free."

Magnus shook his head, grimacing as the air became heavy, pressing against him with a growingly painful force.

"The spell isn't designed to dissipate."

Her beautiful eyes widened as she watched his expression tighten with a grim fear.

"Then what?"

It was the gargoyle who answered. "It's shrinking."

"Shrinking?" she whispered.

"He's right," Magnus muttered, damning Anthony Benson to the fiery pits of the underworld. Most spells were cast to dissolve once the magic-user released their hold on them. But on rare occasions they could manipulate the weave so that instead of melting to nothing, it would collapse like a black hole, destroying everything in its path. "The spell is pulling in on itself. If we don't stop it we'll all be crushed."

"*Mon Dieu.*" The gargoyle glanced toward the distant edges of the illusion that were already turning a sickly gray. "Do something."

Magnus muttered a curse as every eye turned in his direction. What the hell did they expect him to do? It wasn't as if he'd been trained to get out of collapsing spells.

Then his gaze landed on Tonya's pale face and his gut twisted with a fear so deep it nearly sent him to his knees.

For the first time in his life his primary thought wasn't centered on himself. Or what was best for him.

Even the thought of imminent death didn't faze him.

In this moment nothing mattered but this beautiful imp and making sure she survived.

He would sacrifice anything to make that happen.

Still gripping the emerald in his hand, he glanced toward the ashen-faced druid.

"Can you create a barrier?"

The old man gave a slow nod. "Yes, but it will only hold for a few minutes."

"That should be enough time," he muttered, waiting for the three men to grab hands and form a circle.

There was the sound of low chanting, then a thin, nearly transparent shield began to spread from the men, flowing toward the edges of the illusion.

Only when the barrier was in place did he close his eyes as he allowed his innate powers to flow through him.

Instantly a warm glow filled his body. The heat was intoxicating, bubbling through his blood and spreading outward until he felt as if he'd captured the sun and held it deep within.

"Magnus." Tonya grabbed his arm, giving him a small shake. "What are you going to do?"

"Perform a miracle, I hope," he said, abruptly releasing his power with a massive burst.

Heat sizzled in the air, scorching a path of glittering gold toward the nearby breech.

The ground shook as his magic smashed into the wall of the illusion, nearly sending them all tumbling to the ground.

Magnus cursed, realizing that it wasn't going to be enough. His power hissed and crackled, battling against the druid's spell, but unable to penetrate the thick illusion. He clenched his teeth, refusing to give up.

Gathering his strength, he halted the steady onslaught, instead sending out pulses like a battering ram.

Once. Twice. The third time there was a loud pop followed by a series of fine cracks that spread across the backdrop of the sunny meadow.

The fourth at last shattered a large hole, revealing a dark cavern with a circle of tall, standing stones.

"Go," he said between gritted teeth. "Hurry."

The druids didn't hesitate, bolting toward the opening with a speed that was surprising for such elderly men. On their heels was the gargoyle. And then, at last, Tonya was darting forward.

A soul-deep relief surged through him, even as the druids' barrier began to disintegrate beneath the pressure.

Damn.

He instantly turned, using his powers to hold off the collapsing spell long enough for the others to escape.

Close to complete exhaustion, Magnus didn't have time to consider the irony of his exquisite life of utter selfishness coming to an end while he was playing the role of hero.

His only thought was that Tonya had escaped.

And that was enough.

Falling to his knees, he bowed his head in pain, knowing the spell would soon reach a critical mass and explode him into oblivion.

At least it would be quick.

Resigned to his fate, he didn't hear the approaching footsteps.

It wasn't until slender fingers wrapped around his forearm that he realized he wasn't alone.

"Magnus."

Glancing around in horrified shock, he met Tonya's determined gaze.

"What the hell are you doing?" he snarled. "I told you to go."

She jerked him upright with surprising strength, dragging him toward the opening.

"Not without you."

He struggled to break free of her grasp, knowing she'd never make it if she had to drag him along. Damn, the stubborn female. She was supposed to be safe. Now she threatened to ruin his one act of noble bravery.

"No . . . Tonya . . . leave me."

Refusing to release him, Tonya wrapped an arm around his waist, half carrying, half dragging him as his knees gave out.

"We're in this together, prince," she managed to rasp, hauling him ever closer to the opening.

They were less than a few feet away when the pain became unbearable, and Magnus knew the end was near.

Lifting his weary head, he locked his gaze on Tonya's delicately carved profile.

If he was going to die, he wanted this to be his last sight.

Still struggling forward, Tonya gave a soft cry as the spell around them shuddered. She tightened her grip on his waist, moaning at the crushing pain.

Then, as they stood just inches from the opening, there was an ear-splitting screech and the spell exploded into a thousand pieces.

Tonya had endured her fair share of hangovers. Hell, she ran a demon club. There were bound to be a few nights that she overindulged.

Like the night she hosted a mating dance for two wood-land fairies who'd brought an entire wagonload of fermented ambrosia to the club. Or the unforgettable party that Viper had thrown when Styx had taken over as Anasso. The drinks had been on the house and there hadn't been a sober demon in a hundred-mile radius. Including her.

But no matter how hard she'd partied, she'd never felt as if a railroad spike was being drilled into the back of her head and her skin scraped down to the nerve endings.

Careful not to move her throbbing head, Tonya forced her eyes open, baffled by the sight of her barren surroundings.

Where was her pretty canopied bed and walls painted to look like a sunny meadow?

Confusion raced through her as she realized she was in a dark cavern, lying on a smooth slab of rock.

What the hell? That really must have been some bender.

She glanced down, relieved to discover she was wearing clothes. That was something. Or it was until her gaze focused enough for her to see that her dress had several small holes and had been singed at the hem.

It looked as if she'd been in a fire.

No, wait.

An explosion.

Yes. She pressed a hand to her temple. Her memory started to come back.

The labyrinth had been collapsing and Magnus had remained behind, supporting the barriers so they could escape. She'd been furious when she discovered he wasn't with them.

Dammit. He was supposed to be a selfish, arrogant prince. Not a martyr.

The stubborn ass.

So, of course, she'd gone back to rescue him.

And they'd very nearly made it. They'd been only steps away from the opening when everything had gone . . . kablooey.

With a groan, she pressed herself to a seated position on the hard slab, warily glancing toward the towering stone circle.

"Where am I?" she muttered, nearly jumping out of her skin when a male voice spoke directly behind her.

"Beneath the lair of the druid."

"Oh."

She turned her head, warily watching as Magnus strolled to stand directly in front of her.

Like her, his clothing had been scorched and he had a few healing wounds on his impossibly beautiful face, but the explosion clearly hadn't dented his enormous arrogance as he peered down his long nose at her.

"Why did you do that?"

She winched. "Yow, prince, tone it down," she muttered, pressing a finger between her eyes. "My head hurts."

"Of course it hurts." His hands clenched and unclenched, as if he were under a great stress. "You were caught in the backlash of a very powerful spell. I told you to run."

She scowled at his sharp words. She hadn't expected

him to fall on his knees in gratitude for her saving his life. But . . . Christ.

He could at least throw out a "thank you" before snapping at her.

She narrowed her gaze. "Since when do I take orders from you?"

He folded his arms over his chest, his gaze oddly piercing as he studied her upturned face.

"Why?"

"Why don't I take orders?"

His lips flattened. "Why did you come back for me?"

She shrugged. That was a question she didn't want to consider too deeply.

"Because I'm mental," she muttered.

He leaned forward, surrounding her in the scent of aged whiskey.

"Answer the question."

She made a sound of impatience. Dammit. Why couldn't he just let it go?

"Obviously because I was afraid you weren't going to make it out."

The cognac eyes held her gaze with mesmerizing ease.

"Would it bother you if I didn't?"

She bit her lip, a shudder shaking her body. She would never forget the moment she'd glanced back to discover this man wasn't following them out of the collapsing spell.

It'd felt as if someone had reached into her chest and ripped out her heart.

Something she very much hoped never to feel again.

"Of course it would," she muttered.

"Why?"

"Oh, for God's sake, stop saying 'Why?'," she snapped, forcing herself to scoot off the slab and stand on her shaky legs.

Where the hell were Levet and the druids?

Magnus stepped nearer, his fingers closing around her upper arms.

"You think I'm arrogant," he said.

"Because you are."

He frowned, staring at her as if she were a ginormous puzzle.

"You believe I was cruel to Fallon."

She hunched a shoulder. If she had to hear that woman's name on his lips one more time . . .

"You were," she said in clipped tones.

"You don't like me."

His touch was like a brand against her raw skin. So acutely pleasurable it was almost painful.

"You can be an ass," she said, her voice husky.

His fingers skimmed up her arms, the heat of him wrapping around her with an intimate promise.

"So why do you care if I survive?"

Her lips parted to give a flippant response, then snapped shut as her breath tangled in her throat. Just for the briefest second she'd caught sight of something in those amazing cognac eyes.

Something that looked remarkably like vulnerability.

"Oh hell," she muttered, heaving a deep sigh. "You've grown on me."

His brows drew together. "Grown?"

"I . . ." She licked her dry lips. "I would miss you if you weren't around."

The world halted, the air heavy with a sense of anticipation as Magnus slowly lowered his head.

"You've grown on me as well," he confessed, brushing her lips with a soft, reverent kiss. Her toes curled, something deep inside her melting. God Almighty, she was in trouble. He pressed another kiss to her lips, this one staking his claim before he lifted his head to regard her with a brooding gaze. "But if you ever do anything so foolish again I will have you chained to the wall."

Ignoring the pleasure that continued to shiver through her, Tonya went onto her tiptoes so they were nose to nose.

"I'd like to see you try."

He gave a low growl, reclaiming her lips in a kiss that made her forget her aching head, their damp surroundings, and the fact they'd nearly been exploded into a thousand tiny pieces.

There was no telling how long they would have remained lost in one another if someone hadn't loudly cleared their throat, making Tonya abruptly pull away.

Glancing over Magnus's shoulder, she discovered Levet standing near the circle of stones.

"You can kissy-face later," the gargoyle chided. "The druids need you."

Magnus muttered a low curse before he grudgingly released his hold on Tonya.

"Someday I'm going to kill that gargoyle."

Levet gave a flick of his wings. "If only I had a euro for every time I have heard that."

# Chapter Twenty-One

Cyn wasn't happy as he watched as Styx and Viper silently faded into the early-evening darkness before he turned and headed toward the bluff overlooking the Mississippi River.

It had been less than an hour since Fallon had created a portal so they could travel to Chicago.

No surprise that Styx had been waiting for their arrival along with Viper and Dante. But when Cyn had been prepared to insist that Fallon remain in the safety of the Anasso's lair while they travel to the caverns where the Oracles were gathered, the aggravating princess had neatly outwitted him by insisting her brief meeting with Siljar meant that she could use her as an anchor to open a portal.

He'd forbidden her to come, of course.

A total waste of time.

Not only had Fallon ignored him, but Styx had refused to listen to reason. Instead he'd agreed with Fallon, firmly overriding Cyn's protest.

At least the aggravating bastard had drawn the line at letting Fallon go charging into the caves in search of the magic-user, he wryly acknowledged. That was something.

Stepping through the tight cluster of trees, he found Fallon waiting for him exactly where he'd left her. A wry smile touched his lips. It would be nice to think she'd stayed there because he'd asked her to, but the truth was that she was standing at the edge of her portal to keep it open.

There was a very real possibility they would need a quick getaway and she was there to provide it.

He halted at her side, pulling free the large sword he'd strapped to his back before leaving his lair.

"What's happening?" Fallon demanded, her beautiful face pale but set in lines of grim determination.

His heart twisted. The prehistoric male inside him wanted to treat Fallon as a pampered Chatri princess that needed to be protected against the world. But he wasn't entirely stupid. This female had been denied the right to discover exactly who she was and what she was capable of accomplishing for far too long.

He couldn't deny her the right to prove her worth.

Within reason.

He turned so he could keep his gaze locked on the small farmhouse that appeared harmless enough. No one passing by would realize that beneath it was a complex layer of caves that were currently home to the most powerful demons in the world.

"Styx and Viper are more familiar with the caves," he said. "They're going to track down the druid. Once they've found him they'll contact me."

"And Dante?"

He nodded toward the pathway that ran parallel to the river.

"He's going to scout for any unseen enemies."

"And you?" she pressed.

He shrugged. "I'm going to protect our fastest means of escape if things go to hell."

He barely heard her soft sigh. "You mean you've been put on babysitting duty."

"No." He shook his head, his senses on full alert. Everything was eerily still. Understandable, of course. Humans and wildlife might not be aware of the pulses of power that throbbed in the air, but their sixth sense would urge them to leave the area. And no demon was foolish enough to willingly linger so near the Commission. Just because they happened to be the leaders of the demon world didn't make them nice guys. Hell, just the opposite. Which made it easy to keep watch. If anything moved, he intended to kill it. "If Styx believed my place was in the caves, that's where I would be," he assured her. "They hope to locate the druid without alerting him to their presence, so the fewer people with them the better."

"Hmm."

Sensing her continued tension, he turned to study her strained features.

"This is where I belong." His brows snapped together as she gave a violent shiver. "You're cold."

"No." Her hands ran up and down her arms in a convulsive motion. "It's—"

He knew immediately what was wrong.

"You sense something?"

"Magic," she whispered.

He grimaced. Of course it had to be magic. It couldn't be a hellhound. Or even a troll. Anything he could use his big sword to kill.

"The druid?"

She licked her lips. "No. This is demon magic."

The faint sound of a twig snapping had him turning toward the trees to their left.

"Something's coming," he growled, catching the faint

scent of lava. A Manasa . . . fire demon. "Fallon, return to Styx's lair," he snapped.

She turned, as if preparing to retreat, but before she could disappear into the portal she gave a pained cry and collapsed to the ground.

At the same time he was hit with a spell freezing him in place.

"Shit," he rasped, watching in helpless horror as the eerily beautiful demon moved into view. "Phyla."

"You will come with me," the powerful Oracle commanded, her copper hair floating around the pure oval of her face and her green eyes speckled with silver that glowed in the moonlight.

"Phyla." Cyn struggled against the invisible bands that held him immobile. "Can you hear me?"

The female drifted past him, her movements oddly sinuous as she leaned down to grab Fallon by the throat. Then, lifting the unconscious Chatri off the ground, she waved a hand toward Cyn, releasing him from her spell.

"This way."

With a blur of movement, Cyn was standing directly in front of the demon, his sword beneath her chin.

"Wait."

With an unnerving strength, the demon continued to hold Fallon by the throat, the fingers tightening as if she were prepared to crush the unconscious woman's throat.

"You will obey or I will kill the female," she said in a low hiss.

For a crazed second Cyn felt a red mist begin to cloud his mind.

The sight of his female being threatened was enough to tip him into his berserker rage.

It was only the realization that Phyla could destroy Fallon

with one blast of her magical fire that forced back the tidal wave of fury so he could think clearly.

Stepping back, he slowly lowered his sword.

It was obvious the demon was under the control of the druid. Which meant he couldn't physically prevent her from harming Fallon.

He'd have to use his own skills to try and break through the compulsion.

"Fine," he growled. "I'm coming."

"This way."

She headed toward the nearby farmhouse, seemingly indifferent to the massive vampire at her side. Cyn, however, angled himself so he was walking two steps ahead of her and capable of looking her directly in the eye.

"Where are we going?" he demanded, adding a subtle layer of compulsion to his tone.

The damned druid wasn't the only one who could sway the minds of others.

And luckily, Cyn's talent was stronger than most vampires.

Her pace never slowed, but something flickered in the silver-flecked eyes.

"To join your brothers."

Hell. His gut twisted with dread. Styx and Viper must have been caught. He could only hope that Dante hadn't yet been detected.

"What have you done with them?"

"They are preparing to die."

"Phyla." Cyn planted himself directly in front of the demon, his voice low with command. "Stop."

Her steps stumbled, then came to a halt. Her face twisted with obvious pain, her body trembling as she was attacked by two contradicting compulsions.

"We must go," she rasped.

He reached out to touch her face, increasing his pressure on her tortured mind.

"The druid has cast a spell on you," he said. "You must fight it."

Her trembling increased. "I—"

"Concentrate on me," he urged, his hand stroking her cheek. "Release the Chatri."

Her breath came in short, painful gasps. "It's impossible. The death spell I placed on her will trip if I release her."

Cyn swallowed his curse. He was going to need help.

"What happened to the vampires?"

"They're being held in the prisons beneath the caves."

Cyn frowned. Styx had told him about the large holding pens that the previous Anasso had used to confine his drug-addicted humans. He assumed that must be what she was referring to.

"What about the druid?"

She paused, no doubt using the connection the druid forced on her to track him.

"He's in the altar chamber."

"What about the Oracles?"

"They're gathering in the Council Room. I must join them."

"Can you lead me to the druid?"

"Yes. But—"

She made a gagged sound, as if something or someone was cutting off her words.

"What is it?"

The muscles of her neck bulged as she struggled to spit out the words.

"The amulet."

He frowned. "What amulet?"

She didn't answer. Instead, she gave a violent shudder,

pain flaring in her eyes before they abruptly went dull and lifeless.

"We must go," she said, her monotone voice revealing she was once again under full command of the druid.

Cyn continued to stand in her path, desperate to break the spell.

"Phyla."

Fire flickered over the demon's skin. "Move or I'll kill her."

"Damn."

Cyn leaped to the side, his gaze locked on Fallon to make sure the flames didn't touch her vulnerable skin. Locked in the demon's spell, he didn't know if she could survive being burned or not.

Dampening the fire, Phyla started forward again, leading Cyn into the mouth of a cavern hidden behind the farmhouse.

Cyn grimaced as they moved across the smooth floor and into the tunnel that led sharply downward.

He didn't need to be able to sense magic to realize that there was something big happening. He could feel it in the heavy press of air that seemed to cling to his skin and the tiny quakes beneath his feet. There was even a smell of electricity in the air. As if lightning was about to strike.

Not the most comfortable sensation for a vampire.

They followed the main tunnel until they entered a large cavern with a number of openings that branched in every direction.

Cyn frowned as Phyla headed to the very back of the cavern. Where the hell was she going? There was nothing but a large pile of rubble that towered nearly to the ceiling.

As if blind to the mess, Phyla continued forward, her pace never slowing.

Then, as she stepped directly into the stones, he muttered an exasperated curse.

An illusion.

Of course.

Holding his sword in a white-knuckled grip, Cyn forced himself to ignore what his eyes were telling him. Not easy, since he had a moral objection to walking face-first into a stone wall.

Tingles rushed over his skin and the scenery blurred before they'd stepped through the magical barrier to reveal they were standing in a cramped tunnel.

Phyla continued forward, nearly scraping the unconscious Fallon against the jagged edge of the wall as the channel narrowed and curved. Cyn snapped his fangs, trembling with the effort not to snatch his princess from the bitch's hand.

*Soon,* he silently promised himself.

Soon he would have his fangs buried deep in the druid's throat and he would take exquisite pleasure in draining the life from the bastard.

Until then he would have to be patient.

A task easier said than done for a hedonistic berserker vampire.

Grimly reminding himself of the price of failure, he allowed Phyla to lead him to the deepest part of the cavern, the top of his head brushing the low ceiling before they at last came to a heavy steel door that blocked the tunnel.

Phyla used her free hand to shove open the door, revealing a small, barren space that had been roughly carved out of the rock.

Cyn hissed at the sight of the two vampires that were lying motionless in the center of the floor.

Styx and Viper.

But no Dante.

Thank God.

"Enter the cell," Phyla commanded, allowing her hand

to become engulfed in flame as Cyn hesitated. "Do it now or I burn the female."

"Shit." Cyn grudgingly bent down to step through the low opening, whirling to face Phyla with his fangs bared. "Where are you taking Fallon?"

"She will ensure your good behavior," the demon informed him, slamming shut the door.

Shrouded in utter blackness, Cyn tilted back his head and roared in fury.

Fallon remained limp with her eyes closed as the female demon carried her up the stairs that had been chiseled into the side of the wall.

She'd awakened shortly after they'd entered the caverns, but sensing the spell that was wrapped around her, she'd forced herself to feign sleep. Any attempt to free herself from the choking grasp would trigger the death magic.

Her only choice was to remain motionless and wait until the spell was removed. Then she could hopefully catch the demon off guard and escape.

Smoke filled her lungs as they reached a level surface. There was a fire near. And something else . . . blood.

She struggled not to react as the demon came to a halt and rudely dropped her onto the hard floor. Her head banged sharply against a rock, but it was worth the pain as she felt the spell being jerked away from her.

Before she could even think of launching an attack, however, there was the scent of an approaching human male.

"Shackle her to the wall and take your place in the Council Room," the male commanded.

Shit. It had to be the druid.

Forced to maintain her charade, she was roughly yanked

across the floor. If they believed her to be unconscious, they might leave her alone to . . .

That hope was brought to a brutal end as she felt a pair of iron shackles being snapped around her wrists.

Crap.

Iron was one thing that affected fey.

It not only dampened their magic, but it made it impossible for them to create a portal. And, with prolonged contact, it could even kill them.

Thankfully, as a Chatri, the effects were limited on her, but it would definitely make it more difficult to escape.

*Because things just aren't challenging enough,* she wryly acknowledged.

She swallowed her groan of pain as the iron seared her skin, a heavy sense of lethargy spreading through her body. In the distance she heard the female demon leaving the cave, but instead of joining her, the druid contrarily crossed to stand next to her.

Dammit.

The scent of smoke and blood and foulness nearly gagged her as she felt the tip of a boot nudge her shoulder.

"Very convincing, my sweet." The voice was cultured with just a hint of an Irish brogue. "But I know you're awake."

Snapping her eyes open, Fallon shoved herself into a seated position. If helpless didn't work, then maybe she could try intimidation.

She tilted back her head, studying the man who hovered over her.

Surprise flared through her.

This was the deadly enemy who threatened to destroy the demon world?

He looked like a . . . nobody.

Just another human with a round face and fringe of brown hair.

Of course, she knew as well as anyone that appearances could be deceptive.

You didn't have to be a hulking warrior to wield enormous power.

Just look at Siljar.

Shaking off her sense of disbelief, she forced herself to meet his cold gaze as she assumed her best princess manner.

"Release me," she ordered, her voice ringing through the small cave as she took a swift, covert glance around the barren cave.

There wasn't much to see except for the small altar in the center of the floor, but it was enough to make her heart clench with fear.

On top of the altar a fire was burning with a strange blue light.

Magic.

He was in the middle of casting his spell.

"A true Chatri," the druid murmured, crouching down as he studied her with a mocking curiosity. Like she was some bug he'd captured and pinned to the wall. Sicko. "I was beginning to think you were a myth."

She forced a cold smile to her lips. "There will be no mistake we are real when my father arrives."

"Why should I fear your father?"

"He's the King of Chatri."

"Ah." A shockingly intense hatred flared in his eyes. "So you're a royal."

Pure menace crawled over Fallon's skin. This man not only wanted her dead. He wanted her to suffer.

She squashed the urge to panic. Cyn was depending on her.

Hell, the entire demon world was depending on her.

This was her chance to do that big, important thing she'd

always dreamed of doing, she desperately told herself. The opportunity to make her life matter.

Right?

All she needed to do was to keep him distracted for a few minutes so she could gather her power.

"My father will kill you," she said, scooting until her back was pressed against the wall and her hands draped to the side of her body to hide them from the creepy druid.

A human shouldn't be able to see the glow of her powers, but he was clearly more than just another mortal.

"Demons are no match for me," he boasted, thankfully too bloated with his own sense of self-importance to wonder at Fallon's distraction. "Especially not that bastard Sariel. I hope he does come. I would dearly love to watch him die."

Fallon barely listened to the idiot's claims, instead focusing on her magic.

Usually it bubbled through her like vintage champagne. An intoxicating promise that she could tap into whenever necessary. Now it ran through her veins with a sluggish, growingly painful lethargy.

Damn.

There was no way she was going to be able to focus enough power to send a blast toward the druid.

To hurt him, she would actually need to touch him.

"You're mad," she muttered, her mind racing. She had to get him closer.

But how?

"The madness belongs to my forefathers," he was saying, tiny spots of spittle spraying from his lips. "That's the only excuse for them to have sold out the human race to a bunch of filthy fey."

She hid her urge to shudder. What a pathetic, disgusting excuse for a human being.

"Why do you hate demons?"

"They have invaded our world, preying on us like we're nothing more than mindless cattle," he snarled.

Fallon continued to concentrate her power into her hands, silently cursing the iron that was searing into her flesh. Not only was the pain distracting, but it was making it almost impossible to gather enough magic to cause real damage.

"Why do you call it *your* world?" she asked, her voice laced with disdain. Maybe if she could make him angry enough he would be compelled to grab her. Like any petty bully he no doubt resorted to physical violence when he couldn't mentally intimidate his opponent. "Demons were here long before humans began to walk upright."

He sniffed, waving aside the truth of her accusation. "And now the time has come to claim it for our own."

Her lips twisted. "So you're doing this for humans?"

"Naturally."

"And you have no interest in becoming some sort of messiah for your people?" she demanded.

A smug smile curved his lips as he tried to pretend a false modesty.

"The humans will need a leader and I'm not opposed to being worshiped."

Oh . . . bleck.

Her hands warmed, a golden glow beginning to surround them. She pressed them beneath her leg.

"Have you considered what will happen once the demons are dead?"

He leaned forward, slowly enunciating his words. "Every. Day."

He was close. So close. But still too far.

She flicked a dismissive glance down his pudgy form that was swathed in a rough, brown robe.

"Without demons your magic will die," she taunted. "Do

you think you'll be worshiped if you're just another human in a silly costume?"

"I have enough potions in storage to last for several centuries." Without warning the feral hatred transformed into something even worse. Lust. Ew. She struggled not to cringe at the hot gaze that lowered to the swell of her breasts. "In fact, I have enough that I might be willing to share with a female who was willing to please me."

She flattened her lips, biting back her words of revulsion. If she couldn't get him to touch in anger, then she'd settle for a horny grope.

"Really?" She tilted her head, allowing her hair to slide over one shoulder.

He licked his lips. "How long do you think you'll last once the portals are closed?"

She shrugged, glancing beneath her lashes. It's what her older sister, Dellicia, used to do and it always seemed to make the males take notice of her.

"A few weeks, perhaps months," she murmured, dropping her voice until it was a husky whisper.

His gaze remained attached to her breasts. Had he never seen a pair before?

"I could prolong your life . . . at least for a while," he said, his arrogance great enough that he assumed she would be willing to trade her body for a few measly days of life.

"If I pleased you," she murmured.

He inched closer, his foul smell making her shudder. "You're a very beautiful female."

"Do you think so?" Her hands burned against the side of her leg, the magic ready to destroy the bastard just as soon as he got close enough. "I'm a demon."

"My father seemed happy enough to bang a fey." An ugly expression hardened his features. "In my mother's bed. Maybe I should see what the fuss is about."

Was that why he hated demons?

His father had a fey lover?

Ridiculous.

"What would you demand of me?" she forced herself to ask.

"Nothing too painful." His gaze moved to her unmarred neck, perhaps seeking signs of Cyn's feedings. Fallon felt her gut twist, wishing her neck did carry the mark of Cyn's fangs. "Although a princess who chooses to take a vampire lover must enjoy it rough and dirty."

"Sometimes." A secret smile curved her lips as she recalled her berserker's tenderness. It still amazed her that a warrior so large and fierce could touch her as if she were some fragile treasure. "Of course, I do like a man who can be . . ." She struggled for a provocative word. Dammit, why wouldn't he touch her already? "Inventive. You'll need to show me what you like."

He sucked in a slow, shaky breath, his rounded cheeks flushed with his rising lust.

"You are a tempting witch."

"Not witch . . . Chatri." She touched the tip of her tongue to her lower lip. "Touch me."

His brows drew together, his hands curling into tight fists as if barely resisting the urge to give into her soft command.

"Why?" he rasped.

She arched her back. "I want to feel your hands on my body."

He hesitated, his breath rasping between his teeth. "I suppose you also want me to remove your cuffs?"

"Not yet." She rattled the chains while managing to keep her hands hidden. "I think we could have fun like this. Don't you?"

"Ah." He shuddered, clearly excited by the thought of keeping her shackled while he . . . well, whatever the hell he was fantasizing doing to her. Creep. "I knew that your sense of self-preservation would encourage you to play nice."

"Come here and let me show you just how nice I can play," she urged.

For a breathless moment he swayed forward, his hand lifting to touch her cheek. Fallon tensed, her muscles coiled to lunge forward the second he came within touching distance.

Then, as if he were deliberately trying to torture her, he was surging to his feet and shaking a pudgy finger at her.

"Naughty fey. First comes the spell," he muttered, turning to head back to the altar. "And then the pleasure."

Shit.

# Chapter Twenty-Two

For once, the always confident—some might say arrogant—Prince Magnus wavered.

A part of him wanted to demand that Tonya form a portal and return to Styx's lair.

She still looked far too pale, and there were several small wounds that had yet to heal on her arms and legs. She needed a warm bath, a soft bed, and plenty of nectar to finish healing.

But a much larger part of him selfishly wanted her near.

If he wasn't keeping an eye on her, how could he be certain she wasn't in danger? Or that she was taking proper care of herself.

It was at last the impatient sound from the waiting gargoyle that made up his mind.

He'd nearly lost her.

There was no way in hell he was going to let her out of his sight.

Reaching out, he firmly gripped her hand, pulling her with him as he followed the gargoyle through the narrow opening between the standing stones.

There was a cool brush of power as they stepped through

a magical barrier, then, without warning, there was the unmistakable stench of death.

Instantly he was shoving Tonya behind him as he swiftly surveyed their surroundings.

The inner sanctum was larger than he'd expected, with a stone altar set in the middle of a floor that had been worn smooth over the centuries. Along the edges were several small tables that held piles of dried herbs and spices as well as bottles of potions. There were no visible weapons, but he caught the unmistakable scent of gunpowder, which meant there was at least one firearm in the vicinity.

It was the three druids, however, that captured his attention.

They were currently crouched near the altar where a corpse was sprawled on the hard floor.

Even from a distance, Magnus could tell the dead man had been one of the druids. Not only did he wear a similar robe, but the smell of magic clung to his body.

He wrinkled his nose as his gaze took in the deep slash across the front of his throat.

"Was this the druid who trapped us?" he demanded.

The chosen speaker gave a shake of his head as he straightened to face Magnus.

"No, this was our brother." A deep sorrow was threaded through his voice. "Anthony has used him as a sacrifice."

Magnus arched a startled brow. Humans were often violent toward one another, but to choose one of your own brothers as a sacrifice . . .

That took a whole new level of evil.

"Why would he sacrifice him?"

The man pointed toward the flames on top of the altar that flickered with a blue glow.

"The spell has started."

Magnus unconsciously tightened his grip on Tonya's fingers, drawing her close to his side as he scowled at the elderly druid.

"Tell me what it means."

"He's cast the spell of Compulsion on the Oracles. Now they've gathered to combine their powers to complete the spell that will prevent any travel between dimensions. This world will be completely isolated."

Shit. That's what he feared it meant.

"And the demons—"

"Will die," the druid completed his horrifying words. "Along with all magic."

Just a few days ago, Magnus would have shrugged his shoulders and returned to his homeland. What did the fate of this world or any other matter to him?

So long as the Chatri were safely tucked behind their layers of magic, then there was no need to put himself at risk.

Now he knew beyond a doubt he couldn't walk away.

Tonya was a part of this world. And the lesser fey who had once bowed to the Chatri.

Even the vampires . . .

No, wait. He still didn't care what happened to the vampires.

But the others . . . yes, he would do whatever was possible to protect them.

Besides, there was the nagging fear that this might eventually hurt the Chatri.

Magnus pointed toward the flames. "Stop them."

The old man shook his head. "It's impossible."

"Wrong answer," Magnus snapped.

"Only Anthony can halt the spell now that it's been cast."

"Fine, then bring me the druid."

"He's not here."

Of course he wasn't.

Magnus grimaced as the druids covertly stepped backward, knowing that his power was shimmering around him with a golden aura.

"Where is he?" he demanded, trying to leash his temper. It would be a shame to accidentally turn one of the druids into a pile of goo.

"With the Commission."

"Damn," he muttered.

"I've traveled to the caves," Tonya abruptly said. "I can take us there."

He sent her a frown. "No."

"Yes." She shot back. "My decision, not yours, prince."

Magnus bit back the urge to argue. The one thing he knew about this female was that to try and tell her she couldn't do something was the one certain way to make sure she dug in her heels.

And, in truth, he knew that he would need her assistance.

A female as a partner. Who would ever have thought it?

"Very well." He gave her a slow nod, his heart forgetting to beat as he was rewarded with a dazzling smile. Then he grudgingly returned his attention to the men watching him with a completely unwarranted belief that Magnus was going to be their savior. "Will killing the druid break the spell?"

"That is only the first step," the man said.

Magnus knew it couldn't be that simple.

"What else must be done?"

"To cast the Compulsion spell that's controlling the Oracles, Anthony must have a blood sacrifice and a focus object."

Magnus frowned. His magic came from his own powers.

Human magic-users had to manipulate the power that was found in nature. Or steal it from the blood of a sacrifice.

He'd never had to understand what went into casting a spell.

"What object?"

"It can be anything." The druid shrugged. "An amulet. A crystal. Even something personal like a piece of jewelry. It must be destroyed."

Kill the druid and destroy a piece of jewelry. That seemed doable.

"Will it be with him?"

"Not necessarily."

Ah. There had to be something.

"Then how do we find it?"

"It will give off a pulse of magic," the druid answered.

Tonya made a sound of impatience. "Along with a thousand other items. The caves belong to the Oracles," she said. "All of them will have amulets and crystals and God knows what else."

"True." With a frown, the old man turned to share a whispered conversation with his fellow druids. There was a brief discussion, or maybe an argument, before he swiveled around to meet Magnus's impatient glare. "My brothers and I can combine our magic to vibrate any objects that happen to be druid in the cave."

"Vibrate?"

"Yes. The movement will give off a small hum. That should make it easier to find."

Magnus supposed that was as good as it was going to get.

"Fine." He glanced toward his beautiful imp. "Tonya—"

She reached up to place a finger against his lips. "We'll talk when this is over. Are you ready?"

He gave a grudging nod.

The sooner they were done, the sooner he could have this woman alone in his bed.

And he wanted that very, very much.

"Hey, wait for me," a small voice demanded as Levet waddled forward.

"No," Magnus growled. "No way."

Tonya tried and failed to hide her smile. "Actually he's very good at seeing through illusions. We might need him."

The idiotic creature stuck out his tongue. "*Oui,* I am a gargoyle of many talents."

"Fine," Magnus growled. "Let's just go."

Tonya lifted her hand, waving to open the portal. Then she gave it another wave. And another.

"Oh shit," she breathed, her eyes wide with terror. "We're too late."


Cyn's sanity was hanging on by a thread.

Pacing the cramped cell, he searched for any weakness in the smooth stone walls before turning his attention to the iron door that refused to budge.

He grasped the handle, giving it a mighty yank. Nothing happened.

Which meant that it'd been magically connected to the stone that surrounded it.

Dammit.

Whirling on his heel, he moved to where the two vampires lay on the ground. Bending down, he grabbed one of Styx's large shoulders and allowed his power to flow from his hand into his Anasso.

Not all vampires could share power, but as a clan chief he could perform a basic healing.

"Styx," he muttered, his fingers curling around his Anasso's arm to give him a shake. "Wake up."

There was a low groan before Styx was reaching up to shove away Cyn's hand.

"Cyn, you are a vampire with a death wish."

"That's the one thing I don't have," he assured his companion, rising to his feet. "I intend to live. But to do that I need you to get your oversized carcass off the ground."

"Oversized?" Styx went to his hands and knees, giving a shake of his head as if he were trying to clear out the cobwebs. "Isn't that the pot calling the kettle black . . . or some such shit?" With a pained moan, Styx slowly forced himself upright, studying his surroundings with a jaundiced glare. "Damn. We walked straight into a trap."

Cyn frowned in surprise. There weren't many traps that a vampire couldn't sense.

"The druid?"

Styx grimaced. "Yes, but I didn't see him. We were entering the back of the caves, then zap . . . everything went black." He shrugged, glancing toward the heavy door. "I'm assuming there's no way out."

"Nothing obvious," Cyn admitted, his gut churning with fear. Where was Fallon? Was she hurt? Was she . . . no. He clenched his fangs. He had to concentrate on getting out of the cell. It was the only way he could help his mate. "It's magically sealed, but if the three of us can combine our strength we might be able to—"

"Wait."

The choked command came from Viper, who was rolling onto his back, muttering a foul curse as he tried to gather his strength.

Cyn leaned over him, meeting the vampire's dark gaze with a wry smile.

"Welcome back to the world of the living, Sleeping Beauty."

"Bite me." Viper narrowed his midnight eyes. "Where's Fallon?"

Cyn flinched at the pain that sliced through him. "Phyla has her."

"Bitch." With far more grace than either Cyn or Styx, Viper was on his feet, sliding his sword from the scabbard angled across his back. "Move aside," he ordered.

Cyn frowned as he stepped out of Viper's path. "What are you doing?"

The silver-haired vampire halted directly in front of the door, placing the tip of his sword on the ground.

"We can't go through, but we can go under."

Cyn felt the ground tremble beneath his feet, belatedly realizing what his friend intended to do.

As predators, vampires had developed the skill to hide their dinner after a feeding. The humans, after all, were smart enough to ask questions if bodies began to litter the streets. But while most could only use their powers to loosen the soil so it made it easier to bury the dead, there were a rare few that could actually cause enough shift in the earth to collapse large buildings.

Sheathing his own sword, Cyn dropped to his knees at the same time as Styx, using his hands to dig out the large rocks that cracked beneath the pressure of Viper's power.

Dust began to fill the air as they scooped out the earth beneath the doorway, chucking the large rocks to the back of the cell. There was a tense moment as a long crack suddenly appeared in the side of the cavern, warning that the entire cavern was being affected by Viper's tiny earthquakes, but the pace never slowed.

A cave-in would be a pain in the ass, but it wouldn't kill them.

Pulling out one last rock, Styx lay flat on his stomach and began to shove his large body through the hole. There were several curses and the scent of blood as the king scraped off several layers of skin, but eventually he was through the opening.

Cyn was quick to follow, clawing his way under the door and into the narrow tunnel.

With one shove of his hands he was on his feet and headed down the tunnel. He heard Styx call out, but he didn't slow.

He could sense Fallon above them.

Nothing was keeping him from finding her.

Twice he was forced to double back, before he at last reached a pair of stairs that had been carved into the side of the tunnel wall.

He turned to gesture for Styx and Viper to stay behind him. Fallon was near, but so was the druid.

No one was killing that bastard but him.

Cautiously climbing the stairs, Cyn was prepared as a bolt of fire was shot in his direction. With inhuman speed he dodged the lethal bolt, leaping behind a large stalagmite to survey the small cave.

There wasn't much to see.

The druid who was dressed in a plain brown robe. An altar where a fire was burning with an odd, blue flame. And Fallon, who was seated at an awkward angle and shackled to the wall.

The bastard had chained his beautiful princess as if she was some sort of animal.

"How did you get loose, vampire?" the druid rasped, the edge of fear unmistakable despite his belligerent tone.

"Afraid, druid?" he baited, reaching out with his senses to search for hidden dangers.

This was no time to rush into a trap.

A sneer touched the rounded face. "How predictable of a demon to assume that a human would fear them. Your time is past, vampire. The humans will rule this world."

There was another bolt of energy that slammed into the stalagmite. Cyn muttered a curse.

He wasn't going to commit himself until he was certain there were no nasty surprises.

"Ah, how tedious. Yet another mortal drunk on his own sense of self-importance." Cyn clicked his tongue. "It might be amusing if it wasn't so pathetic."

The druid tilted his chin, his eyes darting toward the edge of the cave where Styx and Viper were blocking his retreat.

"The spell is cast. There's nothing you can do to halt it."

Cyn laughed with mocking amusement. He wanted the magic-user distracted.

"I can kill you."

The man growled deep in his throat. "That won't bring an end to the spell."

Cyn inched toward the edge of the stalagmite. He didn't know if killing the druid would end the spell or not. And at the moment he didn't give a shit. All that mattered was getting to Fallon.

"I don't care."

Fear flushed the round face. "Of course you do. You'll die—"

This time Cyn's laughter was genuine. "You're even more of a fool than I first thought."

"Don't pretend you don't want the spell halted."

"My mate is a Chatri," he pointed out. "We can travel to her homeland."

A sizzling bolt flew in his direction. It slammed into the

floor. The entire cave groaned, as if a breath away from tumbling into the tunnel beneath.

"You won't allow your people to die," the druid rasped, no doubt trying to reassure himself that he wasn't effectively cornered.

Cyn stepped forward, his weight balanced on his spread legs.

"I'll take them with me."

The druid licked his lips. "Perhaps we can discuss a compromise."

"Too late."

Without warning, Cyn launched himself at the rotund form. He wanted to be done with this. Grabbing ahold of the druid, he sunk his nails deep into the man's arms as he allowed his fangs to lengthen.

He struck toward the bastard's neck; unfortunately the druid wasn't going to give up without a fight. With a frantic motion, he reached into the pocket of his robe. Then, pulling out a small crystal, he spoke a low word of power.

There was a sudden burst of light, blinding Cyn and forcing him backward as the heat seared deep into his flesh, threatening to burn him to a crisp.

When his sight cleared, he realized the bastard had taken the opportunity to stand close to Fallon, his hand pointed toward her head.

Damn.

He carefully circled forward. Waiting for an opening.

"Stop right there," the druid warned, sending Cyn a warning glare. "If you don't want her dead then you'll turn around and leave this cave."

A red mist began to fill Cyn's mind as his berserker threatened to take command.

"Release her now or I'll rip out your throat."

The druid flinched but his composure never wavered.
"Back to the edge of the stairs and I'll send her to you."

"There's no bargaining. Release her or die."

At last realizing that Cyn wasn't to be bullied or coerced,
the druid stepped backward, as if he intended to try and use
Fallon as some sort of shield.

Coward.

Cyn crouched, but even as he prepared himself for the
coming attack, Fallon was abruptly surging toward the druid.

There was a rattle of chains, then an ungodly scream
from the druid as Fallon grabbed his lower leg.

Cyn hesitated.

It didn't look as if she was doing anything more than
holding on to him, but there was no mistaking the smoke
that was boiling beneath his robe as she released her considerable power. There was another shriek, and Cyn winced
as the stench of charred flesh assaulted his senses.

Accepting that his beautiful princess had quite literally
taken matters into her own hands, Cyn took a step backward,
already prepared for the sudden explosion of light that
rocked the cave.

It was never wise to piss off a Chatri, he wryly conceded,
not surprised to discover there was no sign of the druid as
the smoke finally cleared.

Behind him he sensed Styx and Viper cautiously moving
forward.

"Holy shit," Viper breathed, coming to a halt beside Cyn
as he studied the delicate female who'd just turned the druid
into a small mound of sizzling tar. "That was—"

"Awesome," Cyn breathed. "Fucking awesome."

# Chapter Twenty-Three

Fallon couldn't halt a small smile as she rose shakily to her feet, her hands still tingling from the massive release of power.

She'd felt sick to her stomach as she'd sensed the druid melting beneath her touch. It was, after all, one thing to possess the power to kill, and quite another to actually take the life of another.

Even an evil despot like the druid.

But while she struggled to overcome her moral qualms at killing, she couldn't deny a stab of pleasure as Cyn regarded her with blatant pride.

He wasn't horrified by what she'd done. Or chastising her for taking a risk.

*He thought she was fucking awesome.*

Holding her vampire's gaze, she waited for him to gently twist off the iron shackles as if they were made of clay. She grimaced, belatedly realizing just how much damage the iron had done to her.

Tenderly Cyn lifted her arms so he could kiss the three-inch band of seared flesh.

It would eventually heal, but until then it was going to drain her strength.

Not to mention, hurt like a bitch.

Feeling a cold chill wrap around her, Fallon instinctively pressed against Cyn's large body as the other two vampires moved to stare down at what was left of the druid.

"That was a hell of a trick," a silver-haired vampire with the face of an angel drawled. "But the question is . . . did it stop the spell?"

Ignoring the voice of warning that urged her to remain close to Cyn, Fallon forced her shaky legs to carry her to the altar so she could peer into the blue flames.

She easily sensed the magic that was connected to the druid pulsing in the fire. Unfortunately she didn't possess the ability to actually manipulate the spell, let alone stop it.

"No." She lifted her gaze to discover the three vampires regarding her with unwavering attention. Unlike her own people, it was obvious the vampires had no problem expecting her to pull her own weight. "The spell is still active."

"Damn." Styx scowled. "What about the portals?"

Fallon lifted her hand, releasing a small burst of power.

Even knowing the spell had already started, she still expected a portal to form. It seemed incomprehensible that the dimensions had been blocked.

Like a human might feel to open their front door only to discover there was a brick wall standing in their way.

"They've been closed," she said with a shudder.

Cyn released a low hiss. "So what now?"

Styx grimaced. "We can't fight the entire Commission."

The silver-haired vampire gave a shrug. "The Compulsion spell will have to wear off eventually, won't it?"

"Perhaps, but will it be in time?" Cyn demanded.

"He's right," Styx said. "We have to do something."

Fallon stepped away from the altar, only vaguely aware

of the vampires as they continued to squabble over what should be done next.

There was a strange buzzing inside her skull that had gone from mildly confusing to downright annoying.

What the hell was it?

She pressed her fingers to her temple, concentrating on the strange sensation.

It wasn't until she felt Cyn slide a protective arm around her shoulder that she realized her distraction had been noticed.

"Fallon." He grasped her chin to tilt back her head, studying her pale face with open concern. "What's going on?"

"There's some strange—"

"What?"

Her brows furrowed as she filtered through the buzz to make out actual words.

"A voice in my head," she said.

The jade eyes darkened as he cupped her cheek. "Careful, princess," he said softly. "The death of the druid might have triggered some new spell."

She shook her head. This wasn't magic.

Besides, she'd heard the voice before.

"No, this one is familiar," she said.

He arched a brow. "A Chatri?"

"Gargoyle."

There was a sound from the Anasso who suddenly looked as if he'd bit into a lemon.

"Levet," he growled.

Cyn's arm tightened around her shoulders. "Why is he in her head?"

"He's capable of speaking mind to mind from great distances," the king said.

Cyn pulled back his lips to reveal his fully extended fangs. "I don't like it."

"Neither do I, amigo." Styx gave a lift of one massive shoulder. "But his words might be important."

Cyn grimaced, meeting Fallon's steady gaze. "Can you understand what he's trying to say?"

"I'll try."

She gently pulled away from his arm. There was no way she could think clearly when he had her pressed against his large body. And, in truth, she wanted some space between herself and the two vampires who were watching her with cold expectation.

Okay. She'd wanted to be treated as a competent female with skills to offer, but it was more than a little unnerving to have the powerful vampires expecting her to come up with some sort of miracle.

Standing in a corner with her back turned toward her companions, she closed her eyes and forced herself to focus on the weird chatter inside her head.

"Levet?" she said, speaking out loud since she didn't really know how the whole mind to mind contact worked.

"Ah, thank the gods," the lightly French-accented voice said. "Are you well, *ma belle?*"

With her eyes closed, it was easy for Fallon to imagine the tiny gargoyle with his brilliant wings and stunted horns.

"For now," she reassured him, then gave a sudden shiver. It felt as if an eternity had passed since she'd first awoken in Cyn's caves. Not surprising. In a few short days she'd become a pawn for the Oracles, had her engagement broken, taken a vampire lover, battled a hellhound, killed a druid, and now had a gargoyle speaking in her head. Yep. A pretty eventful few days. "The spell has started."

"*Oui,* I know," Levet said.

Fallon felt a surge of hope. If the gargoyle knew about the spell, he had to be near.

Surely he could help end the magic.

"Where are you?" she demanded.

"At the druid's lair in Ireland."

"Oh." She sighed in disappointment. With the portals closed he was too far away to be of any assistance. "The druid is dead." She felt her stomach clench, the memory of feeling the human disintegrate beneath her fingertips something she was never going to forget. "I killed him."

"*Bon,*" Levet said with fierce satisfaction. "He was an evil man."

He had been.

And while Fallon would always feel guilty for killing a human, she wasn't sorry he was dead.

She was, however, growingly terrified that his untimely demise might have made it impossible to halt the magic that would soon kill off the demons.

"But now we have no way to stop the spell," she said.

"The druids here believe—"

"Druids?" she interrupted. Oh God. The last thing they needed were more enemies.

"They are the brothers of Anthony, but nothing at all like him," Levet hastily assured her. "They have been imprisoned since they refused to participate in his crazy scheme."

"Oh." She ignored the sensation of Cyn moving to stand directly behind her. "Can they help?"

"They say that the magic can be halted if you destroy the focus he used to cast the spell."

"Of course," she breathed, feeling like an idiot for not having thought of such a simple solution.

Cyn's hand touched her shoulder, his patience clearly at an end.

"Fallon?"

Opening her eyes, she turned to meet his searching gaze. "We need to destroy the object that is the focus of the spell."

He arched a brow. "Like an amulet?"

"Yes."

"Damn." Cyn gave an exasperated shake of his head. "That's what Phyla was trying to tell me."

Without hesitation the vampires were moving through the cave, turning over every stone in the search for an amulet.

"I don't see anything," the silver-haired vampire at last muttered.

Cyn turned to glance at Fallon. "Do you know how we can find it?"

She closed her eyes, repeating the question to Levet.

There was an unexpected pause before Levet was clearing his throat, as if embarrassed.

"The druids will cast a spell that will make any druid object hum," he at last said.

"Hum?"

"*Oui,* you should be able to follow the sound."

"Okay." She grimaced. The thought of trying to find one small humming object in the miles of tunnels and caverns was more than a little daunting. Still, it was better than nothing. "Anything else?"

"Hurry, *ma belle.*" Levet's voice was suddenly filled with a tangible urgency. "The lesser demons will begin to die within an hour."

Fallon snapped open her eyes, a shudder wracking her body.

She didn't need the reminder that the demons would soon run out of magic.

It was a sick ball of dread in the pit of her stomach.

Cyn moved to stand directly in front of her, brushing the back of his fingers over her cheek in a gesture of sweet affection.

She briefly studied his strong, beautiful face and clear jade eyes. Her heart slammed against her ribs.

She didn't know when or how this man had become the most important thing in her life, but the thought that she might lose him . . .

No. She fiercely squashed the surge of terror.

Time was running out, but it wasn't over.

As if sensing her grim resolve, he leaned down to brush a light kiss over her lips before straightening.

"What did the gargoyle say?" he demanded in gentle tones.

"We have to follow the hum."

He blinked. "Hum?"

Fallon shrugged. "That's what he said."

The Anasso reached over his shoulder to pull the big sword free of its scabbard.

"We should spread out and—"

"I hear it," the silver-haired vampire abruptly interrupted, headed toward the edge of the cave. "This way."

Fallon moved to follow, only to be halted as Cyn wrapped an arm around her waist and regarded her with a somber expression.

"Fallon—"

She reached up to press a finger to his lips. "We're in this together, vampire."

"You've done enough," he growled. "It's time for you to leave the caves."

"And go where?" she demanded softly, reaching up to run one thin braid through her fingers. "Unless we find the amulet nowhere will be safe."

He nipped the tip of her nose. "Fine. But no more playing Wonder Woman."

Her lips twitched at his disgruntled tone. "Wonder Woman?"

"It's my turn to be a hero."

He gave her a slow, lingering kiss before reluctantly

leading her out of the cave and down the stairs. Then, keeping her fingers grasped in a tight grip, he tugged her down the tunnel, chasing after the silver-haired vampire.

A wry smile curved her lips.

She was quite happy to hang up her Wonder Woman cape.

All she wanted was to find a way to destroy the amulet.

Then they could return to Cyn's lair where the only danger they would ever have to face again was when she informed the superbitch Lise she was no longer welcomed to waltz in and out of the castle unless she was specifically invited.

Oh yes.

That was the first thing on her agenda.

Well, after they saved the world.


Cyn forced himself to concentrate on their surroundings, even as he kept Fallon's fingers firmly grasped in his hand.

She was right.

They were in this together.

But that didn't mean he was going to allow her to take any foolish risks.

Within a few minutes they'd managed to catch up with Viper and Styx who were traveling at a blinding speed through the tunnels that were gradually widening.

Cyn sensed the hum that was growing progressively louder, but he allowed Viper to take the lead, instead focusing on making sure there were no hidden surprises ready to leap out and attack.

The druid hadn't seemed particularly intelligent, but even an idiot could leave behind a few traps for the unwary.

They wound their way from tunnel to tunnel. A fact that

seemed to bother Styx whose lean face was downright bleak as Viper slowed to a mere crawl, as if sensing danger ahead.

"We're headed toward the Council Room," Styx muttered.

"The Oracles?" Cyn demanded.

The Anasso grimaced. "They're all gathered there."

Cyn shook his head. Of course the amulet was in the one place where they couldn't get to it.

"Awesome."

Without warning a dark shape dropped from a ledge above.

"About time you all joined the party," Dante murmured, seemingly indifferent to the three swords that had nearly chopped off his head. "Where's the druid?"

Cyn glanced toward Fallon who went pale at the question.

"Fallon killed him," he said with open pride, not about to allow his princess to regret what she'd been forced to do.

"Damn. Good job," Dante said with an admiring glance. Fallon blushed, and Cyn tucked her close to his side, his gaze narrowing. Hey, he was still a vampire who hadn't yet been able to claim his mate. Taking the hint, Dante swiftly turned his attention back to Styx. "Now what?"

"We're searching for the focus of his spell," Styx said.

"I hear it," Viper murmured softly, peering around the edge of an opening.

Cyn joined Viper, angling his large body so he could peer into the massive Council Room.

His brows lifted at the sight of the long table set in the center of the floor where the dozen Oracles were seated.

They were all different. Different ages, different genders, and different species. But there was no mistaking that these demons were the most lethal creatures on Earth.

It was obvious in the arrogance etched onto their various faces and the thunderous power that was making the floor tremble.

Currently they had their hands and tentacles connected as they continued to perform the spell that was killing them all.

He felt a light touch on his arm as Viper directed his attention toward the center of the table where a small amulet was glowing with a blue light.

"Shit," he muttered. "It would have to be in the middle of the Oracles."

Viper grimaced. "We need a plan—"

"I'll get it," Cyn said, yanking his dagger from the holster at his lower back and heading forward.

They could spend the next half hour debating and arguing and planning how best to get their hands on the amulet. But in the end, there was only one solution.

Someone was going to have to go in and get it.

"Wait, Cyn," Viper rasped, the icy chill of his power swirling through the air. "Dammit."

Cyn ignored his companion's muttered opinion of thick-skulled berserkers as he slid along the edge of the cavern, seeking the most direct route to the table.

There was no possibility of being able to sneak past the entire Commission and destroy the amulet.

He would have to try a snatch and smash before they realized what he was doing.

Not a bad plan.

But as fast as he was, he was still several feet from the table when the nearest Oracle slowly rose from his chair and turned to face Cyn.

The demon had a tall, gaunt body with an overlarge head and tilted, almond-shaped eyes. Then, even as Cyn watched, the creature shifted into a human form, choosing to become a delicate female fairy with a cloud of golden hair and wide emerald eyes.

Recise was a Zalez demon who was part incubus. He was capable of becoming whatever form their companion most desired as well as releasing a sexual pheromone that threatened to cloud Cyn's mind.

Dammit.

Cyn gave a shake of his head, slashing out with his dagger as he tried to dart past the slender form.

The demon, however, wasn't an Oracle just because he could seduce the unwary. He lifted his hand, shooting out a fireball that hit Cyn in the middle of the chest.

Cyn grunted as he flew in a backward arc, slamming into the wall of the cavern with enough force to break a rib.

"I told you to wait," Viper muttered, swiftly at his side. "Damn berserker."

Cyn grimaced, forcing himself back to his feet. His gaze remained locked on Recise who remained standing by the table while the other Oracles continued with the spell. The demon's face was blank, his eyes burning with a strange inner glow.

"The damned druid must have cast a secondary spell to make sure the Oracles protected the amulet," he ground out, his hand pressed against his rapidly healing wound.

Styx silently joined him along with Dante and a scowling Fallon.

They all studied the Oracles who seemed unaware of their presence as they continued their low chanting.

"I wonder if only the Zalez demon is programed to attack?" Styx muttered.

Cyn glanced toward the king. "Do you have a plan?"

The grim warrior gave a shake of his head. "If we all attack at once, then one of us can surely get to the amulet."

Viper lifted a brow. "That's your plan? Everyone attack?"

Styx shrugged. "I'll admit it lacks subtlety, but we don't have time for an elaborate strategy session."

Dante smiled. "Works for me."

It worked for Cyn as well, except for the whole "everyone" attack.

"Fallon, you need to stay outside the cavern."

Predictably she was shaking her head before he finished speaking.

"You need my help."

Styx sent him a regretful gaze. "It's true."

Cyn was prepared. "We'll need her to destroy the amulet once we get our hands on it," he pointed out in perfectly reasonable tones. Not at all like his usual berserker self. "She can't do that if she's in the middle of battling some Oracle or injured."

Styx gave a slow nod. "Good point."

"But—"

The king held up a slender hand. "He's right, Fallon. We need you to be safe long enough to destroy the amulet."

She clearly wanted to argue, but perhaps sensing that Styx wasn't a vampire who was willing to negotiate when he gave an order, she turned her attention to Cyn.

"Fine. I'll wait here," she grudgingly conceded. "But if you get yourself killed—"

He moved to halt her angry words with a short, wholly possessive kiss.

"You're not getting rid of me so easy, princess," he murmured, allowing himself to savor her heartrending beauty. "Just be waiting with whatever magic you need to get rid of the amulet."

She gave a slow nod, her expression somber. "I'll be ready."

"Cyn," Styx murmured.

He reluctantly turned to find his fellow vampires waiting for him, their weapons drawn.

"Let's do this."

Styx lifted his hand, gesturing for them to spread out.

In silence, Viper and Dante slid through the shadows, reaching the far end of the cavern before Styx slashed his hand through the air, giving them the signal to attack.

Cyn waited for the king to circle toward the side of the table, before he moved to capture the attention of Recise.

He grimaced as the demon shifted his appearance again, this time going from the typical image of a fairy to looking specifically like Fallon. The bastard. Logically knowing that the Zalez demon's self-protection was looking like his opponent's deepest fantasy was considerably different than coming face to face with his soon-to-be mate.

Ignoring the false façade, as well as the tug of sexual awareness, Cyn darted forward, slicing his dagger toward the demon's face.

Recise instinctively twisted to the side, the movement making his golden hair swing over his shoulder, just as Cyn had expected. He'd obsessively watched Fallon's every movement. He knew exactly what was going to happen.

Reaching out, he grabbed the silken strands, yanking the demon close enough to sink his fangs into the bastard's throat.

There was a screech of pain as the demon struggled to get away from Cyn's iron grip, his shape changing back to his original form.

Continuing to drain the flaying Zalez, Cyn glanced toward the table where three more Oracles had risen from their seats to meet the vampires.

A Darcole demon was using its tentacles to force Dante against the wall of the cavern, while Viper was dodging the whirling sword of a Mogwa. Styx, meanwhile, was trying not to be burned to a crisp by Phyla, whose slender body was covered from head to toe in flames.

And still the rest of the Oracles continued to chant, the amulet in the middle of the table humming louder and louder.

Recise began to weaken in his arms, but even as he prepared to shove him aside and make a leap for the table, the bastard was placing his hands against Cyn's chest to hit him with another fireball.

Cyn was forced back. Shit. Two more ribs broken and his chest seared to black.

He ripped off his sweater that was smoldering from the burst of flames and grabbed the demon by the throat, squeezing his scrawny neck with enough force to crush the fragile bones.

Recise struggled, his eyes still dull with the force of the Compulsion spell as he used his claws to shred Cyn's arms down to the bone.

Cyn ignored the pain, continuing to squeeze. The demon was already weakened from his blood loss. It wouldn't take much more to disable him long enough to get to the table.

As long as he didn't manage to conjure up another fireball, Cyn grimly conceded.

Recise wasn't the only one who was running on fumes.

He wasn't sure he could survive another blast.

Distantly he was aware of his brothers fighting for their lives, as well as Fallon who had crept closer to the melee, but he didn't dare allow his attention to be diverted from the demon he held in his hands.

His fingers dug into the spongy flesh and Cyn felt the demon begin to grow limp. Then, without warning, the dull eyes flashed with something that might have been terror as Recise was able to break free of the Compulsion.

"Spell . . ." he breathed. "You must stop . . ."

The man slumped forward and Cyn dropped him to the ground. The demon might be pretending to be unconscious to lure him into lowering his guard, but he couldn't afford to wait.

He suspected that it was more than just his wounds that was making him feel as if he was being rapidly drained of his strength.

The spell was clearly affecting him.

And he wasn't the only one, if Styx's grunt of pain and Viper's low curses were anything to go by.

It was now or never.

Leaping over the Zalez demon, he darted straight for the table, hissing in pain as one of the other Oracles rose to their feet to grasp his arm and send jolts of electricity sizzling through his body.

He shoved his hand against the female demon's face even as he leaned over the table, grasping the amulet.

Another jolt shot through him, nearly making him black out.

Moaning, he managed to reach out and grasp the amulet, then spinning around he used the last of his strength to toss it toward the waiting Fallon.

She snatched it out of the air, her face tight with concentration as she placed the amulet on the floor and laid her hands over it.

Instantly he could feel the heat from her spell fill the air.

And he wasn't the only one.

As one the Oracles turned in her direction, ending their spell as they simultaneously gathered their powers to strike at Fallon.

"No." With the last of his strength, Cyn turned to race back to his princess.

He had a last vision of Fallon slamming her fist down

on the amulet as the first bombardment of power exploded directly into her back.

Her pained cry sliced through him and he launched himself forward, fully intending to shield her with his body.

But even as he was flying through the air, there was a sudden shimmer and without warning a tall man wearing a robe of purest white suddenly appeared.

Cyn easily recognized Fallon's father, Sariel.

He had long hair the color of spun gold that was held from his face by a narrow band of silver studded with priceless gems and eyes that were faintly slanted and the color of polished amber flecked with jade.

He was as stunningly beautiful as his daughter, but there was an arrogance etched onto his narrow face that set Cyn's fangs on edge. Not to mention the glittering hatred in his eyes as he glared at Cyn before he leaned down to scoop the unconscious Fallon in his arms.

With one last glower, he spoke a single word and disappeared with Cyn's mate.

Cyn bellowed in rage, barely aware of the magic that was smashing into him as he fell to his knees.

Fallon . . .

# Chapter Twenty-Four

The barren room that had been carved from pure stone was well hidden behind a secret panel.

There were no windows, no furniture, and the fairy lights that danced in the shadows of the low ceiling were deliberately muted.

In the very center of the stone floor was one wooden bowl half filled with water.

Seated next to the bowl, Fallon pressed a hand to her aching heart as she watched Cyn pace the small meadow over and over.

He looked as gorgeous as always with his body shown to perfect advantage in the faded jeans and cable-knit sweater that was stretched across his wide chest. His hair shimmered like pure gold in the moonlight with the two thin braids framing his face threaded with tiny jade beads.

But even in the darkness she could make out the lines of weariness that marred the beauty of his face and the growing tension in his broad shoulders.

No surprise. This was the third night in a row he'd spent pacing the meadow before being forced to hide during daylight hours in a small, cramped hole he'd dug in the ground.

He was there, of course, because it was one of the few openings to her homeland, and while he couldn't see or feel it, he could no doubt sense her presence.

And the fact she couldn't reach him was breaking her heart.

Damn her father.

When she'd awoken to discover she'd somehow been returned to the Chatri palace, she'd instantly tried to return to Cyn.

She not only had to make sure he'd fully recovered from his battle with the Oracles, but she simply needed to be near him.

It was as necessary as breathing.

But she'd swiftly discovered that her father had managed to put a dampening spell around her room, which meant she couldn't create a portal. And worse, she had two guards who constantly stood just outside her door, ensuring she couldn't leave.

Unable to contact her vampire, she'd had to be satisfied with sneaking into her secret room so she could at least catch sight of him.

"Wait for me," she whispered softly, brushing her fingers over the smooth wood of the bowl. "I'm going to find a way to get to you. I swear."

Sensing the approach of her father, Fallon hastily rose to her feet and hurried out of the room, sliding shut the hidden door behind her.

Then, smoothing her hands down her white satin robe that shimmered with priceless diamonds that were sewn along the plunging neckline and hem, she moved to the center of the room.

A second later there was a tap on the outer door and her father made his grand appearance, filling the air with the scent of a rich, full-bodied wine.

Wearing a heavy robe that was heavily embroidered with dozens of precious jewels, he had his golden hair pulled into a dozen complicated braids and his silver crown firmly settled on top of his head.

He looked every inch the King of Chatri.

Moving with a slow elegance, he circled the room, pretending to study the delicate tapestries that covered the walls and the thickly cushioned furniture that had been personally chosen by Fallon. She'd also created the cascade of water that spilled through a wide crack in the flagstone floor, lined by flowers with vivid blooms in shades from crimson to brilliant sapphire.

She loved the sensation that a tiny meadow had just appeared in the center of her room.

Her father, however, wasn't admiring her skill at decorating. Instead he was constantly attempting to discover where she kept her scrying bowls.

"Good morning, daughter," he at last murmured.

She gave a stiff nod of her head. Time moved differently within the palace.

"Father," she murmured.

"How are you feeling?"

She shrugged. It had taken her a full day and night to recover from the blast of magic that had hit her even as she was destroying the amulet.

Which was how her father had managed to trap her before she could escape.

"As I've told you several times, I'm fully recovered," she said, her voice cold.

"Hmm." Sariel ran a slender finger down the length of his jaw. "That is for the healer to decide."

She narrowed her gaze, not fooled for a minute. "Why don't you just admit the truth?"

"I beg your pardon?"

"You aren't keeping me confined to my rooms because you're concerned for my health," she said between gritted teeth. "You merely wish to keep me from leaving."

He tilted his chin to an arrogant angle, folding his arms over his chest.

"A princess belongs in her father's palace."

Her lips twisted with a wry humor. Just a few days ago she'd been sick with the thought of being shunned by her father. Now she was furious that he had not only refused to shun her, but he was insisting that she choose another fiancé and start planning her wedding.

"You allowed Magnus to return to the human world," she pointed out, having used her scrying bowl to watch her former fiancé announce he was leaving to marry the imp, Tonya, who'd captured his heart.

The reaction had been . . . epic.

Not only had the elder members of his House walked out of the public meeting, but Sariel had openly threatened to have him banned from the palace.

Nothing had swayed Magnus, however, who had proudly stalked out of the throne room and back into the arms of his beautiful imp.

"Magnus." Sariel curled his lips in disgust. "A most unsuitable prince. I am deeply relieved that he is not to be a member of our family."

Her heart twisted with envy. "He fell in love."

"Nonsense."

"Why do you call it nonsense?" Fallon gave a slow shake of her head. Like many kings, her father had chosen to keep an extensive harem. Clearly not one of the females he'd taken to his bed had managed to capture his heart. She might have felt sorry for him if he wasn't so determined to steal her own chance for love. "What could be more important than spending your life with the person who fate intended to be your mate?"

Expecting anger, Fallon was caught off guard when something that might have been distress flared through her father's eyes.

"Fallon, this is your home," he said softly, reaching to grasp her hand. "This is where you belong."

"But it isn't." She grimaced. "It never has been."

Sariel's lips flattened at her refusal to play the role of obedient princess.

"I blame that vampire for your discontent," he said. "He stole you from your family—"

"It was the Oracle who took me from this palace, not Cyn," she interrupted. "He's the one who kept me alive."

"Yes, I saw how well he was protecting you when I arrived in the caves," her father snapped.

She rolled her eyes. The second she'd destroyed the amulet the spell had been broken, allowing Sariel the opportunity to use his portal to trace her.

He would, of course, choose the moment that she was being injured.

"I don't want a protector. I want a partner," she informed him. "A man who sees me as more than just a means to improve the status of his family." She squeezed his fingers, willing him to understand just how important this was to her. "I want to be loved."

Sariel pulled his hand free, squaring his shoulders. "Clearly you are still not fully recovered from your ordeal."

Fallon clenched her hands in frustration. "You can't keep me imprisoned forever," she muttered.

"When you are prepared to choose a new fiancé from among the Chatri princes, I will release you." With rigid dignity Sariel marched toward the door. "Until then you will remain in these rooms."

"No." Fallon darted forward only to have the door slammed in her face. Lifting her hand, she slammed it against the wooden panel. "Dammit."

Cyn ignored the King of Vampires who stood at the edge of the meadow watching him pace with an unreadable expression.

He knew that his brothers were worried about him.

Over the past three nights he'd been visited by a half dozen vampires who had all urged him to return to his lair. Dante. Viper. Roke. Jagr. Santiago. Even Lise had traveled from Ireland.

He'd ignored them all.

Clearly they'd finally decided to call in the big guns.

And you didn't get much bigger than a six-foot-five Aztec warrior dressed in leather.

Waiting until Cyn's pacing had brought him within a few feet, Styx at last stepped forward.

"How long do you intend to remain here?" he demanded.

Cyn came to a grudging halt, meeting Styx's searching gaze with a fierce scowl.

He'd awoken three days ago in Styx's lair to discover the threat to the world had been averted. Not that he was in any mood to celebrate.

Instead he'd slipped out of the Chicago mansion as soon as he was capable of moving. And while he knew he couldn't force his way into fairyland, he'd gone to the one place that he knew there was an opening.

Months ago he'd stood in this very meadow while Roke struggled to reach his mate.

It'd been Fallon who'd opened a doorway . . .

His heart clenched, the pain that surged through him so raw that it nearly drove him to his knees.

"Until I have my mate," he rasped.

"Cyn—"

"Don't bother." Cyn sharply interrupted the lecture. He'd already heard it all. Lise had warned him that nothing would have kept Fallon from leaving her home if she truly wanted to be with him. Viper reminded him how fickle the fey could be. Dante had emphasized the difficulties of mating with another species. Especially when she happened to be a royal princess. And even Roke had mentioned the fact that it would be hard for a female trained to obey her father with utter loyalty to turn her back on him. "I'm not leaving until I know for certain that she's fully recovered, and that she doesn't want to be with me. End of story."

Styx grimaced, but he didn't look surprised. "I have called in every fey who owes me a favor to try and find a way into fairyland," he said. "Eventually they'll come up with something." He reached out to grasp Cyn's shoulder. "You're tired. Why not return to my lair and wait there?"

"No." Cyn gave a stubborn shake of his head. "I can feel her presence here. I have to stay."

"What about your clan?"

Cyn shrugged. "Lise has everything under control. And now that Erinna and Mika have returned to Ireland, I don't have to worry about them."

Styx lifted a startled brow. "Where were they?"

Cyn's foster parents had called him each evening, eager to see him although they firmly supported his need to be close to his mate.

They, in fact, insisted that he remain there as long as necessary.

"They haven't given me the full story, but it seemed that Erinna was convinced that she had a vision that the leader of the druids was involved in some nefarious plot and that I was destined to halt him."

"A true vision," Styx murmured. "But why did they leave?"

"They actually were searching for the missing druids. They had been a part of the vision as well," he said, shuddering at what might have happened to them if they'd been around the druids when the spell had been cast. "They had no idea they'd already been trapped by Anthony in the Labyrinth spell."

"I'm sure they're eager to see you," Styx said.

Cyn's lips twisted. Styx had all the subtlety of a freight train.

"I'm not leaving," he repeated for what seemed to be the thousandth time. "Somehow I'm going to rescue my mate."

"Are you so certain that Fallon wants to be rescued?" a male voice drawled as a portal unexpectedly opened and a man with long hair the shade of rubies and eyes that were the color of cognac suddenly appeared. "It's very possible she's happy to be home."

Cyn whirled to glare at Magnus who was dressed in his usual *GQ* style with black silk pants and a jade silk shirt.

"What the hell are you doing here?" he growled.

The Chatri prince strolled forward, looking as if he'd rather be anywhere but the moonlit meadow.

"Tonya insisted that I offer my assistance," he forced himself to say.

Cyn blinked in surprise. He barely knew the imp.

"Where is she?"

A faint smile touched Magnus's face, easing the annoying arrogance.

"Training her replacement."

Styx made a sound of surprise. "She's quitting the club?"

"She will soon be a princess. If she insists on managing a club, then it will be ours, not some vampire's," the Chatri said with obvious pride in his fiancée.

Cyn gave a shake of his head. The thought of Magnus and Tonya opening their own club . . . it boggled the mind.

"I'm sure that went over well with Viper," Styx said, amusement threaded through his voice at the thought of his friend's explosive reaction to losing his best manager.

Magnus shrugged. "She promised him that I would assist in reuniting Cyn with Fallon."

Hope sparked to life as Cyn studied the man he'd so recently wanted to kill.

"You can get me into fairyland?"

Magnus shook his head. "No, but I can see if she is willing to come out."

"Do it," Cyn commanded.

"Wait, Cyn," Styx muttered, sending the prince a suspicious glare. "Do you really trust him?"

Styx hadn't fully forgiven the Chatri for turning his lair into a fey hotel.

"I don't have a better plan," Cyn muttered, his gaze locked on Magnus. "Get her."

"Only if it's what she wants," the prince warned, moving across the meadow and lifting his hand as he opened an invisible door to his homeland. "I won't force her if she decides to stay with her family."

Cyn scowled. He refused to believe for a second that Fallon didn't want to be with him.

It was unthinkable.

"Just go."

Magnus disappeared as he stepped through the doorway, leaving behind a Cyn who was so tense he could barely stand still.

"I don't like this," Styx growled.

Cyn wasn't crazy about it either. It wasn't as if he had a reason to trust the Chatri. Still, he didn't have a lot of options.

In desperate need of a distraction, he turned back to his companion.

"Have the Commission bothered to pass along their thanks for preventing them from nearly destroying the world?" he asked.

Styx rolled his eyes. "No gratitude, but Siljar did say that they have been gathered in one place for too long. They've decided to depart for their individual lairs."

Cyn smiled. It was traditional for the Oracles to remain spread around the world to prevent too much power in one place. It was only because of the numerous threats to the world that they'd remained in the caves for so long.

"I'm sure you're heartbroken to have them out of your territory."

"Good riddance," Styx said with feeling. "I just want a few centuries of peace so I can enjoy my mate without constant interruptions."

"Agreed." Bloody hell. The thought of spending the next hundred years or so with nothing to do but hold Fallon in his arms sounded like paradise. "If I ever get my hands on my mate."

Styx placed his hand on Cyn's shoulder. "She'll come."

As if on cue, there was a tingle in the air and Fallon stepped into the meadow closely followed by Magnus.

His entire body shook with a gut-deep joy, his arms spread wide as she dashed across the frozen ground to toss herself against his chest.

"Cyn," she cried softly, her hands wrapping around his neck as he hugged her so tightly he feared he might leave bruises.

Still, he couldn't loosen his grip.

She'd been stolen away from him.

Taken to a place he couldn't follow.

It was going to take a few decades before he ever let her out of his sight again.

"Fallon," he groaned, burying his face in the silken cloud of her hair to absorb her intoxicating champagne scent. "I've been waiting for you."

"I know." She pressed her lips to his throat, sending a jolt of aching pleasure through him. "I could scry you, but my father had blocked my room so I couldn't leave."

"Bastard," he muttered, lifting his head so he could run a searching gaze over her slender body. "Are you fully healed?"

A brilliant smile curved her lips. "Yes."

He flinched at the memory of watching her collapse beneath the impact of the Commission's magic.

Christ. She was lucky to be alive.

"Forgive me," he rasped. "I should never have allowed—"

"Ssh." She pressed a finger to his lips. "We did what we had to do and now it's over. All I care about is the future."

Cyn cast a quick glance around the meadow, not particularly surprised to discover they were alone.

Styx would have insisted that Magnus return him to Chicago so Cyn could have privacy with his potential mate.

"Aye. The future." He hesitated, knowing that the next few minutes were the most important in his very long life. "You know what I desire."

She arched back, her eyes glowing with a heated awareness that made him instantly hard.

"Tell me," she urged in a husky voice.

Hell. He needed to get her back to his lair.

He could spread her across his bed and gently remove the silk robe before . . .

Desperately he battled to control his primitive urges.

The next time he made love to this exquisite female, he fully intended for them to be formally bound together.

"I want us to be mated," he bluntly admitted, his hand cupping her cheek as he gazed down at the female who'd become a necessary part of his life.

"You're sure?"

He gave a short laugh, his chest feeling as if it were being squeezed by a painful vise.

"Princess, I couldn't be more sure," he said with a fierce sincerity.

"Then what are you waiting for?" she demanded.

He stiffened, half afraid that this was a dream.

"You want to go through with the mating ceremony?" he demanded, framing her face in his hands. He had to make sure she truly understood what she was agreeing to. "Once we exchange blood we can't go back. We'll be permanently tied together."

Going on her tiptoes, she pressed a gentle kiss to his lips.

"Berserker, I couldn't be more sure."

Oh . . . hell.

Relief blasted through his heart, his fangs lengthened, the urge to sink them deep into her flesh an overwhelming force.

Only the knowledge that they could be interrupted at any time by her father allowed him to restrain his primeval impulse.

Leaning down, he kissed her with a barely leashed hunger. "Then let's go home."

"Home." Her face lit with a smile of pure joy. A joy that was echoed deep inside of Cyn. "Finally."

"Eternally," he promised, holding her close as she formed a portal and the world melted away.

# Epilogue

Every one of Viper's numerous demon clubs was a direct reflection of his own taste.

Flamboyant, excessive, and dramatically over the top.

But while all of them were guaranteed to please the most finicky demon, the Viper Pit in Chicago was by far the most exclusive.

The by-invitation-only club was hidden behind a subtle glamour that made it look like an abandoned warehouse to keep away the riffraff.

Inside, however, the public room was decorated with white marble pillars and glittering fountains that served as a perfect backdrop for the dew fairies who were performing a complex dance to the oohs and ahhs of the crowd of demons.

In the back of the club a line of tables had been situated where the guests could gamble. And for those searching for more . . . intimate entertainment, there were private rooms where they could join in the ongoing orgies or start one of their own.

Ignoring the excitement that rippled through the room at his entrance, Styx strolled onto the private balcony where

Dante and Viper were seated at a table sharing a bottle of brandy from Viper's private stock.

As usual, Dante looked like a pirate in his casual jeans and a leather jacket with a golden hoop dangling from one ear. Viper, on the other hand, was wearing a long velvet jacket with a lacy shirt that was more fitting for a Regency ballroom.

Styx had chosen his usual black leather.

Why mess with a classic style?

Both men gave a lift of their brows at his unexpected arrival, but it was Viper who said the words they were both thinking.

"If you've come here to tell us the end of the world is about to arrive then you can shove it. This is my night off."

Styx chuckled. He didn't blame his friends for giving him the hairy eyeball.

Over the past months they'd endured one disaster after another. The Dark Lord, an insane Anasso, a crazed Were spirit, Morgana la Fay, a vampire god . . .

Christ, it made him weary just remembering the enemies they'd faced.

They were all ready to take a break from impending doom.

Styx came to a halt beside the table, folding his arms over his massive chest.

"Is that any way to speak to your king?"

"Don't expect me to kiss your ass," Viper drawled, waving a slender hand toward the dance floor below where the crowd of demons was gazing up at the balcony with unabashed curiosity. "Your adoring masses are waiting for you down there. Up here you're just another schmuck."

"Thank God," Styx muttered, taking a seat and reaching for the bottle.

"So what brings you to my humble establishment?" Viper demanded.

He poured himself a glass and settled back in his chair. "For once all I desire is a few hours to enjoy the company of my friends and your finest brandy."

"No looming apocalypse?" Viper pressed.

Styx took a sip of the aged brandy, savoring the fiery burn. "Not one."

Viper reached for the bottle, his expression one of genuine relief.

"I'll drink to that."

Dante was quick to replenish his own glass. "Here, here."

Styx grimaced. "It's been an . . . adventure."

Dante snorted, his silver eyes shimmering in the overhead chandelier that Viper had liberated from King Louis XIII's palace. Or was it XIV?

"That's one way to put it," the younger vampire muttered.

Styx allowed his gaze to skim over the crowd who had gone back to their entertainments, a fierce surge of satisfaction racing through him at the sheer normalcy of the view.

Never again would he take the mundane things for granted . . .

Strolling along the streets without fear of a nasty surprise leaping out of the dark. Enjoying a casual drink with his friends.

Waking in his comfortable bed with Darcy wrapped in his arms.

"But not all bad," he murmured, a smile softening his harsh features. "We have mates. New friends." He turned his attention back to his companions. "And peace."

Dante rapped his fingers on the table. "Knock on wood."

"And me," a lightly accented voice said as the tiny gargoyle flapped down from his perch among the hidden rafters. "Don't forget you have me."

The three vampires were on their feet at the unexpected intrusion, their fangs fully extended as Levet settled on the railing of the balcony and regarded them with a smug smile.

Styx sent Viper a jaundiced frown. "I thought you had bouncers?"

Viper gave a resigned shake of his head. "I have an entire pack of hellhounds patrolling the neighborhood, but the bastard keeps slipping past them."

Levet sniffed, his wings fluttering in a shimmering burst of color.

"Hey, I am the liver of any party."

Styx scowled. "Liver?"

"Life, you dolt," Dante corrected with a twitch of his lips. "The life of the party."

"If you say so." Levet shrugged. "Tonight, however, I am not here to dazzle you with my sparkling personality. I am here to officially quit my gig as Knight in Shining Armor."

Styx studied the miniature pain in the ass with a suspicious glare.

Levet had appointed himself as the supposed savior of fair maidens throughout the world. A role disputed by most males forced to endure his aggravating presence. Why would he willingly retire from his imaginary position?

"Really?" Viper demanded.

"*Oui.*" The gargoyle looked smug. "I am going to be far too occupied with my new business."

Styx didn't bother to disguise his astonishment. "You have a business?"

With a dramatic wave of his hand, the gargoyle produced a large stack of ivory business cards edged with gold.

"*Voilà.*"

Viper reached to pluck one of the cards from Levet's claws.

"COUP DE FOUDRE?" he read out loud. "What the hell does that mean?"

Levet rolled his eyes. "Can you not read French, you heathen? It means love at first sight."

"I can translate the words," Viper snapped, his dark eyes narrowing. "I simply don't know why you have them printed on a card."

"Because it is the name of my dating service," Levet said with a small sniff.

"Bloody hell." Dante gave a sharp laugh. "You're playing Cupid?"

"Who better?" Levet demanded, acting as if he were shocked by the question. Of course, he labored under the delusional belief that he was a perfect replica of Brad Pitt, not a three-foot gargoyle who regularly created chaos. "I am, after all, an expert in matters of the heart."

Styx swallowed his laugh. "If you say."

"Congratulations." Viper adjusted the lacy cuffs of his shirt. "Shouldn't you be out doing whatever love experts do?"

"But obviously I am."

Dante shared a confused glance with Viper and Styx. "I'm afraid to ask."

Levet turned on the railing so he could peer down at the demons who mingled below.

"Like any new business owner, I am in search of new clients."

"And?" Styx prompted.

"And I must spread word of my services." With a smile Levet lifted his hand and with a low word of power sent the business cards floating down to the gathered crowd. "This is the perfect venue."

"Shit." Lunging forward, Viper grabbed Levet by one stunted horn and dangled him so they were eye to eye. "Toss one more card and I'll rip off your wings and feed them to the hellhounds."

"Fah, you are a pooper of the party." Struggling until he freed himself from Viper's grip, the gargoyle gave a flap of his wings and headed back toward the rafters. "You can all consider yourself crossed off the list for a friends and family discount," he warned as a parting shot.

Waiting until the smell of granite faded, the three friends returned to their seats, each reaching for their glasses of brandy.

Nothing like a small dose of Levet to drive a man to drink.

"Why did you let Shay break him out of the slaver's prison?" Styx demanded, regarding Viper with a chiding expression.

Viper gave a sudden laugh. "You've met my mate. No one tells her what she can and can't do."

"True," Styx agreed with a chuckle.

Dante lifted his glass. "To mates who don't take shit."

Styx joined in the toast. "And to brothers who stand by one another even when facing Armageddon."

Viper tapped his glass to theirs. "To friends."

"For eternity," the three finished in unison.

From the hellhole of a Taliban prison to sweet freedom,
five brave military heroes have made it home—
and they're ready to take on the civilian missions
no one else can. Individually they're intimidating.
Together they're invincible.
They're the men of ARES Security.

Rafe Vargas is only in Newton, Iowa,
to clear out his late grandfather's small house.
As the covert ops specialist for ARES Security,
he's eager to get back to his new life in Texas.
But when he crosses paths with Annie White,
a haunted beauty with skeletons in her closet,
he can't just walk away—not when she's
clearly in danger . . .

There's a mysterious serial killer on the loose
with a link to Annie's dark past.
And the closer he gets, the deeper Rafe's instinct
to protect kicks in. But even with his
considerable skill, Annie's courage,
and his ARES buddies behind him,
the slaying won't stop.
Now it's only a matter of time before Annie's next—
unless they can unravel a history
of deadly lies that won't be buried.

**Please turn the page for an exciting sneak peek of
Alexandra Ivy's**

## KILL WITHOUT MERCY,

**the first book in her new Ares Security
romantic-suspense series,
coming in January 2016!**

# Prologue

Few people truly understood the meaning of "hell on earth."

The five soldiers who had been held in the Taliban prison in southern Afghanistan, however, possessed an agonizingly intimate knowledge of the phrase.

There was nothing like five weeks of brutal torture to teach a man that there are worse things than death.

It should have broken them. Even the most hardened soldiers could shatter beneath the acute psychological and physical punishment. Instead the torment only honed their ruthless determination to escape their captors.

In the dark nights they pooled their individual resources.

Rafe Vargas, a covert ops specialist. Max Grayson, trained in forensics. Hauk Laurensen, a sniper who was an expert with weapons. Teagan Moore, a computer wizard. And Lucas St. Clair, the smooth-talking hostage negotiator.

Together they forged a bond that went beyond friendship. They were a family bound by the grim determination to survive.

# Chapter One

Friday nights in Houston meant crowded bars, loud music, and ice-cold beer. It was a tradition that Rafe and his friends had quickly adapted to suit their own tastes when they moved to Texas five months ago.

After all, none of them were into the dance scene. They were too old for half-naked coeds and casual hookups. And none of them wanted to have to scream over pounding music to have a decent conversation.

Instead, they'd found The Saloon, a small, cozy bar with lots of polished wood, a jazz band that played softly in the background, and a handful of locals who knew better than to bother the other customers. Oh, and the finest tequila in the city.

They even had their own table that was reserved for them every Friday night.

Tucked in a back corner, it was shrouded in shadows and well away from the long bar that ran the length of one wall. A perfect spot to observe without being observed.

And best of all, situated so no one could sneak up from behind.

It might have been almost two years since they'd returned

from the war, but none of them had forgotten. Lowering your guard, even for a second, could mean death.

Lesson. Fucking. Learned.

Tonight, however, it was only Rafe and Hauk at the table, both of them sipping tequila and eating peanuts from a small bucket.

Lucas was still in Washington D.C., working his contacts to help drum up business for their new security operation, ARES. Max had remained at their new offices, putting the final touches on his precious forensics lab, and Teagan was on his way to the bar after installing a computer system that would give Homeland Security a hemorrhage if they knew what he was doing.

Leaning back in his chair, Rafe intended to spend the night relaxing after a long week of hassling with the red tape and bullshit regulations that went into opening a new business, when he made the mistake of checking his messages.

"Shit."

He tossed his cellphone on the polished surface of the wooden table, a tangled ball of emotions lodged in the pit of his stomach.

Across the table Hauk sipped his tequila and studied Rafe with a lift of his brows.

At a glance, the two men couldn't be more different.

Rafe had dark hair that had grown long enough to touch the collar of his white button-down shirt along with dark eyes that were lushly framed by long, black lashes. His skin remained tanned dark bronze despite the fact it was late September, and his body was honed with muscles that came from working on the small ranch he'd just purchased, not the gym.

Hauk, on the other hand, had inherited his Scandinavian father's pale blond hair that he kept cut short, and brilliant blue eyes that held a cunning intelligence. He had a narrow face with sculpted features that were usually set in a stern expression.

And it wasn't just their outward appearance that made them so different.

Rafe was hot tempered, passionate, and willing to trust his gut instincts.

Hauk was aloof, calculating, and mind-numbingly anal. Not that Hauk would admit he was OCD. He preferred to call himself detail-oriented.

Which was exactly why he was a successful sniper. Rafe, on the other hand, had been trained in combat rescue. He was capable of making quick decisions, and ready to change strategies on the fly.

"Trouble?" Hauk demanded.

Rafe grimaced. "The real estate agent left a message saying she has a buyer for my grandfather's house."

Hauk looked predictably confused. Rafe had been bitching about the need to get rid of his grandfather's house since the old man's death a year ago.

"Shouldn't that be good news?"

"It would be if I didn't have to travel to Newton to clean it out," Rafe said.

"Aren't there people you can hire to pack up the shit and send it to you?"

"Not in the middle of fucking nowhere."

Hauk's lips twisted into a humorless smile. "I've been in the middle of fucking nowhere, amigo, and it ain't Kansas," he said, the shadows from the past darkening his eyes.

"Newton's in Iowa, but I get your point," Rafe conceded. He did his best to keep the memories in the past where they belonged. Most of the time he was successful. Other times the demons refused to be leashed. "Okay, it's not the hell hole we crawled out of, but the town might as well be living in another century. I'll have to go deal with my grandfather's belongings myself."

Hauk reached to pour himself another shot of tequila from the bottle that had been waiting for them in the center of the table.

Like Rafe, he was dressed in an Oxford shirt, although his was blue instead of white, and he was wearing black dress pants instead of jeans.

"I know you think it's a pain, but it's probably for the best."

Rafe glared at his friend. The last thing he wanted was to drive a thousand miles to pack up the belongings of a cantankerous old man who'd never forgiven Rafe's father for walking away from Iowa. "Already trying to get rid of me?"

"Hell no. Of the five of us, you're the . . ."

"I'm afraid to ask," Rafe muttered as Hauk hesitated.

"The glue," he at last said.

Rafe gave a bark of laughter. He'd been called a lot of things over the years. Most of them unrepeatable. But glue was a new one. "What the hell does that mean?"

Hauk settled back in his seat. "Lucas is the smooth-talker, Max is the heart, Teagan is the brains, and I'm the organizer." The older man shrugged. "You're the one who holds us all together. ARES would never have happened without you."

Rafe couldn't argue. After returning to the States, the five of them had been transferred to separate hospitals to treat their numerous injuries. It would have been easy to drift apart. The natural instinct was to avoid anything that could remind them of the horror they'd endured.

But Rafe had quickly discovered that returning to civilian life wasn't a simple matter of buying a home and getting a 9-to-5 job.

He couldn't bear the thought of being trapped in a small

cubicle eight hours a day, or returning to an empty condo that would never be a home.

It felt way too much like the prison he'd barely escaped.

Besides, he found himself actually missing the bastards.

Who else could understand his frustrations? His inability to relate to the tedious, everyday problems of civilians? His lingering nightmares?

So giving into his impulse, he'd phoned Lucas, knowing he'd need the man's deep pockets to finance his crazy scheme. Astonishingly, Lucas hadn't even hesitated before saying "yes." It'd been the same for Hauk and Max and Teagan.

All of them had been searching for something that would not only use their considerable skills, but would make them feel as if they hadn't been put out to pasture like bulls that were past their prime.

And that was how ARES had been born.

Now he frowned at the mere idea of abandoning his friends when they were on the cusp of realizing their dream.

"Then why are you encouraging me to leave town when we're just getting ready to open for business?"

"Because he was your family."

"Bull. Shit." Rafe growled. "The jackass turned his back on my father when he joined the army. He never did a damned thing for us."

"And that's why you need to go," Hauk insisted. "You need—"

"You say the word closure and I'll put my fist down your throat," Rafe interrupted, grabbing his glass and tossing back the shot of tequila.

Hauk ignored the threat with his usual arrogance. "Call it what you want, but until you forgive the old man for hurting your father it's going to stay a burr in your ass."

Rafe shrugged. "It matches my other burrs."

Without warning, Hauk leaned forward, his expression somber. "Rafe, it's going to take a couple of weeks before we're up and running. Finish your business and come back when you're ready."

Rafe narrowed his gaze. It was no surprise that Hauk was pressing him to deal with his past. Deep in his heart, Rafe knew his friend was right.

But he could hear the edge in Hauk's voice that made him suspect this was more than just a desire to see Rafe dealing with his resentment toward his grandfather. "There's something you're not telling me."

"Hell, I have a thousand things I don't tell you," Hauk mocked, lifting his glass with a mocking smile. "I am a vast, boundless reservoir of knowledge."

A classic deflection. Rafe laid his palms on the table, leaning forward. "You're also full of shit." His voice was hard with warning. "Now spill."

"Pushy bastard." Hauk's smile disappeared. "Fine. There was another note left on my desk."

Rafe hissed in frustration.

The first note had appeared just days after they'd first arrived in Houston.

It'd been left in Hauk's car with a vague warning that he was being watched.

They'd dismissed it as a prank. Then a month later a second note had been taped to the front door of the office building they'd just rented.

This one had said the clock was ticking.

Once again Hauk had tried to pretend it was nothing, but Teagan had instantly installed a state of the art alarm system, while Lucas had used his charm to make personal friends among the local authorities and encouraged them to keep a close eye on the building.

"What the fuck?" Rafe clenched his teeth as a chill inched

down his spine. He had a really, really bad feeling about the notes. "Did you check the security footage?"

"Well gosh, darn," Hauk drawled. "Why didn't I think of that?"

"No need to be a smartass."

Hauk drained his glass of tequila. "But I'm so good at it."

"No shit."

Hauk pushed aside his empty glass and met Rafe's worried gaze.

"Look, everything that can be done is being done. Teagan has tapped into the traffic cameras. Unless our visitor is a ghost he'll eventually be spotted arriving or leaving. Max is working his forensic magic on the note, and Lucas has asked the local cops to contact the neighboring businesses to see if they've noticed anything unusual."

"I don't like this, Hauk."

"It's probably some whackadoodle I've pissed off," the older man assured him. "Not everyone finds me as charming as you do."

Rafe gave a short, humorless laugh. Hauk was intelligent, fiercely loyal, and a natural leader. He could also be cold, arrogant, and inclined to assume he was always right. "Hard to believe."

"I know, right?" Hauk batted his lashes. "I'm a doll."

"You're a pain in the ass, but no one gets to threaten you but me," Rafe said. "These notes feel . . . off."

Hauk reached to pour himself another shot, his features hardening into an expression that warned he was done with the discussion.

"We've got it covered, Rafe. Go to Kansas."

"Iowa."

"Wherever." Hauk grabbed the cellphone on the table and pressed it into Rafe's hand. "Take care of the house."

Rafe reluctantly rose to his feet. He could argue until he

was blue in the face, but Hauk would deal with the threat in his own way.

"Call if you need me."

"Yes, Mother."

With a roll of his eyes, Rafe made his way through the crowd that filled the bar, ignoring the inviting glances from the women who deliberately stepped into his path.

He was man enough to fully appreciate what was on offer. But since his return Stateside he'd discovered the promise of a fleeting hookup left him cold.

He didn't know what he wanted, but he hadn't found it yet.

He'd just reached the door when he met Teagan entering the bar.

The large, heavily muscled man with dark caramel skin, golden eyes, and his hair shaved close to his skull didn't look like a computer wizard. Hell, he looked like he should be riding with the local motorcycle gang. And it wasn't just that his arms were covered with tattoos or that he was wearing fatigues and leather shit-kickers.

It was in the air of violence that surrounded him and his don't-screw-with-me expression.

Of course, he'd been thrown in jail at the age of thirteen for hacking into a bank to make his mother's car loan disappear. So he'd never been the traditional nerd.

"I'm headed out."

"So early?" Teagan glanced toward the crowd that was growing progressively louder. "The party's just getting started."

"I'll take a rain check," Rafe said. "I'm leaving town for a few days."

"Business?"

"Family."

"Fuck," Teagan muttered.

The man rarely discussed his past, but he'd never made

a secret of the fact he deeply resented the father who'd beaten his mother nearly to death before abandoning both of them.

"Exactly," Rafe agreed before leaning forward to keep anyone from overhearing his words. "Keep an eye on Hauk. I don't think he's taking the threats seriously enough."

"Got a hunch?" Teagan demanded.

Rafe nodded, as always surprised at how easily his friends accepted his gut instincts. "If someone wanted to hurt him, they wouldn't send a warning," he pointed out. "Especially not when he's surrounded by friends who are experts in tracking down and destroying enemies."

Teagan nodded. "True."

"So either the bastard has a death-wish. Or he's playing a game of cat and mouse."

"What would be the point?"

Rafe didn't have a clue. But people didn't taunt a man as dangerous as Hauk unless they were prepared for the inevitable conclusion.

One of them would die.

Rafe gave a sharp shake of his head. "Let's hope we have a culprit in custody when we find out. Otherwise . . ."

"Nothing's going to happen to him, my man." Teagan grabbed Rafe's shoulder. "Not on my watch."


The small but stylish condo on the edge of Denver offered a quiet neighborhood, a fantastic view of the mountains, and a parking garage that was worth its weight in gold during the long, snow-filled winters.

With a muted blue and silver décor, the condo was precisely the sort of place expected of an upwardly mobile young professional.

Not that Annie White was upwardly mobile.

Not after walking away from her position at Anderson's Accounting just six months after being hired.

At the moment, however, she didn't really give a crap about her future in the business world. Instead she was trying to concentrate on her packing. A task that would have been easier if her foster mother hadn't been following behind her, wringing her hands and predicting inevitable doom.

"I wish you hadn't traveled all this way, Katherine," Annie said to her foster mother, moving from the bedroom to the living room to place a stack of clean underwear in her open suitcase.

The older woman was hot on her heels. Still attractive at the age of fifty-five, Katherine Roberts had faded red hair that was pulled into a tight bun at the back of her head, and clear green eyes that could hold kindness or make a child cringe with guilt.

Dressed in a jade sweater and dress slacks, her narrow face was currently tight with concern. "What did you expect me to do when you called to say you were traveling back to that horrible place?" Katherine demanded.

Annie swallowed a sigh. Unlike her foster mother, her honey brown hair tumbled untidily around her shoulders, the golden highlights shimmering in the September sunlight that streamed through the skylight. Her pale features were scrubbed clean instead of discreetly coated with makeup. And her slender body was casually covered by a pair of faded jeans and a gray sweatshirt.

With her wide hazel eyes she barely looked old enough to be out of high school, let alone a trained CPA.

"I shouldn't have called," she muttered.

She loved her foster parents. She truly did. There weren't many people who would take in the ten-year-old daughter of a serial killer. Especially after she'd spent several months in a mental institution.

They'd not only provided a stable home for her on their ranch in Wyoming, but they'd offered her protection from a world that was insatiably curious about the only survivor of the Newton Slayer.

Now, however, she wished her foster mother would dial back on the fussing.

"You think I wouldn't have found out?" Katherine demanded.

Annie grimaced. She tried to ignore the fact that while she'd moved away from the ranch, her parents continued to monitor her on a daily basis.

Not only by their nightly calls, but by speaking with her boss, Mr. Anderson, who happened to be a personal friend of her foster father.

They only wanted to make sure she was safe.

"I don't want you to worry," Annie said.

Katherine waved a hand toward her open suitcase. "Then reconsider this rash trip."

Annie moved into the bathroom, collecting her toiletries as she struggled to smooth her features into an unreadable mask.

Overall, her foster parents had been supportive. They'd urged her to discuss her past with them as well as with a trained therapist. They'd even allowed her to keep a picture of her father beside her bed, despite the devastation he'd caused. But the one thing they refused to accept was her claim that she'd seen visions of the murders as they'd happened.

And they weren't alone.

No one believed the strange images that had plagued her were anything more than a figment of her overactive imagination.

Over the years, Annie had tried to convince herself they

were right. It was insane to think they'd been psychically connected to her father while he was committing the murders.

Right?

Then two nights ago the visions returned.

The images had been fragmented. A woman screaming. A dark, cramped space. The shimmer of a knife blade in the moonlight. Newton's town square.

Annie didn't even try to deny the visions.

Either she was losing her mind. Or they were real.

The only way to know was to return to the town and confront her nightmares.

"It isn't rash," she said as she returned to the living room. "I've given it a great deal of thought."

Katherine made a sound of impatience. "But what about your position at Anderson's?"

"It's possible they'll hold my job for me," Annie said, mentally crossing her fingers.

It wasn't a total lie.

Her supervisor had said they *might* consider rehiring her when she returned.

"Do you realize how many strings Philip had to pull to get you a place at such a prestigious firm?" Katherine demanded, clearly not appeased. "In this economy it's almost impossible to find anything that isn't entry level."

Annie turned to take her foster mother's hands. She knew she should feel bad about leaving her position. It was what she'd trained to do, wasn't it?

"And I appreciate everything he's done for me," she assured the older woman. "That you've both done for me."

Katherine clicked her tongue. "If that was true you wouldn't be tossing it all away on this harebrained scheme."

"I get that you don't understand, but it's something I have to do."

Katherine pulled her hands free, clearly frustrated by

Annie's rare refusal to concede to her stronger will. "Nothing can change the past," she snapped.

Annie turned, unnecessarily smoothing the jeans she'd placed in the suitcase.

This wasn't about the past. The visions weren't memories. They were glimpses of the present.

"I know that," she murmured.

"Do you?" Katherine pressed.

"Of course."

There was a long silence, as if the older woman was considering the best means of attack.

Katherine Roberts was a wonderful woman, but she was a master of manipulation.

"Is this because it's the anniversary of the deaths?" she at last demanded.

The thought had crossed Annie's mind. Within a few days it would be exactly fifteen years since the killings started.

Who could blame her for being plagued with hallucinations?

But her heart told her it was more than that.

"I don't think so," she hedged.

Katherine pressed her hands together. A certain sign that she was trying to maintain her temper. "Maybe you should talk with your therapist."

"No."

"But—"

"I don't need a therapist," Annie said, her voice uncharacteristically hard.

What was going on in her head couldn't be cured by sitting in a room and talking.

She had to go see for herself.

Seeming to realize she couldn't badger Annie into giving up her plans, Katherine glared at her with an annoyance that didn't entirely disguise her concern. "What do you hope to find?"

Annie flinched.

It was a question she didn't want to consider.

Not when the answer meant she was out of her mind. Or worse, that there was a killer on the loose.

"I just need to know that . . ." Her words trailed away.

"What?"

"That it's over," she breathed. "Really and truly over."

A shocked expression widened Katherine's eyes. "What are you talking about? Of course it's over. Your father . . ." The older woman hastily crossed herself, as if warding off an evil spirit. "God forgive him, is dead. What more proof do you need?"

Annie shook her head. "I can't explain."

Reaching out, Katherine placed her hand on Annie's arm, her expression anxious. "Do you know how many nights I woke to hear you screaming?"

Annie bit her lower lip. No one could have been more patient over the years as Annie had struggled to heal from the trauma she'd endured.

The last thing she wanted was to cause Katherine or Philip even more concern.

"I'm sorry."

"Oh Annie." Katherine pulled her into her arms, wrapping her in the familiar scent of Chanel No. 5. "I'm not trying to make you feel bad. I just don't want the nightmares to come back."

"They already have," Annie whispered, laying her head on her foster mother's shoulder. "That's why I have to go."